ASHES IN THE PINES

Borne Back Books
West Egg, New York

First Borne Back Books trade paperback edition May 2023

Cover Design: Damonza.com
Author Photo: Selfie

Manufactured in the United States of America

Publisher's Cataloging-in-Publication Data
provided by Five Rainbows Cataloging Services

Names: Gibbs, Chad Alan, author.
Title: Ashes in the pines / Chad Alan Gibbs.
Description: Auburn, AL : Borne Back Books, 2023. | Summary: Izzy Brown attempts to solve a third murder while struggling with anxiety and opioid dependency. | Audience: Grades 9 & up.
Identifiers: LCCN 2023908545 (print) | ISBN 979-8-9856757-5-7 (paperback) | ISBN 979-8-9856757-2-6 (ebook) | ISBN 979-8-9856757-6-4 (audiobook)
Subjects: LCSH: Young adult fiction. | CYAC: Teenagers--Fiction. | Murder--Fiction. | Drug addiction--Fiction. | Autism--Fiction. | Anxiety--Fiction. | BISAC: YOUNG ADULT FICTION / Mysteries & Detective Stories. | YOUNG ADULT FICTION / Coming of Age. | YOUNG ADULT FICTION / Social Themes / Drugs, Alcohol, Substance Abuse. | YOUNG ADULT FICTION / Neurodiversity.
Classification: LCC PZ7.1.G4991 As 2023 (print) | LCC PZ7.1.G4991 (ebook) | DDC [Fic]--dc23.

a novel

CHAD ALAN GIBBS

Tricia: You don't have to dedicate every book to me.

Me: Yeah, I know ...

For Tricia

"...I went astray from the straight road and woke
to find myself alone in a dark wood."

—Dante, *The Divine Comedy*

ASHES IN THE PINES

1992

Vance Fuller had so many questions.

He struggled to open his eyes as he faced a blackness darker than the sleep from which he'd just awoken. After blinking the world into focus, Vance glimpsed the faint twinkling of a distant star through a break in the cloudy mountain sky. He was outdoors, and it was night-time, but what night, Vance could not say. He was a bear, groggy and confused after weeks of hibernation. Instinctively, he tried to check his Rolex, but his arm refused to obey, then declined to slap the mosquito feasting on his neck. The blood-sucking fly confirmed it was some-time between April and October, and Vance wasn't shivering either. If forced to wager a guess, he'd say it was July. Hadn't there been fire-works a few nights ago? He wasn't sure.

Was he drunk?

Was he hungover?

His pounding head suggested yes.

After shaking the cobwebs from his mind, a memory emerged through the fog. Dinner in the Fuller Farms dining hall with the other counselors and campers. He'd eaten country-fried steak and lima beans, or was that a dream? And did he return to his cabin after lights out? Again, Vance couldn't recall. He'd taken a bite of peach cobbler and woken up here. Wherever here was.

The pop of a floodlight in the distance startled Vance back to the present, and suddenly the world was nothing but blinding light. He closed his eyes, but still, the blaze burned red through his eyelids. Squirming to shield himself from the glare, Vance recoiled as hundreds of twigs clawed into his skin. Was he lying on a pile of straw? No, he was standing, and when he turned his head, he saw why his arms had refused to obey. He was tied to a hay bale. Stretched out like a thief on a cross.

Vance tried to scream for help only to realize he'd been gagged. Someone had stuffed a dirty cloth into his mouth and wrapped duct tape around his head. Squinting toward the light, Vance saw a figure moving in the distance, but it was too bright to look for more than a second. A prank, Vance thought. But who would do this to him? Why?

A whistle and a thud, and Vance turned his head in horror to see the feathers of an arrow sticking out of the hay bale beside him. The archery range. He was tied to one of the hay bales in the Fuller Farms archery range. This wasn't a prank. Someone was going to kill him. He fought to free himself, but the ropes only dug deeper into his wrists and brought tears to his eyes. Vance Fuller would die tonight. He knew it.

Another whistle but no thud. This time the arrow sailed clean over. Maybe his tormentor was trying to miss. Maybe it was a prank. An evil one, but a prank, nonetheless. Some campers didn't like him. Some of the other counselors didn't like him either. Vance had regrets.

He had enemies. But he didn't deserve this torture, and his mind briefly turned to revenge.

His daddy was rich and powerful.

His daddy would make them pay.

Whoever them was.

A third whistle and unfathomable pain. The arrow hit just above Vance's left knee, and he screamed, but the roar never left his head. Now he fought for his life. The ropes burned his wrists, but Vance did not feel it. He felt nothing but an animalistic instinct to escape. If he could have reached his bound hands, he'd have gnawed them off at the wrist to get free.

A whistle and a thud. The fourth arrow missed his neck by mere inches. Vance thrashed, and the hay scraped the skin on his back. Even if the arrows stopped, Vance feared he'd bleed to death on the range. But the arrows didn't stop.

Another whistle and thud, then another, then a blistering pain in Vance's chest that exploded beyond comprehension before receding into nothing.

Dark sky turning darker still.

A gurgling breath.

Oblivion.

Vance Fuller had so many questions, but he would never learn the answers.

CHAPTER ONE

I woke up on June 1, 2009, and like every day for the past week, I had no clue where the hell I was. Bare walls, a hard mattress, and morning sun streaming through the flimsy vinyl blinds that needed replacing five years ago. The musty smell of carpet unfamiliar with vacuum cleaning filled my nostrils, and our upstairs neighbor's stereo, which was always tuned to 104.7 Classic Country, overpowered the white noise from my sound machine with seventies twang.

I sat up, and the day's headache greeted me like a slap to the face. I cursed, rolled over, and fetched a pill from my nightstand before stumbling into the shower. Twenty minutes later, I was ready to face the day.

My name is Izzy Brown. I'm sixteen years old and live with my mother, Brandi, and my brother, Axl, in a three-bedroom apartment in Ashes, North Carolina. Sorry, Ashes in the Pines, North Carolina, as the postcards are quick to remind you. We've lived here for one week after moving from Dandrige, Florida, a sad little speed bump of a town on your drive to the beach.

We were here because of Axl. He'd recently accepted a scholarship to play football at Ashes Preparatory School, an institution that valued a year of its education at roughly the median annual income for North Carolina families. Not possessing any scholarship-worthy athletic prowess, I'd attend the local public school, Ashes High, in the fall. But first, I had to make it through the summer without somehow getting us kicked out of town, something I had a propensity to do.

"Good morning, sunshine."

"Hey, Lenny."

I forgot to mention Lenny Roach, my mother's live-in boyfriend. Lenny was, for lack of a better term, a drug dealer. Sure, he also sold dietary supplements and quasi-legal vitamins out of his windowless van, but his primary source of income was opioids. Lenny ran a crew of guys who hit up Florida pain clinics and cashed in their prescriptions at friendly pharmacies before distributing the bounty throughout the southeast. I hesitate to say Lenny treated my mother well, but he didn't hit her—yet. And he sometimes brought her dying flowers he'd buy on discount at Publix. He also paid half our rent, which is why I suspect she feigned ignorance as to the source of his income. I knew how Lenny earned his living because he provided the bottle of 20mg OxyContin in my nightstand drawer.

"Starting your new job today?" Lenny asked as I dropped a Pop-Tart onto a paper plate and shoved it into the microwave.

"Yep," I said, not particularly interested in conversing with Lenny this early … or ever.

For as long as I could remember, I'd suffered from migraines and bouts of suffocating anxiety. But the year before, after we moved to Bardo, Florida, my boyfriend Blaine gave me a pill to try. The medicine obliterated my headaches, which was great, but it also energized me in a way that's hard to describe. My anxiety was gone, sure, but in its place was what I came to think of as the perfect version of myself. I wasn't some strung-out pillhead. I was motivated, alert, and practically euphoric. Before taking that pill, life often felt like a death march, but now I was coasting downhill with my feet off the pedals. Soon I'd gone from taking a pill whenever I had a headache to taking one every morning and one every night. Then I was arrested for unlawful possession of a controlled substance.

After a few awful days spent detoxing in a juvenile detention center, I returned to my old anxious and headachy self. I still had a bottle of pills, thanks to Lenny, but I decided I'd be more careful. I'd only take a pill when I really needed one. Over the winter and spring, I took about twenty—less than one a week. A perfectly reasonable number, I figured, based on nothing.

But that morning's pill marked the seventh consecutive day I'd woken up with a nasty headache, and the seventh day in a row I'd taken a pill to fend it off. I told myself it was the thin mountain air causing my headaches, and soon my body would acclimate. It was an easy enough lie to believe.

"Good morning, baby girl," my mother said, dressed for her new job running a cash register at Fraîche, one of several organic grocery stores in town, this one specializing in cheese, apparently.

"Morning," I said, hugging my mom.

"You nervous about your first day?"

To the point of vomiting, I thought. "No," I lied. "Are you?"

"Baby girl, a lot of things make me nervous, but swiping the barcode on some yoga-pant-wearing trophy wife's smoked gouda ain't one of them."

I laughed and took a bite of my Pop-Tart, the nuked strawberry filling burning my tongue.

"Hi, bye," my twin brother, Axl, said, stomping through the living room on his way out the door.

"Hug," Mom demanded, and Axl returned and lifted our mother off the ground in a giant bear hug. Mom was small, and I was even smaller, but Axl stood six-foot-four and looked every bit the hot-shot football prospect he was.

"Hug," I said when Axl turned to leave again, but he only shot me a bird.

Axl and I had always fought like Batman and the Joker, but I'd never doubted he cared about me until the last six months. Sophomore year, we attended the prestigious Bardo Academy on scholarships thanks to a wealthy booster who desperately wanted Axl to play college football for his alma mater. But then I began sticking my freckled little nose where it didn't belong. After joining the school newspaper, I investigated a former Bardo student's twenty-five-year-old cold case murder. With the help of my best friend, Elton Jones-Davies, a beyond gangly autistic boy with most of Wikipedia downloaded into his brain, I solved the case, but not before blackmailing our benefactor and getting Axl and me kicked out of school.

Next came my arrest and an invitation to move to London with Elton and his mother in hopes I'd thrive away from all the trouble I'd found on the Emerald Coast. While across the pond, Elton and I solved another murder and saved the lives of thousands of people, but we had to return stateside because Elton's father, a former NFL running back and fat-burning grill spokesman, had filed for divorce and sued for custody.

Now I was back sharing a roof with my brother, who'd hardly spoken to me since I cost him his Bardo scholarship over half a year ago. But he did shoot me a bird, which I took as a good sign since anything was better than indifference.

"Axl Rose Brown, you hug your sister," our mother snapped when she saw his middle finger salute.

"Later, when I'm sweaty," Axl said, and he was out the door, off to work out with the football team before spending the rest of the afternoon lounging poolside while a harem of cheerleaders fanned him and fed him grapes.

"That boy," Mom said, shaking her head while pouring her morning coffee. "And you're sure you don't need a ride this morning? Lenny can take you."

"No, I'm good," I said, knowing I'd walk across Death Valley barefoot before climbing into Lenny's pharmacy on wheels. "A girl from work is picking me up."

"Baby girl," Mom said, grabbing me by the shoulders with a sigh. I suspect she had a speech lined up but figured what was the use. She'd given me speeches before to no avail. I screwed things up. It's who I was. Not intentionally, mind you, but with a consistency suggesting otherwise. I had no plans to seek out another unsolved murder. No plans to ruin our new life in Ashes. I only wanted to work hard at my summer job, then study hard in school, earn a college scholarship, and stop burdening my mother with my existence. But the best-laid plans of Izzy Brown often turn to shit.

A horn honked twice in the parking lot below.

"That's my ride," I said, hugging my mother goodbye, but she still had hold of my shoulders when I tried to pull away.

"Try," she finally managed.

"I always try," I said, fighting back the tears.

My mother, who knew a lot about trying with nothing to show for it, could only smile and kiss me on the forehead.

"Have a great first day at work," she said.

"You too," I replied and headed for the door.

"Later, tater," Lenny said, snapping his fingers and pointing at me like the douche canoe he was.

"Way later, I hope," I mumbled and ran downstairs to the waiting car that would take me to my job at the summer camp where I hoped to pass the next eight weeks in peace.

The camp was called Fuller Farms.

CHAPTER TWO

Ashes in the Pines, founded in 1871 and named after the area's propensity to burn to the ground every hundred years or so, sat tucked in the southern tip of Jackson County, North Carolina, a stone's throw from the Georgia and South Carolina state lines. Perched 4,218 feet above sea level on a plateau in the southern Appalachian Mountains, Ashes was a tourist town, like Highlands, Cashiers, and Sapphire surrounding it. It had a quaint downtown featuring several blocks of two-story boutiques and restaurants I couldn't afford, three golf courses, miles of hiking and biking trails, Doublehead Falls, the most post-card-worthy waterfall in North Carolina, and breathtaking views from Twilight Rock that, in 2009, Instagram influencers had yet to ruin.

Only four thousand people permanently called Ashes home, but the town swelled to five times its size in the summers. Visitors flocked there from May till October, drawn by the natural beauty and low humidity. Before living in Ashes, I did not know a person could step outside their home in July and not immediately sweat through their clothes. I won't lie; it was delightful.

Everyone in Ashes was rich unless they weren't, and the line between the haves and have-nots wasn't blurry. Some women bought their cheese at Fraîche, and others worked at Fraîche and bought their cheese at the Dollar General on Highway 107. There was no in-between. Shelby Ray, the girl who'd offered me a ride to Fuller Farms, fell squarely in the latter category, evidenced by her 1987 Honda Civic with a duct-taped rear window.

"Thanks again for the ride," I said to Shelby as we headed toward Fuller Farms, a twenty-minute drive west of Ashes in the valley below. She had dusty blonde hair under an old Braves cap, and an athletic build. Shelby looked like she might play softball, or more likely, used to play softball before getting into an argument with her coach and putting him in intensive care.

"Yep, no problem," Shelby said, lowering her window and lighting a cigarette while driving with her knees. I didn't think sixteen-year-olds could smoke in North Carolina, but I wasn't sure without Elton and his encyclopedic knowledge of everything around to confirm this. Walking to Fuller Farms wasn't an option, though, so I bit my tongue and tried to take as few secondhand breaths as possible.

Five minutes into our drive, walking felt like a viable option, because Shelby, like every other Ashes local, drove the winding mountain roads like she was running moonshine. The reckless nonchalance with which she took hairpin turns where only a thin metal guardrail stood between us and fiery death below had me shutting my eyes for the first ten minutes of our drive. I don't recall taking a breath until we got stuck behind a slow-moving dump truck forcing a reluctant Shelby to finally tap her brakes.

"Have you lived in Ashes long?" I asked once my heart rate dipped back into double digits.

"All my life," Shelby said, tossing her cigarette butt out the window, much to Smokey Bear's chagrin. Then she turned off the Jason Mraz song on the radio, mumbling something about how people shouldn't be that happy this early in the morning.

"We just moved here," I said, still trying to make conversation.

"Yeah, I know. Your brother is the football star, and you're a druggie."

I'd forgotten why I hated small towns, but now I remembered.

"My cousin Donnie in Franklin can get you weed if you ever need any," Shelby added.

"I'm good," I said. "I got in trouble for pills, but I don't take them anymore." This was a lie. I'd taken one that morning, and I'd likely need one every time I got in a car with Shelby. Still, I preferred thinking of myself as someone who didn't take drugs.

"Donnie can get you pills too," Shelby said, not believing me.

The dump truck turned off, and Shelby resumed her breakneck death wish down the mountain, and it wasn't until we reached a relatively flat and straight stretch of road in the valley below that my jaw unclenched enough to resume our conversation.

"So," I asked, "have you ever gone to camp at Fuller Farms?"

Shelby laughed herself into a coughing fit, leaving me ample time to wallow in the embarrassment of the apparently stupid question I'd just asked.

"Do you know what eight weeks of summer camp at Fuller Farms costs?" Shelby asked. I shook my head, and she took out her phone and began searching the internet, severely limiting her ability to stay in our lane. "Here," she said, and taking her phone, I squinted at the shattered screen and saw summer tuition at Fuller Farms cost $18,000.

"Holy shit," I said, "what sort of kid gets to go to an eighteen-thousand-dollar summer camp?"

"You'll see," Shelby said, taking back her phone. "And if you need an iPhone, Donnie can get them for cheap."

"Yeah, I'm good," I said, thinking about the phone Elton's mother gave me when we moved to London and how much I wished he were here, mostly because he'd insist Shelby drive the speed limit.

Shelby sped past the tall wooden ranch gate marking the entrance to Fuller Farms, and before I could ask if we'd missed our turn, she whipped the wheel and sent her old Honda skidding down a gravel road, kicking up a dust storm that likely baffled local meteorologists.

"Worker bees can't use the main entrance," she said, anticipating my question. Then she winked and added, "They shoot violators on sight."

In 1907, Liston Fuller, patriarch of the Fuller clan, established the West Carolina Pepsi Cola Bottling Company with $8,000 he borrowed from the Bank of Asheville. By 1941, when his third wife, Dorothy, gave birth to his only son, Wellington, Liston had more money than God, a Buckingham Palace-inspired mansion in the Outer Banks, and a 9,500-acre mountain retreat near Ashes in the Pines. Hurricane Hazel destroyed the mansion in 1954, washing all but the fountain into the Atlantic. However, the Fuller clan still owned the mountain retreat, and it was Liston, at the urging of his puritanical fifth wife, Susan, who established a summer camp there in 1963.

"Fuller Farms will be a place of spiritual renewal for children of the upper crust," Susan said in the original brochure for the camp. This quote was removed from all subsequent promotional material, because everyone but Susan, whose mind had likely gone mushy from reportedly drinking thirteen cans of Pepsi a day, realized how terrible it sounded.

Liston died in 1982, suffering a massive heart attack minutes after Michael Jordan sank a twenty-foot jumper to give his beloved North Carolina Tar Heels the national championship. Wellington Fuller, who at fifty-six had just retired after twenty years of running his father's bottling company, took over the day-to-day operations of Fuller Farms. Anticipating the softening of American youth, Wellington built state-of-the-art dormitories with air conditioning, an Olympic-sized swimming pool featuring a seventy-foot waterslide, and added a slew of other amenities aimed at the coddled modern teen. As a result, Fuller Farms' popularity exploded. By the early nineties, everyone who was anyone sent their kids to western North Carolina for eight weeks every summer, mostly to get them out of the house but also to sport the famed "FF" decal on the rear window of their luxury sedan. No one batted an eye at the tuition fee.

"I'm just kidding," Shelby said as the road opened to reveal playing fields of the greenest manicured grass imaginable, a giant pool and waterpark, tennis and basketball courts, an archery range, a climbing wall, zip lines, a ropes course, and dozens of paddle boats moored to a dock in a giant lake, all set against the backdrop of the towering Appalachian Mountains. This wasn't a summer camp; it was Six Flags over heaven.

"Kidding about what?" I asked, only half paying attention to Shelby.

"About them shooting you on sight. There's just no way to get to the employee parking lot through the main gate."

"Gotcha," I said, wondering how stupid Shelby thought I was.

"Old Man Fuller is real nice," she said, parking in the shaded gravel lot behind a long stone building I'd learn was the dining hall, "like a fat Mr. Rogers. His wife was a bitch, but she died back in January. I don't think anyone has been shot out here since their son."

"Wait, what?"

"You don't know about that?"

"Should I?"

"I figured everyone knew," Shelby said. "Back in the early nineties, they found Old Man Fuller's son tied to a hay bale on the archery range and shot full of arrows."

My eyes widened. "What the hell? Who would do that to someone?"

"Beats me," Shelby said with a shrug. "They never caught the killer."

Shit.

"They never caught the killer," I repeated.

"Nope," Shelby said. "Rumor was, some devil worshippers living in the caves around here did it, but they never could catch them because they knew the mountains too well."

"O-kay."

"But other folks figure it was some of those rich camp kids playing a prank that went wrong. Rich kids never get in trouble for anything."

Double shit.

"Well, I'm not getting involved," I said, more to myself than to Shelby.

"What's there to get involved with?"

"I'm not going to try and solve that murder."

"They hired you to serve scrambled eggs and sloppy joes," Shelby said. "I don't think anyone expects you to solve a murder."

"I'm just telling you," I said, climbing out of her Honda, "I don't care who killed the Fuller boy."

But even as the words left my mouth, I knew they were a lie.

CHAPTER THREE

I applied online for my summer job at Fuller Farms a couple of weeks before we left Dandridge, and three days later, they called to say I was hired. Hired to do what, exactly, I did not know. Still, in my mind, I envisioned myself serving as a camp counselor to a horde of sweaty middle-schoolers. Leading them on hikes through the woods, playing games of Marco Polo in the pool, and utterly destroying them all during the end-of-camp shaving cream battle.

I was wrong.

First, there are no middle-schoolers at Fuller Farms. The camp serves high school students only. And second, the counselors are all in college, most of them former campers themselves. It should have been obvious no parent would want someone recently arrested for drug possession leading their children on treks through the Appalachian Mountains. But I hadn't thought of my pills as a barrier to employment until my first day at Fuller Farms, when my supervisor, Julie, gave me a cup to pee in.

"What's this?" I asked.

"Drug test," Julie barked, her vocal cords lined with so much tobacco tar she always sounded like she was whispering at the top of her lungs.

A hot flash began in my spine and radiated out to my hands and feet before returning as a pinprick of panic located in the center of my chest.

"Does, uh, does it pick up like, prescription drugs, because I—"

"How the hell should I know what it picks up?" Julie said. She had all the charm of a prison guard and looked like the women who get arrested on Black Friday for fighting at Walmart. "All I know is Mr. Fuller hates druggies, so if you're a pot smoker, you might as well quit now. That way, I won't waste my time training you today."

"I'm not a pot smoker," I managed, wilting under Julie's glare, then I went and peed in the cup. I had twenty-four hours' worth of dread waiting for the test results that would leave me unemployed or worse. But the following day, Julie marched in without even looking in my direction and sent one of my co-workers home for having marijuana in her system. I could breathe again because the test I'd take every Monday missed opiates.

Or so I thought.

There were several jobs for worker bees, as the back of our sky-blue Fuller Farms T-shirts identified us. A group of mostly guys served on the grounds crew, mowing, edging, and weed-eating the camp's grounds to Augusta National standards. A cleaning crew shined the bathrooms, picked up the dormitories when the campers were out each day, and took care of all laundry. And finally, there was dining services, where I worked. Four old sisters who once ran Pappy Duke's, the most popular meat-and-three restaurant in Ashes, now prepared some of the finest Southern cuisine on Earth for the unappreciative campers, while a dozen teenage girls and I served the food, cleaned the tables, and washed dishes between meals. It wasn't glamorous work, but Fuller Farms paid twice the minimum wage, so it beat any other summer job I was qualified for.

We trained on Monday, served small meals for the counselors on Tuesday, and the campers began arriving after lunch on Wednesday, causing a buzz among my co-workers.

"He's fine."

"The boy with the big nose?"

"No, the tall boy next to him."

"Oh, you're right. He is fine."

"Back to work, ladies," Julie boomed, and the curious crowd around the window dispersed.

There were a hundred campers, half girls, half boys, all dressed in the matching khaki shorts and the red Fuller Farms T-shirts they'd wear every day. I manned the veggie station for the welcome dinner, asking every camper who came through the line, "Carrots, lima beans, or cream corn?" They'd answer some combination of the three, and I'd dump the vegetables on their tray while trying to avoid eye contact.

After having limited interaction with rich kids for the first fifteen years of my life, I'd had more than my share in the last twelve months. But always in a private school setting, where I was their equal, if not in reality, at least in theory. But here in the Fuller Farms dining hall, the line between rich and poor was as stark as the contrasting T-shirts we wore, and I feared if I made eye contact with one of these condescending pricks, my middle fingers would go rogue.

"Carrots, lima beans, or cream corn?"

"Hey, don't I know you?"

I glanced up to see a tall boy with a swoop of blond hair falling over his left eye. Buoyed with confidence from the group of giggling guys surrounding him, his smile bordered on arrogance, and my cheeks reddened, knowing I wasn't in on the joke.

"I don't think so," I said, turning back to my vegetables.

"We all know you. You're the Queen of the Mountain," one of the giggling friends said, and the boy with the hair elbowed him hard in the ribs.

"No, I know you, I'm sure of it," the boy said, turning back to me.

"Not unless you ever spent time in Florida juvie," I said, and I heard Shelby snort from the cornbread station.

Momentarily stunned, the boy opened his mouth but couldn't find his words, so I pointed him down the line with a dismissive wave and said, "Next."

Later, standing outside the dining hall with the other girls waiting on the campers to finish dinner, Shelby winked at me between drags on a cigarette and said, "Looks like you've got an admirer in there."

"I'm pretty sure he was making fun of me," I said, rolling my eyes.

"Right. That's how they flirt," Shelby said, stubbing out her cigarette against the wall and tossing the butt on the ground. "They're idiots. Most go to all-boys schools and haven't been around girls since preschool. If one pulls your pigtail, you'll know he's really into you."

I laughed before peeking through the window to reassess the boy who'd talked to me but couldn't find him in the sea of red T-shirts.

"There are plenty of rich girls here," I said. "I doubt these guys are interested in the kitchen staff."

"Rich girls suck," Shelby said. "Even the nice ones are bitches, and the boys are all scared of them. Trust me. I worked here last summer. That boy was flirting, and by next week, the two of you will be sneaking off to have canoe sex."

Before I could ask Shelby if she meant sex in a literal canoe or if this was something I'd have to look up on Urban Dictionary, Julie, our supervisor, stuck her head out the door and said, "Girls, get in here."

I followed the other girls back into the kitchen, and we huddled around the dining room door. Dinner was over, but a fat old man was now standing at the front of the room, addressing the campers.

"That's Wellington Fuller," Shelby whispered. "He's the richest man in North Carolina."

Wellington Fuller appeared to be in his late seventies, with a bad combover and the physique of someone who'd spent most of his adult life in a chair. He wore the same outfit as the campers, and the blue veins in his legs showed brightly through his translucent skin. Wellington Fuller looked more like a Walmart greeter than the richest man in North Carolina, but in my experience, wealthy old men never look like Daddy Warbucks.

"Now, as most of y'all know, we lost our dear Rosalind back in January," Wellington said, his Southern drawl sounding cartoonish even to me, and I'd spent my entire life in the Florida Panhandle. "She dedicated her life to Fuller Farms, so to honor her, the theme for this year's camp is LEGACY. The L stands for Love. Rosalind loved this camp with all her heart. The E stands for Enthusiasm. Rosalind was always enthusiastic about—"

"People really pay twenty grand for this shit?" I whispered to Shelby, who stifled a laugh.

The old man droned on for several more minutes, going over camp rules, reciting banal platitudes, and seemingly daring the campers to fall asleep at their tables. When his welcome spiel mercifully ended, Wellington Fuller led the room in a drowsy rendition of the camp song, which only rhymed if you pronounced Carolina like you were auditioning for a role in *Deliverance*.

Take me back to Fuller Farms.
Up in the hills of Carolina.
Clean, fresh air and mountain charms.
I can't think of nothing no finer.

"Now, before we leave," Mr. Fuller said at the song's conclusion, "I'd like to introduce y'all to this year's dining staff. Ladies, come on out here."

"Go," Julie said, pushing us all out the kitchen door, and we found ourselves standing in front of a hundred campers who stared blankly at us.

"A round of applause for that delicious dinner," Wellington Fuller said, and the campers clapped politely, if not enthusiastically.

"These lovely ladies will serve y'all breakfast, lunch, and dinner, and it's my heartfelt desire you'll treat them with the respect and—"

While Wellington implored the campers not to be rude to the help, I scanned the room again, looking for the boy with the blond swoop of hair who'd talked to me in line. I found him at a back table, already smiling at me. He smiled bigger when we made eye contact and even dared to wave. I rolled my eyes but smiled back despite myself.

"Thank you again, ladies," Wellington Fuller said, slipping out through the kitchen where the other girls and I waited for the campers to leave so we could clean the tables and go home. We mumbled our reply, and a couple of girls curtsied like he was the King of North Carolina, but Mr. Fuller was now eyeing the leftover cookies from dinner. He pocketed one before giving me a conspiratorial wink and saying, "Good evening, Miss Brown. I'm especially delighted to have you with us this summer."

And then he was gone, leaving Shelby to stare at me in disbelief and ask, "What the hell was that all about?"

CHAPTER FOUR

"I swear, I've never met the man in my life," I told Shelby the following day during another hair-raising trip down the mountain in her Honda Civic. Of course, we'd already discussed this the night before, but she found my answers wanting after a night's sleep.

"Well, he sure is *especially delighted to have you with us this summer*," Shelby said, impersonating the old billionaire.

I shrugged, and Shelby asked, "Are you famous or something?"

"No. Well, sort of. But not really."

"You're sort of famous, but not really? Wait, are you in porn?"

"What? No. I've just solved a couple of murders in the last year," I said, and Shelby squinted at me in understandable confusion. "It's, like, my hobby," I added.

"Gotcha," Shelby said, letting go of the wheel to light a cigarette, "like smoking."

"Something like that," I said.

At breakfast, I served eggs to a hundred sleepy campers who yawned in my face before mumbling thanks and moving on to the bacon. Showing remarkable self-restraint, I refused to glance down the line to see when the boy with the swoop of blond hair would arrive at my station.

"Eggs?"

"Thank you."

"Eggs?"

"Yeah, thanks."

"Eggs?"

"Were you really in juvie?"

I glanced up, and there he was, his bedhead hair defying the laws of physics.

"I like what you've done with your hair," I said.

He tried to flatten several cowlicks with his palm to no effect, and his cheeks reddened when he smiled. "Yeah, I haven't showered yet. Were you really in juvie?"

"Only for a few days," I said. "The judge ruled I acted in self-defense."

The boy smiled, unsure of himself.

"Eggs?" I asked again.

"Yes, please. I'm Sterling, by the way. Sterling Masters."

"Of course you are."

He reddened further. "I know. They named me after my great-great-grandfather. He ran an oil company or something."

The forced nonchalance with which Sterling added, "or something" led me to believe he knew everything there was to know about Eli Ambrose Sterling, founder of Sterling Oil and four-term congressman from Texas, but I let him play this off like it was no big deal.

"Well, I'm Izzy," I said, seeing no reason to add that my mom named me after the rhythm guitarist from Guns N' Roses.

"Nice to meet you, Izzy," Sterling said, offering his hand, but I declined by raising my lunchroom lady gloves.

"Oh, right," he said, blushing again. "So, will I see you at lunch?"

"I'll be here," I said, and he flashed a big smile and moved on toward the bacon while I continued serving scrambled eggs.

"Eggs?"

"Yes, please."

"Eggs?"

"Sure."

"Eggs?"

"Thursday greetings."

I gasped and looked up to see Elton Jones-Davies, all six-foot-eight inches of him, looking particularly lanky in a red Fuller Farms T-shirt and khaki shorts that were several inches too short.

"Elton!" I shouted, silencing the buzz of conversation that had filled the dining hall but not caring. I ran around the egg station and wrapped my arms around my friend in a bear hug he tolerated for several seconds before squirming away.

"What are you doing here?" I asked, shoving him with both hands.

"Attending summer camp," he replied like I was an idiot.

"Why didn't you tell me you were coming here?"

Since returning from London, I'd kept up with Elton as best I could, but he's nearly impossible to talk to on the phone, and he replies to texts with either one-word or one-thousand-word answers, nothing in between.

"I was not aware until yesterday," Elton said. "Mother believes it best I spend time away from the city this summer."

Elton's parents were in the middle of a nasty and public divorce that was of particular interest to the tabloids, and I suspect Holly Jones-Davies relished getting her only son away from the spotlight for two months.

"So she sent you here?" I asked.

"Affirmative. When I informed Mother of your summer employment, she called Mr. Fuller and arranged my attendance."

Since trusting me to look after Elton, I'd almost gotten him killed twice, but apparently, Holly still believed he was better off around me than not.

"But you hate sweating," I said, pointing out the fatal flaw in Holly's plan.

"Affirmative. I had also recently discovered an online game called Minecraft and planned to spend the summer playing it in my room. However, after discussing it with Mother, I concluded sweating outdoors was a small price to pay to spend the summer with you."

I nearly cried. "That may be the sweetest thing anyone has ever said to me, you donkey."

"Do you plan to embrace me again?" he asked, backing away.

"No, but only because we're holding up the line. But I'm hugging you again at lunch and maybe dinner."

I was still smiling an hour later, despite the perilously tall stack of food trays I had to wash before lunch. Elton was here. Elton Jones-Davies was at Fuller Farms, and the loneliness I'd felt in a new town had melted away in his awkward embrace. I hadn't been a good friend to him in London, and I'd felt particularly shitty about it since we returned, but now I had a chance to make amends. Now we could have a normal teenage summer that didn't involve solving murders or nearly dying. It would be great. And I won't lie, that a cute boy was already flirting with me was nice too, though my record with cute boys wouldn't let me get my hopes up yet.

"Izzy Brown!" Julie, my supervisor, barked, stomping into the kitchen like a drill sergeant.

"Here," I said, raising my hand because she hadn't bothered to learn our names.

"Mr. Fuller wants to see you in his office."

What the hell? I turned to Shelby, who gave me a knowing look.

"Now!" Julie snapped, and I left the kitchen in a sprint.

The four main buildings of Fuller Farms formed a giant rectangle, with the girls' and boys' dormitories making up the long sides and the dining hall and recreation center forming the ends. The fieldstone dining hall was built in the early sixties, but the other three buildings were new and constructed of dark-stained pine logs with steep-pitched hunter-green metal roofs and dark tinted glass. They looked rustic, but in the way a billionaire's mountain retreat would look rustic, and I suspected even the splinters in the wood were meticulously arranged by some overpaid decorator and specially designed not to prick your skin. In the middle of the four buildings was a football-field-sized lawn called the commons where several campers played a spirited game of flag football with some Carolina Panthers running back Fuller Farms had paid a fortune to show up for the week. As I jogged past, I spotted Elton under the covered porch of the boys' dorm, hiding from the morning sun.

Camp offices, including Wellington Fuller's, occupied the second floor of the recreation center, above the basketball court, ping-pong tables, and an auditorium where campers watched movies and performed on Skit Night.

"Mr. Fuller asked to see me," I said to the secretary stationed outside the camp offices, a woman who looked old enough to have voted for Abraham Lincoln.

"And who are you?" she demanded, squinting through Coke bottle glasses.

"Izzy Brown."

"Who?"

"Izzy Brown," I repeated, on the verge of shouting.

"Sissy Brown is here to see you," she said after pressing a button on her phone.

"Send her in," Mr. Fuller's voice crackled through the speaker. I was sitting across from his desk a moment later, unsure why.

Wellington Fuller's office was large and rustic, with several animal heads hanging from dark paneled walls. The picture window behind him offered a spectacular view of the lake and mountains beyond, but the sunshine streaming through cast the old man in silhouette, giving the impression of conversing with a shadow.

"Izzy Brown," he said, tapping a pen against a folder on his desk. "Have you enjoyed your short time here at Fuller Farms?"

"Yeah, so far, so good," I said.

"It's a most coveted position you've attained," he said, his accent reminding me of Foghorn Leghorn without the stutter.

"It's not lifeguarding at a male model camp, but I suppose it beats McDonald's."

I cringed as the smart-ass words left my mouth, but Mr. Fuller chuckled, and I knew I hadn't screwed up. Yet.

"Of course, it's not the work people covet but the pay. We compensate our employees well, which gives us the luxury of choice. Choosing the right employees ensures that the camp will run smoothly. We don't have to take chances on applicants with poor references or, say, an arrest record."

And there it was. Shit.

"Mr. Fuller, I swear, I didn't see anywhere on the application to mention my arrest, or I would have. I'm not proud of it, but it's not something I try to hide. If you'll let me—"

"There was no place on the application to mention prior arrests," Wellington Fuller assured me. "We conduct our own background searches to weed out potential problems."

"I ... I don't understand. If you—"

"And, as you know, we also conduct weekly drug tests. I believe we dismissed one of your colleagues in the kitchen on Tuesday. If history is any indicator, two or three more will likely go before the summer is out. I'm afraid there isn't much for teenagers to do up here in the mountains, and sadly, many turn to drugs out of boredom. Opioids are a particular problem of late. Last summer alone, we let three grounds crew members go after they tested positive for opiates."

"The test picks up opioids?" I asked, cringing at how guilty I sounded.

"It does," Mr. Fuller said, letting the silence marinate. "Would you like to see your test results?"

"No," I said, tears welling in my eyes.

"Good, because I've destroyed them."

"Mr. Fuller, I know you—wait, what?"

"Izzy, knowing we conduct thorough background checks on every applicant and dismiss employees who fail their drug tests on the spot, why, do you suppose, are you still here?"

Axl. It had to be Axl. Wellington Fuller wanted my brother to play football for North Carolina, and I was his go-between.

"Look, Mr. Fuller," I said, laughing to myself, "Axl and I are not on the best terms right now, so if you want him to play football for North Carolina, you'll have to—"

"Izzy, my allegiance to the Tar Heels begins and ends with basketball. I don't have the least interest in where your brother plays football, so long as it isn't Duke."

"I'm so confused," I said, shaking my head. "If you knew all those things about me, why did you still hire me to wash dishes?"

"I didn't hire you to wash dishes, Izzy," Wellington Fuller said, leaning in so I could see the intensity burning in his bright blue eyes. "I hired you to solve my son's murder."

So much for my normal teenage summer.

1992

Vance Fuller was humiliated.

Moving back home at twenty-eight was embarrassing enough. In returning, Vance knew he'd fulfilled the prophecy of every Ashes oracle who predicted he'd never amount to anything. Of every mountain seer who foretold this prodigal son's return to live off Daddy's money. So let it be written. So let it be done. When Vance took his seat at the bar in the Ashes Diner, he was aware the hushed conversations of the lunch crowd behind him all followed the same script.

"Who's the long-haired boy at the bar?"

"Vance Fuller. He moved back in with his folks."

"Ha! I told you so."

Never mind that Vance was a hair's breadth away from earning a PhD in art history at Chapel Hill. Or that he'd studied in Paris, Rome, and Tokyo. These mountain bumpkins couldn't tell a Caravaggio from a Cézanne, yet Vance was the failure. And why? Because of a misunderstanding? Because a committee of Vance's supposed peers chose to listen to one side of a story and not the other.

Still, he'd been careless. This much Vance would concede. He'd committed the cardinal sin of wealthy men—getting caught in a compromising situation and presenting the envious, pitchfork-toting horde an opportunity to exact their unwarranted revenge. The facts of the case pointed to his innocence, but the Committee on Student Behavior chose not to see them. They were jealous, just like the fools whispering behind his back in the Ashes Diner. And drunk on their power, the committee punished a blameless man.

That he was back living under his parents' considerable roof was embarrassing in the way all life's setbacks are, but what humiliated Vance most were the conditions his father set for his return. Wellington Fuller would continue to subsidize his son's interminable education into perpetuity at any institution of higher learning that would accept him if, and only if, Vance spent the summer working at Fuller Farms.

Camp counselor.

A twenty-eight-year-old camp counselor.

The shame was palpable.

Back in high school, Vance had no say in the matter. As the founder's grandson, it was a given he would attend Fuller Farms, and Vance recalled those four summers as the worst of his life. The boys' dormitory was stuffed full of dick slaps who'd go on to serve on things like the Committee on Student Behavior, ruining the lives of anyone and everyone who didn't meet their standard of cool. The only people Vance hated worse than Fuller Farms campers were the psychopaths who enjoyed their experience so much they applied to return as undergrads and serve as counselors. These people would be Vance's summer colleagues.

"It's only eight weeks," Vance's mother, Rosalind Fuller, told her despondent son the evening before counselor training began. She'd always played the good cop to Wellington's bad, but Vance was beyond consoling this time. He cried his twenty-eight-year-old self to sleep.

But the next morning, with the stoicism of a martyr entering the lion's den, Vance stuck out his chin and drove to Fuller Farms to face his fate. It was … okay, actually.

The girls were friendly, and the guys were, if not pleasant, at least tolerable, despite none of them being able to carry on a five-minute conversation without quoting *Wayne's World* at least once. Schwing! As the day wore on, Vance felt the unfamiliar buzz of acceptance, and sitting around a lakeside campfire that evening, toasting marshmallows and drinking cocoa, he admitted he'd been wrong. He'd prayed for tolerable, but this summer might be, dare he say it, fun.

"Vance, the man," Tripp, the musclebound alpha of the guy counselors, said as the group made their late-night trek back to the cabins.

"Tripp … a man," Vance replied. He was never good at guy talk.

"Hey, I just want to tell you," Tripp said, putting an arm around Vance and lowering his voice.

"Tell me what?" Vance asked. Did one of the other counselors already have a crush on him? Were the guys getting together to smoke a joint later? The possibilities were endless.

"I just want to tell you I know what you did at Chapel Hill."

Dammit.

"I know what you did, and you're going to pay."

CHAPTER FIVE

"Look, Mr. Fuller, I'm not sure I can—"

"Now hold on there, little lady," Wellington Fuller said, raising a hand and flashing a kind smile. "I know all about that murder you solved down in Florida and the case you cracked in England. You've got a knack for this stuff."

"Not really. I just—"

"Don't be modest, Izzy. It's unbefitting someone of your talents."

"But I'm not being modest," I said, squirming in my chair. "Yes, I solved two murders, but only after bumbling through the investigations, hurting several innocent people, and nearly getting myself killed. Twice."

"You've got to break some eggs to make an omelet," Mr. Fuller said.

I laughed despite myself. "Right, and if it's all the same to you, I'd rather serve those eggs this summer."

Outside, the sun dipped behind a cloud, darkening the office but bringing Mr. Fuller into focus. He continued to smile, but his tone no longer matched his demeanor. "Actually, Izzy, it's not all the same to me. I hired you to solve a murder."

"Well, next time, you might want to mention that earlier in the process," I snapped. I was more annoyed than angry, but Wellington raised his hands to apologize.

"You're right. I'm sorry," he said, spinning around toward the lake. "When you run a large company for half your life, it's easy to fall into the habit of bossing folks around, even when they don't work for you."

"It's okay," I said. "But if the police couldn't solve the murder, what makes you think I can?"

"The police called off their investigation," he said, turning back to face me. "They called off their investigation at my wife Rosalind's request."

"What? Why?"

"Izzy, I don't want to say too much because I don't want to influence your thinking on the case. But there was a slew of rumors going around about Vance, and Rosalind believed them. She was scared if the police dug too deep, the world would learn our poor dead boy was a monster. So, she asked Chief Morrison if he'd let the case go cold, and he did."

"You can do that?" I asked.

Wellington Fuller shrugged as if to say rich people could do whatever they wanted. "The thing is," he said, "I never bought any of that nonsense about Vance, and it's not like stopping the investigation stopped the rumors. But now that Rosalind is gone, I want to know the truth."

"I can appreciate that," I said, "but Mr. Fuller, I promised my mother I'd stay out of trouble this summer."

Wellington chuckled. "Izzy, it sounds like you've found your life's true calling, and that's a scary thing. Don't answer me now, but take a moment and try to remember what it's like working a case."

I didn't have to try to remember because I'd never been happier in my life. While obsessing over a murder, I experienced the utter ecstasy of a fully occupied mind. A focus so intense it left no room for the anxiety that typically inhabited significant acreage in my brain. Now, granted, this hyper-concentration on one thing damaged some relationships beyond repair and caused my schoolwork to suffer, but I had to figure out some way to get through life, and so far, it was either pills or solving murders. At least the latter was legal, if not safer.

"It's exhilarating, finding your life's true calling," Mr. Fuller said after a moment. "But then that devil on your shoulder starts whispering all manner of nonsense in your ear. So many people throw away their best lives because they're worried their happiness might disappoint someone else. You told your mama you'd stay out of trouble this summer, and I can understand that. But, honey, I ain't asking you to get into trouble. Seventeen years ago, someone murdered my boy in cold blood right out yonder. All I'm asking is for you to use your God-given talents to give this old man some closure."

"I'm sorry about your son, Mr. Fuller, but every time I use my God-given talents, someone tries to kill me, and I promised my mother—"

"Fifty-thousand dollars."

"—that I'd ... I'm sorry, what?"

Wellington smiled. "Fifty grand. Find the killer, and it's yours."

Shit, that was a lot of money. It could pay for college. It could pay for so much. The devil on my shoulder started going on about promising my mother I'd stay out of trouble, but the devil on my other shoulder began twerking and singing, "Dolla dolla bills, y'all." Apparently, I don't have an angel.

"I don't have a car," I said, still searching for an excuse. "So I can't—"

"—The camp has several vehicles. You can borrow one whenever you need it."

"Okay, but my mother thinks I have a summer job here."

"You do have a summer job here. You can serve eggs four days a week and investigate the other three. I'll pay you for all seven days."

"That's beyond generous, Mr. Fuller, but—"

"But what, Izzy?" he said, smiling and making a show of checking his watch.

"It's just, I didn't exactly solve those murders by myself. I couldn't have done it without my friend Elton, and he's—"

"Here at Fuller Farms. His mother applied months after anyone could reasonably expect to secure their child a spot, but we accepted him. Why do you think that is?"

"Wait, does Holly know Elton is here to help me solve a murder?"

"No," Wellington said, "but what she doesn't know won't hurt her, will it?"

I thought of Elton, hiding under the dormitory porch in a futile attempt to avoid the summer sun. If this investigation would keep him in conditioned air, he'd be thrilled.

"Well?" Mr. Fuller asked, breaking a long stretch of silence.

I shook my head and smiled. Sometimes you feel in control of your fate, standing tall at the helm of destiny, but it's an illusion. We're all adrift in the storm of life, with no say in which shore we wash up on. I could promise Mom I'd stay out of trouble until I was blue in the face, but, it seems, trouble will find me.

"Fine," I said, "tell me everything you can about the murder."

"Look, I told Mr. Fuller I won't speak for you, so if you don't want to help with this, you don't have to."

"However, if I assist you, I am authorized to use this office whenever my research necessitates?"

"Yeah," I said, and Elton wrapped his long arms around me and squeezed until I couldn't breathe.

"Oh, Izzy, thank you," he said after I fought free. "This is most appreciated."

"Remember that when someone tries to kill us later this summer."

"Death is preferable to capture the flag in this murderous heat."

"Elton, it's only seventy-nine degrees."

"And have you encountered the mosquitoes here? This morning I witnessed one assassinate a hawk."

I laughed, though he wasn't exaggerating about the mosquitoes.

We were in an empty camp office above the recreation center. Mr. Fuller said it could be ours while investigating his son's murder. It only had two swivel chairs, a whiteboard, and an ancient Dell computer, but the internet was fast for the middle of nowhere, so we had all we needed, even if the deer heads on the wall creeped me out.

"Okay," I said, hanging the photograph Wellington Fuller provided me of his son on the whiteboard with a magnet, "this is our victim, Vance Fuller. He was murdered in 1992. What do you know about him?"

"Zero," Elton admitted.

"Wait, for real?"

"Affirmative," Elton said. "There were 23,760 murders committed in the United States in 1992, and I am unfamiliar with most of them."

"Fair enough," I said. "Mr. Fuller told me Vance was working here as a camp counselor the summer he died."

Elton stood and examined the photograph closer and said, "He appears to be of an advanced age for a camp counselor."

"Yeah, he was twenty-eight," I said. "I asked Mr. Fuller about that, and he said Vance had almost finished his PhD at North Carolina but wanted to take one last summer off before joining the real world. I don't believe him, though."

"I concur," Elton said. "Anyone would prefer the real world to this place."

I laughed and said, "No, it's just that part of his story felt, I don't know, overly rehearsed." I leaned in for a closer look at the photograph. In it, Vance stood next to a creepy painting of a woman and her baby while lecturing a small group of students standing close by. His tweed coat, tinted John Lennon glasses, and long frizzy black hair pulled back in a ponytail suggested a man who'd avoid the outdoors at all costs. But looks can be deceiving. Admittedly, I knew nothing about Vance Fuller, apart from how he died.

"Arrows," I told Elton. "They found him tied to a hay bale on the archery range shot full of arrows."

Elton made a pained face and asked, "Did the authorities suspect anyone?"

"Maybe, but they never charged anyone," I said. "The police questioned all the campers, counselors, and employees, but nothing came of it. Mr. Fuller is friends with Chief Jenkins at the Ashes Police Department. He said we're welcome to visit the station and read through the interviews."

"We should go now," Elton said.

I laughed. "We can't go now. I've got to get back to the kitchen. I'm working today." I'd already been gone an hour, and Shelby would have a million questions when I returned. Somehow I'd have to think of a million lies. "I'm off next Tuesday though. So we can go then."

"So I have to go back to camp?" Elton whimpered.

"Nope, Mr. Fuller said he'd talk to your counselor. You can stay here and research until your heart's content. Just show up at mealtime and lights out."

Elton couldn't contain his smile.

"Oh, and Mr. Fuller said he didn't want to taint our investigation but suggested we start with a man named Buster McClellan. The police questioned him in 1992, and Mr. Fuller thinks he's worth looking into again."

"I'm on it," Elton said, and with a dramatic spin in his chair, he began typing furiously on the keyboard. I didn't even make it to the door before he called after me. "Uh, Izzy, I have discovered Buster McClellan's Facebook profile."

"Oh yeah? Let me see."

I walked back and looked over Elton's shoulder at the screen. There he was, Buster McClellan, Ashes, North Carolina. But there was no profile photo, only a black box with red words that said, I DID NOT KILL VANCE FULLER.

CHAPTER SIX

"Good morning, baby girl."

"Morning," I said, stumbling into our kitchen and searching for a Pop-Tart. The box was empty—dammit, Axl—so I nuked a freezer-burned Eggo waffle and doused it with an unhealthy amount of syrup. Bon appétit.

"How are things at the farm?" Mom asked as I sat next to her on the couch. She'd worked the last few nights at Fraîche, and we hadn't seen each other in a few days. "They ain't working you too hard, are they?"

"The farm is good," I said, taking a bite of my waffle and finding it lacking despite the best efforts of Mrs. Butterworth. "Elton is there."

"Elton Jones-Davies at a summer camp?" Mom asked, choking on a sip of black coffee. "Doesn't that boy hate sweating?"

"More than anything, but Holly wanted to get him out of the city for the summer. So the camp came to an arrangement of sorts for him to stay inside most of the time."

"Well, that's good," Mom said with a laugh, and I was thankful she didn't inquire further about the arrangement.

"How's Fraîche?" I asked.

"It's a job," Mom said. "I already know more about cheese than I ever wanted, but these women tip the bag boys with twenty-dollar bills, and they have to split it with the cashiers."

"Well, I'm making pretty good this summer too, so please let me know what you need for my share of the rent and stuff."

"Baby girl, I ain't charging my daughter rent. You save your money up and get yourself a car. Lenny and I are fine."

Lenny. How anyone could take comfort in the thought of Lenny providing for their well-being was beyond me, but my mother seemed happy. Happier perhaps than I'd ever known her. So, I let it slide.

"Shit," I said, standing to throw away my soggy paper plate and realizing the pill I'd taken to wipe out my eleventh consecutive headache had not done its job.

"You okay?" Mom asked.

"Just a headache," I said, wishing I hadn't because Mom would worry.

"You haven't had one of those lately," Mom said.

Yeah, not since yesterday, I thought. "It's been a while," I said, letting her believe it.

"That therapist lady you talked to in London must have done something right."

I grunted without comment.

"If you want to find one around here to talk to, we could probably afford it."

"No, Mom, I'm fine. I read somewhere it takes about a month to get used to the altitude here."

"Well, we've got Advil in the cabinet if you need it."

"Thanks," I said and took a couple for show. Ten minutes later, I puked in my toilet and felt a little better.

It wasn't just my headaches, though. Since moving to Ashes, my baseline sense of dread had risen to levels I hadn't dealt with since Bardo. Typically, my anxiety attached itself to an insecurity or current event that had little to do with me. Over the years, I'd worried myself sick over dirty bombs, mad cow disease, hostile extraterrestrials, friendly extraterrestrials, tumors—both benign and malignant, lead paint, losing my virginity, never losing my virginity, any extinct civilization's end of the world prediction, rogue waves, cloud bursts, and artificial intelligence, to name a few.

"*Izzy, you know*," Dr. Carrick once told me during a therapy session, "*most things you seem to worry about never happen.*"

"*Yeah*," I said, "*because I don't let that shit sneak up on me.*" She was not amused.

My mother's ability to provide for us and the likelihood I'd spend the rest of my life in our sad little hometown of Dandridge used to consume my waking hours and half my dreams. But in the last year, I'd left Dandridge three times, and I now felt certain one of these days, a move would stick. We weren't rich, but things were better now, even if half our financial stability depended on a drug dealer in jorts. I tried not to think about that too much. Plus, I had Elton and his mother and an unspoken understanding they'd take care of me, assuming Mustang Jones didn't take every dime to their name.

No, the anxiety I felt upon moving to Ashes was so hazy and unspecific it took me weeks to realize I was even anxious. The signs were there. The headaches. Insomnia. The tightness in my chest and the tension in my arms that felt like I'd always just finished a hundred push-ups. But when I tried to scratch the itch of my worry, nothing was there. It was like opening your mouth and immediately forgetting what you were about to say.

I got dressed for work, and not wanting to risk bumping into Lenny, I waited outside for Shelby. Axl left for the gym at the same time.

"How's the new job?" he asked, offering a fist bump I hesitated to return. We hadn't been on friendly enough terms for a fist bump since I got back from London, but maybe the ice was thawing.

"It's a job," I said, trying not to resent that our mom never made Axl seek summer employment.

"Any skanks out there you can hook me up with?"

"Did you not know? Fuller Farms is actually a camp for wayward skanks."

"Bitching," Axl said with a laugh, then left to work out, leaving me in the parking lot, staring at the mountains.

After living most of my life at sea level, the mountains unnerved me. Perhaps it was awe. I recalled the way Brother Barry at the Dandridge Church of God and Prophecy used to yell about God. "One day, you will stand in awe of your maker," he'd shout, making the meeting sound more like something to dread than anticipate. Something that would involve a great deal of fear and trembling, like meeting Voldemort. The mountains looked too big to be real, and maybe, subconsciously, I'd conflated them with God. Was that why looking at them made me so nervous? Were the mountains judging me from on high? Threatening damnation for my poor choices? Preparing hellfire for the eleventh pill I'd taken in a row? They weren't, of course. I didn't know it then, but studies had shown a link between higher altitudes and increased anxiety. I only knew those towering peaks filled me with an unexplainable dread. Shelby's driving didn't help.

The morning was foggy, adding an extra layer of horror to our drive down the mountain. Poor visibility didn't stop Shelby from driving with her knees while lighting her morning cigarette or from taking her eyes off the road whenever she'd talk to me. I stared at the floorboard and prayed silently to the mountains for my part.

"It was about my drug test," I lied after Shelby asked me for the millionth time what Mr. Fuller wanted with me the morning before. The girl didn't take "none of your business" for an answer.

She laughed. "I thought you didn't take pills anymore."

"I don't," I said. "But traces of them still showed up on my test. Mr. Fuller said he wanted me to look him in the eye and promise I wasn't still using."

"And that took an hour?"

"No, I sat outside his office for fifty minutes. He wanted to make me sweat."

"You're lucky," Shelby said, apparently buying my story. "Old man Fuller hates drugs."

"So I've heard."

"Rumor is his son was taking when he died."

"Wait, really?" I asked, trying not to sound too interested.

"Yeah. The dude got kicked out of UNC for snorting coke during class or some shit. That's why he had to move back in with his parents."

This didn't jive with Wellington's version of why Vance moved back home, but I figured the truth was somewhere in the middle.

"I mean, why else would he be working as a camp counselor in his forties?"

"Twenty-eight," I said.

"Whatever."

A suicidal squirrel darted in front of us, and Shelby fishtailed her Honda into the oncoming lane before swerving back as if nothing had happened. I stuck my head out the window, but somehow, my waffle stayed down.

"You okay over there?" she asked, laughing.

"Yeah," I said once I remembered how to breathe. "But I don't understand what Vance Fuller being on drugs had to do with him being tied up and shot full of arrows."

"People do weird shit on drugs," Shelby said with a shrug. "Last year, two meth heads in Waynesville went all Aaron Burr and had a pistol duel on Main Street. One got his nose shot clean off. Anyway, you're lucky you didn't get fired on the spot. Fuller let my Aunt Jenny go years ago for pot, and she only smoked because she thought she had glaucoma."

"Your aunt worked here too?"

"Most of my family has. Mom was here the summer Vance Fuller got killed.

"No shit?"

"Yeah, but she won't talk about it. Gets all weird when you ask her. I've always suspected they were hooking up, like you and that Sterling boy."

"I'm not hooking up with Sterling."

"Yet," Shelby said with a laugh, but I was too busy wondering how I could talk to her mother about Vance Fuller to argue.

CHAPTER SEVEN

"Fancy meeting you here."

I looked up from my tray of scrambled eggs to see Sterling smiling at me, his usually floppy blond hair slicked back after a morning shower.

"You can use that line once," I said, dropping eggs on his plate, "and if you use it again, I'll beat you to death with this serving spoon."

His smile faded.

"Next," I said, but Sterling rebounded from the setback.

"When can I see you?"

"Mealtimes."

"No, when can we talk?"

I rolled my eyes but smiled despite myself. "I'm free for half an hour at eleven."

"We've got Bible study at eleven, but I'll skip it."

"Fine, but don't blame me when you burn in hell."

"Totally worth it," Sterling said. "I'll see you here at eleven."

I risked glancing down the line toward Shelby, but quickly turned away when she pointed at Sterling and began humping the biscuit table.

Sterling wandered into the kitchen five minutes early. I was finished washing dishes but made him wait outside until eleven to punish his overeager ass.

"Want to walk around the Mud Lake?" he asked when I finally joined him outside.

"Sure," I said, and we walked through the commons, past the recreation center, climbing wall, and tennis courts, and down to the well-worn dirt trail around the twenty-acre lake.

"I wonder why they call this Mud Lake," I said, tossing a rock into the water that looked like used motor oil.

Sterling laughed. "Can you believe campers used to swim in it? Thank God they built the pool. Have you been down the waterslide yet? It's insane."

I gave him my best are-you-an-idiot stare until he remembered I was an employee and not a camper, then he mumbled an apology and we walked in silence for a moment, the distant screams from his fellow campers going down the waterslide punctuating his embarrassment.

"So, where are you from?" I asked after we stopped to watch some whitetail deer that wandered out of the woods.

"Our family ranch is in Northfork, Texas," he said, "but I attend a boarding school in Houston. There isn't shit in Northfork except oil wells and longhorn cattle." I laughed, and Sterling said, "Seriously, the only restaurant within a hundred miles of our place is Gina's Diner, and I wouldn't eat there if I was starving."

"And I guess you're from here?" Sterling asked, after something spooked the deer and they darted back into the woods.

"No, we just moved to Ashes a few weeks ago."

"Where from?"

"London," I said.

"London, England?" he asked, visibly confused.

"Yeah, via Florida. It's a long story, but I lived there with my friend Elton for a couple of months."

"Elton, the tall Black dude I saw you hugging at breakfast yesterday."

"Yeah," I said.

"He's—"

"He's on the autism spectrum, and he's my best friend in the world, and if I find out you or any of the boys are bullying him, I will murder you."

Sterling laughed.

"No, Sterling, I will poison your eggs and drag your lifeless body into the woods, where raccoons will pick your bones clean. Do you understand?"

"No, he's cool," Sterling said, raising his hands in apology. "That's all I was going to say."

"Good," I said, smiling up at him.

"So, how exactly do you two know each other? If he's …"

"If he's rich enough to camp here, and I'm poor enough to work here?"

"No, I mean—"

"—It's okay," I said, figuring I'd tortured the poor boy enough for one morning. "Elton is rich, and I'm poor. His dad is Mustang Jones."

"The running back?"

"The asshole," I corrected. "Anyway, my brother, Axl, is the fifth-ranked pro-style quarterback prospect for the class of 2011, and last year we were on scholarship at a swanky prep school in Florida. That's where I met Elton. We lost our scholarships after I accused the man paying our tuition of killing a boy twenty-five years ago, and then he had me arrested for drug possession—look, do you want me to keep talking, or have you heard enough to know you don't want to pursue this any further?"

Sterling laughed. "Everyone has their own shit."

"Oh really?" I asked. "And what's your shit, Sterling Masters? You're a male model whose family probably owns half the oil wells in West Texas. So what, did one of your uncles get caught driving a Prius?"

"My family does own half the oil wells in West Texas," Sterling said with a grin, "but God, Izzy, none of them would ever be caught dead in a Prius. What an awful thing to say." I laughed, and Sterling said, "Seriously though, if you want to know my shit, I haven't seen my dad in over a year."

"For real?" I asked, shoving him. "I haven't seen my father since I was three. Does your dad live in Nebraska with a one-legged stripper too?"

"What?"

"Wait, sorry, Destiny is a war hero. I keep forgetting."

Sterling shook his head before saying, "No, my dad lives on his boat."

"Yikes, I'd get claustrophobic living on a boat."

"It's three hundred feet long," Sterling said.

"Oh. Right. I could probably manage that."

Sterling smiled. "Last March, when my grandfather died, everyone assumed my father would take over Sterling Oil. But they passed him over for my uncle, and he must have lost it. He left on Tax Day, April 15th. I remember because when I called home that week, Mom made a joke about Dad doing anything not to pay taxes. We all figured he was just blowing off steam, but we haven't heard from him since.

"That sucks, Sterling. I'm sorry."

He shrugged. "It's hard to miss someone you never saw much of anyway. It's weird, though, because Mom removed all the pictures of him in the house, but there's one here in our dorm."

"What? Why?"

"Tradition. Every summer camp since 1963 gets their group picture on the wall."

"Your dad went to camp here?" I asked, quickly doing the math in my head and breathing a sigh of relief. He was probably here in the early eighties.

"Yeah, sometime in the early nineties."

Shit. That didn't add up. "When in the early nineties?" I asked.

"I don't know," Sterling said, his tone suggesting he'd prefer to talk about anything else than his absentee father. "But it was the year that counselor died."

No, no, no! Elton's voice rang in my ears. *Must you always try to find dirt on the parents of your boyfriends?* But I wasn't looking for dirt, and Sterling wasn't my boyfriend. I just needed to make sure his father wasn't a killer before we made out, that's all. "How old are you?" I asked.

"Sixteen," he said, and noticing the pained look of concentration on my face, he added, "My parents had me when they were eighteen if that's what you're wondering. Freshman year of college."

"Oh," I said. The math did work. I just hadn't considered that rich people got knocked up when they were teenagers too.

"Yeah," Sterling said, blushing slightly. "It was a big scandal, as you can imagine. Quickie wedding. Mom dropped out of college. My grandparents still hate each other. We're all super dysfunctional."

"Okay, Sterling Masters, you win," I said, giving him a little side hug. "You have your own shit." He hugged me back with no intention of letting me go, but I squirmed away and said, "Alright, Romeo, I've got to get back to work. But I'm free every day at this time if you're willing to miss Bible study and risk your mortal soul."

"More than willing," he said, crossing himself. "Oh, and hey, is there any chance you'd want to come back out here tonight?"

"To Fuller Farms?"

"Yeah, on Fridays and Saturdays after lights out, a big group always sneaks down here to the lake to hang out for a few hours. We'll be here by eleven, and you could park at the end of the road, and—never mind, I'm sure you have better things to do than—"

"—I'll try to make it," I said, and Sterling smiled ear to ear.

After lunch, I went to our office and found Elton hunched over the computer, typing like his fingers were on fire and looking like he hadn't slept in a week.

"You missed lunch," I said.

"Friday greetings," Elton replied.

"And breakfast," I added. "The most important meal of the day."

"Recent studies suggest breakfast is no more important than any other meal," Elton said, and I turned off the computer monitor so he'd look at me.

"I said you could work here, but you needed to go to meals and make an appearance at camp now and then. Did you even sleep in your bed last night?"

"Affirmative," Elton said. "The bunkbeds have Sleep Number mattresses and are quite comfortable. Besides, if we are not present at lights out, a search party is formed, and I do not want anyone eaten by a bear on my account."

"Okay, well, promise me you'll go to at least every other meal from now on. I won't have you getting rickets on my watch."

"Rickets is caused by a vitamin D deficiency, and my daily multi-vitamin provides—

"—It was a joke," I said, and Elton forced a laugh. "Okay, what have you found?"

"Apart from his Facebook page, Buster McClellan's online presence is minimal. And even that page has no posts or photos, only the profile picture declaring his innocence in the murder of Vance Fuller. However, I did find his address. 2456 Sour Mash Road ."

"Yeah, I don't know where that is."

"It is between here and Ashes, five miles off State Road 99. Satellite images on Google Maps reveal his is the only house in a four-mile radius."

"Oh great, so no one will hear us scream when he murders us too," I mumbled.

"What?"

"Nothing. Does he have a phone number we can call?"

"Negative. I am not certain he even has electricity."

"Okay," I said, knowing we'd have to go off the grid to visit Buster sooner or later. "Good work, Big E. Now I've got two more people for you to investigate. My friend Shelby's mom worked here when Vance died."

"What is her name?"

"Shelby Ray."

"No, her mother's name."

"I don't know."

Elton stared at me.

"I'll find out," I said, raising my hands in surrender. "In the meantime, see what you can find out about my friend Sterling's dad."

"The boy you were just hugging?" Elton asked, pointing out the window at Mud Lake.

"Yes," I said, ignoring his knowing look. "I don't know his name either, but their family owns Sterling Oil, so it shouldn't be hard to find.

"I'm on it," Elton said with a dramatic salute, and I left him to go wash the lunch dishes.

CHAPTER EIGHT

"You want to come back here tonight? When we're not getting paid?"

"Sterling said a bunch of kids hang out by the lake. It'll be fun."

Shelby rolled her eyes. "You think hanging out with those little rich pricks who won't even say thanks when you serve their eggs will be fun?"

"Yeah," I said without conviction.

"Sorry, bitch, but I've got a date tonight. You're on your own."

I'd played it cool with Sterling at the lake but had every intention of returning to Fuller Farms that night to see him. My problem was transportation. Shelby had a date with some redneck named Buck, who kept a mattress in his truck bed. Mr. Fuller gave me permission to use a camp vehicle if I needed to interview someone, but that wouldn't help me tonight. I had one last hope, but it was a long shot.

"Big plans tonight?" I asked Axl, who was sprawled out on the couch watching SpongeBob.

"Yep," he said, not looking my way.

"Any chance you'd want to drive me to a party at Fuller Farms?"

"Nope," he said, cranking the volume on the television.

I pushed Axl's legs to the floor and plopped down next to him to watch the show. Squidward always cracked me up.

"There'll be girls," I said during the commercial break. "Hot girls."

"Hot girls, where?" Lenny asked as he and Mom walked into the den.

"Fuller Farms," I said. "There's a bonfire on Friday nights at the lake, and employees can go."

"That sounds fun," Mom said. "Y'all should go."

"It's just s'mores and camp songs," I said, "but it's something to do." I knew if I made it sound wholesome enough, Mom would waive our curfew for the evening.

"Sounds lame," Axl said.

"Well, sure, but everything sounds lame compared to a Friday night at home watching SpongeBob with your mom and her boyfriend."

Axl glared at me but didn't reply.

"That settles it then," Lenny said, "y'all are going." He put his arm around Mom and said, "Me and your mamma need some alone time anyhow."

"Gross," I said, trying to leave the room before Lenny elaborated, but he sang, "Bow chicka wow wow" before I could make it to the door.

Back in Bardo, football boosters provided Axl with a shiny new Dodge Charger to drive around town, but Ashes Prep apparently thought a fifty-thousand-dollar education was adequate compensation for my brother's work on the gridiron. So Axl now drove a 1992 Ford Ranger, paid for by pawning all the gifts his ex-girlfriend Sophie

Wolfe gave him during their doomed relationship. The truck was a rolling pile of garbage, but I didn't even own a bike, so I kept my insults to myself lest Axl change his mind about driving me to see Sterling.

"Tell me about these girls," he said, driving down the mountain at more reasonable speeds than Shelby.

"They're rich," I said.

"And hot?"

"Aren't all rich girls?"

Axl shrugged. "I'm a little burnt out on rich people, to be honest," he said.

My brother was the life of any party. Good looking, charming, and as extroverted as I was introverted. But since moving to Ashes, he spent most of his time at the school's gym or home on our couch. Usually, by now, Axl would be dating the head cheerleader after claiming his spot atop the social food chain, but it seemed his classmates hadn't warmed to him yet. No doubt he'd get there. Once Axl threw six touchdowns in his first game, he'd ascend to that rarified peak of popularity known only to handsome quarterbacks. But he wasn't there yet, leaving him slightly off-kilter.

We parked at the locked main gate to Fuller Farms and walked a mile through the woods on the winding gravel road. The sliver of moon hanging high above did little to light our way, and those dark woods freaked me out, even with my giant brother beside me. Hadn't Shelby mentioned cave-dwelling devil worshippers living nearby? But after ten minutes, we reached the clearing and saw the lights of the camp buildings beyond Mud Lake, shimmering under a billion stars.

"I guess they haven't lit the bonfire yet," Axl said.

"No bonfire," I told him. "Some campers just sneak out here on weekend nights to hang out."

"Izzy Rose Brown, did you lie to our dear mother?"

"No. Not exactly. There could be s'mores. You never know."

We spotted half a dozen silhouettes at the edge of the lake, and as we walked toward them, I prayed at least one belonged to a girl. If this was a trust fund sausage party, Axl would drag me back to his truck and never speak to me again.

"Hey," I said as we approached the group, and everyone froze. "Is, uh, Sterling out here?"

"Izzy," Sterling said, emerging from the group, "you scared the shit out of us."

"We thought you were a counselor," one of the other guys said as I scanned the crowd. Six dudes. No girls. Dammit.

"Found it," a third guy said, raising the joint he'd quickly discarded when we walked up. A hushed cheer erupted from the group, and I now noticed none of them had on shirts.

"Uh," I asked, "any particular reason y'all are topless?"

"The smoke would make our T-shirts smell," Sterling explained. "They're piled up on the dock."

"Does the smoke not make your shorts smell?"

"No, because the smoke goes up," one of the guys said like I was the dumb one here.

"Hey, Percy, give Izzy a hit," Sterling said to one of the boys, who stepped forward and offered me the joint.

Under different circumstances, this might have been one of the crises of my young life. Yes, I'd technically taken illegal drugs that morning, but the pills served a purpose: making me feel normal and fending off debilitating headaches. In my mind, there was a clear demarcation line between illegal drugs that got me high and illegal drugs that simply got me through life. But I'm not immune to the charms of cute boys and the suffocating urgency of peer pressure. Thankfully, I had an excuse.

"I can't. They drug test employees," I said, and a murmur of sympathy passed over the crowd.

"They don't drug test me," Axl said, stepping up and towering over the group. "I'm Axl, Izzy's brother."

Introductions and fist bumps followed, and Axl took a long hit on the joint. I wasn't thrilled with him but had to admit he likely needed to be high to spend the night with a group of half-naked guys in a field.

"Hey, want to go for a walk?" Sterling asked me after a while, and when I said yes, he took my hand and led me away to catcalls from his friends. I saluted them with a middle finger.

"I can't believe you came," he said as we rounded the lake.

"It was touch and go," I said. "I don't have a car, so I had to promise Axl there would be girls here. I suspect he'll quickly remind me of that on the drive home."

Sterling laughed. "Yeah, sorry, I may have oversold the party. The girls at camp suck, so they're never invited."

I wanted to ask Sterling about his dad. If he knew Vance Fuller when he was at Fuller Farms. If he perhaps had reason to shoot him full of arrows. But the boy was caressing my fingers in a way that made coherent thought impossible, and instead, I had to focus on remembering to breathe. Across the lake from the group, we detoured off the path into the pines, where a blanket lay waiting in a clearing.

Elton would insist in the multiverse, there exists a universe where blankets randomly materialize whenever you require one, but I suspect Sterling Masters placed this one here in anticipation of some late-night romance.

"Oh, look, a blanket in the wild," I teased. "How lucky for us."

"I thought you might want to get away from the guys," Sterling said, blushing so brightly I could see it in the dark.

"Yeah, if you've seen one group of shirtless guys smoke a joint, you've seen them all."

Sterling laughed. "I really like you, Izzy."

"You don't know me," I said.

"I know I want to kiss you."

"Yeah?"

"Yeah."

"What's stopping you?"

It was all the invitation he needed. A flurry of lips, tongue, and hands put me on my back. Sterling smelled of smoke, sweat, and money, and I kissed him back with my hands all over his bare back. I'll admit it; I got carried away. I hadn't done this in a long time, considering my last boyfriend didn't like girls. But soon, even the devils on my shoulders thought we were taking things a little too fast.

"What's wrong?" he asked when I sat up and wiped my lips.

"Nothing," I said, getting to my feet.

"Something's wrong," he insisted.

"Nothing's wrong," I promised, helping him to his feet and kissing him hard with both hands on his face. "But we've got all summer," I said. "No need to rush things."

I got the feeling Sterling was perfectly fine with rushing things, but he smiled anyway and said, "You're right. We've got all summer."

When we returned to the lake, the pot was gone, and the boys were hungry. The party fell apart after another half hour, and I kissed Sterling goodbye in front of everyone. It was more public affection than I'm comfortable with, but I didn't want him worrying about us all weekend. I just wanted to know him better before …

I drove Axl's truck home while he slept in the passenger seat. He'd taken the joint so casually I wondered if he'd started smoking while I was in London or if he'd ever stopped taking the pills he began taking in Bardo after injuring his ankle. I shook his shoulder, looking for conversation, but he only snored in reply.

"Come on," I said, pulling my brother from the truck when we reached the apartment. "Mom and Lenny might still be awake."

Axl perked up with alarming speed, achieving an allusion of sobriety so convincing I almost fell for it. I suspected this skill had served him well in recent years.

Upstairs, I opened the apartment door like someone cracking a safe, and we slipped into the empty living room to find the lights still on. Nothing irritated our mother more than leaving the lights on when you left a room, so the sight of an empty room ablaze with incandescent bulbs startled me.

"Mom," I called out but got no reply.

Axl followed me down the hall toward the sound of running water. "Mom!" I said, louder this time, noticing the splotches on the carpet but not realizing what they were yet.

My knock opened the bathroom door to reveal our mother standing over the sink, holding a bag of ice over her right eye and a bloodstained washcloth over her nose.

I didn't ask what happened.

I already knew.

Fucking Lenny.

1992

Vance Fuller hoped the worst was over.

The other counselors knew about Chapel Hill, but the campers wouldn't, and that's who he'd spend most of the next eight weeks with. They arrived on Wednesday, and Vance met the three boys he was to mold into young men over the next two months. They were seniors, eighteen-year-olds, and Vance's heart dropped. He'd requested freshmen. Camp virgins who, at least for a few weeks, were unlikely to test the boundaries of Vance's feeble authority. Seniors, while older, were far less mature. These boys fell firmly on the downslope of the inverted bell curve of youthful depravity. A slope that would bottom out sometime during their sophomore year of college when they'd wake up naked in a Taco Bell bathroom stall.

These three were hellions.

Anyone could see it.

Vance prayed he'd survive the summer.

"Okay, icebreaker time," Vance said. "Let's play two truths and a lie."

They were on a Mud Lake dock during a half-hour session designed for campers and counselors to get to know one another, and the three boys had paid minimal attention while Vance rehashed camp rules and regulations.

The boys rolled their eyes.

They were too cool for icebreakers.

Too cool for everything.

"You go first," Vance said, pointing toward the tall boy with a swoop of blond hair falling over his glasses. "Tell us your name, two truths, and a lie."

"Aubrey Masters," the boy said. "My great-grandfather was a US congressman, my family's Texas ranch is larger than Rhode Island, and, uh, my uncle owns the Houston Oilers."

"Okay, any guesses?" Vance asked the group.

"We all know each other," Aubrey said. "You'll have to guess."

"Fine," Vance said, "there's no way your uncle owns the Oilers."

"Right," Aubrey said, "he owns the Houston Rockets."

"The Rockets suck," the boy in the Nirvana T-shirt with Kurt Cobain hair said, and Aubrey shoved him but laughed.

"Okay, your turn," Vance said, pointing at the long-haired boy, who looked faintly familiar.

"Jasper Benson," he said, and Vance nodded in recognition. Jasper was a local kid, and the Bensons were as close to North Carolina royalty as the Fuller clan. "And lying is a sin, so I will not partake in this immoral contest."

Vance rolled his eyes but let the kid have his joke. "Fine, you go," Vance said to the third boy, a tan, athletic kid with Ken-doll features.

"Quinn Westlake," the boy said, "and I was second-team all-state in lacrosse last season." He certainly looked the part, Vance thought. "I drive a 1963 Aston Martin DB5," Quinn continued, but Vance didn't know enough about cars to be impressed. "And finally," Quinn said, "I've killed a man."

Vance knew the story.

Everyone knew the story.

So this was the kid.

Home alone when a vagrant knocked on the door, looking for work. The Westlake estate was gated, of course, but someone left the gate open that morning, and Quinn later told police he feared the man had jumped the fence intent on murder. In the end, authorities concluded Quinn acted in self-defense, never mind he shot the man in the back from twenty yards away. The Westlakes' attorneys were so ruthless, the homeless man would have had to pay to remove his bloodstains from the driveway had he not been dead and penniless. But it was murder at worst, an unspeakable tragedy at best, and certainly not something any normal person would casually drop during a summer camp icebreaker. But Quinn smirked at Vance while the other boys shuffled uncomfortably.

"Well," Quinn said, snapping Vance back to the present, "what's the lie?"

"You don't drive the car," Vance guessed, eager to get this over with.

"Nope. I wasn't second-team all-state," Quinn said. "I was first."

"That's great," Vance said, getting to his feet. "Let's get back to the—"

"—Hold on, Buffalo Bill, it's your turn," Jasper Benson said, making a *Silence of the Lambs* reference that was lost on Vance. "But we'll make it easy on you. Instead of two truths and a lie, why don't you tell us why they kicked you out of Chapel Hill."

Dammit. They knew.

Vance Fuller hoped the worst was over.

But it had only just begun.

CHAPTER NINE

"It was as much my fault as Lenny's."

"Bullshit. Lenny is twice your size, so unless you were chasing him around the apartment with a machete, I don't—"

"—Baby girl, you don't understand. When—"

"—I understand he punched you in the face. I understand he nearly broke your nose."

It had been a minute since a member of the caravan of asshats my mother called boyfriends had laid a hand on her. I was thirteen the last time it happened, and more scared than angry. But this time, I was pissed off. This time I wanted Old Testament vengeance. This time I wanted Lenny Roach's stupid head on a platter.

"It's complicated," Mom said, leaving unspoken the painful truth that Lenny played a significant role in the fragile financial stability we'd found.

"No, it's not complicated. Your boyfriend doesn't get to punch you. Period. And if he shows his stupid face around here again, I'll—"

"—You'll say nothing about it," Mom snapped, catching me off guard with her anger. "We're never talking about this again."

I turned to Axl, who was sitting on the couch. He hadn't spoken since Mom came out of the bathroom. "Say something," I yelled at him, but he only managed a sad-eyed shrug. Seems they'd both conceded Mom's orbital bones were a small price to pay for a 1,200-square-foot apartment with parking lot views.

"Fuck!" I shouted and stomped to my bedroom and slammed the door.

"My cousin Donnie has a guy in Franklin who'd kill him for you," Shelby said on our breakneck drive to work Monday morning. "No questions asked."

I laughed and wiped the tears from my eyes. "Thanks," I said, picturing Franklin as an Appalachian Mos Eisley. A wretched hive of scum and villainy and apple butter shops. "I'm hoping to run him off without hiring a hitman, but I'll keep it in mind."

"My stepdad used to rough up my mom when I was little," Shelby said, blowing the smoke from her morning cigarette out the open window. "But one night, he got blind drunk on Granddaddy's moonshine and drove his truck straight off the mountain. The coroner figured he was alive and trapped under his truck for at least two days before the coyotes came. Some hikers found what was left a few weeks later."

The cheerful tone in which Shelby shared the tale of her stepfather's demise left me unsure how to reply, so I offered a neutral, "Oh, wow."

"Great, huh? So tell your momma to hang in there. Sometimes these things work themselves out."

I shook my head but smiled at the thought of Lenny's van soaring off the mountain. "What's your mom do these days?" I asked, remembering she worked at Fuller Farms when Vance was murdered, and I wanted to talk to her.

"She runs a register at a grocery store in Ashes. The one that sells all the cheese."

"No shit? So does my mom. Her name is Brandi Brown."

"Well, tell her to watch out for Tracie Ray. I love her, but she's got all the charm of a PMS-ing rattlesnake."

Tracie Ray, I thought, committing the name to memory. I'd have to visit Fraîche soon and see what she remembered about the summer of 1992.

"I know how presumptuous it looked, but I'm not that kind of guy, I swear. I just thought it would be romantic, you know? I even had a couple of candles but didn't light them because I was afraid I'd burn down the forest."

Sterling and I were walking around Mud Lake while Bible study went on somewhere without him. He'd spent the first five minutes of our conversation apologizing for Friday night, and I spent the next five assuring him there was no need.

"I told you it's okay, and the blanket was romantic. It's just, my last boyfriend was gay, so I hadn't done that in a while, and it felt like things were moving too—"

"—Wait, your last boyfriend was gay?"

"Yeah. His dad was this asshole soccer manager named Harry Lane, who—"

"—You dated Harry Lane's son? *The* Harry Lane?"

"Pretend dated. But as I said, he—"

"—Hold on, Izzy, are you the girl who foiled that bomb plot at a soccer match back in the spring?"

"Uh, maybe," I said.

"Holy shit. I read about you in *Sports Illustrated*. And you solved some murder in Florida too."

"Well, Elton helped, but I—"

"—This is insane," Sterling said. "What are you doing working in the kitchen at Fuller Farms?"

"I told you. We moved here because my brother got a football scholarship at Ashes Prep. I'm working here because I need the money. I'm not some famous private investigator. I'm a nosey girl who's had an interesting twelve months."

"So, you're not working on another case now?"

I'm an honest person, sometimes to a fault. Introductions are rarely the time to disclose prior arrests, but as I've said before, I like to put my shit on the table early with people. Investigations are tricky, though, and tipping your hand can jeopardize the case. I'd kept my last investigation a secret from my fake boyfriend, Marco, and in the end, it cost me our friendship. I liked Sterling and didn't want him to be angry with me, but I couldn't tell him everything. Not until I knew his father wasn't a murderer.

"Vance Fuller," I said.

"The counselor who was murdered?"

I nodded. "I didn't know it until last week, but that's why Wellington Fuller hired me. He promised fifty thousand dollars if I crack the case."

"Wow," Sterling said, though his grandparents probably gave him fifty-thousand-dollar checks for his birthday. "So, like, how do you go about solving a murder?"

I shrugged. "I just talk to people. Ask a bunch of questions. Then I figure out who lied to me and ask them more questions to see if they're lying to make themselves look better, or to cover up a murder."

"You're something else, Izzy Brown," Sterling said, buckling my knees with a smile.

I rolled my eyes at him. "I've also accused a dozen innocent people of murder," I said, "so I'm no Sherlock Holmes. I'm just lucky. Or maybe unlucky. It's hard to say."

"Do you have any leads on this case?" he asked.

"No," I said. "It's too early. I haven't even spoken to anyone at camp that summer yet."

"My dad was at camp that summer," Sterling said. "Is he a suspect?"

With a capital S, I thought. "Of course not," I said. "Your dad didn't kill anyone. I'd love to talk to him, though."

"Yeah, so would I," Sterling said, and we quickly changed the subject.

"Monday greetings," Elton said when I entered our office that afternoon.

"You missed lunch again today."

Elton checked his watch. "It appears I did. I will set an alarm for dinner."

"Good idea," I said, squeezing his shoulders until he flinched. "How was your weekend?"

"I spent the majority of it in here."

"Elton, you have to go outside some."

"I did attempt to ride the zipline on Saturday, but the camp must first acquire a special harness to compensate for my excessive height."

"Okay, well, what have you got for me?"

"Aubrey Beauregard Masters left Sterling Oil in April 2008. A press release indicated he wished to spend more time with his family."

I laughed. "Dude hasn't seen his family since."

"Using publicly available registration data from the state of Texas and a ten-dollar subscription to a marine traffic website, I have located his yacht, *Sea No Evil*, docked at a marina on the Greek island of Milos."

"Holy shit, you found Sterling's father?"

"I just told you I did," Elton deadpanned.

"Right. Can we call him?"

"No. We would need a VHF radio."

"We could buy one," I suggested.

"And we must be within sixty nautical miles of the vessel."

"Okay, that would prove difficult. Maybe we could call the marina and ask them to hand Aubrey the phone."

"Neither of us speaks Greek," Elton reminded me.

"How long do you think it would take you to learn it?" I asked, and Elton stared back blankly. "Fine, but I'd like to rule him out for, uh, personal reasons. In the meantime, Shelby's mother's name is Tracie Ray. See what you can find out about her, and tomorrow we'll talk to Chief Jenkins at the Ashes Police Department. It would be nice to know who Vance's campers were that summer."

Elton saluted me, but when I turned to leave, he said, "Izzy, I could not help but notice the blood vessels on the surfaces of your eyes have dilated. Have your lacrimal glands been secreting?"

"Come again?"

"Have you been crying?"

I tried to answer but burst out crying again. Poor Elton stood, put an arm around me, removed it, and then put it back. He wasn't great at this, but he tried so hard, and I loved him for it.

"I'm okay," I said, giving him a big hug and ushering him back to his seat. Then I told him about Lenny.

"You cannot return to your apartment," Elton boomed. "It is unsafe. We must alert the authorities."

"I'm fine," I told him. "We're fine. I doubt he'll even come back." God, I hoped that was true.

Elton wasn't convinced, and I'd never seen him more panicked, stomping around the room and clenching his fists so tight I could hear his knuckles pop. "There must be something I can do."

"Seriously, Elton, we'll be—"

"—I will research North Carolina's restraining order laws," he said with a snap of his fingers.

"Elton, you don't have to—fine, if you have a minute, I suppose it wouldn't hurt," I said, and he returned to the computer without another word and began typing at the speed of light.

CHAPTER TEN

Despite having Tuesday off, I rode with Shelby to Fuller Farms that morning because she was my only means of getting there.

"I still don't know why the hell anyone would want to go to work on their day off," Shelby said as we sped down the mountain, blasting "Party in the U.S.A." way too loud for this early in the morning.

"I want to see Sterling," I lied.

"Dear Lord, girl, you can't just show up during camp hours and make out with your boyfriend. Julie will fire your ass on the spot."

"We're not going to make out. I just want to see him," I said. "I mostly plan to hang out with Elton. His mom okayed it with Mr. Fuller."

This was close enough to the truth, and Shelby accepted it with a grunt. "Rich people," she spat. "I guess they can get whatever the hell they want."

"Pretty much," I said, speaking from experience.

I hung out behind the kitchen during breakfast, and when Elton didn't show, I fixed him a plate and took it to our office.

"If you keep missing meals, I'm taking you off the case," I said, walking in and finding him hunched over the keyboard.

"Tuesday greetings," Elton said, ignoring my hollow threat. "I have learned everything there is to know about North Carolina's domestic violence laws."

I sighed. It was impossible to stay mad at someone who cared so much about you. "Fine, you can tell me about it on the drive."

We commandeered one of the camp vehicles Wellington Fuller made available, this one an old Ford pickup without air conditioning, and we drove back up the mountain to Ashes to meet Chief Jenkins at the police department.

"After your mother presses charges," Elton said as we pulled into town, "the court will order a Domestic Violence Protective Order, also known as a 50B, which will require Lenny to stay at least three hundred feet away. Law enforcement can then apprehend him on the spot if he violates the order. Under the circumstances, a judge is likely to—"

"Listen, Elton, I appreciate your work on this, but Mom isn't pressing charges."

"But Lenny struck her," Elton said.

"I know," I said, throwing my hands up in frustration, "but she's already forgiven him. He was back at the apartment last night like nothing happened."

"Did you confront him?" Elton asked.

"No," I said. "I stayed in my room."

"How could she—"

"—I know it sounds crazy, but Mom has done this before. The guys come back all apologetic, and she forgives them, but it never lasts long. Lenny will be gone in a week or two."

"But what if he is not?"

"Then I'll talk to him," I said.

"Perhaps you could press charges against him."

It was a thought, but Mom would flip out if I called the cops to our house. "I don't think so," I said.

Elton was quiet for a long moment. "If my father hit my mother, I would do something."

"I know you would," I said. "I know."

Ashes Police Headquarters was downtown on Main Street, a sort of Appalachian Champs-Élysées with wide sidewalks and beautifully arranged hanging baskets on every lamppost. I swear, this town's flower budget alone could have dented global poverty. Since everything downtown was picturesque to a fault, the police called a converted two-story Tudor house straight out of Pinocchio's village home. It was so ridiculously quaint I suspected we'd find a jail cell inside guarded by a scruffy dog with the key around its neck. Instead, we found Marcy, the grumpiest receptionist in the world.

"He ain't expecting y'all," Marcy snarled when I told her we were there to see Chief Jenkins.

"Chief Jenkins is a public servant, and as taxpayers, we are entitled to—" Elton began, but I hushed him with an elbow to his hipbone.

"Sorry," I said. "We didn't know we needed an appointment. But maybe if you just ask him—"

"—Chief, I got two kids here saying they need to talk to you," Marcy barked into the intercom on her phone.

"Send 'em back," Chief Jenkins said, and I shrugged at Marcy, who only scowled in return.

Chief Jenkins' office was in the back of the house, and we found him leaning back in his chair with his cowboy boots propped on his oak desk.

"Howdy," he said, standing to shake our hands. "Butch Jenkins." He had a handlebar mustache and wore a white Stetson hat with a black band. I suspect he fancied himself a modern-day Wyatt Earp and had waited his entire life for a black-hatted villain to ride into this resort town and rob an organic grocery store. I've no doubt quick-draw Jenkins would have shot the bad guy dead near the free-range eggs.

"Izzy Brown," I said, shaking the chief's hand. "Wellington Fuller said you—"

"—Old Wellington told me y'all might be coming 'round. Said you're going to reopen his boy's case."

"Yeah, I guess," I said, embarrassed to say it to an actual policeman.

"And who might you be?" Chief Jenkins asked, looking up at Elton.

"Elton Jones-Davies," Elton said, shaking the chief's hand with vigor. "My mother is British, and the British are fond of double-barreled surnames. However, once she divorces my father, I plan to drop the Jones."

"Really?" I asked Elton.

"Yes. It would be simpler now than after I have earned my medical license."

"You're going to be a doctor? Since when?"

"I have always planned to attend medical school," Elton said, and I felt awful for somehow not knowing it. "Mother thinks I should choose radiology or another specialty with little patient interaction. However, I am inclined to—"

"—Hey, kids, not to interrupt y'all's conversation, but what can I do for you today?" Chief Jenkins asked, snapping us back to the present.

"Izzy's mother needs a restraining order against her boyfriend, Lenny Roach," Elton blurted out, and I shot him a look that made him flinch.

"Sorry, Chief, he's joking. We wanted to ask you about Vance Fuller's death."

"You can ask me, but I can't tell you much."

"Is the evidence confidential?" I asked.

"Nope, I just don't know much about it, that's all. It all happened before my time. Rusty Morrison was in charge back then, but he's been dead going on ten years now."

"Was he murdered too?" I asked.

"Type 2 diabetes," Chief Jenkins said. "I suppose we could have charged Little Debbie as an accessory, but she's got good lawyers."

"So you've only been here since …"

"Since 1999," the chief said. "Two months before Y2K. Now that was a crazy time. We had us a small doomsday cult come to town and set up shop on Twilight Rock. Most of them stayed and bought property when their spaceship didn't show. You can still pick them out because they all wear the same neon green Nikes. Come to think of it," he added, glancing at the calendar on his wall, "their spaceship is due again later this month. Parks and Rec just issued the permit for their homegoing ceremony."

I didn't know what to say to that, so I tried to steer the conversation back to Vance Fuller. "And did you pick up the Fuller case when you arrived?"

Chief Jenkins laughed, and I felt my face flush. "No, sweetheart, I didn't get to work on a seven-year-old cold case the minute I arrived. To quote the good book, 'Sufficient unto the day is the evil thereof.'"

"Matthew 6:34," Elton said as if he were answering a trivia question.

"Hey, hey," the chief said, pointing at Elton with a snap of his fingers, "we've got us a true believer here."

"Negative," Elton replied. "Mother says I no longer have to attend religious—"

"—Hold on," I said, interrupting Elton, "there's been one murder committed in the history of Ashes, North Carolina, and you're fine letting it remain unsolved?"

Chief Jenkins' eyes narrowed, and I wished I could try my last sentence in a less accusatory tone. "First off, little lady, if Rusty Morrison couldn't solve the case when the evidence was fresh, what makes you think—"

"—Rosalind Fuller told Chief Morrison to stop his investigation."

"Well, I don't know anything about that," Chief Jenkins said, raising his hands to show his innocence. "But like I said, each day here brings its own shit, and I ain't got the time or resources to spend on something that happened nearly two decades ago."

It looked to me like Chief Jenkins had plenty of time and his only pressing issue was when to squeeze in his daily viewing of *Tombstone*, but I kept this thought to myself.

"Can you at least tell us what you do know about the case?" I asked.

Chief Jenkins took off his hat and scratched his surprisingly bald head. "Sure, but it ain't much. I've never looked over Chief Morrison's notes, but I suspect they're a steaming pile of garbage. From what I'm told, he made Barney Fife look like Kojak. So all I know is a decade's worth of rumors. Vance slept with the wrong man's woman. He slept with the wrong woman's man. He was using drugs. He was selling drugs. Folks say he ran into some trouble in Chapel Hill, but no one can agree on what it was. Some say he plagiarized every paper he ever turned in. Some say he got caught pissing in the Old Well. Some say a dean caught him with his sixteen-year-old daughter, but the dean wouldn't press charges because he'd been with Vance too. Small-town rumors, you know, and you can't put stock in any one of them, but taken together, they paint the picture of a pretty screwed-up kid. Wellington is a good man, and he lost his son, and that can't be easy, but maybe his wife was right not to want to know the truth."

I sighed, thinking back to The Red Lion Bombing and how every-one I asked had an increasingly unlikely theory on who had done it.

"Look, I ain't trying to discourage y'all," Chief Jenkins said, pat-ting me on the shoulder, "but this case is so cold rigor mortis has set in."

"We'd still like to look through the files if it's all the same to you."

"I reckoned you would," Chief Jenkins said, and with a press of a button, Marcy walked back in and dropped a stack of brown folders on the desk in front of us.

"Y'all can use the empty office next door. Take your time. Copies are ten cents each."

CHAPTER ELEVEN

Elton and I took the case files to the empty office and got to work. Not knowing where to start, I picked a folder at random and opened it to find dozens of crime scene photographs. I nearly vomited. Sure, I'd solved two murders in the last twelve months, but I'd never seen a dead body, particularly not one shot full of arrows. It was ghastly, and I shook my head, trying to dislodge the image, but it was stuck there forever.

"I wouldn't look in that folder if I were you," I said to Elton, who, of course, opened it immediately. "Told you so," I said after he slammed the folder shut and tried to rub what he'd seen off his retinas.

Like Chief Jenkins predicted, the files were a mess of half-finished reports written in illegible chicken scratch and carbon copies that were even harder to decipher. Someone had typed the interrogation transcripts at least, though the ink had faded on the yellowing paper, and no one had bothered to file them in any particular order.

"I guess these are the original interrogation recordings," I said, pointing to a box full of dusty cassette tapes.

Elton grabbed a tape and examined it, spinning one of the reels with his pinky before tossing it back into the box. "What an impractical way to retain data," he observed.

"At least they didn't use scrolls," I said, and Elton shrugged.

As I shuffled through the rat's nest of evidence, I found a small folder containing transcripts of six interviews conducted by Chief Morrison. A sticky note on top read, "Need to question these again."

"Whoa, I think these were Chief Morrison's prime suspects," I said to Elton, who had found a local newspaper in one of the files and decided to read it cover to cover.

"Did you know that on July 26, 1992, the United States men's Olympic basketball team defeated Angola 116-48 in their first game at the Barcelona Olympics?"

"Of course, I know everything about Angolan basketball, but you're not listening to me. I found Chief Morrison's prime suspects."

Elton reluctantly dropped the newspaper, and we spread the six transcripts out on the table and started reading the interviews, which all followed the same script. Eight questions. No follow-ups. A master detective, Chief Rusty Morrison, was not.

Please state your name, age, permanent residence, and affiliation with Fuller Farms.

Aubrey Masters: Aubrey Beauregard Masters. I'm eighteen, and my family lives on a ranch outside Northfork, Texas, but I go to school in Houston. This is my first summer camping at Fuller Farms.

Jasper Benson: Do I have to do this, Chief? You know who I am. You come to my family's Christmas party every year. Fine. Jasper Benson. Eighteen. Ashes. Camper.

Quinn Westlake: I am Quinn Westlake, eighteen, of Shinnecock Hills, New York, and I am camping at Fuller Farms this summer.

Buster McClellan: Byron McClellan, but folks call me Buster. I'm fifty years old and live back in the woods off Sour Mash Road. As of yesterday, I'm the former archery instructor at Fuller Farms. I'd worked there every summer for twenty-nine years.

Tripp Aston: I'm Phillip D. Aston III, but people call me Tripp. I'm twenty-two and a rising senior at the University of North Carolina in Chapel Hill. This is my third summer serving as a camp counselor at Fuller Farms. Before that, I attended camp here in high school.

Tracie Ray: Tracie Ray. I'm seventeen and live with my mama outside of Ashes. This is my first summer working in the kitchen.

What was your relationship with the deceased?

Aubrey Masters: He was my camp counselor.

Jasper Benson: Vance was my camp counselor, but our families have known each other for decades. We're sort of like the Hatfields and McCoys, only with money.

Quinn Westlake: Vance Fuller was my camp counselor.
Buster McClellan: I've known Vance since he was a baby, Chief.

Tripp Aston: Vance and I were counselors this summer, and we shared a cabin.

Tracie Ray: I just served his food. I mean, I knew who he was. The Fullers are sorta famous around here, but we ain't never talked or nothing.

Did you ever argue with the deceased?

Aubrey Masters: No, I mean, not really. He kept threatening to write me up for skipping Bible study, but he never did. Quinn used to argue with him some.

Jasper Benson: I wanted to argue with him. Ten times a day, I told him the Tar Heels sucked, but he never took the bait. But now that I think of it, I did see Vance screaming at that crazy old archery instructor the morning he died.

Quinn Westlake: Of course not. And please tell me you do not suspect I played some part in his death.

Buster McClellan: Just once, but it was a doozy, and it happened in front of a bunch of campers, so I'm sure they've already told you about it. But here's what really happened. When he was a kid, Vance got bullied at camp, so I always tried to look after him like he was my own. Vance appreciated it back then because his daddy never did anything to stop the bullies. Like everyone else, I'd heard the rumors that Vance had gotten into some trouble at Chapel Hill, and that's why he was back in Ashes. I tried to talk to him about it. Offer some fatherly advice, which, maybe wasn't my place. But Vance wasn't hearing it. He blew up on me, and when I tried to apologize later that day, he blew up again. But that's all it was, Chief. I cared for the boy.

Tripp Aston: Just roommate stuff. I was messier than him. He liked to sleep with the fan running. Nothing big.

Tracie Ray: No, Chief, I told you we ain't never really talked.

When did you last see the deceased?

Aubrey Masters: At dinner the night he died.

Jasper Benson: Lights out.

Quinn Westlake: At skit practice.

Buster McClellan: I suppose I would have seen him at dinner that night, but I don't recall. Actually, no, that was a Friday, so I would've gone home around 4. During the week, I usually sleep on a cot in the archery shed, but I go home on weekends. I probably hadn't seen Vance since lunch.

Tripp Aston: Probably at skit practice that night. Vance hadn't returned to the cabin yet when I went to sleep, but I didn't think anything of it. His parents live in town. I thought maybe he'd gone home to sleep in his own bed.

Tracie Ray: I saw him at supper that night.

Where were you between midnight and 4 a.m. on July 9?

Aubrey Masters: In bed.

Jasper Benson: Sleeping.

Quinn Westlake: Asleep in our dormitory.

Buster McClellan: Home.

Tripp Aston: Asleep in my cabin. Though I woke up around one and walked to the boys' dorm to check on Vance's campers. I mean, if he wasn't going to check on them, I figured someone ought to. Sure enough, two of them were up playing cards, and I made them go to bed.

Tracie Ray: I was home asleep, Chief.

Can anyone corroborate this?

Aubrey Masters: My roommates, I guess.

Jasper Benson: Well, no, Chief, we were all snoozing.
Quinn Westlake: Chief Morrison, I find this line of questioning highly offensive.

Buster McClellan: Yeah, somebody can, but I'd rather not involve her if I ain't got to. I don't want to embarrass anyone.

Tripp Aston: No, I suppose not.

Tracie Ray: I guess my mama could, but she was probably sleeping too, so I don't know.

Do you know anyone who might have a reason to harm the victim?

Aubrey Masters: Not really.

Jasper Benson: Chief, you know as well as I do Vance was a weirdo. Maybe someone killed him for money. Maybe some of those rumors about Chapel Hill are true. I don't know.

Quinn Westlake: I will not be answering any more questions without my attorney present.

Buster McClellan: No, Chief, I don't. Vance … Vance was an odd duck, but he was harmless.

Tripp Aston: No.

Tracie Ray: I don't reckon I do, Chief.

Keeping in mind that lying to or withholding information from an officer of the law is a Class 2 misdemeanor and that violators can face up to sixty days in jail, do you have any other information that might be pertinent to this investigation?

Aubrey Masters: No, I don't think so.

Jasper Benson: Yeah, Chief, I never saw it myself, but I heard Vance touched one of the younger boys. You know, inappropriately.

Quinn Westlake: I know what you are insinuating, Chief, but the man I shot back home was trespassing on private property. He was on drugs and a threat to my family, and I was fully exonerated.

Buster McClellan: Yeah, Chief, I suppose you ought to know that when Vance was a camper, he spent some of his time hanging out in my shed. His mama knew, and she was okay with it because the other boys picked on him. But it wasn't something we advertised, you know, because then all the other campers would want to get out of Bible study or swim relays or whatever else they didn't want to do.

Tripp Aston: I knew Vance at Chapel Hill. Well, I didn't know him but knew of him. He did something horrible to one of my fraternity brothers, Ty Bingham. So yeah, I do know someone with a reason to harm Vance. Or I did know someone. Ty killed himself last week.

Tracie Ray: Yeah, Chief, something weird happened to me that night. I've sort of been seeing one of the campers, a boy named Aubrey Masters, and we snuck off that night and—you know what, never mind, okay? It ain't got nothing to do with Vance.

CHAPTER TWELVE

"Okay, let's try and wrap our heads around all of this," I said to Elton as we sat in our borrowed pickup truck outside the Ashes Police Department with a stack of photocopied police reports between us. "We know Chief Morrison had six suspects."

"Six persons of interest," Elton corrected.

"Whatever. Six people he wanted to question again before Rosalind Fuller called off his investigation." I rubbed my temples and tried to think. We hardly had any leads two hours ago, but now we were drowning in them. "Where should we start?" I asked.

"We should return to Fuller Farms so I can research," Elton suggested.

"You can do that anytime. What can we do in town since we're already here?"

Elton thought for a moment. "There were inconsistencies in the three campers' stories, and one of them had admittedly killed before, albeit in self-defense."

"Yep," I agreed, "and the Benson kid is local, or he was in 1992. "You'll need to find out where he is today, along with Quinn Westlake. We already know Aubrey Masters is on a yacht in the Mediterranean." I left unspoken how suspicious Sterling's father now looked.

"I believe I have located Jasper Benson," Elton announced, and when I turned to him, he pointed out the window toward city hall, where a small, handpainted sign reserved the best parking spot for J. Benson, Mayor.

"Wait, Jasper is the mayor of Ashes? Dammit to hell."

"It appears he is here," Elton said, noting the red Porsche parked in the spot. "Shall we interrogate him?"

"What? No. We can't barge into the mayor's office asking questions about a murder."

"Why not? Barging into offices and asking about murders is your go-to move."

I laughed because he wasn't wrong. "We're going to try some tact this time. We'll talk to him, but let's do our homework first."

Elton conceded this with a shrug. "What about Tracie Ray? We could question her if she is working at Fraîche this morning."

Shelby's mother admitted to hooking up with Sterling's dad, leaving me to wonder if the Masters men had a thing for poor girls in kitchen aprons. I'd have to ask her, but not today. "Bad idea. Mom is working this morning, and she thinks I'm cleaning dishes at Fuller Farms right now."

Elton frowned. "Your dishonesty makes me uncomfortable."

"Me too," I admitted, though Mom would forgive me if I could pocket fifty grand for solving Vance Fuller's murder. "So, who's left?" I asked, changing the subject from my deceits. "There's the roommate …"

"Tripp Aston," Elton said, "but we do not know his current location either. So that leaves Buster McClellan."

"Buster 'I-DID-NOT-KILL-VANCE-FULLER' McClellan," I said, "who conveniently lives between here and camp."

"2456 Sour Mash Road," Elton repeated from memory.

"Let's go."

My seventh-grade geography teacher, Mrs. Clayton, kept a giant globe in her room, and that year I became obsessed with learning about the most remote places on Earth. Places like the Pitcairn Islands, eighteen square miles of volcanic rock over three thousand miles off the coast of New Zealand in the southern Pacific Ocean. Less than fifty people lived there, mostly descended from nine mutinous sailors of the Royal Navy vessel *HMS Bounty* and their Tahitian consorts, and I wanted to hop on the next boat headed that way. I suspect my obsession with these godforsaken locales stemmed from a belief that my anxiety was something I could outrun. An assumption that my fears, both specific and vague, and the chest pains, panic attacks, migraines, and vomiting they produced, were somehow tied to Dandrige, Florida, and the only solution was to get as far away as possible. Of course, by now, I'd lived in enough places to realize I'm still myself no matter where I go, but if I ever did want to test my theory about living at the end of the Earth, 2456 Sour Mash Road would be an excellent place to start.

"So, this is the place?" I asked as the truck idled next to Buster McClellan's mailbox and half a dozen homemade signs warning trespassers they'd be shot on sight.

"Affirmative," Elton said, "but perhaps we should call first."

"Do you have his phone number?"

"Negative. He does not appear to have a phone. But perhaps we could wait until he gets one, then call first."

I laughed. "Elton, are you scared?"

"Of getting shot? Yes."

"Don't be ridiculous," I said, shoving him on the arm. "He's not going to shoot us. People only put up those signs to scare off encyclopedia salesmen and Jehovah's Witnesses."

"What if he mistakes us for Jehovah's Witnesses?"

"We'll duck," I said and turned down the gravel driveway.

After a mile, we still hadn't reached Buster's house, but we had passed several more signs warning us to turn around. We'd just driven past one that read "Last Chance, Morons" when the first gunshot rang out.

I stomped the brakes, and after the truck slid to a halt, Elton and I ducked below the dashboard.

"What do I do?" I whispered.

"Invent a time machine, go back ten minutes, and listen to me."

I rolled my eyes at Elton and raised my head to peek down the driveway as the second gunshot echoed through the woods.

"Shit," I said, diving back onto the floorboard.

"My fear of being shot is not so ridiculous now, is it?" Elton asked.

"He's not going to shoot us," I said without conviction. "Those were warning shots."

"He is warning us he is about to shoot us."

We fell silent at the sound of footsteps on the gravel driveway and waited for a shotgun blast to bring an unceremonious end to our short lives. But instead, a man hollered out in a deep Appalachian growl, "Can y'all not read?"

I dared to raise my head again and saw an old man in a faded safari shirt with white hair and a bushy beard standing twenty feet away. He looked like Hemingway hunting big game in Africa, only his shotgun was pointed at me.

"Buster McClellan?" I shouted through the window after hitting the floorboard again.

"Who's inquiring?" the man shouted back.

"Izzy Brown," I yelled. "We need to talk to you."

"Izzy Brown, it appears you've underestimated my distaste for unexpected guests."

"We would have called, but you do not have a telephone," Elton yelled.

"Who's that?" Buster yelled.

"My friend Elton," I said. "Wellington Fuller hired us to investigate his son's death."

"Then I'll have to refer you to my Facebook page," Buster shouted.

"Buster," I yelled back, "can I get out of this truck and talk to you? This is a stupid way to have a conversation."

There was a long silence. I wondered if Buster was thinking or reloading. But after a moment, he said, "Fine, get on out."

Elton and I crawled from the floorboard with our hands raised, but Buster had lowered his shotgun and was picking at a tooth with his pinky nail. We climbed out of the truck and walked around to the front, and Buster blinked at Elton and said, "God almighty, you're taller than Bill Walton. You play basketball?"

"I prefer not to sweat," Elton answered.

Buster shrugged at this reply and turned to me. "Alright, Red, let's hear it."

"We just left the Ashes police station," I said. "Chief Jenkins let us read over the files from Vance's case."

"That was mighty Christian of him," Buster spat.

"It sounds like you were fired from Fuller Farms soon after Vance died."

"The next day," Buster said. "Wellington needed a fall guy, and he chose me. You see, those were camp arrows Vance got shot with, and I was the archery instructor. Wellington said if I'd locked the shed, none of this would have happened. Look, I get that Wellington lost his boy. I'm sure he felt helpless and wanted to do something, so he fired me. Fine. Whatever. Que sera, sera. But then he starts whispering around town that I was the one who killed Vance, so he can go to hell and die for all I care."

"You did argue with Vance Fuller a few days before he died."

"Yep. I tried to give him some advice he wasn't having, which was fine. Vance was a grown man. He didn't have to listen to me. But I didn't kill him. I'm a lover not a fighter. Namaste and all that," Buster said, flashing a peace sign. "Anyone who knows me knows I wouldn't hurt a fly."

"You discharged your weapon at us twice in the last five minutes," Elton said.

"You ain't dead, are you?" Buster shot back.

"You told Chief Morrison someone could corroborate your alibi for the night Vance died, but you never told him who it was."

"Nope, I didn't."

"Will you tell us?"

Buster laughed. "Maybe if you had a badge and the truth was the only thing standing between me and a jail cell. But you're just a couple of kids hired by a desperate old man. So I'll kindly ask y'all to get off my property before I start reloading."

Elton turned on his heel and quickly headed to the truck, but I stood my ground.

"I know you have a theory on who killed Vance."

"Sure, I got a guess," Buster said, "but if I start throwing out names, I ain't no better than Wellington."

"Fine, but if you were us, where would you start?"

"By quitting," Buster said. "Look, Vance ain't the only one from that camp who turned up dead. There's some scary shit that goes on around here. Shit you don't want to get involved in."

"Wait, someone else from camp was killed?" I asked. "Who?"

"You're the detective," Buster said, raising his shotgun toward the sky and cocking it. "Now get."

<h1 style="text-align:center">1992</h1>

Vance Fuller hadn't forgotten.

The threat Tripp Aston made walking back from Mud Lake their first night at Fuller Farms still rang in his ears. "*I know what you did, and you're going to pay.*" It was the last thing Vance thought about each evening when closing his eyes to try and sleep across the room from the musclebound frat bro who looked like a new species of human evolved specifically to beat up art majors. Vance recalled how unpopular kids were hazed at camp when he attended as a teenager in the early eighties.

Cruel pranks.

Embarrassing initiations.

Outright beatings.

Things considered fun and games back then, but today would be rightfully classified as assault and subject Fuller Farms to an avalanche of litigation. Vance feared he'd wake one morning to a soap in sock beating, or worse, but since the first night, his fellow counselors had treated him with detached disinterest, and he'd lowered his guard.

Twenty thousand students at the University of North Carolina, and Vance had to be summer roommates with a friend of Ty Bingham. The odds were impossible, but here they were. Vance thought back to the cold January day when he passed out the syllabuses for ARTH 151 - History of Western Art. It was a freshman class, full of undeclared majors taking classes at random and struggling upperclassmen looking for an easy A to bring up their GPA. There might be one art major in the class of fifty students, and Vance would soon know them by their eager hand raised high to answer every question he asked.

Ty Bingham did not make an impression that day, and Vance didn't see him again until he failed the final exam in spectacular fashion.

"Is there anything I can do to help my grade?" Ty asked two days later, sitting across from Vance in the supply closet of an office the department had stuck him in.

Vance snorted a laugh. He was used to students showing up this week asking some version of this question, but never with the audacity of Ty Bingham, whose average for the class currently resided in the low single digits.

"I suppose," Vance said, "I could let you take another crack at the essay question on the final. You left it blank."

"What would that bring my grade up to?" Ty asked.

"Well, depending on your answer, you might could pull it up double digits."

"Dr. Fuller, there has to be something more I can do," Ty pleaded.

"I'm afraid not," Vance said. He was still a semester away from his PhD but liked being called doctor and saw no need to correct the boy. "Mr. Bingham, the final was only worth twenty percent of your grade, so even if you aced it, you would still fail this class miserably."

"You don't understand, Dr. Fuller. I have to pass this class. I'm supposed to graduate next week. My parents are flying in from Chicago to see me walk."

Vance stood to show Ty Bingham the door. Later that night, he'd retell this story to howling laughter from his fellow PhD students over drinks at Linda's on Franklin Street, but right now, he was sick of hearing this kid whine.

"Mr. Bingham," Vance said, standing next to the boy with one hand on the door, "if you are truly that close to graduating from this university, you already know you cannot expect to pass a course you skipped for sixteen straight weeks."

"Please, Dr. Fuller," Ty Bingham said, moving Vance's hand from the doorknob, "I'll do anything."

It happened so fast—the boy dropping to his knees, his hands reaching for Vance's belt.

Please stop, Vance thought, but he didn't say it. He didn't say anything, so stunned was he at how the last sixty seconds had unfolded like the what-not-to-do chapter of the HR handbook.

Vance had to stop him.

He was about to stop him.

He would have stopped him after another moment or two …

But then the Associate Dean entered the office without a knock, ending Vance's academic career before it began.

Vance Fuller hadn't forgotten.

He hadn't forgotten any of it.

But he prayed he'd been punished enough.

CHAPTER THIRTEEN

"You do not appear well," Elton said later that morning after we'd returned to our office so he could use the computer.

"I'm fine."

"You do not appear fine."

I tried to roll my eyes at him, but the movement brought fresh new hell to my head.

"It's just a headache," I said, squeezing my temples in a feeble attempt to squash the demon who'd taken up residence between my ears.

"I did not know you still suffered from headaches," Elton said, concerned enough to spin away from the computer monitor and almost look me in the eyes.

"I told you, I'm fine," I said.

"Have you resumed taking medication without a prescription?"

"No," I lied. "I took some Advil. Plain old over-the-counter Advil."

The truth was, I'd popped enough Advil that morning to blow out a horse's kidneys and washed them down with enough caffeine to wake the dead. This cocktail had valiantly fended off my headache for several hours, but now it was back with a vengeance. The adrenaline rush of having a shotgun pointed at my face did not help matters, digging up memories I'd tried to bury of Professor Taylor holding me at gunpoint in the River Bones and Katherine Park doing the same in the *Bardo Breeze* newsroom. My God, I'd had a lot of guns pointed at me lately.

Relief waited in my nightstand drawer, but yesterday marked fourteen straight days of taking OxyContin in the morning, and I'd decided two weeks was long enough. Part of it was self-preservation. If Lenny left, and I prayed nightly to every God of every major religion, my unlimited supply of pills left with him. Sure, I could get more. Shelby's cousin Donnie in Franklin apparently could get me anything from opioids to a suitcase nuke. But I needed to ration because buying drugs was a line I'd vowed not to cross. The line was admittedly arbitrary, but most lines are.

"Okay," Elton said, taking my dishonest word for it because he always did.

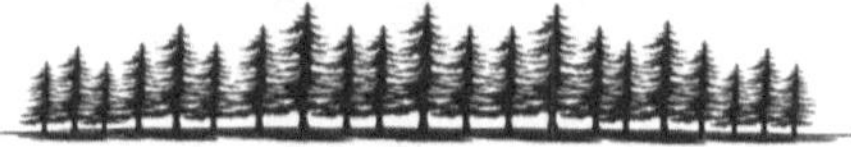

While Elton researched the six people Chief Morrison wanted to question again back in 1992, I walked down to Mud Lake to see Sterling, who'd skipped the afternoon tennis lesson with a two-time Wimbledon champion to see me.

"How's your day been?" I asked.

"Lame," he said. "The pretty girl who usually serves eggs didn't work this morning."

I tried to hide my smile but couldn't.

"How's your off day been?" he asked.

"Not bad," I said. "A crazy mountain hippie fired a shotgun at Elton and me."

"You're joking."

"Nope. I mean, it was mostly our fault. We drove past two dozen no-trespassing signs to get to his house. I don't think he would have hurt us, though."

"He shot at you."

"Over us. Warning shots. It was all very civilized."

Sterling shook his head. "I'm guessing this has something to do with your investigation."

"Yeah," I said. "Buster McClellan was the archery instructor at Fuller Farms when Vance died. Mr. Fuller fired him after the murder and still suspects him of having something to do with it."

"What do you think?" Sterling asked.

"I don't know. In 1992, he told the police there was someone who could confirm he was home in bed when Vance died, but he'd rather not involve her because he didn't want to embarrass anyone. So, I'm guessing his alibi is someone he was sleeping with, but he didn't seem interested in discussing it with me this morning."

Sterling took my hand. "Please be careful," he said. "It freaks me out to think you spend your off days getting shot at in the woods."

"I'm always careful," I lied. "By the way, did you know your dad was one of Vance Fuller's campers?"

"No," Sterling gasped. "Shit. Do you think—"

"—No, I don't," I said, squeezing his hand to reassure him I didn't suspect his father of anything ... yet. "But I did learn he hooked up with one of the girls working in the kitchen."

Sterling blushed and laughed despite himself. "Okay, that is funny."

"Yeah, you Masters men have a type."

"We do," he said, leaning in to kiss me, but I turned away at the last second to tease him.

"By the way, Elton found your father's yacht," I said, turning back to catch his reaction.

"Still in Milos?" Sterling asked.

"Yeah. How'd you know?"

"It's been there for a year. Mom assumes he's shacked up with some Greek skank—her words, not mine. All the bills still get paid, so I don't think Mom cares anymore, to be honest."

"I have successfully located Chief Morrison's six persons of interest," Elton said when I returned to the office.

"Nice work, Big E," I said, offering a fist bump he tried to high five. "Let's hear them."

Elton cleared his throat and began. "We know Buster McClellan."

"All too well."

"Phillip Dean Aston III, also known as Tripp, is thirty-nine years old and a partner at the law firm of Day, Dorminey & Aston in Charlotte. Licensed to practice in North Carolina, Florida, New York, and Texas, he is married with two young children, active in several civic organizations, and was recently named North Carolina Attorney of the Year."

"Okay," I said, not thrilled one of our suspects was a hotshot attorney.

My standard operating procedure on the two cases I'd solved was to catch people in lies, then blackmail them into giving me information they'd otherwise withhold. This probably wouldn't work with a lawyer. Well, it worked with shirtless Tanner Cobb in Cowden, but no one would mistake him for Attorney of the Year.

"Tracie Ray is thirty-four and lives with her daughter in a mobile home east of Ashes. Her Facebook page consists entirely of pitbull photographs and invitations to join a pyramid scheme."

"Helpful," I said, and Elton huffed at me.

"We previously located Aubrey Masters," Elton continued.

"Yeah, but apparently that wasn't a secret. Sterling said his dad's yacht has been there for over a year. Aubrey's wife thinks he's shacked up with a Greek skank." Elton scribbled this down, and I said, "But please don't search the internet for Greek skanks. They'll take away our computer access."

Elton wrote this, too, before continuing with his list. "Jasper Benson is thirty-five and, so far as I can tell, does nothing."

"Nothing? I thought he was the mayor of Ashes."

"The J. Benson on the sign outside city hall referred to his father, Jeremy."

"Wait, you were wrong about something?" I teased.

Elton didn't dignify this with a response and continued recounting the Benson family's history. "Jasper's great-great-great-grandfather, Willoughby, was a railroad and hotel tycoon and built a 150-room mansion outside Franklin called Benson House. Locals refer to it as Baby Biltmore. Jasper has never married and lives off his substantial trust fund. I found an article about him in *Maxim* titled "The Last American Playboy." I can print it off for you if you like."

"Sure," I said. "Do you know where Jasper is now?"

"Negative. The *Maxim* article does not list a permanent residence, and Jasper claims to spend his days flying around the world, frequenting night clubs, and having sexual intercourse with beautiful women."

"Lovely," I deadpanned. "We'll have to call Mayor Benson and ask when he expects his son home from his latest world sex tour."

"World sex tour," Elton mumbled, earnestly writing down everything I said.

"What about the other camper?" I asked. "Quinn Westlake of Shinnecock Hills."

"He is deceased."

"Wait, what?"

"Quinton James Westlake committed suicide on April 12, 2008, by leaping from the roof of his Manhattan high-rise."

"Holy hell," I said, not sure what, if anything, this had to do with Vance Fuller, but shocked the boy I'd just read an interview with was dead. "Buster told us Vance wasn't the only person from camp to turn up dead. Do you think he meant Quinn?"

"I do not know," Elton said, "but I have no desire to return and ask him."

I laughed. "Yeah, me neither." I sat next to Elton and rubbed my temples. It was hard to think with my head throbbing, but I was stuck here until Shelby got off that evening. "I guess Tracie Ray makes the most sense to talk to next since she's local. Do you want to try and—"

The landline next to the computer rang and nearly startled us out of our chairs.

"Should we answer?" Elton asked.

I shrugged and grabbed the receiver.

"Izzy Brown?" a man asked.

"Uh, yes."

"This is Mayor Jeremy Benson."

"It's the mayor," I whispered to Elton, covering the receiver with my hand.

"Mr. Mayor, I was about to call your office. Do you know if Jasper is—"

"—Chief Jenkins told me you came by the station this morning," Mayor Benson continued, not letting me finish my sentence. "Said you and some giant were digging into Vance Fuller's death."

"Yes, sir, we were. Wellington Fuller hired me to—"

"—Well, look here," Mayor Benson said, again cutting me off, "you two need to cut it out. I've known the Fullers all my life. There couldn't be a sweeter family. But since Rosalind died, Wellington hasn't been himself. Otherwise, he wouldn't hire a couple of teenagers to investigate his son's death twenty years after the fact."

I wanted to argue, but there was some logic to this.

"Listen, I've heard about you. I know you caused a stir with those murders you solved. But folks around here aren't looking for a stir. Besides, the 25th annual Twilight Rock Film Festival is this October. Chase Foster and Bridget Bell are premiering their new film right here, in Ashes, and the last thing we need—"

"—Oh, sorry, I didn't know about the film festival. That's an excellent reason to let someone get away with murder."

"You listen here, young lady, Vance Fuller's death was an accident. The sooner Wellington accepts it, the better off he'll be."

"An accident? Mr. Mayor, I saw the crime scene photographs. Vance Fuller's death was no accident."

Mayor Benson was quiet for a long moment. "Maybe not, but if you start looking hard enough, you'll soon realize all the garbage Vance was caught up in. Learning the truth would only break his father's heart again. So, you need to let this one go. It's the right thing to do."

CHAPTER FOURTEEN

In my admittedly limited experience with murder investigations, when someone tells you to stop digging, you should totally keep digging.

I believed Mayor Benson's concern for Wellington Fuller was at least partially sincere. I've no doubt losing his wife had filled him with grief, and perhaps in that grief, he'd begun making decisions he wouldn't otherwise make—like hiring a couple of kids to investigate his son's death. But there was fifty grand on the line, so I wasn't going to call off the investigation just because some small-town mayor didn't want me to cause a stir. I'd seen *Jaws*. I knew how small-town mayors thought. If I solved this murder, it would bring a lot of publicity to Ashes in the Pines, and none of it good. But if the only other option was to let someone get away with murder, what choice did I have?"

I had to work at Fuller Farms the rest of the week, so we did put our investigation on hold, but only until Saturday, my next day off.

"Is your mother working today?" I asked Shelby on our light-speed descent down the mountain, this one set to Lady Gaga's "Poker

Face," a song I've since associated with double and triple checking my seatbelt.

"Why do you care?" she asked, squinting at me like I'd asked how often she brushed and flossed. She already thought I was weird for coming to work on my days off. Continually asking about her mother, whom I didn't know from Eve, only cemented her opinion. "You in the market for some fancy-ass cheese?"

"No, Mom just said they had some big sale today, so I figured it was all hands on deck."

This wasn't true. Mom was off that morning. She and Lenny were hiking to Doublehead Falls, pretending he hadn't punched her in the face. But I needed to talk to Tracie Ray and wanted to know if I'd find her at home or at Fraîche.

"Yeah, she's working," Shelby said, and I changed the subject to boys so she'd think I was normal.

Half an hour later, Elton and I were in our Fuller Farms pickup truck driving back up the mountain into Ashes. Fraîche was a couple of blocks from the center of town, in a brick building with roses climbing the walls and late-model luxury SUVs filling the small parking lot. Fraîche wasn't a large grocery store. None of the gourmet grocers in Ashes were. That would be tacky, I suppose. It was about the size of a Dollar General, but with polished hardwood floors, fresh produce displayed in rustic wooden carts like farmers had pulled it there straight from the field, and cheese, my God, the cheese. An island counter took up a third of the store selling Brie, Blue, and everything in between. The rumor was you could even get some of the illegal unpasteurized French stuff if you knew how to ask. I took a toothpick sample of Gouda from one of the women behind the counter and looked around the store in awe. If every grocery store in Ashes was this specialized, it would take two dozen stops to buy a week's worth of groceries.

"Cheese constipates me," Elton announced to the woman who tried to offer him a sample of Colby Jack. She quickly pulled it back and found another customer to help.

"A simple no thank you would do," I told him, but he just shrugged.

There were three registers at the front of the store, all manned by women in the same uniform Mom wore to work every day, a hunter green Fraîche polo shirt and khaki pants. One woman looked a hundred years old, and another was Hispanic, but the third woman looked like she could be Shelby's older sister, with the same dusty blonde hair and permanent scowl. I grabbed a pack of organic chewing gum from the impulse purchase shelf near the register and dropped it on the conveyor belt. Tracie Ray swiped my gum, tossed it in a recyclable Fraîche tote bag, and said, "Sixteen thirty-seven."

"For a pack of gum?" I asked, choking on the words.

"The bag is ten," Tracie said.

"I don't need the bag. I can—wait, the gum is six dollars?"

Tracie Ray glanced at me, and in a conspiratorial whisper, said, "If you don't want six-dollar gum, the gas station across the street sells Juicy Fruit for a quarter."

"No, it's fine," I said, handing her a ten-dollar bill and wincing as she rang up the world's most expensive pack of gum.

"You're Tracie Ray, aren't you?" I asked when she handed me my change.

"Who's asking?"

"Me. I'm asking."

"And who the hell are you?" Tracie barked before looking around to ensure her manager wasn't in earshot.

"I'm Izzy," I said, backing up a step because Tracie Ray looked like a woman who'd carry a switchblade. "I work with your daughter, Shelby. And this is my friend, Elton."

"Salutations," Elton said, and Tracie Ray glared at him before turning back to me.

"You said you work with Shelby?" Tracie asked, looking skeptical.

"Yes, ma'am," I said. "She drives me to work most days."

"Oh, so you're the girl with the pill problem who solves all the murders," Tracie said, and I figured it was safe to assume everyone in Ashes knew my life story by now.

"The pills were a while ago," I lied, and Tracie shrugged her indifference.

"Well, I guess it's nice to meet y'all," Tracie said. "Enjoy your six-dollar gum."

"Wait," I said, "we wanted to talk to you for a minute if you have time."

"What the hell do you want to talk to me about?"

"Vance Fuller," I said, and Tracie Ray stared at me so hard I prayed I was dreaming, so when I woke up, I could reconsider walking into this cheese fetish store and asking Tracie Ray about Vance Fuller. "But, we can see you're busy, so we'll just—"

"My next smoke break is in half an hour," Tracie said. "I'll meet you out back."

The rear of Fraîche wasn't nearly as fancy as the front. Weeds instead of roses, an overflowing dumpster, broken glass, and the employee parking lot full of cars that looked like they'd recently lost a demolition derby. Elton and I stood against the wall, next to some penis graffiti, waiting on Tracie. Half an hour later, she burst out the rear door, blinking into the morning sun while lighting a cigarette.

"Well," Tracie said, blowing smoke into our faces and sending Elton into a coughing fit, "I hate to disappoint y'all after keeping you waiting, but I didn't know Vance Fuller."

"But you worked at Fuller Farms the summer he died," I said.

"So did a lot of people. Don't mean I knew him, does it?"

"That summer, you saw a boy named Aubrey Masters."

Tracie Ray stubbed her cigarette out on the wall and tossed the butt on the ground. "How the hell do you know that?"

"Wellington Fuller hired me to solve his son's murder," I said, "and Chief Jenkins let us look over the case files. We read the interview you gave the police after Vance died."

Tracie Ray spat on the ground and said, "Wellington Fuller has more money than sense."

"Maybe," I said with a shrug, "but that doesn't change the fact someone shot his son full of arrows, and I'm going to find who."

Tracie shook her head but didn't argue.

"Did you know Aubrey Masters left his family a year ago?"

"I ain't talked to Aubrey Masters since 1992."

"What do you think he's running from?" I asked.

"Aubrey didn't kill Vance Fuller if that's what you're asking."

"How do you know?"

Tracie started to reply but caught herself.

"I'm friends with Aubrey's son, Sterling," I said. "He's at camp this year."

"Hugging friends," Elton clarified for me.

"You listen to me," Tracie said, jabbing a finger into my chest, "you'll stay away from that boy if you know what's good for you. You'll stay away from every boy at that camp. They're all rotten to their cores."

"I am a boy, and I attend Fuller Farms," Elton protested, but Tracie ignored him.

"I've warned Shelby about them. Told her I didn't even want her working out there, but they pay so good I couldn't talk her out of it. But she knows to stay away from those boys. Working there was the worst thing that ever happened to me. Aubrey Masters was the worst thing that ever happened to me."

"You began telling Chief Morrison about something that happened to you the night Vance died, but—"

"—I ain't talking to y'all about this," Tracie snapped.

"Please, if you saw anything that night, it might help us solve Vance's murder."

"Y'all get out of here and don't ever come back talking to me about Aubrey Masters again. You hear me?"

"Please, if you'll just—"

Tracie stormed back into Fraîche and slammed the door behind her, leaving Elton and me with nothing but questions and a pack of six-dollar gum.

CHAPTER FIFTEEN

Shelby was off Sunday, so Mom offered to drive me to work. But as we walked out the door, her manager from Fraîche called.

"What about Rhonda? Can't she drag her lazy ass out of bed?" Mom asked, then rolled her eyes at the man's reply. "Fine, give me half an hour."

"Trouble at the cheese factory?" I asked.

"Tracie didn't show up this morning, and they need me to work. Sorry, baby girl, but your brother can take you to work."

Shit. Did Tracie Ray skip work because of me? Surely not. It was a coincidence. Right?

It took me ten minutes to wake Axl from his slumber, and he said he couldn't drive me to work because he had to get ready for church.

"Since when do you go to church?" I asked.

"Since the chick I want to bang invited me," Axl replied before performing a vulgar dance best left undescribed in these pages.

This left me with only two choices—miss work or bum a ride off the piece of shit who hit my mother last weekend. Half an hour later, I was in the van with Lenny, driving down the mountain toward Fuller Farms.

"You want me to drive?" I asked after he drifted onto the shoulder a third time.

"Like I'd let you drive Tina," he said, patting the dashboard of the van he'd apparently named Tina.

"Well, try and stay on the road. I don't want you to die a virgin."

Lenny snorted a laugh, and then we drove in silence for a few miles.

"You know, I'm glad it worked out for us to have some time together this morning," Lenny said after a moment.

I'm not, I thought. "I'm not," I said.

"Your mama said you were mad at me, you know, for what happened last weekend."

"You mean when you punched her in the face and nearly broke her nose? Yeah, Lenny, I was mad. I'm still mad. I wish she'd thrown you out on your ass. I wish she'd called the police and—"

"—Whoa, whoa, whoa, hold on there, Izzy. You and I both know we don't want the police anywhere near our apartment."

He was right, but I wasn't going to give him the satisfaction of saying it.

"But listen, what I did was wrong, and I don't blame you for being angry. I love your mama, but sometimes she can be—

"—Nope. I'm not letting you blame her for what happened."

"No, you're right," Lenny said, raising his hands to apologize before snatching the wheel to keep us from driving off the mountain. "This is on me, one hundred percent. But you've got to understand, I've been under a lot of stress lately with my job. Moving to the middle of nowhere has made things hard for me. I've got guys running all over Florida and up and down the east coast, and I used to could keep close tabs on them, but now it's difficult. Deliveries ain't showing up. Payments ain't being made. And my bottom line is suffering. Look, I don't plan to do this forever. This ain't a sustainable lifestyle. But I have an opportunity now to make enough money to set us up for life, and I don't want to blow it. You know I love your mama. I wouldn't have moved here with y'all if I didn't love her."

I glanced over at Lenny while he drove. He looked worse than I remembered. Way worse than he had the day I met him back in Bardo when he had his fake Air Jordans propped on our coffee table. His face was hollowed out, and his arms looked like he'd recently fought several large cats in a phone booth. I had no doubt his line of work was stressful. Most jobs are, even when you're not worried the police could kick down your door at any moment. I wondered if he'd started taking his own product to cope but didn't ask.

"I promised your brother I'd be better going forward, and I'm promising you the same thing."

"You talked to Axl about this?" I asked.

"He talked to me," Lenny said. "Picked me up by the collar and threatened to bash my skull if it ever happened again."

I looked out my window so Lenny wouldn't see my smile. I loved my brother again. Loved him the way I did when we were kids, and he'd walk in front on our treks through the woods surrounding Pineview Villas to make sure I didn't step on a rattlesnake. Loved him the way I did in eighth grade when he threw Lincoln Barber in a dumpster for pinching my ass during gym.

"But it ain't gonna happen again," Lenny said. "I promise you."

"Okay," I said, feeling as good about the situation as my faith in Lenny Roach would allow. He seemed his goofy, harmless self, but I'd now seen his dark side and vowed to never lower my guard again.

"By the way, how's your supply holding out?" he asked as we pulled into the employee lot at Fuller Farms. I couldn't be sure if he was genuinely concerned about my headaches or just reminding me that running him off would have consequences.

"Fine," I lied, climbing out of the van. "I've hardly touched them."

"Good for you," he said, with his trademark snap and finger point. Then he drove away.

On Sundays, campers at Fuller Farms attend a mandatory morning worship service, then have the afternoon free to race yachts around Mud Lake or sample beluga caviar or whatever rich kids do in their spare time. I didn't see Sterling until after lunch when we went for a walk on one of the trails winding through the woods behind Mud Lake.

I never cared much for hiking before moving to Ashes. Of course, what we called woods back home were, in essence, just pine tree farms infested with rats and snakes. But these woods were peaceful. Serene, even. Here the trees grew tall and ancient, safe in the knowledge they weren't destined for the sawmill and later Home Depot. The air was fresh and clean, and a babbling stream or tiny waterfall hid behind every bend. Even the wildlife was idyllic. Singing birds, playful foxes, and frolicking deer that seemed to only be waiting for an invitation to crawl through your window and help you get dressed like some helpless Disney princess. Having Sterling there with me didn't hurt.

"I missed seeing you Friday night," he said, taking my hand in his.

"Me too," I said. "Axl has started ascending to his perch as king of Ashes Prep, so he claimed to have better things to do than drive me back here. But Mom said I can borrow her car next weekend if she isn't working."

"I can't wait," Sterling said, kissing my cheek. "How's your murder investigation going?"

"Okay, I guess," I said with a shrug. "The former Ashes police chief had six people he wanted to question more about the case. One is dead, one shot at us, and one told us never to talk to her again."

"A solid start," Sterling said with a laugh. "And the last three?"

"One is the mayor's son, and the mayor strongly encouraged us to drop our investigation because he doesn't want any bad publicity for the town. One is a hotshot attorney in Charlotte. And one ... is your dad."

"The police chief wanted to talk to my dad again about Vance Fuller?"

"Yeah, but only because he didn't mention sneaking around that night with Tracie Ray, the kitchen girl he was seeing. I'm sure Chief Morrison just wanted to ask your dad if he saw anything that might help the case."

"Okay, so you really don't think my dad had something to do with the murder?"

"No, I don't," I said, squeezing Sterling's hand to reassure him.

"Okay, good," he said, letting out a sigh of relief. "I mean, I hate my dad right now, but I'd rather him not be a murderer, you know?"

"Yeah, I know," I said with a smile. "That said, Elton and I did talk to Tracie Ray yesterday, and she wasn't a big fan of your father. She said he was the worst thing to ever happen to her."

"She and Mom would hit it off," Sterling said with a smile.

"Any idea why she'd say that?" I asked.

Sterling shrugged. "No clue. You'll have to ask her, I guess."

"I guess so," I said, with Tracie Ray's words ringing in my ear. *Y'all get out of here and don't ever come back talking to me about Aubrey Masters.*

That evening, one of the other kitchen girls drove me back to Ashes after dinner, saving me from having to call Lenny and ask for a ride home. I went to bed thinking about Tracie Ray and what happened to her that summer that made her so reluctant to talk to us. She appeared in my dreams, screaming at Elton and me to stay away from her. Of course, Elton had a horse's head in my dream, and Tracie Ray wore a straitjacket, but I still woke up feeling painfully anxious about the whole thing. I took a pill. The sixth in a row of what I swore would only be a seven-day streak this time, and after my shower, I waited in the parking lot for Shelby. When she arrived, I could tell she'd been crying.

"Shelby, what's wrong?" I asked, climbing into her car, and putting a hand on her shoulder.

"It's Mom," she said, bursting into tears again. "She's run away."

CHAPTER SIXTEEN

On the outskirts of Ashes, Shelby pulled over and let me drive the rest of the way to Fuller Farms while she chain-smoked and told me about her mother.

"I didn't come home Saturday night," Shelby said. "This guy I'm seeing on and off has an apartment outside Cashiers, and I stay there sometimes."

"Your boyfriend has an apartment? How old is he?"

"He's not my boyfriend," Shelby said. "Just a guy I sometimes see on weekends. He's twenty, or maybe twenty-one."

"And your mother doesn't care you're shacking up with some twenty-one-year-old?"

"No," Shelby said in a tone that made me feel dumb for asking. "I'm almost seventeen, so it's not illegal unless he's a teacher, and I don't think Toby finished eighth grade, so he ain't no teacher."

"Oh," I said, because what else could I say?

"Anyway, I didn't get home until late Sunday morning. Mom was gone, but that ain't unusual. I figured she had a shift at Fraîche, so I crawled into bed and slept all day. Didn't wake up until about five on Sunday afternoon, and I was starving. So, I went to the kitchen and fixed myself a ham sandwich, and that's when I saw the note. She probably left it on Saturday night, but I didn't see it when I came home."

Shelby handed me the note, scribbled on a wrinkled sheet of notebook paper, the blue ink blotched from tears.

Shelby Bear,

I got to go away for a while. Don't you worry about me. I'm okay. But I can't stay in Ashes right now, and maybe one day I'll tell you why. You might hear some things about me while I'm gone. Some might be true, but don't you believe all of it. You just keep your head down, mind your business, and I'll be back soon, I promise. There is enough money in the bank to pay the bills for a few months, and I left a checkbook in the top drawer of my dresser. Aunt Jenny in Franklin probably won't turn you away if you need anything. I'm sorry I can't tell you more, Shelby Bear, but it's better this way. Trust me. I love you, and I'll see you soon.

Love,
Momma Bear

"Has your mother ever done this before?" I asked, hoping this was a common occurrence but knowing it wasn't.

"No," Shelby said and started crying again. "Last time I remember her spending a night away from home was when we won a trip to Dollywood some local radio station gave away. I'm worried about her, Izzy. What if she's in trouble?"

If Tracie Ray was in trouble, it was my fault. I could still see the fear in her eyes when I told her I'd read the interview she gave the police after Vance Fuller died, and I couldn't forget her visceral reaction to just the mention of Aubrey Masters. She knew something about Vance's death. Tracie Ray saw something that night at Fuller Farms. Either that, or she had something to do with the murder. And now she was gone, lost in the North Carolina pines.

"Did you talk to anyone at Fraîche?" I asked, hoping Shelby hadn't tied her mother's disappearance to me.

"Yeah, I called Robbie, her asshole supervisor, but he wasn't any help. Said Mom left her shift early on Saturday with a headache and didn't show up for work on Sunday. Said to tell her she's fired if I ever talk to her again."

"Shit, Shelby, I'm so sorry. If you're afraid to stay in your trailer alone, you're always welcome to sleep at our place. Mom won't mind if—"

"—I sleep with a Glock 43 under my pillow," Shelby said. "I ain't afraid of shit. But there is something you can do for me."

"Anything," I said.

"You're the famous investigator, right?"

"Not really, I just—"

"Find my mama."

"Shelby, I'm not sure I can—"

"Find her, Izzy," Shelby said, sniffling as she wiped the tears from her eyes. "If she's in trouble, I've got to help her. So please."

"I'll try," I said, knowing if Tracie Ray had something to do with Vance Fuller's murder, Shelby should be careful what she asked for.

"Tracie Ray was adamant she did not wish to discuss Vance Fuller's death with us any further, so her disappearance does not alter our investigation."

"People tell us they don't want to talk to us all the time," I said, wadding up a sheet of paper and throwing it at Elton's head, "but once we uncover some shady shit they've done, they tend to change their tune."

"True," Elton said, throwing the paper ball back and missing me by a mile.

"But if we can't find Tracie Ray, we can't blackmail her, and she knows something about Vance Fuller. She knows something we need to know. We have to find her."

"Izzy, I do not believe opening a second front to this investigation is an appropriate use of our time and resources."

"Opinion noted and ignored," I said, and Elton frowned.

"The logical course of action is to continue interviewing the suspects we can locate."

"Thanks, Mr. Spock."

"A week searching for Tracie Ray or Aubrey Masters is a week wasted if they were to return of their own volition. We should turn our attention to Jasper Benson and Tripp Aston."

Elton was right, of course. He was always right. But Jasper Benson's father had already gently warned us to drop our investigation.

His next warning might not be so gentle if we tried interrogating his son. And the idea of calling the partner at some giant Charlotte law firm and having him talk circles around me until I felt dizzy wasn't appealing. But those were my choices.

"Fine, I'm off on Wednesday. If Jasper Benson is in town, we'll pay him a visit. In the meantime, see if you can find any dirt on him."

"Aye, aye," Elton said with a heel-clicking salute. "I have already sent him a Facebook request he has failed to accept, but I will double my efforts." Then Elton turned serious and asked, "Is Lenny Roach treating your mother better? I still worry about you living in such proximity to a violent person."

"You don't need to worry about me," I said, giving him a hug he tolerated for half a second. "I talked to Lenny, and so did Axl. He'll be on his best behavior from now on."

That night when I got back to the apartment, Mom was working at Fraîche, and Axl was off doing who knows what, but Lenny was home, his fake Jordans on the coffee table, his Taco Bell wrappers strewn across the couch while he watched his Tampa Bay Rays on ESPN.

"Dizzy Miss Izzy," he said, snapping his fingers and pointing at me when I walked through the door.

"Hi, Lenny, bye, Lenny," I said, hurrying past him to my room because I preferred not to breathe the same oxygen as Lenny for long.

"Hey now, the man of the house deserves more respect, don't you think?" Lenny called after me.

I bit my tongue until I tasted blood but couldn't help myself. "Lenny, there are no men in this house. Just women and boys."

I took a shower to wash off the shitty day, and after throwing on some gym shorts and a T-shirt, I sat still long enough to feel the day's vanquished headache rising from the grave. It wasn't too bad. Nothing a couple of Advil with dinner couldn't handle. I didn't need another pill. Two pills a day was a bad idea I did not intend to repeat. But I reached for my nightstand drawer anyway because seeing my bottle always gave me a jolt of peace of mind, and I needed it then. But when I opened the drawer this time, the pills were gone. Dammit, Lenny.

"Hey, Lenny," I said, walking back into the living room.

"Yeah, Izzybell," he replied without looking up.

"By any chance have you seen the bottle I keep in my nightstand drawer?"

"You mean the giant bottle of twenty milligram OxyContin I was so kind to give you back in Dandridge?"

"Yeah, that one," I said.

Lenny paused his game and walked across the room to stand so close I could smell the Taco Bell Fire sauce on his breath.

"Yeah, I took it back because you've been a little bitch lately. Everyone under this roof needs to get it through their heads that I'm the man of this house, and what I say goes."

He seemed a different person from the groveling, apologetic man who'd given me a ride to work just a day earlier, and I backed up a few steps out of fear.

"So, when you start showing me the respect I deserve, you'll get your little bottle back. But until then," he added, brushing my face as he ran his hand through the side of my hair, "you're shit out of luck." Then he popped me on the cheek with an open hand, no harder than a small child would, but it still stunned me to tears.

I turned and ran for my bedroom with Lenny's mocking laughter chasing after me.

1992

Vance Fuller could see the light at the end of the tunnel.

After crawling from bed and marking off the previous day on his wall calendar, Vance took a moment to celebrate making it this far through the summer camp from hell. He'd survived five long weeks of campers not listening to him and counselors ignoring him—he could survive three more.

Vance took the first shower, part of an unspoken agreement he and Tripp reached, which afforded his roommate an extra fifteen minutes of sleep. That morning, after he dressed, he found Tripp sitting on his bed, reading through a stack of mail.

These days it's impossible to disconnect Fuller Farms campers from the rest of the world. Disregarding rule 3A in the camp handbook, they bring their smartphones, smartwatches, tablets, laptops, and the like. But in 1992, the United States Postal Service provided campers with their only link to the outside world, and letters arrived on Wednesday mornings in a batch.

"Anything good in the mail?" Vance asked Tripp, because out of common courtesy, he tried at least once daily to converse with his roommate. But, as usual, Tripp did not acknowledge Vance's existence, so Vance left the cabin and headed toward breakfast.

Halfway across the commons, Vance heard the footsteps, fast and pounding, and on him before he could even turn around. Tripp hit Vance like the all-state linebacker he once was, sending them both to the ground in a heap, and the first fist connected with Vance's face before he saw who or what had run him over.

A second fist followed.

Then a third.

Then a twentieth.

Blood was all Vance could see or taste, but he could hear the shouts of campers and counselors. Shouts of condemnation or encouragement, Vance could not say. But the pummeling continued into eternity until this beating was all he knew—past, present, and future. Then, by some miracle, it stopped, and he found himself in the archery shed, turning up the jar of moonshine Buster McClellan offered him.

"Our secret family recipe," Buster said when Vance recoiled and shook violently after his first sip.

"Diesel fuel is not a secret recipe," Vance managed.

Buster laughed. "No, maybe not, but this stuff will numb you, and trust me, you're not gonna want to feel your face for the next several days."

Vance touched his puffy face, winced from the pain, and took another sip of whatever Buster kept in that jar.

"What the hell did you do to that boy anyhow?" Buster asked. "I've seen roommates scuffle over all sorts of shit, but he looked intent on killing you."

During the beating, as Tripp Aston rained down punches and

insults, Vance pieced together what news the mailman delivered. Ty Bingham, the UNC student who'd ended Vance's academic career, had killed himself. Tripp blamed Vance. Everyone would blame Vance.

"Do you know why I left Chapel Hill?" Vance asked Buster.

The archery instructor shrugged. "I've heard rumors but figured most were bullshit."

Vance told him the truth.

Well, a version of the truth.

Vance's version of the truth.

Tripp was fraternity brothers with Ty Bingham, and he'd aligned the other counselors against Vance from day one. "They planned to ignore me all summer," Vance said. "Treat me like I didn't exist. But I guess when Tripp got the news about his friend this morning, he lost it." Vance took a third sip of moonshine and handed the jar back to Buster because any more of the stuff would likely send him into organ failure. "Christians couldn't hate the Colosseum more than I hate this place."

Buster laughed and put a hand on Vance's hand. "Now, son, you don't—"

Vance yanked his hand away and knocked over the table while scrambling to his feet, all the painful memories of the last time he'd been in this shed ten years ago flooding his brain. "I always hated it. Every minute. Every second. And if you don't leave me alone, I'll tell Dad everything."

Buster called after him as Vance burst out the door heading back toward the dorms, but Vance kept running. Only three weeks of camp left. It might as well be three million.

And that light at the end of the tunnel?

Choo-choo.

CHAPTER SEVENTEEN

Sleep ran from me Monday night, and I chased it until exhaustion hit sometime after four in the morning, when I finally drifted off into restless rest. Two hours later, I awoke to my terrible new reality. My pills were gone. The pills I'd taken almost daily for the last three weeks. The pills whose mere presence in my nightstand drawer gave me the peace of mind I needed to make it through life.

Dammit to hell.

I sat up, expecting the mother of all headaches to knock me back on my ass, but, to my surprise, I felt okay. Okay enough to inhale a Pop-Tart and glass of milk while standing next to the sink, ready to run back to my room if Lenny made an early morning appearance. Panic didn't hit until I was in the shower, when after losing my breakfast, I thought I was drowning in the steam. I fumbled with the knobs, my lungs so full of water the world around me grew black. I don't even remember stumbling into my bedroom and falling to the floor, but that's where I came to, gasping for air.

I reached for my phone to text Shelby. I wouldn't need a ride to work. I couldn't fathom ever needing a ride anywhere again. But then, I remembered Shelby's offer the day I met her. *My cousin Donnie can get you pills.*

Sure, buying pills was a line I'd vowed not to cross, but this was different. Shelby was a friend, and I was already doing her a favor by looking for her mother. She'd just be doing me a favor in return, nothing more. I wasn't buying handshake drugs in a dark alley from some dude in a trench coat. I wouldn't even have to meet her cousin. I needed this medicine to be a functioning member of society, and no one would begrudge me getting it however I could. Right?

Oxygen returned to my lungs. This would be okay. I'd be okay. I got dressed for work.

Tuesday wasn't great. My headache was tardy, not absent, and after it showed up mid-morning, I spent the rest of the day battling it with extra-strength Goody's powders, the strongest non-narcotic in my arsenal.

"Twenty milligrams?" Shelby asked after I finally found the nerve to make my request on our drive home from work.

"Yeah, or whatever he can get," I said, playing it cool like my very existence didn't depend on those little pink pills.

"No problem," she said. "Give me a couple of days."

I was off Wednesday but returned to Fuller Farms to work on the case with Elton. He was in our office when I arrived with bacon and eggs.

"Have you even met any of the other campers?" I asked.

"Several," Elton said without looking up. "Though I have yet to encounter one with which I have anything in common."

"But they're not being mean to you, are they?"

"Negative. Your hugging friend Sterling insisted they treat me well."

I smiled and dropped his plate on the desk. "Good, but you still missed breakfast again."

"I knew you would provide," he said, inhaling a piece of bacon in one bite. To be on the autism spectrum, Elton wasn't a particularly picky eater. Well, he was particular about eating his food in a certain order, but he'd inhale whatever you put in front of him. His issue, I realized now, was if you didn't feed him, he'd never go looking for food on his own.

"Okay, I guess it's Jasper Benson's day," I said, watching Elton move on to his eggs. "What do we know about him?"

"As you know, *Maxim* magazine once published a feature on Jasper referring to him as the last American playboy," Elton said through a mouthful of breakfast. "However, it appears that was likely a paid promotion meant to hype his directorial debut, *Ghost of Judas*."

"Jasper Benson is a film director?" I asked.

"Was. And barely. *Rotten Tomatoes* lists *Ghost of Judas*'s approval rating at 7 percent based on thirteen reviews."

"And that's bad?"

"Historically bad," Elton said.

"Okay. Well, apart from that, what do we know about him?"

"Frustratingly little," Elton admitted. "I canceled and resent my friend request, but he has still not accepted it."

"Maybe because he's not your friend?" I offered.

Elton cocked his head in thought before scribbling something on his notepad.

"So, do we even know if he's in town?" I asked.

"No, but if he is, we will find him at Benson House."

"Benson House? What, does he give tours or something?"

"Negative. The publicly visible section of his Facebook profile claims he resides there."

"Wait, he lives in that giant house people pay fifty bucks to walk through?"

"They offer student discounts," Elton said. "We will only pay forty dollars, plus tax and a small service fee."

I squinted at this information. "So, we have to pay this guy to go to his house?"

"We pay the Benson Trust, which maintains the home and the 5,000 acres it sits on. Jasper Benson just lives there. So far as I can tell, he has nothing to do with tours or the day-to-day operations of the house."

"Well if he doesn't work in the gift shop, do we just search room to room until we find him?"

"Negative. A map on the Benson House website labels part of the west wing as 'private residence.' I suspect we will find Jasper Benson there."

"Okay," I said, trying to wrap my head around all of this, "so you're suggesting we pay forty bucks plus taxes and a small service fee to enter Benson House, then, during our tour, sneak off to the west wing to look for Jasper Benson?"

"Affirmative," Elton said, now gulping down his orange juice.

"And if we get caught?"

"Benson House is 107,345 square feet," Elton said. "We can claim we got lost."

I felt a twinge of guilt that Elton, who valued the truth over everything, could suggest lying so casually after only a year of my bad influence. But I didn't have a better plan, so we got in the truck and drove to Benson House.

"The World Health Organization has not declared a pandemic since the 1968 Hong Kong Flu," Elton said as we wound through curvy mountain roads in our old truck toward Benson House. The WHO had declared swine flu a pandemic the week before, and it's all he wanted to talk about.

"Well, I don't eat bacon, so I'm not particularly worried."

"Izzy," Elton said in his most exasperated tone, "H1N1 is spread mainly by droplets made when people cough, sneeze, or talk, not consumption of pork byproducts. In fact, most experts believe—"

"Hold that thought," I said as we turned into the visitor's entrance to Benson House, which starts on Highway 64 east of Franklin and winds for three miles through a picturesque forest and formal gardens, stopping just shy of a twenty-acre striped lawn rising gently uphill to the 150-room gilded age monstrosity Willoughby Benson once called home.

Unlike the Biltmore Estate in tourist-friendly Asheville, Benson House is off the beaten path. Still, over half a million visitors a year fork out fifty bucks to tour the second-largest house in North Carolina. That morning, Elton and I were among hundreds of them, most of whom, judging by their matching T-shirts, belonged to the Golden Eagles, an old folks' ministry at some big Baptist church in Chattanooga.

We waited in line to buy tickets, retrieved our self-guided tour headsets, and walked through the front doors into the entrance hall, a space more cavernous than any of the ancient cathedrals I visited in London.

"On doctor's orders," said the folksy tour guide in our headsets, "Willoughby Benson began visiting the North Carolina mountains in 1881 in hopes the clean mountain air might reverse the effects of tuberculosis, the dreaded disease that would take his life only six years later."

"Tuberculosis was fatal until 1943 when Selman Waksman and Elizabeth Bugie discovered streptomycin," Elton shouted over his headset. I tried to shush him, but he kept going, his voice drowning out even the Golden Eagles, who shouted over their own headsets. "Doctors once recommended inhaling hemlock to ease the symptoms, and before that, people would wait in line to be touched by the king of England."

I grabbed Elton by the arm and pulled him into the next room, a frescoed-ceilinged banquet hall the size of a basketball gym containing a forty-place table and a fireplace so large you could burn entire trees in it.

"Today, four drugs are commonly used to treat tuberculosis. Rifampin, pyrazinamide, iso—"

"I need you to focus," I said, pulling the headphones from Elton's head. "We're here to find Jasper Benson, remember? Now, where is the west wing?"

"On the west side of the house," Elton said without a hint of sarcasm.

"And which way is that?" I asked.

He pulled a small compass from his pocket, because of course he did, spun around twice, then pointed toward a door at the end of the banquet hall. "That way."

I followed Elton down a long hallway, past guest bedrooms, where everyone from Teddy Roosevelt to Oprah had once spent the night. Our trek west led us to the basement, alongside the indoor swimming pool and bowling alley, before returning upstairs, where we reached a door with a sign reading, "Staff Only: Do Not Enter."

"We are not staff," Elton said, the sternly worded sign quickly causing him to abandon his plans to lie and say we got lost if someone caught us in an off-limits part of the house.

"I'm on staff at Fuller Farms," I said.

"That does not help us."

"Sure it does. We have a reciprocal relationship with Benson House. They can enter our "Staff Only" rooms, and we can enter theirs."

"That is not true," Elton said.

"Like you would know," I said, and he huffed but conceded my point with a grunt. Then I opened the door, and he followed me inside.

We entered another long corridor, though this one was not decorated with John Singer Sargent portraits and other priceless trinkets like the rest of Benson House. This could have been a hallway in any random three-star hotel, with dark red carpet and half a dozen closed doors. I was about to open the first door and look inside when the opening riff of Nirvana's "Smells Like Teen Spirit" came blasting from further down the hall.

Elton and I stared at each other with wide eyes before walking toward the source of the music.

"Ready?" I asked, reaching for the knob.

"Negative," he said.

I turned the knob anyway, and we stepped into what looked like a teenage boy's bedroom, only it was the size of a Walgreens. Posters featuring early nineties movies, rock bands, and athletes plastered the walls, and couches, beanbags, a ping-pong table, vintage arcade games, and a larger-than-king-sized waterbed filled the room.

"Did we just time travel?" I asked Elton, but before he could pontificate on Einstein's Theory of Special Relativity, a scruffy guy in a flannel shirt stumbled out of the bathroom and blinked at us in confusion before asking, "Dude, do you two like, work here or something?"

CHAPTER EIGHTEEN

"No, I'm Izzy, and this is my friend Elton," I said to the man in the flannel shirt, who proceeded to scratch his ass and say, "Excellent. Well, nice to meet you." He then plopped down on one of his many threadbare couches, turned on an old-school Sega Genesis, and began a game of *NHL 92*.

"I now consider your time travel hypothesis as the most likely explanation for what is happening," Elton said. I shrugged at him and we stepped further into the room.

"Excuse me, sir," I said, "are you Jasper Benson?"

"In the flesh," Jasper said without taking his eyes off his game. His voice had that slow, relaxed stoner tone, and the room reeked of pot. "And who might—oh wait, you already told me, Dizzy and Elvis."

"Izzy and Elton," Elton corrected.

"That's what I said, man," Jasper said, and Elton huffed in frustration.

"Mr. Benson," I said, "we need to ask you—"

"Out the door you came in, make a left, no, sorry, make a right, then turn east down the third hallway. If you follow it to the end, you'll be in the gift shop near old Willoughby's library. If you take a detour, you may never be seen again."

"Wait, what?"

"Sorry, dude, I thought you were like, looking for the way back to your tour or whatever," Jasper said, pounding the buttons on his Sega controller in frustration after the computer scored a goal. "Most people who end up in my room are like, totally lost."

"Actually, Mr. Benson, we were looking for you," I said.

Jasper paused the hockey game and squinted at us. "No shit?"

"You are Jasper W. Benson, son of Mayor Jeremy Benson, heir to the Benson fortune, right?" I had to ask, because Jasper Benson looked more like the bassist for a Pearl Jam tribute band than a trust fund baby.

"The same," Jasper said with a laugh like he couldn't believe it either.

"Jasper Benson, whom *Maxim* magazine called the last American playboy?" Elton asked.

Jasper laughed at the skepticism in Elton's voice and explained, "Dude, my dad paid them to write that article like ten years ago, back when he thought I was his ticket to Hollywood. But I'm long past trying to impress him or anyone else. Besides, if you've smashed a thousand European skanks, you've smashed them all. You know what I mean?"

Elton did not know what he meant and turned to me for an explanation I could not provide.

"I'm guessing I'm like, not what you expected," Jasper said.

"Not exactly," I admitted.

Jasper laughed. "Yeah, I'm not exactly what my father expected either. He wanted me to be the next Spielberg or some shit. Went so far as to build Southern Cal a new library so they'd accept me into film school. If you've had the misfortune of viewing *Ghost of Judas*, you know that dream didn't work out too well for either of us. Shit, I've been a terrible host," Jasper said, jumping from the couch and heading toward the industrial-size refrigerator against the wall. "Y'all want a beer or something?"

"We are underaged," Elton snapped.

"I won't tell if you won't, Manute."

"We're fine," I said, "but we needed to ask you about—"

"Yeah, I'm like, one massive disappointment to Mayor Jeremy Benson," Jasper said, returning to the couch with a breakfast Heineken. "But let me ask you, do you have any idea how much cash my family has?"

"3.65 billion dollars," Elton answered automatically.

"Hey, that's right," Jasper said, pointing at Elton with an approving nod. "3.65 billion dollars. If you lived to be like, a hundred, you'd have to spend …" Jasper mumbled in concentration. "… you'd have to spend like, a million thousand dollars a day, every day, to blow through it all. And that's if the money is like, stuffed in a mattress or something. If it's invested, you'd never spend it. It multiplies, like wet Gremlins. Have y'all ever seen *Gremlins*. I've got a copy on VHS somewhere around here. It's the freakiest shit."

Jasper began flipping over couch cushions while I tried to comprehend everything he'd just said.

"I'm the only person in my family who enjoys our wealth," he said, quickly giving up on his search for *Gremlins* and returning to his couch. "It's like my mom and my sister think maybe we'll be punished for it in the afterlife. And I'm like, whatever, maybe it's a prize for being good in a past life. They don't get it though, so they give back." Jasper Benson put air quotes around the phrase "give back," rolling his eyes so hard I feared they'd get stuck in the back of his head.

"My dumbass sister like, flies around the world chasing natural disasters, feeding orphans like some sort of Gucci-clad Mother Theresa. And Mom spends every waking hour fretting over the Benson Family Foundation, visiting charities to decide who gets the next stack of cash."

"What's wrong with giving back?" I asked.

Jasper exhaled dramatically like he shouldn't have to explain it to me. "Dude, when you finally open your eyes and see the world, I mean, truly see it or whatever, the only logical conclusion is that it's all meaningless. It's more random than a casino, but I'm the only person in my family who recognizes that the great blackjack dealer in the sky dealt us a winning. So these days I do what I want, like, all the time. It's what my dad should be doing, but he's somehow worse than my mom and sister, with his stupid little film festival, trying so hard to impress all these Hollywood phonies who don't give a shit about him. I'm like, dude, you're a billionaire, who cares what Tom Hanks thinks about you, just enjoy your life. But he cares too much what other people think."

Jasper bobbed his head to the bass riff of "Come as You Are" and said, "But not me. I do what I want. This morning, I wanted to get high and play Sega. Tomorrow, I may want to eat crepes in France, snorkel the Great Barrier Reef, or buy a Picasso and take a shit on it, and that's what I'll do."

"Defecating on a Picasso would significantly decrease its—"

"He was being facetious," I said to Elton.

"I assure you, I was not," Jasper said, unpausing the Sega and resuming his hockey game.

Elton and I exchanged a look and joined Jasper on the couch.

"Make yourselves at home," he said with a snort. "Mi casa, su casa."

"Mr. Benson, we need—"

"God, please stop calling me that. Mr. Benson is my father, and he sucks balls."

"Fine, Jasper, we came here to ask you about Vance Fuller."

Jasper Benson paused his game again and dropped the controller. "Dude, what could you possibly want to ask me about Vance Fuller?"

"Wellington Fuller hired us to investigate his murder."

"Old Man Fuller hired two children to investigate his son's murder?" Jasper asked, and when I nodded, he shrugged and added, "I mean, like, who am I to criticize how another man blows his fortune? But this makes shitting on a Picasso look prudent, no offense."

"None taken," I said, pressing on. "Vance was your camp counselor at Fuller Farms the summer he died, correct?"

"Yeah, but I've known him all my life. Our families constitute like, the upper echelon of West North Carolina society, or something."

"You told police you were asleep the night Vance died."

"Yep."

"You also told the police your roommates were asleep, but Tripp Aston claimed he caught two of Vance's campers playing cards after midnight."

"If you say so," Jasper said. "I suppose it was like, presumptuous or whatever to assume. For all I know, Aubrey and Quinn could have been down at Mud Lake for one of the famous Fuller Farms orgies. They do still have those, right?"

I opened my mouth to reply but couldn't find the words, and Jasper laughed and said, "I'm joking, dude. Fuller Farms is way too lame for orgies. The truth is, I don't know what Aubrey and Quinn were up to the night Vance died. You'll have to ask them."

"One is missing, and the other killed himself."

Jasper shrugged to say it wasn't his problem.

"You told Chief Morrison you'd heard a rumor Vance touched a younger camper inappropriately. Do you recall where you heard that?"

Jasper laughed. "I can like, barely remember my own birthday, man. But Vance Fuller rumors were a dime a dozen. He was weird as shit. I remember the kid's name, though, because it was like, the dumbest-sounding name I'd ever heard. John Wayne Crumpet." Vance laughed like Butthead and added, "Dude got arrested a few years ago for kiddie porn. I saw his name on the news and knew it was him."

"Okay," I said, while Elton scribbled down the name John Wayne Crumpet, "but you also told Chief Morrison that Vance's murder may have had something to do with an incident at Chapel Hill. Can you tell us about that?"

"Dude, you don't know about that? I thought everyone in Ashes knew that story."

"Enlighten us," I said.

"Vance and a student got caught, how do I put this delicately, earning extra credit. Vance got canned, kicked out of the PhD program or whatever he was in, and returned to Ashes in shame. That's why he was back working at his family's camp the summer he died."

"So, do you think that student had something to do with Vance's murder?"

"Not unless you believe in zombies. That dude killed himself a week before Vance died."

"Ty Bingham," Elton and I said in unison.

"Dude, you said you didn't know the story," Jasper said.

"We only knew part of the story," I said. "Tripp Aston told the police Vance did something awful to a friend of his at UNC, but he didn't say what."

"Yeah, and Tripp Aston like, beat the shit out of Vance the day before he died."

"Wait, what?"

Jasper nodded. "The morning he learned about Ty's suicide, Tripp ran Vance down in the commons and turned his face into abstract art."

"Like a Picasso," Elton said, and Jasper giggled.

"There was nothing about that in the police report," I said.

Jasper shrugged before tapping a button on the coffee table. Seconds later, a tuxedoed butler appeared by our side. "Yes, Lord Benson," the butler asked.

"Lord Benson," Jasper said, snickering to himself. "You can make these people call you whatever you want." He then turned to the butler and said, "Lucian, would you be so kind as to show Dizzy and Elvis here back to the main house. And like, hook them up with some credit at the gift shop or something while you're at it."

"Of course," the butler said.

"And Lucian, find me a copy of *NHL 94.* I want to make Gretzky's head bleed."

"Right away," the butler said. "And do not forget, sir, you're having lunch with your father today to discuss the film festival this fall."

Jasper greeted this news with a childish tantrum, then waved us toward the door to show our meeting was over.

"Wait," I said, as the butler put a hand on my shoulder to escort me from the room, "do you think Tripp Aston had something to do with Vance's murder?"

Jasper Benson laughed and shook his head. "Dude, Tripp Aston is like, the most powerful attorney south of the Mason-Dixon Line. If his mom said he was a fussy baby, Tripp would sue her for slander, so I'm not about to accuse him of anything." He shrugged and added, "But, if anyone at camp had a reason to murder Vance Fuller, it was totally that dude."

CHAPTER NINETEEN

"Charlotte is approximately 151 miles from Ashes," Elton said as we climbed back into the truck to return to Fuller Farms. "If we leave now, we could interview Tripp Aston and return in time for dinner."

"We're not going to Charlotte," I said. I didn't trust our pickup to make it halfway there, but more than that, I was scared of Tripp Aston. His smirking profile photograph on Day, Dorminey & Aston's website confirmed my every assumption. This man had the means to crush me if I didn't watch my step, and I tended not to watch my step. I had to talk to him, but a phone call from an untraceable number while disguising my voice was preferable. And under no circumstances could I let on I suspected he had something to do with Vance Fuller's murder. Otherwise, he'd likely join Dalton Wolfe and Marley Craven in the growing list of powerful men with reason to destroy my life. It wasn't hard to envision a scenario where I slipped up, and Tripp Aston caught something accusatory in my tone. Moments later, I'd be served papers, sued into oblivion, and burnt at the stake after a daring yet unsuccessful escape from debtors' prison. No, I needed to call Tripp

Aston when my head was clear. I would wait for Shelby's cousin to get me more pills.

"That'll be two bills," Shelby said on Friday morning when she handed me a small pill bottle.

"Two ten-dollar bills?" I asked, shaking the bottle and finding it lacking.

Shelby's laugh told me I'd asked a dumb question. "Hey, it could have been worse. Donnie gave you the family discount."

When Axl and I were in middle school, Mom dated a guy who worked at Wild Bill's Go-Karts & Arcade in Dandridge, and he gave us game tokens and free go-kart rides for several weeks until the inevitable breakup. Not concerned with the potential awkwardness of Mom running into her ex, Axl and I begged her to take us back to Wild Bill's for weeks until she finally relented one Saturday evening. But when the woman behind the counter told us how much a five-minute go-kart ride cost, Mom laughed in her face and dragged us back to the car without another word.

Opening my two-hundred-dollar bottle and looking inside to see only eight 20mg OxyContin tablets, I had a similar experience. Lenny had easily given me four thousand dollars' worth of pills before I left for London, but I couldn't appreciate it because I didn't know just one of those little pink miracles cost twenty-five freaking dollars until now. Holy shit, drugs are expensive.

If I took one every morning, these would barely last a week. Spending most of my paycheck on pills didn't seem like a great idea, so I'd need to conserve. I'd take one every other day unless I woke up feeling especially shitty, and in the meantime, I'd have to try like hell to get my big bottle back from Lenny.

"I appreciate it," I said to Shelby, handing her most of my money. Then I popped one of the pills and swallowed it without water. Shelby raised an eyebrow but didn't say anything.

Before lunch, I walked to Mud Lake and met Sterling. I hadn't had much time to talk to him that week and was happy to see him again.

"You look pretty," he said, taking my hand as we began our slow orbit around the lake.

"My shirt is covered in bacon grease, and I have scrambled eggs in my hair," I said.

Sterling laughed. "Well, you've looked better, but I stand by my original statement."

I smiled and let him kiss me on the cheek.

"How's camp?" I asked.

"Lame," he said. "Some perverted first-year kid got busted watching porn in the bathroom, and the counselors confiscated all our phones. How's your investigation going?"

"Elton and I went to Benson House this week and met Jasper Benson."

"I've heard he's crazy."

"More like rich and bored."

"Yeah, I've got an uncle like that. He built a miniature London in his backyard and spends most of his time reenacting the Blitz with remote control planes."

I laughed and said, "Okay, well, Jasper hasn't reached the pretend-he's-the-Luftwaffe stage of his wealthy boredom yet."

"What about your friend's mom?" Sterling asked. "The one who knew my dad."

"She disappeared," I said.

"What do you mean?"

"She skipped town. Shelby doesn't know where she is. She was pretty agitated after I asked her about Vance Fuller, and a day later, she's gone."

"Shit," Sterling said. "Do you think she killed Vance Fuller?"

"Not really, but I think she knows something and she's too scared to tell me. She mentioned something weird happening to her the night Vance died. I bet she saw something."

Sterling was quiet for a moment, then asked, "Any chance of you coming back here tonight?"

"Maybe," I teased. Mom had told me I could use the car that evening.

"Well, if you can make it, I won't be so presumptuous as to set up a candlelit blanket in the woods again."

"I don't think that would be presumptuous at all," I said with a wink, and Sterling nearly fell into the lake.

After washing the lunch dishes, I visited Elton in our office. My pill had kicked in, and I felt like myself for the first time in several days. I wasn't exactly brimming with confidence, but it seemed as good a time as any to call Tripp Aston.

"Friday greetings," Elton said when I walked in, almost successfully returning my fist bump.

"Have you cracked the case?" I asked, sitting in the office chair next to him and spinning until I made myself dizzy.

"Negative. I have spent most of this afternoon corresponding with Zadie Carrick. We have unreconcilable differences over whether Jaffa Cake is a cake or a biscuit."

"It does have cake in the name."

"Yes, and Ladyfingers have fingers in the name," he said, shaking his head in disappointment that I had sided with his ex-girlfriend in a culinary debate.

"Well, tell Zadie I said hello, and I'm sorry about all that business with her mother."

"Zadie bears no grudge," Elton said, and I could tell how much he missed her, so I gave him a hug he didn't want, then I called Tripp Aston on speakerphone.

"Day, Dorminey, and Aston," a woman said after picking up on the first ring. "How may I direct your call?"

"Tripp Aston, please."

The phone rang again, and another woman answered, "The office of Tripp Aston. How may I help you?"

"I need to speak to Tripp Aston," I said.

"Mr. Aston is currently unavailable. If you leave your name, number, and reason for your call, an associate will be in touch shortly."

I should have known I couldn't just call a partner at a giant law firm, particularly on a Friday when he was likely on the golf course. So,

I gave the assistant my name and number and said, "Tell Mr. Aston I called to talk about the murder of Vance Fuller." Five minutes later, Tripp Aston returned my call.

"Have I met your acquaintance, Miss …"

"Brown," I said, "and no, you haven't. Wellington Fuller hired me to investigate his son's murder, and I hoped you could provide some information."

"Miss Brown, may I inquire as to your age?"

"Sixteen," I said and heard Tripp Aston let out a deep sigh.

"I'll catch up on the next hole," Tripp shouted to the rest of his foursome before saying to me, "I heard Wellington had been acting irrationally since Rosalind died, but I didn't realize he was to the point of hiring minors to investigate his son's murder."

I shouldn't have deemed this worthy of a reply, but his condescension pissed me off. "I've solved two cold-case murders before my seventeenth birthday, Mr. Aston. What about you?"

He chuckled. "No, I suppose I wasn't quite so accomplished at your age," he admitted. "How can I help you, Miss Brown?"

"You were Vance Fuller's roommate at camp."

"I was."

"And you beat the shit out of Vance the morning you found out Ty Bingham had killed himself."

"I did, and given a chance, I'd do it again."

"Given the chance, would you kill him?"

"Over Ty Bingham? No, I would not. Ty and I were fraternity brothers but not particularly close. My actions that day were motivated by a sense of honor. I couldn't return to Chapel Hill in the fall and face my fraternity brothers if I'd shared a cabin with the guy who pushed

Ty to suicide without confronting him. So, I addressed the situation with physical action."

"You mean you beat his ass."

"That's one way of putting it. Either way, the matter was resolved as far as I was concerned."

"Okay, but—"

"Why didn't I inform law enforcement of my altercation with Mr. Fuller?" Tripp asked. "Because I was a scared kid, and I knew how it would look. But I'm no longer a scared kid, Miss Brown, and I think this line of questioning has gone far enough."

"Sorry," I mumbled and hated my cowardly self for it.

"Well, if that's all, I'll—"

"Wait," I said, "Jasper Benson told me there were rumors Vance acted inappropriately with a camper named John Wayne Crumpet."

Tripp snorted. "I wouldn't put much stock in anything Jasper Benson told me, but I can't say I didn't hear the same."

"So, do you think the Crumpet kid killed him?"

"What I think is irrelevant," Tripp Aston said, "because what I know is this. If you choose to move forward with this investigation, it will take you down a dark road. Yes, Vance Fuller abused Ty Bingham, and yes, he likely abused others as well. And one of those others might have killed him for it. I couldn't blame them. But I've also practiced law long enough to know most abusers don't exist in a vacuum. Many were abused themselves. I don't say this to make excuses for Vance, only to warn you that the truth doesn't always set you free. Wellington Fuller thinks he wants to know what happened to his son, but he might shoot the messenger when he hears it. And now, Miss Brown, I bid you a good day."

With that, Tripp Aston hung up, and Elton said, "We can add Tripp Aston to the list of people who told us the truth about Vance Fuller will be dark."

"And the list of people who have tried to get us to end our investigation," I said, wondering what Tripp Aston had to hide.

CHAPTER TWENTY

That evening, Shelby dropped me off after work, and I showered and got dressed to turn around and drive back to Fuller Farms to hang out with Sterling and his friends by Mud Lake.

"Partying with the camp nerds again?" Axl asked, entering my room without a knock while I put on makeup.

"Maybe," I said, not bothering to look at him.

"Well, watch yourself," he said, grabbing the stuffed raccoon off my bed and pretending it was a football.

"First," I said, snatching the raccoon from him, "don't touch Mr. Bigglesworth. And second, I always watch out for myself."

Axl laughed. "I know you do. And you could probably take out all those dudes by yourself if you had to. But sometimes these Uber-rich jerkoffs think they can get away with anything because they usually can, so be careful, even with the harmless ones."

I wasn't sure if Axl said this because he wanted to boss me around or if he was truly worried, but when I turned around, I saw genuine concern on his face.

"I'll be careful," I said, grabbing him by both arms and shaking him. "You don't have to worry about me."

"Yeah, I know," Axl said, playing his concern off like it was nothing.

He turned to leave, and I said, "Hey, by the way, do you still …"

I was about to ask if he still took pain pills for his sprained ankle. Partially because I was concerned about him, but mostly because I was curious if he had a giant bottle Lenny hadn't taken away. But that conversation could go in a million different directions, some ending in Axl telling Mom I still took pills for my headaches, and Lord knows where things would go from there.

"Do I still what?" Axl asked.

"Do you still suck?" I said, and he rolled his eyes and left my room.

"Hot date tonight, baby girl?" Mom asked as I hurried through the living room on my way out the door, hoping to avoid any Lenny interaction. I had on black tights and a sweatshirt, but considering most days I left the house in a grease-stained Fuller Farms T-shirt, I suppose I did look dressed up.

"Sitting by the lake with Sterling while his friends giggle every time he tries to hold my hand," I said, making my evening plans sound so lame that Mom couldn't even find it in her heart to tease me.

"You feel alright lately?" Lenny asked out of the blue, and Mom and I both looked at him.

"Yeah, fine," I said.

"Have you not been feeling well?" Mom asked.

It had been five days since Lenny took my bottle of pills away, and he knew I should be feeling the full force of withdrawal by now. I'd experienced it before, back in Florida, and were I feeling that way again, I wouldn't be on my way to see Sterling; I'd be in bed, praying for death.

"Oh, right," I said, shaking my head with a forgetful sigh, "I was just cramping earlier this week."

The mention of cramps confused and embarrassed Lenny, like it does all men, throwing him off his game.

"But I'm fine now. Never felt better."

Axl stomped into the living room, looking for the Duke hat he'd worn every day since our move, and when Mom glanced his way, I shot Lenny double birds.

"Well, good," Mom said, turning back to me. "You have fun tonight."

"I will," I said, all but sprinting for the door. "Love you."

Driving down the mountain by myself for the first time at tortoise speeds, I thought about the case and everyone we'd spoken to so far. My working theory was Vance Fuller had done something to a camper, or campers, who got their revenge by shooting him full of arrows. This jived with Rosalind Fuller pressuring Ashes Police to end their investigation early, thus saving her dead son's reputation. Jasper Benson and Tripp Aston mentioned a kid named John Wayne Crumpet, and locating him was now Elton's top priority. Wellington Fuller fired Buster McClellan because he blamed him for his son's death, but Buster had an alibi, or so he claimed. Buster also told us we should call off our investigation, as did Mayor Benson and Tripp Aston, moving them all up my suspect list. Then there was Tracie Ray, who said something weird happened to her the night Vance died, but she'd gone AWOL. I let out a long sigh. This case was a giant knot of fishing line, but I hadn't even found an end to pull on in hopes of unraveling it.

"Shit," I shouted when a whitetail deer darted from the woods in front of Mom's car. I stomped the brakes and swerved onto the gravel shoulder to miss it, sliding back onto the pavement a hundred yards later with a jolt.

The highway was deserted, minus the antlered psychopath now eating grass by the edge of the woods as if nothing had happened, so I stopped the car to catch my breath and let my hands stop shaking. It took five minutes, but when I felt calm enough to operate a motor vehicle again, I put the car and drive and started again, only to feel the rhythmic bump of a flat front right tire. Perfect.

I got out and cursed the tire for going flat as far from civilization as possible, but this did nothing to fix it, so I opened the trunk and prayed Lenny hadn't traded the spare for Kid Rock tickets. He hadn't, but knowing how to change a tire and being able to change a tire are not the same. I wrangled the jack, spare, and crowbar from the trunk, but try as I might, my hundred-pound self couldn't budge the first lug nut. I called Axl first, but he didn't answer. So I tried the lug nuts again, hoping I'd somehow grown stronger in the interim, but no luck. I had to call Mom, and she'd send Lenny, and dying of starvation here in the North Carolina woods seemed the better option, but then headlights topped the hill in the distance, and I knew I'd soon be saved or killed, but either way, I didn't have to call Lenny.

The headlights belonged to an old Ford Bronco that sounded like it could give up the ghost at any moment. It sputtered past but stopped a ways down the road, then backed up until it was even with me.

A gray-bearded man in a trucker hat rolled down the window, looked my car over, and said, "You got yourself a flat tire there."

No shit, I thought. "Yes, sir," I said.

"Don't know how to change it?" he asked.

"I know how, but I can't get the lug nuts off," I said.

He turned off his ignition, and the Bronco clanged and shuddered before falling silent. "I got you," the man said, taking the crowbar from me as he walked by. He got to work, making quick work of the lug nuts, and while jacking up Mom's car, he asked, "Where was you heading this late at night?"

"Fuller Farms," I said. "To see some friends."

The man stopped what he was doing and looked at me to see if I was joking.

"I work there," I explained. "In the kitchen."

"That makes more sense," the man said, getting back to work. "If your parents could afford Fuller Farms, I didn't figure you'd be out here driving the ugliest damn car in creation." I laughed, and the man said, "Rhonda, my old lady, worked out there for a few years. Cleaned the dorms while those little shits played croquet or whatever the hell they do all day."

"Did she work there when Vance Fuller died?" I asked.

"Before," he said, taking off the flat and putting on the spare. "That Fuller boy was a camper when she worked there."

"Did she know him?" I asked.

"Hell naw," the man said with a laugh. "She knew some of them boys. They're always looking to slum it with a mountain girl for the summer. But she said Vance was a weird one. Spent most of his time with that crazy McClellan fella who lives out in the woods and shoots buckshot at anyone who turns down his driveway."

"Buster," I said.

"That's the one," the man said with a nod. "He wanders into the hardware store where I work about once a month and buys the weirdest shit. Wouldn't surprise me if he's not making bombs out there in the woods."

The man lowered my car off the jack and put the flat tire in my trunk for me.

"Is there any chance I could talk to your wife about Vance Fuller?" I asked. "I'm sort of investigating his murder." The man squinted at me, so I added, "It's a hobby of mine."

"Well, there wasn't much Rhonda liked more than gossiping about Fuller Farms, but you'll have to find her first. She left me for my cousin Doobie three years ago, and I ain't seen neither of 'em since."

"Oh, I'm sorry," I said.

"Don't be," the man replied. "I hated 'em both."

I thanked him several times for fixing my tire and offered him money he refused to take. "It's the neighborly thing to do," he said, climbing back into his Bronco, which cranked right up, much to my surprise. "Just like it's the neighborly thing to tell you to stay away from that McClellan man. I know crazy when I see it, and Rhonda used to swear he was into devil-worshipping."

"Wait, what?"

The man nodded. "Vance Fuller wasn't murdered. Buster McClellan and his Satanic doomsday cult sacrificed him to the devil. But they shut all that up. Didn't want to scare off the tourists, you know?" Then the man put his Bronco in drive and sputtered away, leaving me alone in the moonlight.

1992

Vance Fuller had a decision to make.

Leaving camp wasn't an option. He asked. He fell to his knees and begged. His father said no, either ignoring Vance's swollen face or believing it was a fitting punishment for what happened at Chapel Hill. So, Vance would stay at Fuller Farms, but where would he sleep?

Under no circumstances could he continue sharing a cabin with Tripp Aston. How would Vance ever fall asleep knowing he might wake to another beating from the psychotic frat bro? The extra cot in Buster McClellan's shed wasn't an option either, the trauma from a visit ten years ago still fresh in Vance's mind. And he couldn't just find an empty bunk in the boys' dorm without giving his campers yet another reason to despise him. Lights out was the only time camp-ers felt free from the prying eyes of adults, and having a counselor in the dorm would feel suffocating. Besides, Vance avoided the Fuller Farms boys' dormitory at all costs, though he often returned there in his nightmares.

Mitch was his name.

Mitch, who was Vance's camp counselor.

Mitch, who brought locker room-style hazing to the dorms of Fuller Farms.

It began each morning in the showers. Those miserable, wretched showers. Vance would never understand why locker room architects assumed guys wanted to stand naked in a giant open room under communal shower heads. At least the campers had an unspoken agreement to stare at the ceiling, not say a word, and get clean as fast as humanly possible. Mitch, however, was not bound by this agreement. He'd shower with the campers several times a week, despite having a private bathroom in his cabin. Mitch slapped asses, commented on anatomy, and on the bad days, picked a camper at random for naked wrestling. "Just like the Greeks," Mitch would yell, with some poor kid pinned underneath him on the cold tile floor.

But the showers weren't anything compared to what happened at night when Mitch visited the dorms. Unlike the random and widespread terror of shower time, Mitch targeted his nocturnal victims. Chose them, most likely, based on their unlikeliness to say anything. Vance was one of the unlucky number, and on the nights Mitch crawled into his bunk, he'd close his eyes until it was over, taking small solace in the fact no one ever got it two nights in a row.

Buster McClellan came to Vance's rescue that July, the extra cot in his archery shed a refuge—a safe harbor from Hurricane Mitch. Buster never asked, and Vance never told, but there was an unspoken gratitude. You could hear it when Vance laughed at one of Buster's dumb jokes. You could see it behind the boy's tortured eyes. The two grew close over the following summers, like friends, like family. But then, one night, Buster McClellan went and ruined everything.

Vance would likely have always been confused about himself, even without Mitch's torture. If pressed, Vance would say he was asexual, but that wasn't true. He was attracted to men, though his abuse and ultra-conservative upbringing left him conflicted about this. He'd vowed never to act on his urges. A vow he'd kept until the day Ty Bingham walked into his office. And even then, he hadn't exactly acted, just not reacted quickly enough. Vance swore he'd never get caught in such a compromising situation again.

But then it happened.

The evening of his ass-beating at the hands of Tripp Aston, Vance's campers missed dinner. Vance assumed they were off doing something stupid but harmless, and he enjoyed his peach cobbler without giving them another thought. But then the boys didn't show up for Wednesday night skit practice either, a glaring absence considering Jasper and Aubrey both had speaking parts. Vance knew the other counselors would be beyond eager to inform his father he was slacking on his duties, and that day had been bad enough without capping it off with a condescending lecture from his old man. So, Vance went in search of his missing wards.

"Aubrey? Jasper? Quinn? You guys in here?" Vance asked, daring to stick his head inside the boys' dorm for the first time in over a decade. "You're late for skit practice." But there was no answer, and Vance darted back onto the porch before he hyperventilated, never mind that this dorm building was new, and the communal showers had been replaced by individual stalls with rainfall shower heads. That's when he noticed a light flickering in the archery shed.

Buster left early on Fridays, but maybe he stayed late today. Perhaps he hung around in hopes of clearing the air with Vance. He'd already tried at lunch and Vance shouted him down again. Or was Tripp Aston down there stealing a bow and arrow to finish what he started? Vance would have laughed at the thought if laughing didn't hurt all the places Tripp punched and kicked that morning. But most likely, Vance thought, his campers were in the shed, smoking a joint and listening to Pearl Jam or Sir Mix-a-Lot or some other terrible cassette tape they'd snuck into camp. He had to take a look.

Walking across the archery range toward Buster's shed, Vance saw shadows dancing on the wall through the window. His heart raced, but he couldn't say why. Something just seemed off, but Vance didn't know what until peeking inside and witnessing the unimaginable.

My God.

This was wrong.

So wrong.

Again, Vance Fuller had a decision to make. Only this decision was much more important than where he'd lay his head that evening. This decision was between right and wrong, good and evil. This was the sort of decision that will gain a man his soul—or lose it. This was the most important decision Vance Fuller would ever make.

In the end, it cost him his life.

CHAPTER TWENTY-ONE

Donut spares are only good for about fifty miles, and the man who fixed my flat said ours looked like it might have ten miles left on it if I was lucky. So, instead of risking another stranding in the middle of nowhere, I abandoned my Friday night plans and drove back to our apartment in Ashes.

Shelby picked me up for work on Saturday morning, disappointed I had no juicy details to share about the night before with Sterling. Then she railed against her Aunt Jenny most of the way down the mountain.

"I called her all upset about Mama leaving, and she didn't even care," Shelby said. "She said, 'So what? Your mama does it all the time.'"

"Wait, does she?" I asked.

"No. Well, not all the time. When I was in third grade, she went on a ten-day bender with some man she met at the Indian casino over in Cherokee. Then, three years later, she drove to Blockbuster to rent *Ocean's Eleven* and didn't come back for a week. And then a couple of summers ago, we took a big family trip to Myrtle Beach and didn't see her the entire time we were there."

"And you'd forgotten about all that?" I asked, now unsure whether

Traci Ray's disappearance had anything to do with Vance Fuller's murder.

"Well, no, not entirely," Shelby said, lighting what was probably her third cigarette of the young day. "I've just learned to block out some of that shit through the years." She blew a cloud of smoke out her window and added, "Otherwise, life can get unbearable."

"Don't I know it," I mumbled.

Say what you will about my mother's parenting abilities, but she was always frustratingly present in our lives. Of course, I'm not sure what I would have done differently without her around. I'd always been the responsible child in the Brown house, while Axl played the role of irresponsible rebel. A skeptic might point to my recent purchase of drugs from Shelby's cousin as evidence I was less responsible than I thought. But even my opioid problem, which I didn't see as a problem yet, was further proof I cared.

For as long as I remember, I've worried about my mother. Even as a kid, I recognized she didn't have it together like other parents. Mom tried. Lord knows she tried. But even her best efforts barely kept our family afloat. I'd blame my father, who ran off with half our stuff when I was three, but his presence would have only served as an albatross around our necks.

No, Mom just ticked every box on the how-to-struggle-through-life checklist. Teenage mother, check. Didn't finish high school, check. Married a deadbeat, check. But perhaps more than all that, the woman was straight unlucky. Her streak of shitty boyfriends defied all odds, and she had an uncanny knack for securing employment with busi-nesses that would go belly-up within six months. And then, on those rare occasions when fortune smiled on her and she found herself living in a seaside mansion, sending her kids to a private school that cost more money than she'd make in a year, I went and blew it all to hell.

It's not that Mom didn't have a plan to pull us up a few rungs on the social ladder. It's that her plan was stupid. She believed Axl was only a few years away from a multi-million-dollar NFL contract. On more than one occasion, I pointed out the foolishness of a long-term financial plan resting solely on the shoulders of my idiot brother, but Mom wouldn't hear it. So I took it upon myself to save her, even if she wouldn't admit she needed saving. For the longest time, I planned to earn a college scholarship, get a good-paying job, and rescue Mom from her life. This proved unlikely. Not because I wasn't smart, but because I hyperventilated anytime I got within twenty feet of a stan-dardized test. Even trying to solve Ricky Lee's murder in Bardo was at first an attempt to catch the eye of some college admissions board, though by the end, that investigation became more personal. My rela-tionship with Elton and his mother gave me a short reprieve from worrying about my family's future. Holly Jones-Davies loved me and had more money than a small country. Surely she wouldn't let us go under. But now, she and Mustang Jones were in the middle of a nasty divorce, and who knew where she'd be when the dust settled.

Axl's football future was Mom's only consideration before moving us to Ashes, but it had worked out okay so far. She'd remain gainfully employed so long as rich people enjoyed fancy cheese, and I had a good-paying job. We'd be okay even if Lenny Roach packed up and left, though his departure might cost me more in the end because

Shelby's cousin charged full retail. But I also had the Vance Fuller case and the promise of fifty grand if I could crack it. Fifty thousand dollars would get us ahead and keep us there. The only problem was I wasn't anywhere close to solving the case. I needed my wits about me. I needed my pills.

You see, I didn't take the pills to feel good. I didn't take them to get high. I took them to feel normal, or what I'd started to consider normal. Normal was not debilitating headaches that only abated after half an hour of vomiting in the toilet. Normal wasn't paralyzing anxiety that struck in waves, taking me under for weeks at a time before washing me up on strange shores, exhausted and depressed. All I had to do was look around to see normal people didn't deal with this shit. Normal people didn't feel like me. They laughed. They smiled. They got things done. And when I took a pill, I was one of them. That's why I felt responsible when I took them. I was doing what I had to do to help my family.

But with Shelby's revelation that her mother had a propensity for running away, I was perhaps even further from earning Wellington Fuller's fifty grand than I'd thought.

Sterling didn't talk to me in the breakfast line that morning. He didn't even look at me when I shoveled the scrambled eggs onto his plate. I suppose he was mad I'd stood him up the night before, which made me mad he hadn't even considered I was stranded on a North Carolina backroad, my fate in the hands of whatever redneck happened to drive by next.

After washing trays and helping wipe down the tables, I sat on a bucket behind the dining hall and watched Shelby and the other girls smoke. This was usually when Sterling and I walked around Mud Lake, but I wasn't about to go out there and wait for him and look like an idiot.

"Want one?" one of the girls asked, offering me her pack of Camels.

"No thanks," I said. I already had one expensive habit and didn't need another.

"More for me," the girl said, lighting her next cigarette with the fading embers of her last one.

A tall, raven-haired girl, whose name I couldn't remember, so I called her Tattoo Neck in my head, walked outside to join us, and seeing me, she asked, "Not having canoe sex with your rich boy today?"

"He's mad at me," I said, "so I'm mad at him."

"Well, he's standing out yonder by Mud Lake," she said, "and he don't look mad to me."

I stood and yawned, trying to downplay my excitement. Still, the girls could tell, and as I headed toward Mud Lake, they shouted inappropriate things until I was out of earshot.

"I'm sorry," Sterling said when I reached the lake. "I assumed you'd stood me up, and I was mad, but your friend Shelby told me you had a flat before calling me a bunch of incredibly vulgar names. I swear, I didn't know you—"

"It's okay," I said, kissing him on the cheek. "It's sweet, in an unhealthy, possessive sort of way."

"I'm not possessive," Sterling huffed, frustrated I wasn't letting him off the hook that easy. "I was excited to see you last night, and … you could have called."

"They confiscated your phone."

"You could have sent a carrier pigeon."

"I tried, but it flew to my side dude's house by mistake. So now he's mad at me, and I'm out one pigeon."

Sterling smiled and took my hand.

"So you were excited to see me?" I asked.

"A little," he said.

"Is the blanket still out here?" I asked, and when Sterling looked my way, I buckled his knees with a wink.

Thirty seconds later, we were in the woods, making out like the world was ending. I hadn't kissed a boy like this since Bardo and Blaine and one too many cups of punch that tasted like strawberries and fire. His mouth moved down to my neck, and his hands … his hands went everywhere, ignoring red lines I'd drawn to keep from getting pregnant before finishing high school like my mother, and setting off alarms in my head. Although, to be fair, Sterling didn't ignore the red lines. He didn't know about them. I ignored them … until I couldn't any longer.

"Sterling."

"I love you, Izzy."

What the hell? This set me back several seconds but didn't slow Sterling down in the least. Now I wasn't sure if I should address his declaration of love or the other thing.

"Sterling … hold on … I've got to … Sterling."

Like a wrestler escaping a pin, I slipped from under him and scrambled to my feet.

"I've got to get back to work, Casanova," I said as he smiled up at me.

"But you'll come back tonight?" he asked, making praying hands and batting his puppy dog eyes.

"I'll try," I said, and the devils on my shoulders tossed confetti into the air.

CHAPTER TWENTY-TWO

Saturday evening after work, Shelby dropped me off at our apartment just as Mom and Lenny walked out.

"Taking him back for a refund?" I asked.

Mom laughed, Lenny didn't.

"Leonard and I are having dinner at Cafe Forêt tonight," Mom said with her best attempt at a fancy accent.

"The swanky French place downtown?" I asked. "No wonder Lenny dropped the jorts."

Another laugh from Mom. Another glare from Lenny.

"You're on your own for dinner," Mom said. "There's leftover pizza in the fridge."

"The pizza from last weekend?" I asked, making a disgusted face.

"Oh, right," Mom said. "Maybe toss that out and have Axl take you to pick something up. If you need the car later, we'll be back in a couple of hours."

"Au revoir," I said and went inside to find my brother.

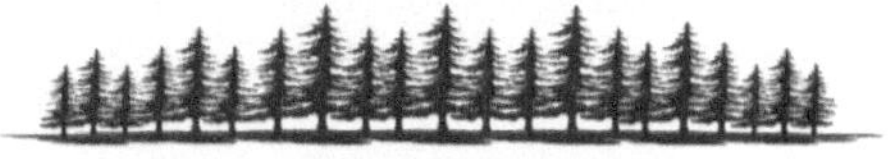

"Mom said you have to take me to get dinner," I told Axl since asking nicely would get me nowhere.

"Fine, I'm starving anyway," he said, rolling off the couch and stomping toward the door.

"Aren't you going to wear a shirt?" I asked.

"Nope."

We left Ashes heading north toward Cashiers on 107, windows down, Axl's arm out the window, making waves in the air. It was almost 8 p.m., but the summer sun wouldn't set for another hour. Growing up in Florida, where the sun is only about twenty miles from the Earth's surface, this was the only time of day I wanted to be outside during the summer. But in the mountains, summer evenings could be downright chilly, and I wished I'd brought a jacket. Judging by the goosebumps on his arms, Axl was cold, though he was too stubborn to admit it and put on a shirt.

A couple of miles outside of town, we pulled into the gravel parking lot of an old-timey A-frame restaurant called Jo-Jo's Dairy Barn. Jo-Jo's sat perched on a rocky bank overlooking a rushing creek, and when we arrived, a group of teens were toweling off from an afternoon spent leaping off the rocks into the water below.

Axl and I ordered burgers and shakes—he made me pay—then we took them to the picnic tables where the kids were hanging out. After handshakes and fist bumps, I gathered Axl knew most of the guys. And watching the girls watch him, I understood why he'd opted not to wear a shirt. But then they packed their beach towels and coolers into their Audis and Land Rovers, leaving Axl without an invitation to wherever the party was heading next.

"Friends of yours?" I asked as the group sped away toward Ashes.

"Most of those dudes play for Ashes Prep," Axl said, and after a long silence, added, "They're okay."

"But you prefer rich Florida kids to rich North Carolina kids," I teased.

Axl laughed. "Rich kids are rich kids," he said. "Things are just weird right now because the other quarterback on the team is a senior, and he's this Brad Pitt-looking dude all the guys worship and all the girls line up to sleep with."

For my Ken-doll brother to be intimidated by some guy's looks likely meant this other quarterback was so handsome he could impregnate you from across the room with just a glance.

"But you're better than him, right? They wouldn't have brought you in on scholarship to ride the bench."

"Of course I'm better than him," Axl snapped. "He sucks. But his folks give a shit-ton of money to the school, and Coach Denham is under a lot of pressure to play him too. He's already floated the idea of us splitting time next season."

"What did you say?"

"I told him that was fine if he didn't mind looking like an idiot every time he pulled me out of the game."

I laughed and said, "You could always transfer to Ashes High with me."

"It's crossed my mind," Axl said, surprising me. "I don't know. I just want to play football and ..."

"And be king of the school?"

"Maybe," Axl admitted with a smile.

We ate in silence for a while, then my brother asked, "How's Elton enjoying camp? I don't remember him being much of the outdoors type."

"Oh, he's not," I said. "Bugs and sweating are on his top ten list of things to avoid. Thankfully, they're letting him stay inside most of the time to work on our ca—"

"Work on your what?" Axl asked.

"Our case," I said, and he closed his eyes and let out a long sigh.

"Izzy, after everything that happened in Bardo, are you seriously—"

"This is way different," I said, raising my palms to show my innocence. "Mr. Fuller, the old billionaire who owns Fuller Farms, hired me to find out who murdered his son. I'm not going to get you kicked out of school. He paid for half of your school. Besides, if I crack the case, he's promised me fifty thousand dollars."

"Okay, but—wait, fifty thousand dollars?" I nodded, and Axl said, "Yeah, that would help."

"No kidding. Mom might finally feel like she could kick Lenny to the curb."

"Lenny's not that bad," Axl said.

"He punched our mother in the face."

"And I talked to him about that."

"And he slapped me after you had your talk."

"He did what?" Axl said, the color rising so fast in his cheeks, it scared me.

"Not hard," I said, wishing I hadn't mentioned it. "He probably meant it as a joke. We had an argument and—"

"I'll talk to him again."

"You don't have to do that. Surely he'll be gone soon."

"It's been nine months, Izzy. I think he's here to stay."

Axl dropped me off at the apartment after dinner, saying he was going to some party. However, I suspected he'd just drive around until he got sleepy and come home. To my surprise, Lenny was on the couch when I walked in, watching his Tampa Bay Rays beat the Mets.

"Cafe Forêt kick you out for not wearing deodorant?" I asked, but Lenny didn't immediately reply.

I was halfway to my bedroom before he said, "The soup was cold, so I said something to the waiter, who got all smart-ass with me, saying it was supposed to be served cold. I asked to see his manager, and he asked us to leave, so I shoved him. Didn't knock him down or anything. Hell, I was still sitting when I did it, but he started threatening to call the cops, so we left. Your mama is in bed with a headache."

"I'm talking to her headache," I mumbled, and Lenny was on his feet.

"How you feeling these days?" he asked, getting in my face.

"Fine," I said, backing up until I hit the kitchen counter and ran out of room.

"I don't see how," Lenny snarled, standing so close I'd soon suffocate on his Axe body spray. "I've seen what happens to people when they stop taking those pills. They look like death, and they feel even worse."

"Yeah, well, I don't know what to tell you, Leonard, but I feel fine."

"You know what I think?" Lenny said.

That the Earth is flat, I thought. "No, Lenny, I don't," I said.

"I think you're stealing from me."

I rolled my eyes. "The alarm on your van goes off every time a leaf lands on the hood. Everyone in Ashes would know if I tried to break into it."

"You could have used my keys."

"The keys you keep hooked around your belt loop at all times?"

The truth was, stealing pills from Lenny was my first thought when he took my bottle away. But he drove the Fort Knox of drug vans, and he slept and showered with his keys, so it wasn't happening.

Lenny bit his lip as the gears in his rusty brain slowly turned. "You're buying from someone else."

"Seriously, Lenny, who would I—"

"That's it," Lenny said, smirking and shaking his head. "After everything I've done for this family. All the bills I've paid, all the food I've bought. After everything it cost me to move up here to Sherwood Forrest because I love your mama and can't stand not being near her."

Lenny was shouting now, and I prayed Mom would hear him and come stop what was about to happen, but her bedroom door remained closed.

"After all that, you go and buy from the competition."

"Lenny, I didn't—"

"The fucking competition," he shouted, rattling the walls.

"Look, Lenny, let's talk about this tomorrow when you're not act-ing insane," I said, trying to squeeze past him, but he grabbed me by the shoulder.

"I've let it slide for too long," Lenny said, "but from now on, every-one living under my roof will give me the respect I deserve."

"And how much respect does a white-trash pill-pusher deserve?" I asked, watching with regret as the words left my mouth and floated through the air into Lenny's ears. There was a moment of calm while he registered the insult, then came the punch.

Lenny's fist caught me hard in the left eye, his high school class ring cutting me open and leaving a faint 1989 on the side of my nose. I hit the linoleum floor in a heap and woke up there sometime later, my face bloodied, my head pounding, concussed either from the blow, the floor, or both. Lenny was back on the couch, watching his baseball game as if nothing had happened.

He didn't say a word when I crawled to my feet.

Didn't say a word as I stumbled down the hall toward my room.

Lenny Roach would never say another word to me again.

CHAPTER TWENTY-THREE

Most days, even when my anxiety is running full throttle, I'll enjoy a few seconds of normal each morning. A glorious beat or two where the worries that will consume me the rest of the day have been momentarily deactivated by a pleasant dream. I'm often parasailing in these dreams, floating high above the ocean, looking down on sunbathers and shell collectors. I read somewhere floating dreams express a desire to escape the pressures of your life, and I can only assume people who grew up in Florida parasail away from their troubles instead. But I didn't have a parasailing dream that night. I dreamt Lenny Roach was chasing me down a long, dark alley. He cornered me, snarling like a rabid dog, and I pulled a gun out of nowhere, but it wouldn't fire. Lenny was closing in when I awoke, my head still pounding from the punch, my pillow wet with tears.

I took one of the precious few pills I had left and showered for work. My eye was red, and I knew it would turn black and purple in a day or two. I hoped, at least for today, I could conceal it with makeup.

"Good morning, baby girl," Mom said when I wandered into the kitchen, looking for a quick breakfast.

"Morning," I said, trying to keep my left eye turned away from her.

"You and Axl have a nice dinner last night?" she asked.

"Yeah, it was fine," I said. "How about you and Lenny?"

Dammit. I already knew their date went down in flames, but I was trying to make small talk and act normal. Now I was in for a story.

"It was a disaster," Mom said with a long sigh. "After working at Waffle King for as long as I did, you know nothing in the world makes me madder than someone being rude to a waiter. But Lenny does it all the time, trying to get a free appetizer or dessert. The jerk. I let him have it when he came to bed last night, and he stormed off."

"Wait, he's gone for good?" I asked, spinning around.

"No, baby girl, but I told him he wasn't sleeping in my bed last night, so he—Izzy, what the hell happened to your eye?"

Okay, so makeup didn't do the trick.

"It, uh …"

I'd have to answer this question a million times for the next couple of weeks, and I'd meant to think of a believable lie, but I hadn't yet, and when I hesitated, Mom knew.

"That son of a bitch," Mom said. "I swear to God, if—"

"Mom, it was my fault."

What the hell? I didn't believe that. Why did I say it?

"What was your fault?" Axl asked, bounding through the living room on his way to work out.

Mom pointed at my face, and Axl began shaking with anger.

"That fucker hit you again?"

"Again?" Mom shouted.

"The first time was a slap," I said, "and not hard, but—"

I broke down crying, and both of them rushed and held me.

"I'm going to kill him," Axl said.

"No, you ain't," Mom scolded him. "I'm killing him. You can watch."

This made me laugh, and Mom held me out at arm's length, tears in her eyes as she examined my face.

"What time do you get off work today?" Mom asked me.

"I should be home by seven," I said.

"I'm off at six," she said. "Have Shelby drop you off at Mason's Jar for dinner. Axl, can you be there?"

"Yeah, sure," my brother said.

"We're having a family meeting. Lenny has to go. Ain't no arguing that. But he pays half the bills, so we've got to talk through some things and make some decisions, alright?"

Axl and I nodded.

"And you're okay?" she said, gently touching my face, but I winced anyway. "Nothing broken?"

"Nothing broken," I said, though it felt like something had broken inside.

Mom smiled, and I could see the faint outline of her own black eye, covered with makeup.

She hugged me again, and Shelby honked from the parking lot.

From the passenger seat, there was no good way to hide my eye from Shelby without getting a nasty crick in my neck. But it took her a while to notice because she was too busy singing along to "Gives You Hell" by the All-American Rejects.

"This is mine and Toby's song," she said, cranking up the volume until I thought her old Honda would rattle apart.

"This is your song?" I asked.

"Why not? I mean, this way when we do break up, at least—holy shit, girl, what happened to your eye?"

I told her and she shook her head in sympathy.

"Mama had a boyfriend who hit me once," Shelby said, blowing smoke out her window. "My granddaddy killed him."

"Like, he shot him?" I asked, my eyes widening.

"No, nothing like that," she said, shocked by what I thought was a perfectly reasonable accusation. "He just snipped the brake lines on his truck. It's a pretty steep downhill when you leave our place. The asshole crashed straight into a tree."

I laughed, though Shelby wasn't joking.

"Hitting women is the only sin my granddaddy cares about. He'd be happy to help y'all with Lenny if you want him to."

"I'll keep him in mind," I said.

Sterling skipped the egg line altogether that morning and took his breakfast plate back to his dorm to eat. I understood why he was mad at me. Technically, I'd stood him up two nights in a row. But he'd feel awful when he found out why I didn't make it back to Fuller Farms the night before. Assuming he ever spoke to me again.

We cleaned the dining hall after breakfast, and after washing the plates and trays, I went to our office to check on Elton.

"Sunday greetings," he said, taking his belated breakfast plate from me and inhaling the bacon in one bite.

"Good morning," I said, rubbing his head and making him flinch. "Solved the case yet?"

"Negative," Elton said, closing his chat box with Zadie. "Per your request, I spent some time outdoors yesterday. The swimming pool is quite nice."

"Well, yeah, it's the size of a Walmart."

"I was also asked to join a beach volleyball team but declined."

"Because you don't like to sweat."

"Correct."

"Either way, I'm proud of you for getting out of your comfort zone a little."

"Thank you," Elton said, "but I did spend several hours working on the case and can unequivocally rule out John Wayne Crumpet."

"Wait, really? How can you do that?"

"His grandmother died, and he left camp the day before Vance Fuller's murder to attend her funeral in Birmingham."

"How'd you figure that out?"

"I returned to the Ashes Police Station and read more of the interviews. Crumpet was part of the initial interviews, but Chief Morrison saw no need to question him again since he could not have killed Vance, being several hundred miles away at the time of death."

"Hold on, how did you get to the police station without me?"

"I drove the truck. I am licensed to operate a motor vehicle in all fifty states."

"Well, yeah, I know that, but—"

As far as I knew, Elton had never driven outside the 15mph red-brick roads of Bardo by the Sea, Florida. It was hard to imagine him driving our old Fuller Farms truck up the mountain to Ashes, and even harder to picture him driving it back down. But the boy would never cease to amaze me.

"Are you not pleased?" Elton asked.

"No, I am. Great work, Big E. It's nice to rule out at least one suspect. I guess now tracking down Aubrey Masters is our top priority, and finding Tracie Ray is a close second. In the meantime, maybe we can—"

"You are injured," Elton said after turning away from his computer screen and looking at me for the first time.

"What? No. I just ran into a—"

Elton would believe any semi-plausible lie I could concoct, but I'd lied to him once at Bardo and felt shitty about it for weeks after. He was my friend, and he deserved the truth, but I burst into tears when I tried to tell it to him.

Elton, bless his heart, reached out to pat my shoulder, thought better of it, reached out again, then sat there awkwardly rubbing his arms.

"It was Lenny," I finally managed, "He—"

I couldn't get through the story, but Elton had heard enough, and he stood and paced the floor with window-rattling stomps. "You cannot return to your apartment," he boomed. "It is unsafe. I am contacting the police."

"You're not calling the police," I said.

"Someone must do something," Elton said. "Living with a man who punches you is not an option."

"Axl and I are having dinner with Mom tonight. She's dumping Lenny, and we'll figure out how to get along without him. It's going to be okay."

Elton looked skeptical.

"Look," I said, "I think Lenny deserves punishment just as much as you do, but he's into some bad stuff, and if the police get involved, it might come back on Mom somehow."

Elton shook his head and bit his lip in frustration. I'd never seen him so angry, and I loved him for it. But I had to talk him off this ledge, or the Ashes PD would show up at our apartment, and who knows what Lenny would tell them when he went down.

"Do you vow you will never put yourself in a situation where he can hurt you again?" Elton asked. "Because if not, I will—"

The door opened with a knock, and Wellington Fuller stepped into our office. "Hello, Izzy, Elton," he said.

"Sunday greetings," Elton said, and I waved.

"Izzy, if you have a moment, there is something I need to tell you about Vance that might help your investigation."

"Uh, yeah, sure," I said, getting up to follow Wellington to his office.

"Izzy, do you vow?" Elton asked again, tears of fear and anger welling in his eyes.

"I vow," I said, smiling and reassuring him with a pat on the back. "And look, I appreciate you caring so much. It means the world, honestly. But Lenny will be gone after tonight, and you won't have to worry about me again."

CHAPTER TWENTY-FOUR

"Goodness gracious, what happened to your eye?" Wellington Fuller asked, leaning back in his overstuffed desk chair.

"I made the mistake of throwing football with my brother," I lied.

Mr. Fuller winced but accepted this without further comment, then asked about my investigation.

I shrugged. "Not much to report."

"Well, it's still early," the old man said, "but I've seen you and young Elton hard at work. Surely there's something you can update me on."

I took a deep breath and considered what to share with Mr. Fuller. It's not that I didn't trust him—he'd hired me to begin with. But in London, I'd learned a painful lesson about oversharing details of my investigation and, in the process, assured the real killer was always a step or two ahead of me. I'd vowed from then on to hold my cards closer to my chest.

"You'll have to forgive me," Wellington said, holding up an apologetic palm while I thought. "I was always a bit of a micromanager. When I'm paying folks to do a job, I like to know they're doing it."

"No," I said, "that's fair. Elton ruled out John Wayne Crumpet."

"And who might that be?" Wellington asked.

"He was a camper the year Vance died."

Wellington's face scrunched in strained thought, but he couldn't place the kid.

"He was arrested a few years ago in a child pornography sting."

The light went on, and Wellington snapped his fingers. "Ah, yes, I'd forgotten John was here that same year. Bad egg, that one. We never caught him but suspected he killed several ducks in Mud Lake. You believed he had a hand in Vance's death?"

"I didn't have any reason to, but Tripp Aston and Jasper Benson mentioned his name."

"You've spoken with Tripp and Jasper?"

I nodded. "I called Tripp last week. He hated Vance for something that happened at UNC."

Wellington nodded. He knew the story, and I was angry he didn't tell me from the beginning.

"We met Jasper at Benson House. He was … uh …"

"Jasper is a product of his raising," Wellington said. "Neither Jeremy nor I did a stellar job with our sons. We were busy, I suppose, but that's no excuse."

Wellington Fuller looked skyward, perhaps seeking forgiveness for being an absent father, and I tried to steer the conversation back to the case. "Anyway, Jasper and Tripp both suspected the Crumpet kid had something to do with Vance's murder, but he wasn't even at camp that week. His grandmother died, and he went home for the funeral. I don't know if they were trying to throw me off the scent or if it's just been twenty years and their memories are fuzzy."

Wellington scratched his chin. "Who else have you spoken to?"

"Tracie Ray," I said. "She worked in the kitchen that summer. Her daughter, Shelby, actually works here now. Tracie was hooking up with one of the campers, Aubrey Masters." Old man Fuller shook his head at the thought of his campers hooking up, but I continued, "She began telling police about something weird happening the night Vance died, but never elaborated. I believe she saw something but was too scared to tell."

"Well, what did she say?"

"Told us never to talk to her again, and now she's skipped town. That could be a coincidence though."

Wellington scribbled something on the notepad in front of him, and it dawned on me I likely wasn't the only person he'd hired to investigate Vance's murder.

"What about Buster McClellan?" Mr. Fuller asked, spitting out the name like sour milk.

"Yeah, we drove to his house, and he fired buckshot at us."

Wellington huffed. "I'm sorry, I should have warned you more about Buster. He's a lunatic. That's one of the reasons I fired him."

"Mr. Fuller," I said, clearing my throat, "I'm not exactly sure how to say this, but some people we spoke with mentioned that Vance may have abused campers. Do you know if—"

Mr. Fuller stopped me with a raised palm, I assumed to keep me from disparaging the name of his deceased son, but I was wrong. "Izzy, I should have told you this earlier, but I didn't want to taint your investigation. I believed it was best for you to talk to folks without my opinions influencing you. I shouldn't have even said what I did about Buster, but I couldn't help myself there. But now that you've spoken to most everyone around that summer, I think I should fill you in on Vance.

"He was a troubled boy. Did something at Chapel Hill that broke our hearts. Not the sort of things we raised him to do, I promise you that. But Vance—" Mr. Fuller's voice cracked, and he pulled a handkerchief from his pocket to wipe his eyes. "Vance, I believe, was abused when he was younger. Now, I don't have proof. Not the kind of proof you'd need to convict someone in court. But I'll tell you what I do know, and you can make up your own mind."

Mr. Fuller took a deep breath to compose himself, then said, "Vance camped here for four summers as a kid, and sometime that first year, he began sneaking down to Buster McClellan's shed to spend the night."

"Wait, spend the night?" I asked. "Buster told the police that Vance used to hang out in his shed some during the day, but only because the other boys were picking on him."

"Well, he lied," Wellington said, shaking his head in disgust. "Now, I obviously didn't know about this while it was happening, or I would have put an end to it and shot Buster in his damn head. Excuse my language, Izzy, but this makes me so angry I can't hardly speak."

Wellington was shaking now, but he kept talking. "I learned about all this after Vance died, when Chief Morrison questioned the campers. Turns out, Vance was still going to Buster's shed the summer he died. Twenty-eight years old, and his abuser still had that much sway over him."

"Mr. Fuller, I'm so sorry," I said after Wellington burst into tears again, but I didn't think he heard me over his sobs.

"I've heard the rumors," Mr. Fuller finally said. "I know what people say Vance did to some of the boys at camp. I don't know if they're true or false, and I'm not trying to make an excuse for Vance either way. But I want you to know he was abused, and victims of abuse sometimes become perpetrators. So maybe he did. And maybe a camper killed him for it. That's a theory. But a better theory is Vance was about to talk, so Buster McClellan silenced him for good."

Before dinner, I relayed everything Wellington Fuller told me to Elton, both of us agreeing we needed to talk to Buster McClellan again, though preferably on public property where he'd be less likely to shoot at us. Then, after cleanup, Shelby drove me back to Ashes and dropped me off downtown for some overpriced veggies and cornbread with Mom and Axl at Mason's Jar.

"I spent most of my break time looking for apartments," Mom said while stirring a packet of Splenda into her tea. "It's slim pickings in Ashes city limits."

This wasn't shocking. We could barely afford the worst apartment complex in town, even with Lenny paying half the rent.

"There's a trailer park with a couple of units for rent just outside of town, and we could probably afford it, but I know you kids don't really want to live in—"

"How many beds?" Axl and I asked in unison.

"Three," Mom said, and my brother and I exchanged a shrug. The worst part about Pineview Villas, apart from the rattlesnakes, was sharing a bedroom and bathroom with my twin brother. We could make three bedrooms work.

"Now, Izzy, I know your job at Fuller Farms will end come August, but I've talked to my manager at Fraîche, and he said you could come on as a bagger once school starts."

That Mom expected me to earn my keep while Axl got to play football was a given. Still, it stung to hear it out loud.

"Yeah, that's fine," I said.

"Okay, but what about Lenny?" Axl asked.

"We'll tell him tonight," Mom said. "All of us, together."

Axl and I nodded.

"He should have never moved here to begin with," Mom said. "It put a lot of stress on him, and—"

"Don't make excuses for him hitting you," I snapped, "or me."

"No, you're right," Mom said, putting her hand on mine. "He's got to go. We'll all be happier in the end. I honestly don't even think he'll fight me on it. But I want y'all there, especially Axl."

I could tell Mom was worried. Thanks to the caliber of man she typically dated, her breakups were often violent affairs involving smashed windows, broken televisions, and slashed tires. Lenny would be no different, but Axl could break him like a twig, and his presence would likely keep things civil.

"We're going to make it, kids," Mom said, reaching out and taking both of our hands. "Look how far we've already come."

The truth was, we'd just moved our poverty north a few hundred miles to a milder climate. Mom's plan to save us still revolved around Axl making the NFL, and right now, he wasn't even guaranteed to start for his little North Carolina private school. Still, we'd soon rid ourselves of Lenny Roach, and that was a start.

After dinner, we spent a few minutes walking around downtown, where Twilight Rock Film Festival posters had popped up in every storefront window. In October, Chase Foster and Bridget Bell would premier their latest rom-com, *Cupid's Crossbow*, right here in Ashes, which I had to admit was rather exciting, considering no celebrity had ever been within fifty miles of my hometown of Dandridge, Florida.

"Ice Cream?" Mom asked after staring into Chase Foster's dreamy eyes for the better part of a minute.

"Yes," Axl and I said in unison, and the three of us stepped into Ashes Creamery in what I suspect was a subconscious effort to delay our confrontation with Lenny. Half an hour later, we finally left for the apartment—Mom in her car, me riding with Axl.

"I need to stop for gas," Axl told Mom, "so it'll be a minute."

"I'll wait in the parking lot, and we'll go up together," Mom said.

Axl pulled into a Chevron, just missing a head-on collision with some crazy redneck in a truck who came barreling out of nowhere on two wheels.

"Holy hell, can no one around here drive?" Axl asked.

"Not that I've seen," I said.

We both got out of his truck, slightly shaken from the near wreck, and while he pumped gas, I asked, "You ever wonder why Mom can't meet a nice dentist?"

"I hate dentists," Axl said, and I laughed.

"A veterinarian, then."

My brother smiled and thought for a moment. "I don't think Mom thinks of herself as the sort of person who could date a dentist or veterinarian. So, she settles for ass potatoes like Lenny. Maybe when I'm rich, she'll have more confidence."

"Yeah, maybe," I said, trying hard not to roll my eyes. Then I waited as Axl went inside for a pack of gum, a process that took five minutes because he bumped into some cheerleaders he knew while walking out.

A few minutes later, we pulled into our apartment complex and noticed the door to our unit was wide open, light streaming out.

"That's weird," Axl said, just as a silhouette filled the door, then fell to their knees. What the hell?

Axl slid into a parking spot, and we both jumped from the car and ran upstairs to find Mom sitting in the doorway, gasping for breath and shaking with fear.

"Mom, what's wrong?" I asked as Axl and I bent down to check on her.

There was blood on her hands. Blood on her shirt. I thought Lenny had hurt her again, but I was wrong. Dead wrong.

"Holy shit," Axl said, scrambling to his feet and backing up several steps. I turned to look into the apartment and saw what my brother saw.

Lenny Roach, dead on the floor.

1992

Buster McClellan could fix anything.

Refrigerators, air conditioners, dishwashers. You name it; Buster could repair it. His was an innate ability, perfected through countless hours of tinkering in the back of his father's automotive garage outside of Ashes. Taking apart machines and putting them back together in working order was as easy for Buster as reading and writing were difficult. Mr. Harrison, the principal at Ashes High, recognized this and began pulling Buster out of class whenever a freezer went down in the kitchen or the boiler started making strange noises. When Buster graduated by the skin of his teeth in 1961, Mr. Harrison offered him a job as the school's maintenance man.

A steady paycheck.

Summers off.

Where do I sign?

Fuller Farms opened two years later, in 1963. That March, the camp ran several ads in *The Ashes Tribune*. They needed kitchen staff, a grounds crew, and maids, among other things. But the listing for an archery instructor caught Buster's eye. He'd been bowhunting with his old man since kindergarten and could put an arrow in a squirrel's eye from eighty yards away. Plus, at three bucks an hour, three times the minimum wage, Buster could stash away enough cash over a couple of summers to buy the Ford Thunderbird he'd been dreaming about for as long as he could remember. So, he filled out an application and got the job without an interview.

By 1963, Liston, the Fuller clan patriarch, was already old as Methuselah and had little to do with the day-to-day operation of the summer camp that bore his name. He greeted campers on opening night, led the camp song, and showed up at lunch about once a week. Liston's crazy fifth wife, Susan, was around more, but only to conduct Bible studies. Bible studies which, as far as Buster could tell from what little he overheard walking past the chapel, consisted mainly of Susan's accounting of everyone she thought should burn in hell. No, it was Rosalind, Liston and Susan's daughter-in-law, who did most of the work at Fuller Farms, and Buster loved her.

Tall, pretty, and about ten years Buster's senior, Rosalind Fuller actually acknowledged the staff, greeted them with smiles, and thanked them for their work. Buster correctly assumed Rosalind had grown up comfortably but not with Fuller millions in the bank. She seemed normal. Down to Earth. Nice, even. This was more than he could say for the campers. They ignored instructions, insulted Buster when they thought he wasn't listening, and lost more arrows than you'd have believed possible. The campers were only a few years his junior, but Buster wanted nothing more than to take off his belt and teach them a lesson. But his job was to teach archery, not discipline the campers, something Susan Fuller reminded him when Buster sent an idiot kid back to his cabin early after he'd shot an arrow at two girls swimming in Mud Lake.

"At least she's not your mother-in-law," Rosalind Fuller whispered to Buster after witnessing Susan dress him down in front of the campers.

"But I'd be rich," Buster countered with a smile.

"Trust me," Rosalind said after considering this for a moment, "there's not enough money in the world."

Buster bought his Thunderbird, wrapped it around a tree one wild Saturday night, then bought another one a couple of years later. He sold that second car to buy an engagement ring he never gave away, then resigned himself to a lonely life in the woods.

Fifteen years slipped by before Rosalind and Wellington's son, Vance, attended his first camp at Fuller Farms. He was an awkward kid. Shy and pimply. Bully bait, no doubt.

"Keep an eye on him for me, will you?" Rosalind asked Buster at the welcome dinner.

"Of course," Buster said.

"And if you see the other kids picking on him, please—"

"Shoot them full of arrows?" Buster asked, and Rosalind smiled.

"Seriously," Buster said, "if it gets bad, he can always sleep in my shed."

It did get bad, and about halfway through his first summer, Vance showed up at Buster's door in the middle of the night, his face streaked with tears. The boy never said what happened, and Buster didn't pry, but Vance slept in Buster's shed every night from then on.

Buster and Vance grew close.

Closer than friends.

Until one night Buster ruined it all.

Things got weird in 1983 when Liston died, and a freshly retired Wellington took over the camp. Vance had moved on, off to Chapel Hill, and Buster missed him, but the boy would probably never speak to him again anyway. Not after what Buster did.

Rosalind wasn't the same with her husband around either. She adopted the Fuller family posture of not consorting with the hired hands, and Buster was lonely. He thought about quitting, but what the hell else would he do with his summers?

Time marched on, and a decade later, Vance came back. It seemed he'd gotten into trouble at UNC, but Buster didn't believe the rumors he heard. The problem was, the boy wouldn't talk to him about it. He wouldn't talk to him about anything. Vance avoided Buster entirely until the day he got his ass beat and wound up in the shed, drinking moonshine and nursing his wounds.

Buster wanted to mend fences that day, but it all unraveled so quickly. One minute they were talking for the first time in ten years, and the next minute, Vance was screaming at him and storming out of the shed. They'd find the boy dead the next morning, and Wellington Fuller pointed his finger squarely at Buster. Blamed him for Vance's death in front of campers, counselors, and anyone with ears to hear, then fired him on the spot.

The cops questioned him, and Buster feared for a while he might go to prison, so angry was Wellington Fuller, and so firm was his grip on the local police. But the investigation faded into nothing, and the town seemed to collectively forget what happened that night at Fuller Farms. Still, nothing was ever the same after the night Vance died.

Buster McClellan could fix anything.

But not this mess.

It was beyond fixing.

CHAPTER TWENTY-FIVE

Someone called the police. It may have been me, but it's hard to recall. The fifteen minutes after finding Lenny Roach dead on the apartment floor are a blur of shouts and sirens.

Detectives arrived, filling the parking lot with flashing red and blue lights, and roping off the scene with their yellow tape. In my mind, a town the size of Ashes only needed like three cops to keep the peace, but there were at least ten there that night, two of them arriving in an armored tank-looking thing I suspect they'd been waiting years to take for a spin. Neighbors stood in their doorways and peeked out their blinds for a look. Every so often, one would dare to approach a cop and ask what was going on, only to be told there was no immediate threat of danger and they should return home.

Someone sat Mom in the back of an ambulance and wrapped her in a blanket. Axl and I stood beside her, watching people go in and out of our apartment. They'd bring Lenny out in a body bag soon, and our neighbors would all begin searching for a new place to live. I can't say I blamed them.

"There was so much blood," Mom mumbled after a long time. Axl put his arm around her, but I don't think she noticed. I don't think she knew the world was still spinning.

Scanning the parking lot, I spotted Chief Jenkins beside an unmarked black sedan talking to a gray-haired man in a fleece vest. I walked over to see what he could tell me, and as I approached, the man in the vest slipped away.

"Izzy," Chief Jenkins said, taking off his Stetson hat and placing it over his heart. "How's your mama?"

"Shook up," I said. "She's not used to this stuff, I guess."

"And you are?" Chief Jenkins asked, his eyes narrowing.

"I have solved two murders, and you showed me some rather graphic photographs of Vance Fuller just a few days ago."

"I suppose that's true," he said, snorting something like a laugh. "Look, we're gonna need to talk to you all about this, but not out here in front of God and everyone. Would y'all mind coming into the station?"

"Sure," I said, "do you want us to come in the morning, or—"

"Nah, we should do it tonight. I mean, y'all ain't getting into that apartment anytime soon, and I doubt you'd want to sleep there anyhow. We can get this out of the way now, and y'all can spend the night at the Ashes Inn downtown."

"Okay, yeah," I said. "Let me talk to Mom, and we'll drive over there."

"We'll take you," Chief Jenkins said, putting a firm hand on my shoulder and calling one of his deputies over with a whistle. "You all have been through enough tonight to get behind the wheel of a car. Detective Elroy here will drive you, and I'll be there to take your statements soon."

Detective Elroy took us in his black unmarked Chevy Suburban, me up front, Axl and Mom in the back. So, at least it didn't appear to our peeping neighbors the police had hauled the three of us off in the back of a paddy wagon. The folks at the station were friendly enough. They offered us drinks and snacks, which none of us wanted, then ushered us into separate rooms to wait. I was in the room where Elton and I sifted through the Vance Fuller files a couple of weeks earlier. Sitting at the table with nothing to do, I texted Axl.

ME – You don't think they think we had something to do with Lenny, do you?

AXL – No. Why would we call the police if we killed him?

ME – Good point. Who do you think killed him?

AXL – Hell if I know. You know the shit Lenny was into. Getting murdered is part of his job description.

I dropped my phone when a firm knock on the door startled me. Chief Jenkins and a cop with a beer belly and permanent scowl walked in, taking their seats across the table from me. Chief Jenkins introduced me to Detective Hootkins before offering his condolences.

"Thanks, Chief, but Lenny Roach was a piece of shit who hit my mother. So, I'm not exactly torn up he's no longer among the living."

Detective Hootkins exchanged a glance with Chief Jenkins, then asked, "So, you wanted Mr. Roach dead?"

"Yep," I said. "But I want Osama bin Laden dead too. If y'all find him behind Ashes Creamery with a knife in his chest, are you going to suspect I had a hand in it?"

Hootkins huffed, and Chief Jenkins raised a hand to calm the conversation. "Izzy, we ain't saying you had anything to do with Mr. Roach's death. But I need you to walk us through the last few hours so we can piece together a timeline."

"Fine," I said and told him about our evening.

"You and your brother stopped for gas, so that took, what, five minutes?"

"Maybe ten. Axl went inside to buy a pack of gum and ran into a couple of cheerleaders from school."

"If the store has a security camera, we can get an exact time," Detective Hootkins said, and Chief Jenkins nodded.

"Then you drove straight to the apartment complex?" Chief Jenkins asked.

I nodded. "We both noticed the door was open, and when we got upstairs, Mom came stumbling out and fell on the ground."

"You said your mama was going to throw Lenny out tonight," Hootkins said.

I nodded.

"Because he abused her, correct?" Hootkins asked.

"It is legal for women to break up with abusive boyfriends in North Carolina, correct? Or do we have to let them hang around until they get tired of punching us?"

Again, Chief Jenkins tried to lower the temperature. "Izzy, Detective Hootkins didn't mean to—"

"Now, hang on a minute, Butch," Hootkins said. "I'm just trying to make sure we've got this all straight. Your mama was gonna toss her no-good boyfriend out on his ass tonight, and she wanted your big strong brother there in case Lenny got violent. Y'all leave downtown around 8:45, but you and your brother stop for gas. You're at the gas station for twenty minutes or so—"

"Ten, at most," I interrupted.

"And when you finally get to the apartment complex, the door is wide open, and your mama is already up there covered in blood, despite telling y'all she'd wait for you in the parking lot."

"Yeah, because when she got there, the door to our apartment was wide open, and—"

"And when you and your brother finally show up, Lenny Roach is dead on the floor."

An ache in my chest rose to my throat, and I fought back the tears as I tried to argue with Detective Hootkins. "Yes, but you've seen my mother. She isn't much bigger than me. There's no way she could have killed Lenny. He'd have—"

"He could have been asleep on the couch when your mama got there," Hootkins offered.

"Or, somebody could have killed him six hours ago while y'all were all somewhere else with witnesses to verify it," Chief Jenkins said, coming to my rescue. "We'll know more once the coroner files his report."

"Yep, we sure will," Detective Hootkins said with a smirk. "The truth will come out. It always does."

Chief Jenkins' phone buzzed. "It's the coroner," he said to Hootkins, then stood to leave the room. "Izzy," he said, reaching the door, "is there anything else we need to know about Lenny Roach? Anyone who might have had a reason to hurt him?"

I opened my mouth but hesitated. Telling the police my mother's boyfriend was a drug dealer seemed a horrible idea. Still, it would likely move Mom down their list of potential suspects.

"Uh, yeah," I said, "I think maybe Lenny used to sell drugs."

Detective Hootkins snorted. "Yeah, no shit."

An hour passed, or maybe it was a year. The battery in my phone died, so I sat in that room alone with nothing to do but stare at the walls and try not to picture my mother strapped to the electric chair. Seasons changed, empires rose and fell, and finally, Chief Jenkins opened the door and said, "Alright, Izzy, come with me."

I followed him down the hallway to the front of the station, where Axl stood next to a plump woman in a night robe with curlers in her hair. My brother's eyes were bloodshot. He'd been crying.

"Izzy, this is Martha Dawson. She's a foster parent with Jackson County DCS. You and Axl will stay with her until your dad can get here."

"Our dad?" I asked, confusion flooding my brain. "What the hell are you talking about?"

"Dad is our next of kin," Axl said, and I looked at him, then back to Chief Jenkins.

"Y'all won't be going home with your mama tonight," Chief said. "We've charged her with the murder of Lenny Roach."

CHAPTER TWENTY-SIX

Back in the spring, while I was across the pond in London, Axl flirted with the idea of moving to Nebraska and living with our estranged father, Rodney Brown. I was adamantly against this plan for several reasons, not the least of which being our father left us alone in a trailer when we were three years old, and we hadn't seen him since. My brother and I locked horns over this for several weeks, tossing accusations of selfish assholery back and forth like grenades. Axl stayed with Mom in the end because, according to him, Ashes Prep had a better football program than the high school in Nebraska. But Mom told me Axl found out our dad had already accepted a bribe from a University of Nebraska booster in exchange for his son's commitment to the Cornhuskers, and it pissed off my brother something fierce. I only reminded him I was right about this several times a day.

You can say what you want about Rodney Purvis Brown—and there is a lot to say about him—but I must give the man credit when it's due. When the North Carolina Department of Children's Services woke him up around midnight that Sunday, he showered off, jumped in his truck, and made the seventeen-hour drive from the Lincoln suburbs to Ashes in thirteen hours flat. It was close to suppertime the next day when he knocked on our foster family's door.

Axl and I were in the den when he knocked, watching the Braves game with Mrs. Dawson, a kind woman who'd fed us so much since our arrival, I feared she might be fattening us up to go in a pie.

My brother and I exchanged a glance and a sigh.

"You ready for this?" Axl asked.

"No," I said, and we both stood while Mrs. Dawson answered the door.

Now, I must admit here everything I knew about my father came courtesy of my mother, who painted a bleak picture of a man who cooked meth in his Nebraska trailer and was married to a one-legged stripper. I would learn this narrative was mostly false, but I do not fault my mother. If one parent abandons their children, the remaining parent is legally exonerated from any and all falsehoods they wish to spread about the other. It turned out Destiny wasn't a one-legged stripper. She was a one-legged Army veteran who lost her leg to an IED in Kandahar. Dad didn't cook meth either. He worked construction, flipped houses on the side, and was doing okay, evidenced by the big-ass Chevy Silverado he drove to Ashes. He was even a deacon at some non-denominational church in Lincoln, and thanks to the photograph on their website, I knew he was skinny as a rail and had a DIY buzzcut with a wispy goatee. Still, the man who walked in the door was a stranger to me, and when he said, "Hey, kids," Axl and I just stared back, speechless.

Hugs were aborted, awkward handshakes exchanged, and Dad shuffled nervously in the doorway for the better part of a lifetime before asking, "So, y'all hungry?"

We weren't hungry, but we went to Porch Dog Burgers anyway, and Axl and I sat across the booth from our father while he wolfed down a double cheeseburger.

"So, son, how's football going?" Dad asked between bites.

"Oh, so you're still trying to sell your son to the highest bidder?" I snapped, referencing the twenty grand he'd supposedly taken back in the spring to secure Axl's commitment to play football at Nebraska.

"Now hold on," Dad said, "that Nebraska booster approached me with an offer for your brother. I wasn't going around with my hand out looking for—"

Dad's version of the story painted him more the clueless middleman, and less the conniving father pimping out his own son for profit, but either way, I didn't really care.

"Please shut up," I said, silencing our father with a raised hand. "Our mother is in jail for murder, and the only thing we're going to talk about his how to get her out."

Dad's words caught in his throat, then he snorted a little laugh and smiled. "Gracious, Izzy, you're the spitting image of your mama."

"Thank God," I mumbled.

"Act just like her too," he said, shaking his head.

I didn't dignify this with a response and instead turned to Axl. "When Rodney drops us off at the apartment, I need you to drive me back to the police station to talk to Chief Jenkins. If we can prove—"

"Now, Izzy, hold on a second," Dad said. "I didn't drive all this way to drop y'all off at your apartment. You're coming back with me to Nebraska."

"Like hell we are," I yelled, and Dad flinched. "We're staying here and getting our mother out of jail."

"Izzy, they ain't just gonna let your mama out of jail," Dad replied. "She murdered her boyfriend."

"She did-fucking-not, and if you ever insinuate otherwise again, I'll knock every cavity-filled tooth out of your tiny little skull."

"Nope, you're right," Dad said, raising his hands in surrender, "ain't no violent tendencies in this family whatsoever."

An awkward silence overtook the booth, broken only by Dad slurping the last of his Dr Pepper. "Look," he finally said, "we're all tired. Let's check into a hotel for the night, get some sleep, and we can figure out what we're going to do in the morning."

Dad was right; I was exhausted. Though I don't recall this, when Chief Jenkins told me he'd arrested Mom for murder, it apparently took three grown men to drag me kicking and screaming from the police station and strap me into Mrs. Dawson's van. Since then, I'd slept maybe ten minutes and taken two pills because I thought I was having a heart attack when the first one wore off. But I couldn't relax until we had a plan to help Mom.

"Better idea," I said, pulling out my phone, "we're figuring this out now."

I scrolled through my contacts and found Tanner Cobb, the often-shirtless attorney from Cowden, Florida, who'd helped get me out of juvie after my run-in with Dalton Wolfe.

"Pippi Longstocking," Tanner said by way of hello. "Did I see something on the news about you foiling some bomb plot over in England, or was that a fever dream?"

"Hi, Tanner. Nope, that was Elton and me."

Tanner Cobb chuckled. "Well, so much for staying out of trouble. I hope at least this time y'all managed not to piss off the richest man in the county."

"This time, he was one of the richest men in England," I said, "and he had ties to organized crime, but we left the country before he could get us kicked out of school."

My father squinted at this information and turned to Axl, who only shrugged in return.

"But Tanner, I'm calling because I could use your help right now."

"Sure thing. What can I do for you?"

"My mother was arrested last night and charged with murdering her boyfriend."

Tanner Cobb choked on whatever he was drinking, coughed for several seconds, then managed, "Okay, yeah, I can help. Y'all moved back to Washington County, right? So they must have your mama locked up in Chipley."

"Actually, we moved to Ashes, North Carolina, right after school let out in May."

"Oh," Tanner said. "Well, shit."

"What?"

"Izzy, I ain't licensed to practice law in North Carolina."

"Why not? You're a lawyer, right? Who says you can't do your lawyer stuff wherever you want?"

"The North Carolina State Bar, for one," Tanner said. "I'd have to pass their exam first."

"That's the dumbest thing I've ever heard," I said.

"Well, we attorneys ain't known for making things simple and easy."

I let out a long sigh. "What are we going to do? They think Mom stabbed Lenny. She needs a lawyer, and you know we can't afford one. Hold on—" I looked across the table at Dad and asked, "Can you pay for Mom's lawyer?"

My father raised his hands and said, "We've only got about five thousand dollars in the bank right now. All our cash is tied up in a couple of houses I'm trying to—"

"Never mind," I said to Tanner, "my father remains useless."

"What about Stretch?" Tanner asked. "His daddy is rich enough to bring Johnnie Cochran back from the dead to represent your mama."

"Elton's parents are going through a nasty divorce," I said, "so now's probably not a great time to ask his mother to pay more attorneys."

"Yeah, probably not," Tanner agreed. "But look, Izzy, it ain't like they're just gonna throw your mama in front of some hanging judge without a lawyer. They'll assign her a public defender if y'all can't pay."

"But public defenders aren't any good, are they?"

"I beg your pardon," Tanner said. "I'm a public defender." When my silence grew uncomfortable, Tanner said, "And Atticus Finch was a public defender."

"Yeah, and how'd his case turn out?" I asked.

"Touché," Tanner said with a laugh, then after some thought, added, "Okay, Pippi, I'm sure some folks from my law school class ended up in North Carolina. Let me make some phone calls, and I'll get back to you."

"Thanks, Tanner."

"Don't thank me yet," he said.

"You have an attorney on retainer?" my father asked when I hung up.

"Something like that," I said.

Dad accepted this with a shrug, then stood to leave, saying, "Alright, that Dawson lady y'all was staying with said the Ashes Inn had clean beds and free breakfast. Let's go get us a couple of rooms, and then—"

"Hold on," I said, staring at my father until he sat back down. "I need you to understand we're not going back to Nebraska with you. We're staying here, in Ashes, and we're getting Mom out of jail."

"Look, Izzy, I don't think—"

"I'm still talking, Rodney," I snapped, and Dad shut up. "Currently, you're in sixth place on the Top-10 Worst Dads of All-Time list, just above Darth Vader. But, if you stay and help us, you'll fall off the list entirely and start to make up for all the shit you've put this family through."

Dad frowned. "Sweetie, I've got a job back home. I can't just—"

"Do you have any vacation days?" I asked, ignoring the fact I didn't want him calling me Sweetie.

"Well, yeah, I've got a few, but Destiny and I have a cruise booked in August. It's our fifth anniversary, see, and we're going to Cancun and—"

"Rodney."

"Yeah?"

"I appreciate you dropping everything and driving here to get us. Seriously, I do. Before today, the nicest thing you'd ever done was send us two wrinkled five-dollar bills months after our birthday. But if you have any aspirations of being part of our lives again, you'll stay here and help us get Mom out of jail. Otherwise, we're never talking to you again."

Dad looked to Axl for help, but my brother offered none.

"Okay," Dad said, with a defeated sigh, "let me go call Destiny."

CHAPTER TWENTY-SEVEN

On Tuesday morning, Axl and I went to our mother's arraignment hearing at the Jackson County courthouse in Sylva, a forty-five-minute drive from Ashes. We told Dad it was best he stay behind at the hotel since just the sight of him would likely send Mom into a profanity-filled tirade the prosecution would later use against her at trial.

A scowling judge read the charges against our mother, and her court-appointed attorney, who somehow looked younger than me, entered a plea of guilty. "Shit, sorry, I meant not guilty," her attorney corrected himself, drawing a round of laughter from the gallery that persisted until the judge banged her gavel. This was depressing enough but was compounded by the fact Tanner Cobb had called on the drive over to say none of his classmates were licensed to practice in North Carolina. Well, one was, but he was currently incarcerated for mail fraud.

No bail was set, not that we could have paid it anyway, then a couple of sheriffs came to take Mom back to the county jail. She looked like a skinny little kid in her ill-fitting orange jumpsuit, and it took every ounce of willpower I had not to cry in the courtroom.

"I love y'all," Mom said over the divider keeping us from rushing forward to give her hugs.

Axl and I told our mother we loved her too, his voice cracking worse than mine.

"I didn't do what they're saying I done, Izzy," Mom said as the men led her toward the door. "I swear I didn't do it. You gotta prove I didn't do it."

"I will," I mouthed to her, even though I had no idea how I'd pull it off. I didn't even know where to start.

The enormity of the pressure I felt hit me on the walk back to Axl's truck, and I fell to my knees in the parking lot, sobbing uncontrollably. I was a fish out of water, gasping for air, or water, or whatever it is fish gasp for.

Axl helped me to his truck before returning to the courthouse to find me something to drink. While he was gone, I snatched one of my few remaining pills from my purse and swallowed it dry. God, I hoped it kicked in quick.

Sitting there, trying hard not to hyperventilate, I saw Chief Jenkins across the parking lot, talking to the man in the fleece vest from Sunday night. He waved at me, said goodbye to the man in the vest, and walked over.

"Izzy, you okay?" Chief Jenkins asked, noticing I looked pale even for a redhead.

"No," I said, fighting the strong urge to kick his shins, "You're trying to send my mother to the electric chair."

Chief Jenkins tried to put a hand on my shoulder, but I recoiled at his touch, and he reconsidered. "Izzy, first off, we don't use the electric chair in North Carolina. It's lethal injection."

If this was meant to somehow comfort me, it achieved the exact opposite, and I burst into sobs again.

"Wait, hold on," Chief Jenkins said. "And second, your mama was charged with second-degree murder, so the death penalty ain't even on the table."

"Go to hell," I muttered through my tears.

"Now, Izzy, you, of all people, should know I'm just doing my job here. This isn't some—"

"We need to get into our apartment," I said, cutting him off. "I've worn the same clothes for two days straight."

"Yeah, of course. I don't think forensics is through yet, but we've got an officer posted over there. I'll make sure you can get back to your room to grab some things."

"You're a real hero," I muttered, before slamming my door in his face.

A young police officer met us at the door to our apartment and walked us back to our bedrooms one at a time. Investigators still had parts of our living room marked off with tape, and those little numbered crime scene markers covered the floor. There were dark blood stains on the carpet from where Lenny lay dying. I felt terrible for whoever would have to clean this place when the cops were done, even worse for whatever unsuspecting family moved in next and was haunted by the douchiest ghost of all time.

As the cop escorted me through the living room with my duffle bag full of clothes, I stopped and leaned down to examine one of the crime scene markers. I wanted to stay here for hours, take it all in, and look for clues. But the crime scene's overwhelming complexity quickly reminded me I was a sixteen-year-old girl with no forensics training. If fact, I had no investigative training whatsoever. I'd just stuck my freckled-little nose where it didn't belong a couple of times, nearly gotten myself killed, and somehow solved two murders. I could spend weeks combing over this murder scene and not come out any wiser as to who killed Lenny Roach or why. Dammit to hell.

"Get up, keep moving," the officer barked, and I obliged because what choice did I have?

Back in the truck, I confessed to Axl I didn't think I could solve Lenny's murder. "Honestly, I don't even know where to start."

"Well, where do you usually start?" he asked. "You know, with your other cases."

"I usually have suspects," I said. "But I don't know who would want to kill Lenny."

"Apart from Mom?" Axl asked.

"Apart from Mom," I conceded with a sigh. "I mean, Lenny was in a dangerous line of work. I suspect there isn't a shortage of rival drug dealers who wanted him dead. But I can't exactly look those guys up in the Yellow Pages."

"So you're giving up already?" Axl asked.

"No," I snapped. "We've just got to think of another way to help her, like … like hiring a real attorney."

"You mean that guy on TV who's always screaming, 'Hey North Carolina! If you're hurt, call Curt.'"

"No, I mean a real lawyer. The fancy suit, slicked-back-hair kind that charges a thousand dollars an hour."

"Yeah, right," Axl said. "We could pay him for about ten seconds."

"True, but …"

"But what?"

"But if I can solve Vance Fuller's murder, I'll have fifty grand."

"Then you have to solve Vance Fuller's murder," Axl said, snapping his fingers.

"Okay, let's go to Fuller Farms. We need Elton."

We found Elton in our office, hunched over the computer.

"Tuesday greetings," he said, not bothering to look away from the screen. "You were absent from work yesterday."

"Yeah, it's been a weird couple of days. We've got a lot to—wait, why are you wearing wingtips?"

Elton turned and stood, his camp shorts barely reaching midthigh, his feet covered in a pair of shiny dress shoes. "I … I no longer wish to support Nike, as they are one of my father's endorsement sponsors."

"Fair enough," I said, "but I'm going to find you some size 16 Adidas because those can't be comfortable."

"I would be much obliged," Elton said, then he waved awkwardly at my brother. "Tuesday greetings, Axl."

"Hey, Elton," Axl said, then pointed at the bandage on his arm and asked, "you okay?"

Elton examined his arm like it belonged to someone else, then said, "I was assaulted by one of the camp's mutant mosquitos and fear the wound has become infected."

I rolled my eyes and sat on the desk next to Elton. "Okay, Big E, I've got good news and bad news. The good news is Lenny Roach is dead."

Elton nodded without emotion. "That is preferable to him hitting you."

"The bad news," I said, "is they think Mom killed him. She was charged with second-degree murder this morning."

"What? No," Elton said, the color draining from his face. "They cannot—we must—"

"It's okay," I said, patting him on the shoulder until he noticed and squirmed away. "She needs a lawyer. A good lawyer. And we can't afford one until we solve Vance Fuller's murder and get our fifty thousand dollars."

"My mother can afford excellent attorneys," Elton said. "I will call her now and—"

"Elton, if your mother finds out about this, she'll make you come home."

Elton considered this for a moment. "That is probable."

"We just have to hope she doesn't read about Mom and Lenny in the *New York Times* or something."

"There are, on average, over fifty murders a day in the United States. The national media ignores most of them."

"Good," I said. "Well, good for us. Besides, your mother has enough shit to deal with right now. And if your father somehow found out, he'd use it against her in the divorce. So we're going to solve Vance's murder, hire Mom a hotshot lawyer, and get her out of jail."

I'm not sure if Elton was convinced, but after a moment of intense consideration, he nodded vigorously and said, "Agreed. We will solve Vance Fuller's murder."

"Great," I said, standing to pace the room. "Here's what I need from you. See if you can find any random connections between our suspects."

"Random, how?" Elton asked.

"I don't know exactly," I said, "but back in Bardo, we found out Mason Driscoll was in Dalton Wolfe's pocket, and in London, we busted Dr. Carrick and Harry Lane for having an affair."

"Holy hell, y'all are snoopy," Axl said.

"It's hard to solve murders without being snoopy," I snapped, then turned back to Elton. "Just dig. We need to find something someone doesn't want us to know so we can bust their balls with it and get to the bottom of this."

"Aye, aye," Elton said with a salute.

"But first," I said, "find out what a round-trip flight from Pensacola to Milo, Greece costs."

Elton spun around and began typing furiously.

"Why the hell do you want to go to Greece?" Axl asked.

"I'm not going to Greece. I'm sending Tanner Cobb to look for Sterling's father."

"Aegean Airlines has the lowest current fares," Elton said. "$1,290 for an economy seat with three stops and two checked bags."

"Can you get that much from your mother without raising too much suspicion?" I asked.

"I currently have three times that in my Capitol One Teen checking account," Elton said before explaining, "I receive a large weekly allowance."

"Alright," I said, clapping my hands together, "we're getting somewhere. You keep digging, try and remember to eat dinner, and I'll be back in the morning."

"Where are you going now?" Elton asked.

"To visit Buster McClellan," I said. "He didn't tell the police Vance slept in his shed nearly every night he spent at camp, and I want to see his face when we ask him why."

Elton considered this for a moment. "He will likely shoot at you again."

"Don't worry," I said, walking toward the door, "I'll duck."

"So, when Elton said this guy would likely shoot at you again," Axl asked as we walked from the office toward the employee parking lot, "he meant metaphorically, right?"

"Literally," I said, "with bullets."

Axl began loudly doubting my sanity, but I wasn't listening because I'd just spotted Sterling sitting on the porch of the boys' dormitory with some friends. He looked right at me, but when I waved, he stood and walked inside.

Dammit to hell.

I'm sure, as far as Sterling was concerned, I'd stood him up several nights in a row. He probably thought I was some sort of tease who tortured boys for fun. Maybe I could smooth it all over next time we spoke, but for now, I had more important things to worry about than boys.

CHAPTER TWENTY-EIGHT

"Tell me again what we're doing here," Axl said as we parked downtown outside the fairytale house the Ashes Police Department called home.

"I need to look at Buster McClellan's file from 1992 again," I said. "Make sure there's nothing I missed before we talk to him."

"Wait, so you can just stroll into a police station and ask to see their files?" my brother asked.

"Sure, well, no, not exactly," I said as we entered the Tudor-style house, "but after Wellington Fuller put in a call for us, Chief Jenkins was more than obliging. Rich people can do whatever they want."

"Ain't that the truth," Axl said before shuffling behind me after receiving a stern glare from Marcy, the world's orneriest receptionist.

"What," Marcy growled before begrudgingly adding, "can I do for you?"

You can stick your head in an oven, I thought. "We'd like to see Chief Jenkins," I said. "There are some files—"

"He ain't expecting y'all," Marcy snapped.

"We're taxpayers," I snapped back, trying Elton's method of getting past the old bag.

"Food stamp recipients, more like it," Marcy said with a snort.

"Listen, you old bitch, if you don't—"

"Izzy, Axl," Chief Jenkins said, stepping out of his office to check on the commotion, "what can I do for you this afternoon? Were y'all able to get your things out of the—"

"We need to look through Chief Morrison's file on Buster McClellan," I said. "We're going to talk to him about Vance again, but I need to see if I missed anything first."

Chief Jenkins frowned while steering us away from Marcy's desk. "Look, Izzy, I know I told Wellington y'all could look through those old files, but under the circumstances—"

"Are you referring to the circumstances of you falsely accusing my mother of murder?"

"Well, yeah, them's the circumstances. But I won't stand here and listen to you insinuate—"

"Do you even have a murder weapon?"

Chief Jenkins hesitated. "No, not yet. But your mama had plenty of time to dispose of it."

"She had five minutes, and, if you recall, she was in traumatic shock."

"Listen, we wouldn't just charge her if we didn't believe—"

"Whatever, Chief, it's fine. We'll catch Vance's killer without your help. Then we'll hire Mom a real lawyer who'll expose you for the incompetent buffoon you are."

"You know, you're kind of a badass when you're trying to solve a murder," Axl said as we drove out of town, heading toward Buster McClellan's house on Sour Mash Road.

I laughed. "Sometimes it feels like a different person is saying those things. Like, I'm watching it on television or something. I think the part of my brain that should keep me from talking to adults that way is broken, because the panic is always twenty minutes late, then I hyperventilate."

Axl started talking about football and how he's calm on the field but often pukes in the locker room, but I tuned him out because I didn't care.

"There," I said, interrupting a football story that was somehow taking longer than an actual game. "Turn in there."

"I'm not turning in there," my brother protested.

"Why not?"

"Because of the giant 'No Trespassing' sign in the shape of a shotgun."

"I swear, you and Elton are the biggest babies when it comes to—"

"Getting shot? Sure, I'll accept that criticism. I'm a baby when it comes to getting shot."

I ignored this and said, "Look, it's like I told Elton, Buster puts up these signs to keep out salesmen."

"He literally shot at you."

"Sure, but after he realized we weren't trying to get him to switch cable providers, we had a pleasant conversation."

"A pleasant conversation at gunpoint?" Axl asked.

Our argument lasted several more minutes, but in the end, Axl could only sigh and turn down the long, gravel driveway. We made it a mile and had just passed the "Last Chance, Morons" sign when Axl stomped the brakes, and we slid to a halt. Buster McClellan was sitting on the hood of a rusty old Ford truck blocking our way, his shotgun lying across his lap.

Buster hopped off his truck and took a couple of steps toward us. "Where's the tall boy you was with last time?" he yelled.

"Back at Fuller Farms," I shouted through the window.

"Who's this then?"

"My brother, Axl."

"Izzy and Axl? Y'all weren't named after members of Guns N' Roses, were you?"

"I'm afraid so," I shouted.

"Bitching," Buster said with a laugh, then added, "Alright, y'all get out."

"Thanks for not shooting at me again," I said as Axl and I climbed out of his truck and walked around front to face Buster.

"Well, I recognized you on the security camera this time. Figured there was little use in firing warning shots at someone who don't listen to warnings anyhow. Seems I told you not to come back here."

"You also told me you didn't kill Vance Fuller," I said, and Buster's eyes narrowed.

Axl elbowed me in the side and whispered, "Maybe tone down the badass stuff when the other guy has a shotgun."

I ignored him and said to Buster, "You told Chief Morrison that Vance used to spend time in your shed because he was bullied."

"Yeah, so?" Buster said.

"I'm just wondering why you didn't tell the police the whole truth that Vance slept in your shed nearly every night for four straight summers?"

"What are you trying to say?"

"It's just weird, that's all. I mean, if something happened in your shed, and Vance was about to tell, it makes sense you'd—"

Buster raised his shotgun so fast my life didn't even have time to flash before my eyes.

"I want you to think long and hard about what you say next because I didn't shoot you for trespassing, but I sure as shit will shoot you if you ever insinuate I laid a hand on that boy."

I raised both hands in apology, holding my breath until Buster finally lowered his gun. "I didn't insinuate it," I said. "Wellington Fuller did."

Buster spat at the mention of old man Fuller. "Look, Vance was an odd duck. Got picked on something fierce his first summer at camp, so his mama asked if I'd mind him sleeping on the extra cot in my shed." Buster's voice began to crack. "I cared for that boy. Cared for him like he was my own son."

"But why didn't Mr. Fuller know Vance spent the night in your shed?"

"I guess Rosalind never told him," Buster said with a shrug. "But it wasn't some secret. Listen, I see what Wellington is at here. If I abused Vance, it explains why he did what he did at Chapel Hill. Well, it don't explain it, but it shifts the blame away from Wellington's shitty parenting and puts it on me. Or, maybe, if I abused Vance, and he threatened to tell, then I killed him to shut him up. Only problem is, I never touched the boy."

"Do you ... do you think someone else at camp abused Vance?" I asked.

"Maybe," Buster said after some thought. "I don't know what

happened those first few weeks at camp because he never talked about it, but something shook him up pretty bad."

"And do you think Vance abused his own campers?"

Buster rubbed his temples, took a deep breath, and let it out slowly. "I've heard all the same rumors as everybody else, but I don't know. I hope not. But if he did, and they killed Vance in revenge, I don't suppose that's a story Wellington will want to hear. That man's mind is made up. He blamed me the morning they found Vance, and he's blamed me ever since. And now that Rosalind is gone, he's coming after me. That's why he hired you, right? To find dirt on me?"

I started to argue but couldn't. So far, whenever I'd spoken to Wellington Fuller about the case, he'd pushed me toward his former archery instructor. Perhaps he didn't so much want me to find Vance's killer as he wanted me to prove it was Buster McClellan.

"Well, I didn't kill Vance, and I didn't abuse him, so you can stop wasting your time."

"Want to tell me your alibi then?"

Buster's face softened, and he let out a low laugh. "Is this how you solve murders? Pester folks until they can't stand the sight of you anymore and spill the beans? Look, there's nothing I'd like to do more than tell you my alibi. It would clear up a lot of things. But I made a promise, and I keep my promises."

"I guess you know about the woman arrested in Ashes on Sunday night and charged with stabbing her boyfriend?" I asked.

Buster nodded. "Yeah, I heard that yesterday while I was in town buying cheese."

"That's our mom," I said, motioning to Axl. "She needs a good lawyer, but we can't afford one until I solve Vance's murder and Wellington pays me fifty grand. So please, Buster, is there anything you can tell us that might help me crack this case? Last time Elton and I were here, you said Vance wasn't the only person from camp that year who turned up dead. Were you talking about Quinn Westlake?"

"Who the hell is Quinn Westlake?" Buster asked.

"One of Vance's campers," I said. "The one who killed the homeless man that wandered onto his family's property. He jumped off the roof of his Manhattan high-rise last year."

"Shit," Buster said. "I remember the kid but didn't know that. To be honest, I just made up all that stuff about other people from camp turning up dead to try and scare you off. What about Vance's other camper?"

"Jasper Benson? He's at Benson House smoking pot and playing old video games."

"No, not Jasper. That jackass is useless but probably harmless. The other one, from Texas."

"Aubrey Masters."

"That's the one," Buster said, snapping his fingers. "He was sneaky as hell. I can't count how many times I caught him out of his dorm after lights out. Where is he now?"

"Hiding in Europe, it seems."

Buster shrugged to say there's your man, and I silently vowed to start vetting my boyfriends better.

"You really think Aubrey Masters killed Vance?"

"Sure. Maybe. Hell, I don't know. I'm just thinking out loud here. It could have been Aubrey. It could have been that frat boy who beat Vance's ass. It could have been devil worshippers like all the morons around town say. Look, I'd love to help you, but the truth is, if I knew who hurt Vance, I'd have killed them myself years ago.

I cursed under my breath and said to Axl, "We're never getting that fifty grand."

"Well," Buster said, "I told you to quit the case three weeks ago. Want me to tell you again?"

"You can, but I won't listen."

Buster chuckled, and Axl and I walked back to the truck.

"Thanks for your help," I called back to him.

"You're welcome," Buster said. "Don't come back."

"Okay, see you soon," I said, and when I glanced back, Buster shook his head and smiled.

1992

Tripp Aston held himself in high esteem.

And why not? He was president-elect of the Delta Nu fraternity at the University of North Carolina. Fraternity chaplain, too, the first man to hold both offices in the organization's proud 102-year history. Unprecedented, yes, but for his fraternity brothers, the choice was obvious. Tripp was a natural leader, captaining the intramural football team to three straight Greek championships. And on Wednesday nights, he led a well-attended Bible study in the Delta Nu house basement.

Tall, handsome, and charming.

Tripp was the poster boy.

The alpha among alphas.

But Tripp also knew how to have fun. He partied hard on weekends. Partied hard some weeknights too. He brought dates back to the Delta Nu house, though rarely the same girl twice, and in the morning, they'd make the well-trod walk of shame across campus from Tripp's bedroom back to the girls' dormitory. Tripp's reputation, however, remained unblemished.

Still, Tripp wasn't perfect. He never failed a class, but his As and Bs were few and far between. His 2.4 GPA kept him off academic probation but miles away from the Dean's List. Nevertheless, finding work after college would not be difficult. Tripp smashed every interview he ever sat for, and he knew his looks and charisma would trump any shortcomings on his resume. Besides, the Delta Nu alums loved him, and several owned Fortune 500 companies. But that was a backup plan because Tripp wanted to go to law school, and entering his senior year at UNC, he had a lot of work to do.

But first, one last summer at Fuller Farms, Tripp's favorite place in the world. He'd camped there in high school, and this would be his fourth and final summer serving as a counselor. After eight weeks of fun, games, and fresh mountain air, Tripp would return to Chapel Hill refreshed, recharged, and ready to buckle down and crush his senior year. But then he met his cabin mate.

The rumors started late in the semester after most students had already finished finals and moved out for the summer. A graduate assistant had used their position of power to sexually abuse a student and was caught in the act by their dean. The University tried to protect the student's name, but people talk, and Tripp learned just before leaving for Ashes that the victim was Ty Bingham, a Delta Nu brother whom Tripp knew but not well. Fearing a lawsuit, the University tried even harder to protect the grad assistant's identity, but Tripp was sleeping with a girl on the Committee on Student Behavior, and she let slip the name. Vance Fuller

And now, that same Vance Fuller would spend the summer sleeping across the room from Tripp, leaving him with a moral dilemma. Tripp had to teach Vance Fuller a lesson. He had to avenge Ty Bingham, or he'd never be able to face the brothers of Delta Nu when he returned. But he couldn't do too much because Vance's father ran Fuller Farms. So Tripp decided his revenge would be psychological. He'd threaten

Vance, put the fear of God in him, and ruin his summer the best he could without laying a hand on him. Then came news Ty Bingham had killed himself, and Tripp had no choice but to act. The beating on the commons in front of half of the camp was fast and brutal.

Tripp knew he'd be sent home. Feared the Fuller family might even take legal action against him. But then, nothing happened. No one told Tripp to pack his bags. No one said anything. Wellington Fuller was at dinner that night, and so was Vance, but everyone enjoyed their peach cobbler like the morning's beating never occurred. Maybe camp leadership didn't approve of Tripp's actions, but they appeared to understand them. Tripp certainly believed he'd done the right thing. The honorable thing. And he went to bed with a clear conscience, but sleep was hard to find.

That night, Vance didn't return to the cabin, which was okay with Tripp. But where was he? Back at his parents' house? Sleeping in the dorms? Or out in the woods, plotting his revenge? Tripp lay in bed, eyes wide open, long past midnight, so worried was he that his psychotic former roommate would slip through a window and slit his throat. Tripp's paranoia amplified every little bump in the night, and after hearing a commotion from the archery range, he got dressed and went to investigate.

Tripp Aston held himself in high esteem.

But not after that night.

Not after the archery range.

Now a great attorney, Tripp could easily convince a jury he did the right thing that night; some days, he could even convince himself. But deep down, Tripp Aston knew there was hell to pay, if not in this life, then maybe the next.

CHAPTER TWENTY-NINE

Wednesday morning, I awoke to a migraine that felt not dissimilar to the sensation of someone bludgeoning my skull with a hammer. However, this particular headache was seemingly accompanied by actual banging noises in what I feared was a new and horrible feature. Thankfully, it was just someone knocking on our hotel door.

"Answer that," I mumbled across the room to Axl, who threw a pillow at me but eventually crawled out of bed and let our father inside.

"Rise and shine," Dad said, stepping into our room and setting a couple of sacks from Blue Valley Bagel on the entertainment center next to the television. "I've got overpriced bagels and coffee."

I groaned a reply, and Axl flopped back into bed and covered his head with the comforter.

"Thanks for breakfast, Dad. We really appreciate it," Dad said, but we both ignored him. I couldn't ignore my headache, though, so I stumbled to the bathroom and took a pill and a hot shower. By the time I got out, I felt okay-ish.

"Thanks for breakfast," I said between bites of my bagel.

"No problem," Dad said. "Do you have work today? Need a ride?"

"Shelby's picking me up," I said. "I'm going to quit when I get there."

Dad laughed. "Speaking as someone who has quit their fair share of jobs, you could save yourself the trip and do that over the phone."

"I'm just quitting the kitchen staff part. If I'm going to solve this case and get mom a real attorney, I can't spend half my time serving eggs."

"Well, I'm rooting for you," Dad said. "When I called Destiny yesterday and told her I'd be here a while, she was madder than hell. Said if I'm not back in ten days, I'd better not come back at all."

I was reminded then it cost Dad something to be here. Granted, missing a cruise should be a small price to pay to keep your children from state custody, but Dad hadn't seen us in thirteen years. Ignoring that phone call from child services would have been a hell of a lot easier than driving across the country and pissing off your Army veteran wife. Maybe he had ulterior motives for being here. Perhaps he was still trying to work his way back into Axl's good graces to get some of that NFL money if it ever came, but I didn't think so. I believed he was trying to make amends for a lifetime of shitty parenting, and I couldn't help but appreciate it. "Well," I said, "I'm glad you stayed."

Dad started to reply but just smiled instead.

"I told you there was ways to get rid of your mama's trash-ass boyfriend, but stabbing him in the chest wasn't one of them," Shelby said on our high-speed drive to work.

"She didn't stab him," I said. "At least, I don't think so. I mean, I guess she had enough time before Axl and I got back, but you've seen my mother. No way she could kill a grown man with a knife. He'd have wrestled it away from her easily."

"Unless he was asleep when she got home, and she got him Van Helsing-style," Shelby said, pretending to drive a stake into a vampire's heart.

"Yeah, that's what one of the cops said. But I didn't see any blood on the couch. So he'd have seen it coming unless he was sleepwalking through the den."

"Well, a good lawyer should be able to get her off. Who's she got?"

"Dennis, somebody. He looked about twelve."

"Dennis Strewberry? Oh, God, Izzy, I'm sorry. That's who the court assigned my cousin Donnie a few years ago when he got arrested for mooning a school bus—long story, but those stupid kids had it coming. The judge gave him the maximum sentence. Four months in jail and a two-thousand-dollar fine. Just for showing his ass to a bunch of sixth graders."

"Shit," I said. "I really do have to get her a better lawyer. Any word from your mom?"

"Nope," Shelby said. "But even Aunt Jenny is freaking out now. I'm really worried about her."

"Yeah," I said, "me too."

"No, Izzy, considering the circumstances, I understand why you need to step away from your duties here," Wellington Fuller said. I'd looked for him in his office that morning, but his secretary told me I'd find him down at the pool, getting his laps in.

"Just my kitchen duties," I explained, wishing I'd waited until Wellington had a shirt on to have this conversation. "I want to focus all my energy on Vance's case. My mother needs a better attorney, so I need the reward money more than ever."

"I'm sure," Mr. Fuller said. "Lady justice may be blind, but when it comes to legal representation, you get what you pay for."

"Which is why I wanted to ask if, perhaps, you'd consider …"

"Consider what, dear?"

"Paying me in advance for solving Vance's murder?"

Wellington Fuller chuckled to himself, then let me dangle in the breeze for a moment. "Izzy, please do not interpret what I'm about to say as callousness toward the situation your family finds itself in, but I did not make it this far in life by paying folks for jobs they've yet to complete."

"Right," I said, not even trying to hide my disappointment.

"You keep working hard," he said, patting me on the back, "and you'll get that money and help your mama. I've got faith in you."

Thanks, asshole, I thought. "Thanks, Mr. Fuller," I said, then I went to see Elton.

"Wednesday greetings," Elton said as I walked into our office.

"Morning," I said, and it must have sounded extra glum because even Elton noticed.

"You sound sad," he observed, spinning around in his computer chair.

"Just feeling a little defeated," I admitted. "This case is going nowhere, and I'm afraid Mom will go to prison."

"But she is innocent," Elton said.

"I know, but what can I do? Looking for Lenny's real killer is more of a lost cause than the case we're already on. Any pill-pusher in a five-hundred-mile radius has motive."

"You are correct. Finding Lenny's killer would prove impossible," Elton agreed, turning back to face his computer.

"So, how's the digging going? Any leads?"

"One," Elton said, shuffling through a stack of paper on his desk. "The internet is overrun with ten-year-old articles chronicling Jasper Benson's sexual exploits. However, it was not until I began searching his name combined with the names of other suspects that I discovered this story buried deep in the Google results." He handed me an old article from the *Miami Herald*, with the headline "Charges Dropped Against North Carolina Playboy."

MIAMI, FL

Jasper Benson, North Carolina socialite and director of the Razzie-winning film Ghost of Judas, has reportedly reached a plea deal with Miami-Dade prosecutors in his Miami Beach DUI case. Sources tell the Herald Benson won't face drunk driving charges if he agrees to take anger management classes.

In February, Benson was arrested for driving 125 mph through a school zone. According to police reports, his blood alcohol level was recorded at .24 percent, three times the legal limit.

Benson will reportedly have to attend a 6-hour anger management course and make a $100,000 charitable donation to Mothers Against Drunk Driving.

Prosecutors were disappointed in the ruling but could still charge Benson with misdemeanors stemming from the several exotic animals found in his trunk at the time of his arrest, including a rare albino panther cub. However, Benson's attorney, Phillip Dean Aston III of Dorminey, Day & Aston, believes his client's legal troubles in the Sunshine State are behind him. "My client has seen the error of his ways and now understands the 'Yo Mama' jokes he told the arresting officer were highly offensive and inappropriate. Mr. Benson looks forward to fulfilling the court's requirements and continuing to give back through his family's charitable foundation."

No stranger to legal trouble, Benson also cut a deal late last year in North Carolina, in which he pleaded no contest to misdemeanor vandalism after launching several dozen eggs into his neighbor's pool with a homemade catapult. Then Jasper Benson received two years probation and was ordered to pay his neighbor $47,500 in damages.

"Wait," I said, putting down the article and looking at Elton. "Tripp Aston is Jasper Benson's attorney?"

"Affirmative."

"That's weird, right?"

"Negative," Elton said. "Tripp Aston is an accomplished attorney, and the Benson family is wealthy."

"Well, it's weird Tripp Aston never mentioned he's Jasper Benson's attorney."

"Negative," Elton said again. "He was under no legal obligation to reveal such information."

I huffed and said, "Well, it's weird that Jasper Benson told us if anyone had reason to kill Vance Fuller, it was Tripp Aston."

"Yes, that is weird," Elton admitted.

"You know what I'm thinking?"

"Izzy, we have discussed this several times. I cannot read minds, and even if I could—"

"I think we need to call Tripp Aston back right now."

I reached for the phone just as a knock came on the door, and Sterling peeked inside.

"Hey, Izzy," he said, "can we talk?"

CHAPTER THIRTY

"Your friend Shelby told me about your mom this morning," Sterling said as we walked from the office building toward Mud Lake. "I'm so sorry, Izzy. I can't imagine how hard this all must be."

"Yeah, it sucks," I said, putting my hand in my pocket when he tried to hold it.

"And I'm sorry if I seemed mad the other day when—"

"When you turned your back on me the second we made eye contact?" I snapped. I wasn't really mad at Sterling. Whatever we were or weren't was the furthest thing from my mind. But it felt good being mean to him. A sort of unhealthy therapy I'd feel guilty about later.

"Yeah, then," Sterling said sheepishly. "I assumed you'd stood me up, so I was angry. How could I have known your mom was arrested?"

"Mom wasn't arrested Saturday night," I said. "That happened Sunday. I didn't show up on Saturday night because her boyfriend Lenny punched me in the face." I turned so Sterling could see my eye better, and he was horrified.

"Oh my God, he punched you? I'm going to kill him."

"He's dead," I reminded Sterling.

"Right, your mom."

"She didn't do it. At least, I don't think so. But the police say she did, and her attorney is the dictionary definition of incompetence."

"Are you looking for the real killer now?" Sterling asked, making me sound like O.J. Simpson.

"No," I said. "Lenny was into some shady shit, and there are probably more people in the world with a reason to kill him than not. I'm going to solve Vance Fuller's murder. Mom needs a new attorney. One who didn't go to law school in a strip mall. But we can't afford one until I get the fifty grand Wellington promised. So Vance's case has to be my focus."

Sterling seemed to think all this over as we walked silently around the lake, watching campers race two small daysailers across the muddy water. His family had money. His family probably employed an army of attorneys. Perhaps he was thinking of a way to help or, more likely, searching for a way to end whatever we were. Slumming it with a poor girl at camp was probably all fun and games until her mom got arrested for murder.

"Hey, Izzy," Sterling said, "maybe—"

And here it came, the end of Sterling and me. I couldn't blame him. Still, I wondered how he'd go about it. *Maybe we should just be friends. Maybe you should just serve my eggs. Maybe you're too damaged for anyone to love.*

"Maybe we should hang out tonight."

"You're probably right. We should—wait, really?"

"Yeah, I mean, I know you have a lot going on right now, and I know you want to catch Vance's killer, but it would probably do you a lot of good not to think about those things for an hour or two."

I glanced over at Sterling, who smiled weakly and shrugged.

"But if you can't, I understand. Like I said, you've got—"

"No, Sterling, I'd love to hang out tonight. Just meet you here at the lake?"

"Yeah, I can be here by ten."

I smiled and kissed him on the cheek. "I'll be here, I promise." Then I went back to the office to call Tripp Aston.

"Day, Dorminey and Aston, how may I direct your call?"

It was Wednesday afternoon, so I figured Tripp Aston wasn't on the golf course. However, it still took several minutes navigating his law firm's phone tree of receptionists and personal assistants before I finally got the man on the line."

"Miss Brown," he said, not unkind, "I did not expect to hear from you again."

"What can I say? I don't scare off easily."

Tripp laughed. "I wasn't trying to intimidate you when we last spoke, only warn you this little investigation of yours will only bring pain. To Wellington Fuller. The town of Ashes. Perhaps even to yourself."

"I've had plenty of pain in my life," I said. "I can handle a little more."

"I heard about your mother," Tripp said. "I'm sorry. I know that cannot be easy."

Something in his tone pissed me off more than it should, and I couldn't stop myself. "You don't know shit, you little trust fund brat."

Tripp Aston laughed hard.

"What's so funny?"

"Someone thinking my parents would even know what a trust fund is. My father worked in a tire factory when he wasn't drunk, and my mother cleaned houses."

"Then how did you camp at Fuller Farms?"

"I was good at football, which, as you well know, opens a lot of doors. I finished high school at a private school in Charlotte on a scholarship. My best friend's parents paid my way to Fuller Farms. Paid my way to Chapel Hill, too. They even paid my fraternity fees so I could keep an eye on their son."

"But … but your name is Phillip Dean Aston III. No poor person could have a name like that."

Tripp laughed again. "You're not wrong there. My birth certificate says Phil Aston. I added the rest at UNC to try and fit in."

This completely changed my picture of Tripp Aston but didn't change the fact he was Jasper Benson's attorney and never mentioned it to me.

"Fine, whatever," I said. "But when I called you and said Jasper Benson told me some Crumpet kid killed Vance Fuller, you told me not to put much stock in whatever Jasper Benson said."

"Because I wouldn't," Tripp replied.

"But you failed to mention you're Jasper Benson's attorney."

Silence.

"I said you failed to mention you're Jasper Benson's attorney."

"Yes, Miss Brown, I heard you, but I'm waiting on a question."

"Fine. Why didn't you tell me you were Jasper Benson's attorney?"

"Miss Brown, we spoke for perhaps five minutes. There are several things I did not tell you. I take an ACE inhibitor for hypertension. My youngest son was born eight weeks premature. Our next-door neighbor plays wide receiver for the Carolina Panthers. It would take forever to list everything I did not tell you during our first phone call."

God, I hated lawyers.

"You knew I was investigating Vance Fuller's death, and you knew your client was a suspect. You should have—"

"Miss Brown, I knew no such thing. Jasper Benson is a hot mess. Of course, having met him, you already know that. But never once has anyone accused him of murder."

I cursed under my breath because I didn't have anywhere to go from here without throwing out wild accusations against this powerful attorney and his client. I took a deep breath, trying desperately to think of something to ask that might start the case unraveling, but Tripp Aston broke the silence first.

"Miss Brown, I've looked into your mother's case."

"Okay," I said.

"I heard the guy she was living with abused her."

"Where'd you hear that from?"

"Doesn't matter," Tripp Aston said. "But I also know the legal counsel the court provided her with is, how should I put this, less than ideal."

"I'm pretty sure her lawyer started eating glue in kindergarten and never stopped."

This made Tripp laugh. "Listen, Izzy, I like you. You've got spunk. You're a lot like me when I was your age. You're driven, despite your circumstances. I'd be happy to take over your mother's case. She was abused. That's well documented. I put her on the stand, let her tell her side of the story, and no jury in the world would convict. They'd be more likely to throw her a parade. And when she's out, I can probably help you too. College. Maybe law school. You'd make a hell of an attorney."

"Wait, you'd do that? Why?"

"As I said, you remind me of me. And someone helped me out when I was your age, or God knows where I'd be. I'm just paying it forward, as they say. The only thing is, you'd …"

"I'd what?

"You'd need to drop this Vance Fuller stuff. Like I told you last time we spoke, Wellington Fuller thinks he wants the truth, but he doesn't. Letting it go is the best thing for everyone. So, we got us a deal?"

Holy shit. Even the devils on my shoulders were conflicted by this offer, and it took a moment before I could manage, "Can I … can I think about it?"

"Sure," Tripp said, "you think about it, then call me back when you're ready to say yes."

I hung up and turned to Elton, who'd been surfing Facebook and not paying any attention to my conversation. "What did Tripp Aston say?" he asked absently.

Oh, he just offered to buy me off, I thought. "Not much," I lied, wondering if I was for sale.

CHAPTER THIRTY-ONE

"I, uh … I need to, uh … I need to get up with your cousin Donnie again," I told Shelby that evening on our drive back to Ashes.

"How soon?" she asked, no hint of judgment in her voice.

I shrugged like my life didn't depend on it. "Soonish, I guess." I'd taken another pill that evening and only had one left. They'd all be gone tomorrow, unless, by some miracle, I woke up a completely different person. "Friday would be nice."

"Yeah," Shelby said, "that shouldn't be a problem. Same order?"

I wanted a full bottle. I needed a full bottle. Only having a few pills at a time just added to my anxiety as I watched my supply quickly dwindle. But I didn't have the money for a bottle. I didn't really have the money for eight pills, but what choice did I have? I'd never solve Vance Fuller's murder in bed with a migraine, and then Mom would never get out of jail. What's the old saying? You've got to spend money to make money. Well, I was investing in myself. I'd cut back once Mom was free and life returned to normal, maybe even start seeing a thera- pist again. These are just a couple of the lies I told myself before I told Shelby, "Yeah, eight more will do for now."

Shelby dropped me off at the Ashes Inn, and I found Axl in our room watching a baseball game but dressed for a date.

"Shit," I said, "do you have plans tonight?"

He smiled. "I have a date with the Ashes Prep cheerleader voted most likely to put out."

I shot him a bird. It annoyed the hell out of me he had a date while our mother was in jail, but then I remembered I had a date too, assuming I could find a way to get back to Fuller Farms. I begrudgingly conceded Axl probably needed to forget about life for a couple of hours tonight just as much as I did.

"Why?" My brother asked when I told him I needed a vehicle. "Do you need to go talk to more crazy rednecks who'll pull a shotgun on you?"

"No," I said, "I was going back to Fuller Farms to see Sterling tonight."

Axl made porn music sounds until I threw one of his smelly football cleats at him.

"Well, I'm sorry," Axl said with a shrug. "But you could always ask Dad to borrow his truck."

I'd almost forgotten the man staying in the next room was our father. Our father who left us when we were three. Our father, whose mere existence used to piss me off so bad I couldn't see straight. Sure, he'd done one nice thing by showing up and keeping us out of a group home. Okay, two nice things by canceling his anniversary trip so I'd have ten days to catch Vance Fuller's killer and get Mom a real attorney. But still, two nice things don't make up for thirteen years of neglect. The man owed me.

"Uh, I don't know, Izzy. I'm afraid you'd—"

"Drive off and not come back for thirteen years?" I asked, and Dad frowned. "I need your truck for my investigation."

"Fine," he said with a defeated sigh, "you can borrow the truck."

"Thanks, Rodney," I said, snatching the keys from his hand and running toward the parking lot before he changed his mind.

Around ten, I pulled up to the locked main gate of Fuller Farms and saw Sterling waiting with a flashlight.

"The counselors are keeping a closer eye on the lake at night," he said, climbing in the passenger side. "I thought maybe we could go someplace else. Nice truck, by the way."

"It's my dad's," I said.

"Wait, your dad who left you when you were a baby and lives in Nebraska?"

"The same," I said. "He showed up after Mom was arrested and is trying to do the right thing for once in his life, it seems."

"Well, that's good," Sterling said. "I called Mom from the camp payphone last night, and she never mentioned Dad, so I don't think he's had a sudden change of heart."

"I'm sorry," I said, though I knew if my plan worked, I might hear from Sterling's dad soon. Tanner Cobb had said yes to a free trip to Greece before I even finished asking, and he was set to fly out of Pensacola in the morning.

"So," I asked, pulling back onto the road, "where do you want to go? Everything in Ashes closes at ten except that swanky martini bar we'd never get in."

"I thought maybe we could go to Doublehead Falls," Sterling said. "I hear it's beautiful, but I've never been there."

"Yeah, I'm pretty sure it closes at sunset."

"But there's not, like, a security guard out there, right?"

"I guess not," I said with a shrug. "We can try."

We drove back toward Ashes, turning down Sour Mash Road like we were going to see Buster McClellan, but pulling over a couple of miles shy of his driveway at the gravel parking lot for Doublehead Falls. A gate blocked the trail to the falls, and a hard-to-miss sign informed us the park closed at sunset—its small print detailing all the punishments violators would face. But as Sterling predicted, there wasn't a guard, so we hopped the gate and started walking.

The falls were a half-mile hike from the road, mostly uphill. Sterling's flashlight helped some, but I still tripped several times during our ascent, skinning both knees in the process. This would not be a great place to break an ankle. You'd likely be eaten by bears before help arrived.

I heard the falls long before I saw them. The water from two rushing creeks poured over the mountain's side and plunged ninety feet below. The winding trail emerged at a clearing across from the plunge pool, leaving us with a near-vertical look up the falls. I'm sure it's nice during the day, but the way the falling water sparkled in the moonlight was perhaps the most beautiful thing I'd ever seen.

"Wow," Sterling said, craning his neck up at the falls.

"It's okay, I guess," I teased, then put my head on his shoulder.

I had to admit, this was way better than okay. It was absolutely perfect, and I needed it so badly. There'd been way too much adult shit going on the past few weeks, and I needed to be a teenager again, if only for a couple of hours. I needed to stay out late and miss my curfew no one was around to enforce. I needed to make out with this cute boy until my lips chapped and not think about Tripp Aston's offer or Vance Fuller's murder or pills or headaches or any of it.

Sterling leaned down to kiss me, and before I knew it, we were on the ground, me on top, his hands in my hair. This went on for maybe ten minutes. Ten glorious minutes. The best ten minutes I'd had in God knows how long. I was so—I'm not exactly sure how to say it, but—so present. So in the moment. So unburdened by my stupid brain and all the stupid shit it usually threw at me. Then it all went to hell.

At some point, we'd rolled over, Sterling on top, kissing my neck and whispering sweet nonsense in my ears. His hands slid down from my hair and kept going.

"Sterling," I said, my tone implying that was enough.

"What?" he said, going back to my neck. "You could be going back to Nebraska with your dad soon. This might be our last chance."

"Our last chance for what?" I said, my body going stiff.

"You know," he said, his hands back on the attack.

Of course I knew, and with Sterling, yeah, maybe, one day. He was nice and cute, but this was a decision I'd need to overanalyze for several months. I'd need a SWOT analysis, or at the very least, a pros and cons list of losing my virginity to Sterling, plus a risk assessment of how likely I'd be to end up a pregnant teenager like my mom. Then I'd want to hire an actuary, write to several teen magazines that offered advice in these situations, and consult a Magic 8 Ball. All this to say, I wasn't the sort of person who could make a decision this big on the fly, no matter how romantic the moonlight shimmered off Doublehead Falls or how good Sterling's lips felt on my neck.

"Sterling, stop," I said, trying to laugh a little as I said it because I didn't want him to think I was mad.

He misinterpreted my stop sign as a yield and blew right through it.

"Sterling, please."

"I love you, Izzy."

Again with the love shit, though I was ready for him this time.

"Sterling, I can't—"

"Sure you can."

"Stop. Sterling, please. No, Sterling—dammit, Sterling, stop!"

It took so much effort to get out from under him, it scared me, but I got away and scrambled to my feet. Sterling looked up at me, and I couldn't tell if he was angry or hurt or what, but honestly, I didn't give a shit.

"We should go," I said.

Sterling reached out a hand, but when I tried to help him up, he pulled me back toward the ground.

"No," I said, snatching my hand away. "Let's go."

"Oh, come on, Izzy," Sterling said. "I'm sorry, for real. Please sit back down. We don't have to do anything you don't want to do."

I've often wondered about this moment and what Sterling's next move would have been. Would he have relented and moped back to the truck? Would we have stood there arguing until sunrise? Would I have blinked first and resumed the make-out session against my better judgment? Would something worse have happened? In the end, I never found out, because as I stared down at Sterling's sad face, a flash of light sparkled in his eyes. He squinted, and I turned to see two men with flashlights coming down the trail toward us.

I knew it was the cops even before one of them yelled, "Hands up, nobody move!"

CHAPTER THIRTY-TWO

I didn't get into trouble. Well, I didn't get into real trouble. Trouble is a sliding scale, and for someone who has spent several nights in a juvenile detention center, having to call your dad to pick you up at the police station isn't so bad. But thank God I'd left my last pill in my other purse back at the hotel. Otherwise, who knows?

One officer drove Sterling back to Fuller Farms, where I suspect he got a stern talking-to from his worried counselor, but nothing more. The other cop took me back to the police station in Ashes and spent the entire drive trying to scare me by making up punishments for trespassing on state property, but I tuned him out after he mentioned a firing squad.

"Izzy, I can't pick you up. You have my truck," Dad reminded me when I called.

"Oh, right, sorry," I said. "They towed your truck here. The cop said you'll need to pay $135 to get it out."

Dad sighed but held his tongue. I suppose he believed a parent needed to have at least provided the bare minimum of parenting before earning the right to scream at their child, and he'd yet to pass that threshold. "Let me see if your brother is back yet so he can drive me up there," Dad said. "I'll be there soon as I can."

The police made me wait in the same room where they interrogated me on the night Mom was arrested; teenage trespassing not deemed a serious enough offense to necessitate throwing me behind bars with the hardened criminals. Still, the flickering fluorescent light overhead felt like a form of punishment, threatening to summon my headache from whatever abyss the day's pills had sent it. After half an hour, there was a knock on my door, and I said, "Come in," expecting a cop who'd tell me my dad was here and I was free to go. Instead, the gray-haired man in the fleece vest I'd seen talking to Chief Jenkins several times stepped through the door.

On closer inspection, the man was older than I thought, but how old was hard to say. He was built like a marathon runner, with hair styled like George Clooney's and a face overly familiar with the plastic surgeon's knife. He smiled at me, but only his mouth moved, Botox holding his other facial muscles against their will.

"Izzy," the man said, reaching out his hand for me to shake. "I'm Mayor Jeremy Benson."

"Shit," I said, "I'm sorry they woke you up, Mr. Mayor. Sterling and I just wanted to see the waterfall at night, and we didn't know—"

Mayor Benson laughed with kindness in his eyes and said, "Izzy, teenagers have been making out at Doublehead Falls since the dawn of time. Chief Jenkins and his boys wouldn't even bother patrolling up there if it weren't so dangerous at night. One slip and fall, and we've got a tragedy on our hands, you understand?"

"Yes, sir," I said.

"But you're not in trouble," he said. "I even told the boys at the impound yard to waive the fee when your daddy comes to pick up his truck."

"Thank you," I said. "That's very kind."

Mayor Benson waved off my gratitude, pulled a round keychain from his pocket, and handed it to me. "We just got these in today. They'll go in the swag bags at the premiere in October."

I examined the keychain. One side featured Chase Foster and Bridget Bell locked in a passionate kiss, and the other side read *Cupid's Crossbow*, World Premiere, Ashes in the Pines, October 10, 2009.

"Uh, cool," I said, not really knowing what I was supposed to say.

"You can keep that one," Mayor Benson said before taking the seat across from me and taking a more serious tone. "Now, Izzy, I'm glad you and I got this chance to talk, because I'm afraid I didn't make myself clear enough on this Vance Fuller business the last time we spoke."

"You were pretty clear," I said. "I just ignored you."

Mayor Benson laughed again, but this time his eyes narrowed. "As you know, Tripp Aston provides legal services for our family. I know you spoke to Tripp after I asked you to end this little investigation, and I know you called him again today, still digging for dirt. Well, Izzy, if you want the dirt, here it is. Vance Fuller abused his campers. Did horrible things to them. Unspeakable things. Now, did someone do those same things to Vance years ago? Perhaps. But that's no defense, and it doesn't change the fact Vance hurt those boys, and one of them hurt him back. End of story. Now, Tripp told me he offered to help you."

"Was Jasper one of the boys who hurt Vance back?" I asked.

"Dammit, girl, what does it matter? A child abuser is dead."

"Mr. Benson, I saw the photographs of Vance Fuller. Someone tied him up. Someone tortured him."

"Okay. So, a boy tormented his tormentor. Who am I to say he went too far? Who are you? If I was Quinn, I'd have—"

"Wait, Quinn?" I asked when Mayor Benson abruptly stopped talking. "Quinn Westlake?"

Mayor Benson closed his eyes and slowly exhaled. "Chief Morrison knew. Figured it out pretty quickly. The Westlakes knew too, and so did Rosalind, but she kept it from her husband. Everyone had reasons to sweep it under the rug and never look back. No jury in the world would have ever convicted Quinn, not after the things Vance did to him. In fact, it was the Westlakes who could have pressed charges against Fuller Farms. They could have sued Wellington back to the Stone Age and taken every dime from that old miser's name. But they didn't need the money and didn't want the publicity, not after all they'd already been through. It haunted the boy, though. I'm told the note he left detailing what Vance did to him would bring a man to tears. You do know how Quinn's sad story ended?" I nodded, and Mayor Benson said, "So, the way I see it, you've got two choices. You can tell Wellington the truth. Break his old heart into a million pieces and spit on Quinn Westlake's grave while you're at it. Or you can quit trying to dig up bones everyone agrees should stay buried."

"You hungry?" Dad asked an hour later as we left the police station.

"Sort of, but we don't have many options at one in the morning."

"Hush your mouth," Dad said. Five minutes later, we pulled

into the Waffle House on the outskirts of town and got a table next to a drunk man who, for unexplained reasons, played "What's New Pussycat" fifteen consecutive times on the jukebox.

"So tell me," Dad said after we ordered waffles and bacon, "what exactly did going to Doublehead Falls in the middle of the night with some boy have to do with your investigation?"

I rolled my eyes at him.

"I'm only teasing," he said. "Lord knows you deserve a little fun."

"The crazy thing is, I solved the case tonight."

"Wait, for real? Izzy, that's great."

"No, it's not. Mayor Benson told me a boy named Quinn Westlake killed Vance Fuller. Killed him because Vance had abused him all summer."

"Oh, God, that's horrible," Dad said.

I nodded. "Apparently, it haunted Quinn for the rest of his life. He killed himself last year."

Dad closed his eyes and shook his head. "Still," he said, "you found out who killed Vance. That's what you were asked to do, right? You can tell Mr. Fuller what happened, collect your reward, and get your mama a lawyer."

"It's not that simple," I said. "Mr. Fuller wanted me to prove what he already assumed happened to Vance, and this isn't it. This would crush him … if he even believed me. I mean, it's not like I have proof. There's no evidence. And Mayor Benson isn't going to repeat what he told me to Mr. Fuller. All he really cares about is his stupid film festival, and he's scared if Vance's murder starts making headlines again, it'll scare off Chase Foster and Bridgett Bell."

"I do like that Bridgett Bell," Dad said, and I glared at him until he apologized.

"Mayor Benson is convinced everyone involved will be better off if no one ever talks or thinks about Vance again. So much so, he's willing to let his attorney represent Mom and help me with college if I drop the case. Well, his attorney made the offer, but I now suspect the mayor is behind it."

Dad nodded. "That's a tough one."

"Yeah, no shit," I said, and he laughed. "Any advice?"

"I guess you'll have to figure out the right thing and do it."

"And what's the right thing here? Mr. Fuller hired me, but if what I learned gets out and other campers come forward, Fuller Farms would get sued into oblivion. If a jury thinks Wellington covered up abuse at his camp, he'll lose everything. And maybe he deserves to. Maybe Vance deserved every arrow Quinn Westlake hit him with. God, I hate this case."

"Yeah, sometimes figuring out the right thing to do is harder than other times," Dad said.

"And what do you know about doing the right thing?" I snapped.

Dad took the blow and smiled sadly.

"Sorry, I'm just—"

"No," my dad said, rubbing his eyes, "that's fair. But listen, Izzy, we was just stupid kids when your mama got pregnant. Not much older than you and Axl. How do you think your brother would handle fatherhood right now?"

Not well, I thought but refused to concede Dad's point.

"He'd be scared shitless, right? Well, I was no different, only there was two of y'all, which somehow makes things more than twice as hard."

"But you didn't leave for three years," I said. "You weren't a kid anymore."

"I was an adult, sure, but about as mature as a fifth grader. The thing is, I felt trapped. Felt like if I didn't run, I'd be stuck forever in that little trailer with two toddlers we couldn't get potty trained to save our lives. It was a mistake to leave, Izzy. It was the worst mistake I ever made, and I'll pay for it the rest of my life."

"You could have come back," I said, wiping a tear from my cheek.

Dad smiled. "I tried. Tried more than once. Every time I called your mama and said I wanted to come home, she informed me if I ever stepped foot back in Washington County, she'd blow my head off with her daddy's shotgun."

"Okay, that does sound like Mom."

"I believed her too."

"But still, we needed you," I said. "Mom has barely kept us afloat all these years, and if not for anything else, we could have used the money."

"I know," Dad said, raising his hands to show his innocence, at least in this one matter, "but I sent money. I sent y'all checks for six straight months, and each time your mama sent them right back with a bunch of swear words scribbled across the front."

I shook my head and laughed despite myself. I couldn't help but appreciate my mother's unflinching righteous indignation. Still, it would have been nice to have had money for new clothes occasionally.

"You know, Izzy, sometimes you screw things up so bad you can't ever make them right again. I was afraid that's what I'd done with y'all. I was afraid I'd never see you or your brother again. But Destiny, she's made me a better man. She taught me the best any of us can hope to do is the next right thing, and that's how I try and live my life. I ain't perfect. I ain't even close. But I'm trying. You gotta believe I'm trying."

I reached across the table and squeezed his hand. "I know, Dad. I know. But what if there isn't a right thing to do?"

Dad thought for a moment and shook his head. "I guess you pick the least wrong thing and go with that."

1992

Quinn Westlake felt no remorse.

Not for the first thing. The thing with the bum outside his parents' oceanside mansion in Shinnecock Hills. He'd told the cops the man was a stranger, but that wasn't true. Quinn knew the man. He'd seen him around town. Everyone had.

Asking for food.

Asking for money.

Asking, asking, asking.

The guy wasn't right in the head. Any first-year psych resident could spot it a mile away. And Quinn didn't just think that because the man was homeless. He knew most men and women who mowed lawns and scrubbed toilets around town couldn't afford to live in the Hamptons. Some camped in the woods off Cold Spring Pond during the high season, and they were nice enough. Quinn had bought weed from a few of them. They were contributing to society, not stumbling down County Road 39, drooling all over themselves and shouting nonsense at everyone waiting outside the Lobster Shack for lunch.

Usually, by now, the police would have bought this troublemaker a one-way Greyhound ticket to Anywhere, USA. But this guy had been in town for over a month now with no intentions of leaving.

He'd been to the Westlake house once before, looking for work, or so he said. He caught Quinn's mother off guard. Frightened her. Mrs. Westlake said to come back when her husband was home just to get the guy to leave. He thanked her and said he would, but the Westlake Family never relayed this information to the police.

A week later, while his parents were attending a Bush-Quayle re-election fundraiser, Quinn saw the guy coming down their long oyster shell drive again. He met him outside with the shotgun his father took pheasant hunting in South Dakota.

"Hey, man, I'm not looking for any trouble," the bum said.

"Then you had better turn and run," Quinn replied, his hands shaking, whether from fear or excitement, he couldn't say.

The guy turned and ran, and Quinn shot him in the back, just like he'd planned.

It was horrible, really, seeing a man die. If Quinn was remorseful about anything, it was that he had to watch this guy cough and gurgle through his last breaths. The police came, and one of them called the Westlake family attorney. Later, once his story was straight, they took Quinn's statement and patted him on the back. It was an awful business, but thank God no one was hurt.

There was no arrest.

No charges.

And Quinn Westlake felt no remorse.

Quinn felt no remorse for the other thing either. The thing at Fuller Farms.

God, he didn't even want to go to camp, but his parents insisted, their desire for an FF decal on the back of their Land Rover trumping their son's desire not to spend his summer in the North Carolina backwoods. Aubrey and Jasper, the two guys in his group, were bumpkins. One kid was local, mountain trash. The other was from Texas, oil trash. Sure, they were both technically richer than Quinn, but their accents dripped of brisket, moonshine, and new money, and their Beavis and Butthead laughs could drive a man to jump in Mud Lake with a pocket full of rocks. Still, Aubrey and Jasper liked to smoke weed, and they liked to gamble, and despite himself, Quinn began to enjoy their company.

Twenty bucks. That was their typical wager. Gambling was always big at Fuller Farms, but these three would bet twenty bucks on literally anything.

"Twenty bucks says Jasper won't push that black-haired bitch from Atlanta into Mud Lake."

"Twenty bucks says Aubrey won't sneak into the kitchen and piss in the sweet tea."

"Twenty bucks says Quinn won't call Vance 'Professor Molester' in front of his dad."

It was Quinn who upped the ante one night. Partially out of boredom, but mainly because he owed Aubrey a thousand dollars and wanted it all back in one swoop. "Okay, Aubrey, a cool grand says you won't slay the Queen of the Mountain."

"Bet," Aubrey said, and Quinn began counting his money because he knew this wannabe cowboy didn't have the balls to pull it off. But then Vance Fuller went and ruined everything.

Now losing a few hundred bucks was the least of Quinn's worries.

Now his future was at stake, and if word got out, it would ruin him. Ruin his family. Ruin everything.

Something had to be done.

Something terrible.

But Quinn Westlake felt no remorse.

CHAPTER THIRTY-THREE

After whatever the hell happened with Sterling the night before and a late-night heart-to-heart over waffles with, of all people, Rodney Brown, Thursday morning's alarm hit me like an ill-tempered train. Before slapping the clock off the nightstand, I reached for my bottle and swallowed my last pill. Shelby honked while I was getting out of the shower, so I threw on some clothes and met her in the parking lot with water dripping from my hair.

"Here," she said, tossing the bottle I'd asked for the day before onto my lap. "It's a pleasure doing business with you."

"Wow, that was fast," I said, stashing the pills in my purse while a warm tingle rose up my spine.

Shelby shrugged. "Donnie went ahead and gave me two bottles last time. Said you'd be asking for more soon."

This stung more than I cared to admit, but I paid her anyway, then went through my justifications for needing more pills in my head, but they didn't work as well as they had before. I'd solved the case. Quinn Westlake killed Vance Fuller, and when I told Wellington, he'd either pay me fifty grand or he wouldn't, but either way, my work was done. The story I'd told myself about needing pills to clear my head while I investigated Vance's murder no longer held water, and now was a good time to start weaning myself off them like I'd promised I would. But I didn't want to think about that just then, so I didn't.

"I may be back working in the kitchen today," I said as Shelby drove down the mountain with her knees while lighting a cigarette, a high-wire act I hardly even noticed anymore. It's amazing what you'll get used to.

"Bitch, it's about time," she said with a laugh. "We've been short-handed since you quit, and Julie has been extra-ornery."

"I didn't quit. I just took time off to …"

"Solve Vance Fuller's murder," Shelby said.

"Wait, you knew?"

"Of course I knew. I ain't stupid. Why else would old man Fuller let you run around camp doing whatever the hell you want?"

Apparently I hadn't kept my investigation as close to my chest as I'd hoped. I prayed Shelby hadn't figured out I was the reason her mother skipped town.

"But hold on, are you saying you solved Vance's murder?" Shelby asked, nearly driving us off the mountain. "Holy shit. Who do you think—wait, don't tell me. Was it those devil worshippers who live in the caves near Fuller Farms?"

"What? No. There aren't any devil worshippers living in the caves near Fuller Farms."

"Oh, so you checked every cave?" Shelby asked, and when I didn't dignify this with a response, she said, "Fine, tell me who did it."

"Quinn Westlake."

"Who the hell is Quinn Westlake?"

"A rich kid from the Hamptons who was one of Vance's campers the summer he died.

"How'd you figure that out?" Shelby asked.

"Mayor Benson told me last night, but he doesn't want me to—"

"Hold on, back up. Why were you hanging out with Mayor Benson last night?"

"Sterling and I were sort of arrested for sneaking up to Doublehead Falls. I bumped into Mayor Benson at the police station."

"Doublehead Falls? At night? With Sterling?" Shelby asked, raising both eyebrows.

I blushed. "Yeah, I know, but that's all over now because he's a piece of shit."

"A 'no means yes' piece of shit?" Shelby asked.

"How'd you know?"

She shrugged. "The boys at camp have a reputation."

This information would have been useful on the first day of work, but whatever. "Anyway," I said, "Mayor Benson told me what happened. Vance abused Quinn at camp, and Quinn took his revenge one night and shot Vance full of arrows."

"Well, I'll be damned," Shelby said. "So, who all knew about this?"

"Chief Morrison, Rosalind Fuller, the Westlakes. Seems they all agreed sweeping it under the rug was their best option."

"Oh, shit, do you think my mom knew too?"

"I don't know, she, uh, never said—"

"Like, maybe that Quinn dude threatened her never to tell and … wait, you talked to my mom, didn't you?"

"Yeah," I admitted, seeing no reason to lie to Shelby now.

"Oh my God, Izzy. You're the reason she ran away. This Quinn dude probably threatened her, and when you came snooping around trying to get her to talk, she freaked out and—"

"Quinn Westlake is dead," I said.

"Wait, really?"

I nodded. "He was a screwed-up kid even before the stuff with Vance. Shot and killed a homeless man trespassing at his parents' home when he was, like, fourteen. He killed himself last year. Jumped off the roof of his New York penthouse. So even if your mom was scared of him, he can't hurt her now."

Shelby considered this before shaking her head.

"What?"

"I don't know," she said. "Folks around here have been speculating on what happened to Vance Fuller for as long as I've been alive, and this just ain't the most satisfying answer."

"Not satisfying? Why, because it wasn't cave-dwelling devil worshippers?"

"No, it's just—"

"It's the truth," I said. "And it's what Wellington Fuller wanted to know."

Shelby frowned. "It may be the truth, but it ain't what Wellington Fuller wants to know."

Wellington Fuller kept me waiting half an hour outside his office that morning, his ancient secretary asking questions, then making me repeat my answers half a dozen times over the buzz of her hearing aids. I was scared. Scared Wellington wouldn't accept what I told him. Scared I was making the wrong choice. All morning, I'd replayed my father's advice to do the next right thing, which eventually brought me back to the vow I'd made after solving Ricky Lee's murder in Bardo. A vow to keep sticking my freckled little nose where it didn't belong and be a pain in the ass to anyone hiding the truth. Mayor Benson was hiding the truth. So were the Westlakes and Rosalind Fuller. Sure, the truth was horrible, but telling the truth, I believed, was always the right thing. I hoped I wasn't about to be proven wrong.

When Mr. Fuller's door finally opened, he escorted Sterling out by the arm. Sterling's eyes were bloodshot from tears, and Mr. Fuller patted him on the back the way authority figures do sometimes when they realize their punishment perhaps went too far.

Sterling smiled weakly at me, but I didn't smile back, and once he was out the door, Mr. Fuller nodded for me to follow him into his office.

"Miss. Brown," he said as I sat down, "before we go any further, I need you to understand some things. If you were an ordinary employee here at Fuller Farms and trespassed on camp property after-hours, then lured a camper off to Doublehead Falls for all manner of debauchery, I would be terminating your employment today."

I shrugged in reply, figuring this went without saying.

"I'm of a right mind to fire you anyway because what you did last night goes against everything we teach here at Fuller Farms."

My God, this man was naive. If he spent five minutes around his campers, he'd know they didn't need me to lure them into debauchery. Shit. Maybe he wouldn't accept the truth about Vance. It certainly didn't harmonize with his rose-colored view of the world.

We sat there in silence for what felt like most of the summer, Mr. Fuller waiting expectantly for an apology I wasn't about to give. After a while, he finally said, "Okay, you had something to tell me?"

I nodded and cleared my throat. "I think I know who killed Vance."

"You think?" Wellington said, sitting up straighter.

"Yeah," I said. "I mean, I can't be one hundred percent sure, but it all makes sense."

"Tell me," Wellington said.

"Several people, including yourself, told me they thought Vance was likely abused as a young man."

"Yes, by Buster McClellan," Wellington said.

I shook my head. "I don't believe Buster abused Vance. It was probably a counselor, or perhaps—"

"Horse shit," Wellington Fuller barked, then apologized for swearing. "We screen our counselors. We thoroughly vet everyone who attends or works at this camp. There's no way—"

"And Buster McClellan worked here for nearly thirty years," I said. "You can't have it both ways."

Mr. Fuller didn't like this but told me to go on with a grunt and wave of his hand.

"And like you said the last time we spoke, abused children sometimes abuse others later in life, which could explain, though not justify, what Vance did at Chapel Hill."

"I don't want to hear any more about Chapel Hill," Wellington said, gritting his teeth. "I want to know who killed Vance."

"Quinn Westlake," I said, and old man Fuller's mouth fell open. "It was Quinn Westlake from Shinnecock Hills, New York. Quinn Westlake, who was Vance's camper that summer. Quinn Westlake, who, as you'll recall from your thorough vetting process, had a penchant for violence. Vance abused Quinn, and Quinn killed him in retaliation."

"How could you possibly know that Vance—"

"Quinn killed himself last year, and he left a note. It mentioned Vance. It mentioned Vance a lot."

Wellington Fuller sat silent, rubbing his temples and digesting everything I'd said. It can't be easy to learn something so terrible about your son. But he wanted the truth, and I gave it to him. And now he'd give me the fifty thousand dollars I needed to hire my mother a competent attorney.

"Izzy?"

"Yes, sir."

"I don't believe a damn word that just fell out of your pretty little mouth."

So much for my fifty grand.

"Tell me truly, did you come up with that little theory, or did someone put you up to it?"

"No one put me up to anything," I said, the crack in my voice not helping my case. "I'm sorry the truth doesn't paint the nicest picture of Vance, but it—"

"I hired you," Wellington boomed, his fist slamming hard on the desk, "to put Buster McClellan behind bars."

"You hired me to find out who killed your son," I yelled back.

"I know who killed my son. I needed you to prove it. But all that garbage you just came in here and spewed, and it was a load of garbage, was a waste of my time. Now get out of this office, and don't dare come back until you can prove Buster McClellan put those arrows in my boy."

CHAPTER THIRTY-FOUR

I left Wellington Fuller's office in a defeated stupor and stumbled down the hall to find Elton hunched over his computer, chatting with Zadie Carrick in London.

"Working hard," I said, and he quickly closed the chat box. "Elton, I don't care if you chat with Zadie. I know you have a life. You don't have to work on Vance's case 24/7."

"But your mother is depending on us," Elton said, "and I vowed not to rest until she was free."

"Okay, well, why don't you ask Zadie if her father will hire Mom a new attorney then."

Elton frowned. "That scenario feels unlikely, considering you destroyed his marriage."

"Destroyed his marriage, my ass. His cheating wife did that."

"True," Elton said, "but still, I would not anticipate his financial support. He does not even know Zadie and I remain in communication, and if he learned, he would be most displeased."

"Elton, I'm joking," I said, giving him an air hug because he didn't mind those as much. "I don't want you to ask Zadie's dad for money. But we'll have to think of another way to pay for Mom's attorney because I just told Wellington Fuller who killed his son, and he didn't believe me."

Elton sat up straight in his chair. "You solved Vance's murder?"

"Yeah. Well, no. I mean, sort of," I said, and Elton squinted at me. "Mayor Benson told me who killed Vance last night after I was arrested."

"Izzy, nothing you just said made any sense whatsoever. I fear one of us has suffered a stroke."

I laughed and gave Elton a consoling pat on the shoulder, then told him about my conversation with Mayor Benson the night before.

"Hiking to Doublehead Falls at night is extremely dangerous," Elton boomed, missing the point of my story entirely. "One misstep on a slippery rock and authorities would still be searching for your corpse."

"I appreciate your concern," I said, thankful I didn't share any more details of my night out with Sterling, "but what about the Mayor Benson part?"

"It is plausible," Elton said after some thought, "but also convenient."

"Convenient? How?"

"Mayor Benson has twice asked you to end your investigation," Elton reminded me.

"True," I said, "but nearly everyone we've spoken to about Vance told us to stop digging. Mayor Benson isn't special. In fact, his motivation actually makes sense. If Ashes starts making national headlines for murder and sexual abuse, Chase Foster and Bridget Bell would likely take their movie premiere someplace else."

"I have read the synopsis of *Cupid's Crossbow*," Elton said. "It seems unlikely two people with amnesia would even take vacations, much less on the same cruise ship."

I ignored this and said, "Besides, how many people told us they'd heard Vance abused a camper? Now we know it was Quinn Westlake. His suicide note proves it."

"His suicide note you have not read," Elton reminded me.

"Well, I can't exactly call up his parents and ask to see it, can I?"

"No, their number is unlisted," Elton said, missing my point again.

I cursed and let my forehead hit the table in frustration.

"You should have informed me of these developments before reporting to Mr. Fuller," Elton said.

"I considered it," I said, "but was afraid you'd talk me out of it."

Elton huffed, and I stood to pace the room, stopping to reach inside his backpack on the floor because he usually kept Skittles in the front pocket.

"Izzy," he bellowed, "do not tamper with my belongings."

I flinched and took a step back, raising my hands in apology. "Chill, dude. I was just looking for candy."

Elton snatched his backpack off the table and put it under the computer desk, but not before fishing inside and handing me a few Skittles. "I did not mean to yell."

"All good," I said. "I should've asked."

I'd been a shitty friend to Elton in London. Ignoring boundaries and constantly forgetting he had a life of his own and didn't exist solely to solve murders with me. He was always particular about his things, and I should have known better than to dig through his backpack without asking. Still, his reaction was over the top, even for Elton.

"So," I said, getting back to the case, "you don't believe Mayor Benson?"

"I did not say that," Elton said, "only that his story is convenient. The suspect is dead, and his motive for killing Vance is justifiable, if not provable. It is also not a story Wellington Fuller would want to hear. Perhaps, Mayor Benson told it to you in hopes you'd drop the case."

Dammit. Of course he did. Mayor Benson gave me the choice between taking a sweet deal or telling an old man something unspeakable about his dead son. There's no way he thought I was stupid enough to choose the latter, yet here we were.

"Or perhaps it's the truth," I said, hopefully.

"If so, you are done. You cannot force Wellington Fuller to accept an awful truth about his son. The question is, do you believe Quinn Westlake killed Vance Fuller?"

"Yes, no, I don't know," I said, throwing my hands up in frustration. "I thought I did, but now you've got me all confused. See, this is why I didn't want to talk to you before I saw Mr. Fuller."

Elton shrugged, and I asked, "So, if Mayor Benson lied to me, what is he trying to cover up?"

"Perhaps nothing," Elton said. "It is possible he does not know who killed Vance Fuller but does not want you to continue your investigation. As you noted earlier, as mayor of a resort town that relies heavily on tourism and founder of the Twilight Rock Film Festival, Mayor Benson has ample reason for not wanting Ashes in the Pines making national headlines for abuse and murder."

"So, back to square one?" I asked.

"Perhaps not," Elton said, spinning in his chair and pointing toward the computer screen. "Last night, Jasper Benson finally accepted the Facebook friend request I sent using a fake profile."

I leaned in and squinted at Elton's fake profile, which featured a woman with boobs the size of my head. I was afraid to ask where Elton found this photo.

"Elya Petrovich?" I asked, reading the woman's name.

"Affirmative. In Jasper's *Maxim* profile, he expressed an affection for Eastern European women."

"Well, great," I said, "now Jasper and Elya can play FarmVille together."

"I do not believe you grasp the significance of this development," Elton said. "We should visit Jasper again at Benson house."

"Why? Did Elya get him to confess to murdering Vance on Messenger?"

"No," Elton huffed. "He just …"

"Oh, God, you just want to see all his old video games again, don't you?"

"Do you have any better leads?" Elton snapped.

"One, I don't like your tone," I said, punching him on the arm, "and two, yes, I do have a better lead. The man who fixed my flat a couple of weeks ago told me Buster McClellan belonged to a Satanic doomsday cult, and they sacrificed Vance Fuller to the devil."

Elton's face lost all expression while he processed this, but when I laughed, he grunted at me and said, "Izzy, this is no time for jokes."

"I'm not joking," I said. "The man actually told me that, but I don't think Satanic doomsday cult is a rabbit hole we have time to go down."

But we did have time, and while Elton scoured the web for rumors about devil worshippers, I played Michael Jackson songs on my phone. The King of Pop had died earlier that day, and I remembered being in London when he announced a fifty-concert residency at the O2

Arena. Elton's mother promised she'd to take us to see him, but life had taken several wrong turns since then. Later that afternoon, as the shadows grew long, I texted with Tanner Cobb, who'd arrived safely in Athens and was currently on a six-hour ferry to Milos.

ME – Well, the ferry was your idea. Flights from Athens to Milos only take like half an hour.

TANNER – Nope. No way I'm getting on one of those little propellor planes. And I'm not saying a ferry should have a 3-star Michelin restaurant either, but I've had better gyros at the Circle K in Cowden.

"According to this anonymous post," Elton said after spending most of the afternoon on the *Ashes Tribune*'s message board, "devil worshippers mutilated a local farmer's prized goat in 1981."

"Seems legit," I said.

"There are also several anonymous posters who claim the Nike-wearing doomsday cult that moved to Ashes in 1999 are devil worshippers. However, most locals believe they are harmless."

"Okay, well this has been a productive after—"

"Izzy," Shelby said, bursting into our office and breathlessly holding a piece of paper for us to see. "My mom just called. She wants you to call her back."

"Here," Shelby said, shoving the paper into my hands. "I've got to get back to the kitchen. Julie is already pissed I took a phone call at work."

"Wait," I asked, "is your mom back in town?"

Shelby shook her head. "That's a pay phone number. Just call her quick. She said she'll wait for ten minutes. And come tell me what she says."

I dialed the number on speakerphone, and Tracie Ray answered on the first ring.

"Mrs. Ray," I said, "this is Izzy Brown. Shelby said—"

"Shut up and listen. You're in a shit-ton of trouble."

"Okay, then help me," I said.

"That's what I'm trying to do," she said, "but for the life of me, I don't know why. Maybe I'm just tired of the secrets."

"What secrets?" I asked.

"I'm trying to tell you," Tracie Ray barked, and I shut up. "You already know I worked at Fuller Farms the summer Vance died. Same job you and Shelby got—serving breakfast, lunch, and dinner to a bunch of trust fund assholes. I'd been there a week before I started sneaking off to fool around with Aubrey Masters."

"History doesn't repeat itself, but it rhymes," Elton said, and I shot him a bird.

"I liked Aubrey," Tracie said. "He was sweet. Shy. Different than the other boys at camp. They were all so spoiled and privileged. If you worked at Fuller Farms, they thought you were less than human. You could see it in their eyes. I mean, the girl campers were bitches, but at least they ignored us. The boys would pinch our asses when their counselors weren't around. Cop a feel when no one was looking. It was humiliating, but not enough to quit over. Not with what old man Fuller paid. Still, Aubrey said the right things, at least to me. He thought it was all disgusting, but how could one boy stand up to forty-nine others. He told me one night it was mostly bets and dares. Twenty bucks says you won't slap her ass. Twenty bucks says you won't grab her tit. The boys kept a notebook with running tabs on every bet, every dare, every dollar owed, and every dollar paid."

"The bastards," I said. "That's horrible."

"It ain't even the worst part," Tracie said. "Apparently, all the boys put a hundred bucks in a pot at the start of camp, and the twelfth graders picked a worker bee to be the Queen of the Mountain. Slay the Queen of the Mountain before camp was over and walk away with all the cash."

Tracie Ray kept talking, but her words grew muffled and distant as a cold sweat ran down my spine. My stomach soured, my breath caught in my throat, and for a moment, I wasn't sure if I was about to vomit, suffocate, or both. The mixture of panic and anger was unlike any emotion I'd ever felt in my life, and try as I might, I could not stop replaying what Sterling's giggling friend said the night I met him in the dining hall.

"Hey, don't I know you?"

"I don't think so."

"We all know you. You're the Queen of the Mountain."

Son. Of. A. Bitch.

CHAPTER THIRTY-FIVE

I'm not sure how much of Tracie Ray's story I missed while consumed with blinding rage, but after a moment, I shook my head back to the present and asked, "I'm sorry, Mrs. Rae, could you repeat that?"

"I said, Aubrey used to tell me he loved me," Tracie Ray said, "but he was full of shit. I let myself pretend, though, because we was poor as dirt, and his family owned half of Texas. Wouldn't it be nice, I thought. Now, I wasn't no prude, but both my older sisters got knocked up in tenth grade, and I swore to myself that wouldn't happen to me. I'd get through high school at least, and maybe even go to that junior college in Franklin and try to make a nurse." She laughed bitterly and added, "Just saying, I had bigger dreams than working at a damn cheese shop."

I nodded, wondering what my mother's dreams were before Axl and I came along. I doubt they involved a cheese shop either.

"So, I wasn't about to get pregnant," Tracie Ray continued, "even with some rich boy's baby. It wasn't easy. Aubrey and I messed around, but things never went too far. I won't say he was a gentleman, but he took no for an answer, which is more than I can say for some of the men I've been with. Of course, he sort of had to, considering I could have kicked his skinny little ass."

I laughed at this, and Tracie said, "But one night, he asked me to meet him in the archery shed during suppertime. We knew Buster McClellan left early on Fridays, and we'd have the place to ourselves. Aubrey brought a bottle of wine he stole from somewhere, and I drank one cup, then another. I knew what he was up to, but I went along with it because I also knew it wouldn't work. My grandpappy had been giving me moonshine for my cough since kindergarten, so I could handle two cups of wine without losing all inhibitions. But I'll be damned if I didn't wake up several hours later half-naked in the parking lot. That little bastard drugged me. He drugged me, and he …"

"Oh my God, I'm so sorry," I said as Tracie Ray burst into tears.

"I told Shelby to stay the hell away from Fuller Farms," Tracie said through muffled sobs. "Outright forbid her from working there, but she ain't never listened to me once in her life."

The line went silent for a while, and I thought Tracie had hung up, but then she said, "I came back the next morning with the German Luger my grandpappy brought back from the war. I came back intending to shoot Aubrey's balls clean off. But when I got there, cops was everywhere, roping off the place and questioning everybody."

"You started to tell Chief Morrison about something weird that happened to you that night," I said, my mind now churning as it shifted away from Sterling and back to the case, "but then you told him to forget it. Said it didn't have anything to do with Vance."

"I didn't tell him because he'd never believe me anyhow," Tracie Ray said, not hiding her bitterness. "It was the word of poor mountain trash against the crowned prince of Texas. I didn't know Aubrey killed Vance until later that morning."

Elton and I stared at each other with wide eyes, and I said, "Wait, what?"

"Jasper Benson told me. Caught me in the parking lot right after I'd quit. He was pale as a ghost, raving about how Aubrey had lost his mind. Seems Vance walked in on us the night before when I was passed out, and Aubrey killed him to keep him quiet."

My God. This was a lot to process.

"Why didn't you tell the police that?" I asked, but Tracie Ray didn't respond. "Mrs. Ray, did Aubrey threaten you not to tell? Did his family threaten you? Why didn't you—"

Tracie mumbled something that sounded like, "He sends me—"

"Who, Aubrey? What does Aubrey send you? Money? Mrs. Ray, please—"

"I've done said too much," Tracie Ray said. "You … you do what you gotta do. But leave Shelby out of it. You hear me?"

The line went dead, and I hung up and stared at Elton in disbelief. "Oh my God. Aubrey Masters killed Vance Fuller."

"Izzy, I owe you an apology," Elton said. "Finding dirt on your boyfriends' parents now appears to be a sound investigative method."

I stood and paced the room, overcome by a gumbo of emotions. "Aubrey Masters killed Vance Fuller," I repeated, starting to cry but not sure why. "Vance didn't abuse his campers. He caught one of them doing something horrendous, and it cost him his life. I've got to tell Mr. Fuller. He was right. He was right about Vance all this time. He—"

"Izzy," Elton said, in the tone he often used while raining on my parade, "we do not know any of that for a fact."

"Yes, we do. Tracie Ray told us so."

"And Tracie Ray was a person of interest in Vance Fuller's murder," Elton reminded me. "A person of interest who recently fled town."

"Because she's scared," I argued.

"Perhaps. But Wellington Fuller will be rightfully skeptical of information gleaned from someone who admittedly withheld facts from the police."

Elton was right. I understood why Tracie Ray never mentioned the assault to the police and assumed Aubrey Masters had kept her quiet about the murder all these years through bribes and fear. But Mr. Fuller would want more than my assumptions. We needed someone else to verify her claims. We needed Jasper Benson.

"Jasper knew Aubrey killed Vance," I said to Elton, "and he lied to the police. I'm guessing he could get into serious trouble for that."

"Making a false report to law enforcement is a criminal offense under North Carolina Criminal Law 14-225 and punishable by up to sixty days in jail. However, Jasper was a minor at the time, and the statute of limitations has long since passed." I shook my head and blinked at Elton, who added for clarification, "I have read a lot about North Carolina law of late."

"Okay," I said, thinking out loud, "we can't really threaten Jasper with any legal trouble, but maybe we can threaten him financially."

"How do you propose we do that?" Elton asked.

"Simple," I said, pacing the floor faster as my mind raced. "We tell him what we know. Aubrey Masters drugged and assaulted Tracie Ray. Vance Fuller caught him in the act, and Aubrey killed him. Then we tell Jasper that old man Fuller only wants the truth. He doesn't want the case reopened. Doesn't want justice. He just wants to know what happened to his son before he dies. All Jasper has to do is confirm Tracie Ray's story to Wellington Fuller, and this all goes away."

"And if Jasper declines?"

"We threaten to go public. Threaten to tell the newspapers, TV stations, and anyone who will listen that Jasper Benson knew who killed Vance Fuller but kept it from the police. A scandal like that will put Ashes in the Pines on the map in the worst way possible. It'll keep tourists away. It'll ruin their precious film festival. And who will Mayor Benson blame?"

"Apart from us?" Elton asked.

"Well, yeah, apart from us."

"Jasper."

"Exactly," I said, snapping my fingers. "He'll blame Jasper and cut off his funds, and I can't imagine anything scares that stoner more than the thought of going through life without access to his family's fortune."

"That might work," Elton said after some thought.

"Of course it will work," I said, hitting him on the arm.

"Are we going to see Jasper now?" he asked, standing up.

"It's too late," I said, checking the clock on the wall. "Benson House would be closed by the time we got there. We'll go in the morning. But in the meantime, I've got another mission for you."

I left our office and headed toward the dining hall to update Shelby on her mother, but then I saw Sterling in the commons, chipping golf balls with his asshole friends. I could just imagine him replaying for the drooling herd how close he came to slaying the Queen of the Mountain the night before, and it made me so angry I wanted to puke. I hadn't planned on confronting him yet, but there was no time like the present, so I changed direction and stomped his way, regretting I didn't have a hand grenade on me.

Sterling saw me coming and waved. I didn't break stride but extended both middle fingers in his direction. His smile faded, and he looked to be assessing his escape routes, but he was saved, momentarily, by my buzzing phone.

"What?" I barked at Axl, skipping the pleasantries.

"Mom's lawyer just called," he said, his voice shaky. "He wants her to plead guilty to voluntary manslaughter."

"What? Why?"

"He said the prosecution is willing to cut a deal. This way, Mom would only go to prison for a few years. If she goes to trial for murder, they might lock her away for life."

"Oh my God, this is insane. They don't even have a murder weapon. How the hell could they lock her up for life?"

"I don't know, Izzy, but I'm scared, and—"

"Did you tell him I'll have enough money to hire a real attorney soon?"

"No. I mean, you're not really that close to solving—"

I hung up on my brother and resisted the urge to throw my phone on the ground and stomp it into a million pieces. We couldn't call Mom in the detention center. She could only call us, and so far, she'd chosen not to. So, I called Dennis Strawberry instead.

"Strewberry & Strewberry, Attorneys at Law," a man answered.

"Dennis Strewberry, please."

"Speaking," Dennis said, and I cursed under my breath. If Mom's attorney was answering his own phone, things were even worse than I feared.

"Dennis, this is Izzy Brown. My mother did not kill Lenny Roach, so she's not pleading guilty to manslaughter, murder, jaywalking, or anything else."

"Izzy, I'm sorry, but I'm not at liberty to discuss your mother's case with—"

"I don't want to discuss anything with you, Dennis, especially not her case, because this time tomorrow she'll be represented by a competent attorney. You know, one whose diploma isn't written in crayon."

"Izzy, I'm not—"

"Manslaughter? Seriously? The police have no evidence. They don't even have a murder weapon, and you're just going to let my mother go to prison?"

"She could have stabbed him with an icicle," Dennis suggested.

"It's June, Dennis."

"Look, Izzy, your mother is in a tough spot here. Taking the prosecution's deal is likely her best chance to—"

"Her best chance is to hire anyone besides you," I snapped. "The prosecution has nothing. Otherwise, they wouldn't offer you a deal after a week. I don't even watch *Law & Order*, and I know that."

"You're not listening to me, Izzy," Dennis said again through gritted teeth. "Your mother is in a tough spot here, and I'm under a lot of pressure to ..."

Dennis thought better of finishing his sentence, but I wasn't letting him off the hook. "Pressure? Pressure from who, Dennis? Who is pressuring you to put my mother in prison?"

"I misspoke," Dennis said. "Your mother is—"

"It's Mayor Benson, isn't it? He thinks I'll call off my investigation if you hang prison time over my mother's head."

Dennis was dumb, but not dumb enough to admit to this. I knew, though. Mayor Benson was pulling the strings. It was the only thing that made sense.

"Listen to me, Dennis. I don't care who is pressuring you. I don't care if they've threatened to cut off your balls and feed them to you with syrup. Skip town. Hide in a cave if you have to. But don't you dare accept any plea deals because I've just solved Vance Fuller's murder, and as soon as Wellington's check clears, you're off the case."

"Izzy, I don't know if—"

Click.

CHAPTER THIRTY-SIX

I slept through my alarm on Saturday morning—a consequence, I suppose, of the 20mg Oxycontin pill I took at midnight, and the one I took four hours later after waking up with a blinding headache. I'd admittedly taken too many of late. Slipped into some bad habits I'd vowed not to repeat. But in my defense, it had been a rather stressful summer. However, Mom would be out of jail by the time I extinguished my small supply, and then I was done. Forever this time. At least, that's what I told myself.

"Girl, did you take all those pills at once?" Shelby asked on our drive to Fuller Farms.

"What? No. I told you I just take them when I have headaches."

Shelby grunted disapprovingly. I didn't think she really cared about the pills. She was just mad I didn't come downstairs when she honked, and she had to crawl out of her car to wake me up. "Well, me and your brother thought you were dead. I ain't never seen nobody sleep through two glasses of water to the face."

"I was tired," I said with a shrug.

"I'd be tired if I could get ten minutes alone with that Axl."

"Gross."

"I'd make him put those tight football pants on, and—"

"La la la la la," I said, sticking my fingers in my ears.

"Well, don't do nothing stupid, okay?" Shelby said after a while. I glanced at her, and she glared back. "I said, okay?"

I can't always help it, I thought. "Okay," I said, "I won't."

"Saturday greetings," Elton said as I walked into our office later that morning. He was still wearing his wingtips because none of the boutique sneaker shops in Ashes carried size sixteens, and the pair I'd ordered wouldn't be in for another week.

"It's a beautiful day to bust Jasper Benson's balls," I said. "You ready to go?"

"Affirmative."

Elton grabbed his backpack out from under the desk, and when he stepped aside, I saw Jasper's Facebook profile open on the computer monitor.

"Find anything interesting on his Facebook page?" I asked.

"His relationship status is complicated," Elton said.

"Join the club."

"And he has requested nude photographs from Elya Petrovich thirteen—"

The computer dinged.

"Fourteen times."

"You know, it's a shame he's not the killer. I'd really enjoy watching the police drag him kicking and screaming from Benson House."

"There is always hope," Elton said with a smile.

An hour later, we paid our forty bucks to tour Benson House and snuck into the west wing, searching for Jasper. It must have been cleaning day for that side of the mansion, because we had to dodge several dozen maids along our route, once by hiding in a storage room containing enough priceless art to start a North Carolina branch of the Louvre.

More Seattle grunge music blasted through the walls of Jasper's room, Alice in Chains this time, and we entered without knocking to find our person of interest passed out on a couch. A paused game of Super Mario Kart flickered on the television screen, pizza boxes and beer cans littered the floor, and the smell, well, it wasn't great.

"Mr. Benson, we require a word," Elton boomed, but Jasper Benson did not stir. He turned to me and said, "I believe he is deceased."

"He's not dead. He's hungover," I said, feeling slightly ashamed that I probably looked no different when Shelby and Axl tried to wake me up earlier. I leaned down and shook Jasper with both hands, but only elicited a grunt. "Wake up, dammit," I growled, pulling him toward me until he rolled off the couch with a thud.

"Fine, Dad, I'm getting up," Jasper mumbled, stumbling to his feet only to find Elton and me. "What the hell are you two doing back here?"

"We know Aubrey Masters killed Vance Fuller," I said.

I watched Jasper's face for any sign of emotion, but there was none. Of course, he'd only been awake six seconds and was understandably confused. I tried again.

"I said, we know Aubrey Masters killed Vance.

"Dude, I like, heard you," Jasper said, blinking himself awake. "Who told you that?"

"Tracie Ray."

There was a flash of something. Anger, maybe. But it disappeared as quickly as it came.

"Who's he?" Jasper asked.

"*She* worked in the kitchen at Fuller Farms. But you already know that."

"Yeah, okay, I think I like, remember a Tracie," Jasper said. "Local girl, maybe? Where is she these days?"

"In hiding," I said, "from Aubrey Masters." The last part was conjecture on my part, but it made the most sense.

"She's smart," Jasper said. "Aubrey would totally kill her if he knew she told."

Elton and I looked at each other with wide eyes. "So Aubrey really did kill Vance Fuller?" I asked. "Did you ... did you see him do it?"

Jasper glanced around the room, perhaps looking for more strangers who'd snuck in while he slept, then said in a low voice, "No. Just like, the aftermath or whatever. Aubrey ... Aubrey had a thing for Tracie, and she—"

"Was the Queen of the Mountain," I said.

Jasper's face twitched, then he forced a laugh and started to lie. "I, uh, I never heard anyone call her—"

"We know, Jasper. We know all about the little bets you assholes made. What was it, five grand to anyone who could slay the Queen of the Mountain? Now finish your story."

"Fine, what can I say?" Jasper said with a shrug. "We were stupid. It's like, the defining trait of teenage boys. But Aubrey liked Tracie. They were a couple, sort of, only Tracie wouldn't, you know, give it up."

Jasper again laughed like Butthead, but when I tried to kill him with a glare, he backed up a step.

"The problem was, Aubrey wasn't the sort of dude to take no for an answer. He had these pills, right, I guess he'd brought them from home or whatever, and one night when he and Tracie were down in the archery shed fooling around, he slipped one in her drink. Then Vance Fuller showed up at like, the worst possible time, and Aubrey killed him."

It was true. Everything Tracie Ray told us was true. Still, there was something I needed Jasper to clarify.

"If you didn't see the murder," I asked, "how did you find out Aubrey killed Vance?"

"He like, told us," Jasper said. "Aubrey needed an alibi, and Quinn and I weren't about to tell him no. Not after he showed us what he did to Vance. Not after he told us we'd be next if we didn't help him. Dude, you should have seen him that night. There wasn't like, any trace of sanity left in his eyes."

"And you told Tracie the next morning?" I asked.

"Aubrey made me," he said, fear still shaking his voice. "He wasn't sure if she remembered anything from the night before, but he like, couldn't risk it, you know? So he made me threaten her."

"Okay, I get that you were scared of Aubrey, but you could have told Chief Morrison the next day when he questioned you. The police would have protected you from him."

Jasper shook his head and laughed. "Like, you still don't get it, do you? Aubrey was fucking crazy, and his family—look, Quinn and I were rich, but the Masters family is like, Texas oil rich. The Masters are standing-invitation-to-the-White House rich. That family has so much power, I'd have totally fallen up the stairs the next day if I'd squealed."

While I processed this, Jasper stood and walked away. "Hang on, we've got more questions," I called after him.

"And I've got to piss," he called back, disappearing into his bathroom.

Elton wandered off, looking under couches and behind shelves of CDs for who knows what, and I sat on an old recliner, rubbing my temples and trying to decide my next move.

"Hey, come here," I called to Elton, who was now halfway under the waterbed. "What do you think?"

"He is lying," Elton said, dusting himself off from crawling around on the floor.

"About what?"

"Everything," Elton said, then continued exploring the room.

Elton's lie-detecting skills were notoriously poor, but I had to concede Jasper Benson wasn't the most credible witness. Still, he didn't need to convince a jury, just Wellington Fuller. The problem was we'd caught him hungover and half-asleep. Stone-sober, Jasper might balk at retelling a story that incriminated him in several ways.

"The greatest athlete of all time," Jasper said, stumbling out of the bathroom to see me admiring one of the Bo Jackson posters in the weird early-nineties museum that was his bedroom. "And *Wayne's World*," he said, pointing to the poster next to it. "Could there like, be a better film? Party on, Wayne. Party on, Garth."

"Who else knows about Aubrey?" I said, snapping Jasper back to the present and praying someone slightly more credible could corroborate his story.

"Me, Tracie, Aubrey, and now you and Elvis over there," Jasper said, pointing at Elton who was digging through a box of *Playboys*.

"But you're going to totally wish you didn't. Aubrey Masters is like, a psychopath or something, and if he got freaked out and left his family, he's more dangerous than ever. I bet he like, pushed Quinn off that building in New York, and he'll come for me one day too.

"And Tracie Ray?" I guessed.

"That one's trickier," Jasper said, "but now that she's talking, all bets are off."

"Why is she trickier?"

"She's got like, a daughter, right? Sixteen or seventeen? You do the math."

Holy hell, this was way too much to take in. I had to sit back down in the recliner.

"You'll like, never catch the dude," Jasper said. "But he might catch you."

"I … I don't want to catch him," I said, knowing it was a lie. I wanted to bury Aubrey Masters under the jail, but that's not what Wellington Fuller hired me to do. The killer might walk this time, and I had to wrap my head around that because, so far, all my efforts to lure him out of hiding had led to zilch. "But you've got to tell Wellington Fuller what happened to Vance."

"Dude, no way."

"He deserves the truth."

"Maybe, but I'm not giving it to him. I'm high as a kite and still know better than to cross Aubrey Masters."

"Then we're going public," I said. "We're going public with everything we know about you and Aubrey and the Ashes Police and Fuller Farms. I still get emails from reporters wanting to talk about The Red Lion. I suspect they'd be more than interested in a story about this crooked town too." This wasn't true. I hadn't heard from the tabloids since leaving London, but Jasper didn't need to know that. "I've spoken to your father. I wasn't sure if a man could be more disappointed in his own son. But if you bring a lot of nosy reporters to town and ruin his film festival, he just might cut you out of the Benson family all together. Bye-bye, trust fund."

"That," Jasper warned, looking more sober than I'd ever seen him, "would be like, a terrible mistake."

"Well, you know how to stop me from making it," I said, grabbing Elton and moving toward the door. "You've got twenty-four hours. Tell Wellington what happened, or I talk."

1992

Aubrey Masters liked the girl.

Sure, Tracie Ray wasn't exactly marriage material, but Aubrey was eighteen and not in the market for a wife. His mother had made it perfectly clear a young man of his social standing should be married between the ages of twenty-five and twenty-eight. Any sooner, and people would ask questions. Any later, people would ask different questions. Aubrey knew before he even considered getting down on one knee, he'd have to complete four years of undergrad at UT Austin, where his family name graced the facades of several buildings, then an MBA at whatever Ivy League school his parents could get him into. A year spent learning the ropes at Sterling Oil would follow, and only then should Aubrey Masters take a wife. A wife that ticked all the boxes. A wife who, unfortunately, would be nothing like Tracie Ray.

Tracie was funny.

Tracie was foul-mouthed.

Tracie was ... a little forward.

She'd kissed him first one lazy Saturday afternoon after Aubrey skipped dodgeball to hike with her through the woods behind Mud Lake. They'd stopped to sit on a fallen tree, and after the better part of eternity, Aubrey worked up the nerve to hold her hand. But when the conversation lulled, Aubrey couldn't summon the courage needed to do what he wanted to do more than anything in the world. So, Tracie took pity on the poor boy, grabbed him by the face, and put him out of his misery.

Before that summer, Aubrey didn't have much experience with girls. Okay, technically speaking, he had none. Since fifth grade, he'd attended St. George's, an all-boys preparatory school in Houston. Yes, there were rare occasions when the boys were permitted to socialize with pupils from their sister school, Blackburn Hall. But any time one of those girls in their plaid skirts and blue blazers looked Aubrey's way, he froze in panic.

Camp could be different, though. Camp could be a fresh start if Aubrey just tried harder. But five minutes into orientation, he knew it was no use. The girls at Fuller Farms were every bit as snobbish and intimidating as the ones from Blackburn Hall. Oh well, he thought, at least it would be over in eight weeks. But then, one fine morning—the prettiest worker bee in the dining hall asked Aubrey if he'd like scrambled eggs, and instead of saying, "Yes, I'd love some," he said, "Yes, I love you." Aubrey blushed, but the girl laughed and smiled, so he said it again the next day as a joke, and the next, and the next. A week later, they were together anytime she could slip away from the kitchen.

Sex wasn't on Aubrey's mind. Well, it was always on his mind the way it's always on the mind of any teenage boy. Still, he was under no delusions that sex was where his relationship with Tracie Ray was headed—partly because he was terrified of the prospect, but mostly because Tracie had told him point-blank it wasn't happening. Sure, they made out hot and heavy in the woods whenever possible. But both of Tracie's older sisters had gotten pregnant in high school, and that, she told him, wasn't going to be her.

The bet caught Aubrey off guard. He knew Tracie was that year's Queen of the Mountain. He'd voted for her the first night of camp before he ever met her. He knew the rules too. Everyone did. Slay the Queen of the Mountain and get a hundred bucks from every boy at camp. But the thing is, it was all a joke. A way for the older boys to talk big in front of the younger ones. So far as anyone knew, no one had slayed the Queen of the Mountain since 1973, and even that mythical conquest wouldn't hold up to strict historical scrutiny. The other boys knew Aubrey and Tracie were an item, and they teased him unmercifully. Still, no one was worried about losing their hundred dollars until Quinn Westlake pressed the issue.

"Okay, Aubrey, a cool grand says you won't slay the Queen of the Mountain."

Aubrey would have laughed it off had a crowd not gathered around. But under the suffocating crush of teenage peer pressure, there was only one acceptable answer to Quinn's challenge. "Bet."

Aubrey had saved face, but he knew he'd lose the bet. This wasn't the end of the world. He'd already taken hundreds off Quinn. Now he'd give it all back when camp was over and leave no worse off than when he arrived. But then, half the camp wanted in on the action, all taking Quinn's side, all anticipating an easy payday. This put tremendous financial pressure on Jasper Benson, the camp's unofficial bookmaker. Now, with rooting interest, Jasper made Aubrey's success his raison d'être.

It was Jasper who asked Aubrey nightly how far he'd made it with Tracie.

Jasper who offered unsolicited advice on everything from condoms to the Kama Sutra.

Jasper, who provided the bottle of wine, and said, "This will get her in the mood."

That night in Buster's shed, it all happened so fast. Aubrey had laid off the wine like Jasper told him to do. "Get too drunk, and you won't be able to perform," he'd teased. Tracie drank one cup, then another, then she was on the floor, shaking like a live wire. With tears already falling down his face, Aubrey sprinted from the archery shed, searching for help. My God, what if she died?

He'd never meant to hurt her.

He'd never meant for any of this to happen.

Aubrey Masters liked the girl.

CHAPTER THIRTY-SEVEN

"Dammit! What the hell?"

On our way back from Benson House, just as we passed the hand-painted city limits sign welcoming us to Ashes in the Pines, flashing blue lights filled my rearview mirror.

"You were exceeding the speed limit by seventeen miles per hour," Elton said, not taking his eyes off his phone.

"I was not."

"Evidence points to the contrary," Elton said.

"Then why didn't you tell me to slow down?"

"I requested you lower your speed no fewer than four times since leaving Benson House," Elton said, still typing away on his phone. "Each time, you ignored me and increased the volume on that Black Eyed Peas song you know I despise."

"Pull over, now!" The policeman said into his PA speaker, so I stopped arguing with Elton and steered the truck onto the gravel shoulder.

The black SUV behind me was unmarked, apart from blue lights on the grill, and the man who climbed out of the driver's seat wore street clothes. I didn't think about the pills in my purse until he was halfway to my door, and cold sweat dripped out of my every pore. Without being too obvious, I kicked my purse under my seat the best I could, drawing a confused glance from Elton.

"Good morning, ma'am," the officer said after I rolled down my window. He flashed his badge, then added, "I'm gonna need you to step out of the truck."

"What? No. You can't make me get out of the truck."

"I'm afraid I can," the cop said, sounding more bored than angry.

I wanted to argue, but my only knowledge of traffic stop law came from a Jay-Z song, and telling this cop I wasn't stepping out of shit and all my papers were legit seemed like a bad idea. So, I asked Elton, "Can he make me get out?"

"In *Pennsylvania v. Mimms*, the United States Supreme Court ruled that a police officer ordering a person out of a car following a traffic stop and conducting a pat-down to check for weapons did not violate the Fourth Amendment."

The cop pointed at Elton with an approving nod, and I said, "I don't have a weapon. Why would you think I have a weapon?"

"Ma'am," the cop said, raising his hands in peace, "I don't suspect you have a weapon, and you're not in trouble. However, Mayor Benson is in the SUV behind you, and he would like a word."

I sighed and climbed out of the truck, leaving Elton and the cop to discuss constitutional law.

"Hello, Izzy," Mayor Benson said as I opened the back door to the SUV. He patted the seat next to him and said, "Please, have a seat."

I climbed in and closed the door, wondering if this guy ever took off his stupid fleece vest or if he slept in it too.

"I understand you've learned our town's dirty little secret," Mayor Benson said. "It was Aubrey Masters who killed Vance Fuller."

I nodded, figuring Jasper must have called his dad the moment we left Benson House.

"Well done. You're a clever girl, Izzy Brown. I'm not surprised you cracked the case."

"No thanks to you," I snapped. "You told me Vance abused Quinn Westlake, and Quinn killed him in revenge."

Mayor Benson shrugged. "I'd hoped if you believed the truth about Vance was nightmarish and sickening, you'd spare Wellington the pain and take my deal."

"You were wrong," I said. "Mr. Fuller wants the truth, and I'm going to give it to him."

"But does he?" Mayor Benson asked. "Would Wellington still want the truth if he knew it would cost him everything? A girl was raped under his watch, and if you believe it only happened once, you're fooling yourself. There are things people don't talk about, Izzy. Secrets people are resigned to take to their graves. If you're quiet, if you listen, you can hear whispers of the horrors that have gone on at Fuller Farms for decades. But if you speak aloud the things no one will say, the floodgates will open, and a torrent of victims will drown Wellington Fuller. Drown him in an ocean of lawsuits."

Mayor Benson smiled and patted my knee while I considered this, and I recoiled at his touch, scooting closer to the door.

"Now, in full disclosure, I have my reasons for dissuading your little quest for the truth. My idiot son isn't completely innocent here. He witnessed a crime and lied to Chief Morrison. But in Jasper's defense, he was terrified of Aubrey Masters, and for good reason. His family wields more power than Caesar, and if you try to bring them down, they'll crush you like a bug."

"I'm not trying to bring anyone down," I said. "Mr. Fuller paid me to find out who killed his son, and that's what I did."

"And you think Wellington Fuller will accept any answer that isn't Buster McClellan?" Mayor Benson asked with a knowing smirk. "Look, I understand Floridians relish insanity, and London is a bustling metropolis, but Ashes is a sleepy mountain town. Folks retire here for peace and quiet. If they wanted to read about rape and murder, they'd have stayed in Atlanta. Now, as you know, the 25th annual Twilight Rock Film Festival is this October, and—

"Oh my God, I don't care about your stupid film festival."

"But I care," Mayor Benson yelled, his voice echoing in the SUV. "I care a great deal. You see, Izzy, I love the movies. Dreamt of Hollywood my entire life, and do you have any idea, any clue how long I've tried to get my foot in that door? 1984. I founded the Twilight Rock Film Festival in 1984, right after I retired as CEO of Benson Properties. Do you know who came that first year? No one. Not a soul, and first prize went to some freaks from Brevard College who made a short film about vampires with a camcorder." Mayor Benson shook his head at the memory and said, "So, I tried to take a shortcut. Jasper was always a creative kid. I thought maybe he was my ticket. I bribed his way into film school and financed his directorial debut—money I might as well have set on fire."

"That one critic liked *Ghost of Judas*," I said, remembering its 7 percent rating on Rotten Tomatoes.

"Because I paid him five thousand dollars," Mayor Benson said, looking like he wanted to punch me for reminding him. "But I kept at it with the film festival," he continued. "I increased the prize money, which helped, and I paid some hefty appearance fees, which helped even more. After a few years, we started getting C-listers, then a B-lister or two, and now, after twenty-five years, two genuine bona fide Hollywood stars are coming to little Ashes in the Pines to premiere their latest film. And believe me, there is no way in hell I'm going to let you screw that up for me. I've already provided you with one off-ramp from your stupid case. Tripp Aston would have had your mother out of jail in minutes, and with your college taken care of, your future never looked brighter. But no, you kept at it, and in a way, I respect you for it. Your virtue remains unblemished. Well, apart from that pill business back in Florida," he added with a wink. "But now I have a new offer, and unfortunately for you, this one isn't so sweet. Drop the case, leave Ashes forever, and your mama pleads guilty to involuntary manslaughter. She'll have to serve two years, but that's not so bad considering the alternative. Because if you tell Wellington Fuller what you've learned, if you go public with any of this like you just threatened my son you'd do, I can guarantee we'll find a bloody knife with your mother's fingerprints all over it. That's life in prison unless the prosecutors can prove it was premeditated. Then your mother will be choosing her last meal. I'll need your decision by the end of the day. Now get out of my fucking car."

"Hold on, you solved the case?" Axl asked. "That's awesome."

Elton and I were back in my room at the Ashes Inn because I couldn't return to Fuller Farms. Not yet. There was too much to think about.

"Yeah, awesome," I said without enthusiasm.

"What is wrong with you?" Axl asked. "Tell the old man what he wanted to know, get your money, and we can hire Mom a real attorney."

"It's not that simple," I said, shaking my head.

"Of course it is. He hired you to—"

"Hey, I thought I heard you come in," Dad said, walking in from next door.

Elton stood and extended his hand. "Elton Jones-Davies. My mother is British, and the British are fond of double-barreled surnames."

"Rodney Brown," Dad said, looking up at Elton. "I'm Izzy's father."

Elton jumped back like Dad had just announced he had swine flu.

"You abandoned Izzy and Axl when they were three years old."

"Not my finest moment," Dad conceded.

"Izzy is my best friend, and I would never abandon her. I will protect her at all costs."

"I don't doubt it, Elton," my dad said with a smile. "I'm thankful Izzy has friends like you."

Elton remained skeptical. "I still do not like you."

"Understood," Dad said, nodding in acceptance. "I'll have to earn your trust, just like I'll have to earn Izzy and Axl's. But I'm trying, Elton, I really am." Dad then turned to me and asked, "How goes the murder solving?"

"The murder is solved," I said.

"But she's not going to tell the old man," Axl interrupted.

"Wait, why not?" Dad asked.

"Because she always screws things up," Axl snapped, and I was on him in an instant, clawing at his face and pulling out his hair. He fought back like a man being mauled by a tiger, but Dad and Elton still had to pull me off, and once they did, it took us all a moment to catch our breath.

"I can't tell him," I said, once I'd composed myself, "because Mom will go to prison for murder."

"Izzy, that doesn't make any sense," Dad said.

"It will," I said, then told them the whole sordid story. About Quinn, Aubrey, and Jasper. About the Queen of the Mountain and summers full of disgusting wagers. About Vance catching his camper in the act. About the murder, the cover-up, and the perpetrator sailing away to hide on his mega-yacht.

"Holy hell, Izzy," Dad said when I finished. "What sort of camp are you working at?"

"A miserable one," Elton replied, though I suspect he was referring to the outdoors in general.

"I still don't see what any of that has to do with Mom," Axl said, still rubbing his face where I'd clawed him.

"Mayor Benson is making it about Mom," I said. "He wants this all swept under the rug, and he's already tried to bribe me to drop the case."

"Bribe you with what?" Axl asked.

I closed my eyes and said, "One of the top attorneys in North Carolina offered to take Mom's case and pay my way through college."

"And you didn't take it?" Axl yelled. "Oh my God, Izzy, what the hell is wrong with you?"

"Some of us have principles," I shouted back.

"Principles? You've been in juvie," Axl screamed. "Where's my phone? I'm calling the mayor right now and taking the stupid deal for you."

"It's too late," I said, hanging my head. "He changed the deal. The mayor pulled us over this morning and gave me an ultimatum. I can drop the case, leave town, and Mom pleads guilty to involuntary manslaughter. Or, I can tell Wellington the truth, hope he pays me fifty grand for information he doesn't want to hear, and be guaranteed the Ashes PD will find some damning evidence against Mom, including a murder weapon with her fingerprints on it."

The four of us were quiet for a long time, and I finally asked, "So, what should I do?"

"You should have fucking asked us that weeks ago, before—"

"Son," Dad said, raising a hand to tell my brother to chill. Then he turned to me and said, "Izzy, I don't think you've got a choice. Take the deal, we'll get out of town tonight, and—"

"And just let Mom go to prison?"

Dad shrugged. "I don't see an alternative."

"If Mr. Fuller pays me, we could still hire a good attorney and—"

"And they wouldn't stand a chance against a town this corrupt."

He was right. As much as I wanted to tell Mr. Fuller the truth, expose Aubrey Masters, and shine a light on the cesspool that was Ashes in the Pines, I couldn't risk Mom going away for life ... or worse.

"Come on," I said to Elton. "Let's go tell Mr. Fuller we're quitting the case.

CHAPTER THIRTY-EIGHT

I let Elton drive us back to Fuller Farms because I was too upset to get behind the wheel. Mom was going to prison. She was going to prison for at least two years, and it was all my fault. She'd miss our graduations. She'd miss Axl's football games. She'd miss so much. I wondered then if Mayor Benson was somehow behind Lenny's death. If he knew I was getting close to the truth and set up a scenario where he could extort me. Or maybe Lenny was just murdered because he was a drug dealer, and Mayor Benson took advantage of the situation.

"Hey, what's that shaving thing you told me about where the simplest answer is usually correct."

"Shaving thing," Elton said, squinting at me, then his face brightened. "You mean Occam's Razor."

"That's it," I said, wondering what ol' Occam would think about this, not that it mattered much in the end. The mayor was already sending my mother to prison. I couldn't fathom what he'd do if he thought I was snooping around trying to pin Lenny Roach's death on him.

"Hey, take the next right," I said to Elton about halfway to Fuller Farms.

"That is not the way to camp."

"Shortcut," I said.

"Izzy, even without consulting a map, I know this route will take us significantly longer to—"

"I'm joking, you donkey. I want to talk to Buster before I leave town."

Elton turned down Sour Mash Road but wasn't happy about it, and after driving another mile, he admitted, "I would rather not have a shotgun aimed at my face this afternoon."

"Don't worry," I said. "Buster and I are on much better terms these days. Now he only aims his gun at me when I accuse him of heinous crimes."

"Then it is a good thing you are not prone to accuse people of heinous crimes," Elton said, and when I glanced over at him, he cracked a smile.

We turned down Buster's driveway, past his sundry no-trespassing signs, including some new ones featuring graphic cartoon depictions of what would happen to those who didn't turn around. As usual, Buster sat waiting past the "Last chance, morons" sign, but this time he wasn't toting a shotgun, just a coffee thermos.

"Hey, no gun. Does this mean we're friends?" I asked as Elton and I climbed out of the truck.

"I suppose so," Buster said, "but don't expect a Christmas card."

"Well, you'll be happy to know this is the last time I'll ever show up uninvited again. We're leaving Ashes tomorrow."

Buster nodded like he knew we'd never make it here long.

"But I had to come to see you first because I know who killed Vance."

Nearly every human emotion flashed across Buster's face before settling on a mixture of sorrow and relief. I thought he was about to cry, but instead, he asked, "Would y'all mind coming to the house? I want to hear this, but I need to be sitting down."

We rode with Buster in his truck the rest of the way down the never-ending driveway to his home, which was even further off Sour Mash Road than I'd have thought possible.

"Don't you get scared living all the way out here?"

"Having neighbors is a lot scarier," Buster said.

Soon, we started seeing the strangest sculptures out in the woods. Giant, colorful metal figures that looked half-insect, half-human.

"Some of my handiwork," Buster said before I could ask. "Sarah dreams up the designs, and I do all the welding."

"Who is Sarah?" I asked.

"My girlfriend," Buster said, "but don't tell her I called her that. She prefers cosmic consort."

Elton and I exchanged a glance, and Buster said, "There she is now." We turned to see a blonde woman doing yoga in the woods without a stitch of clothes apart from a pair of neon green Nikes. Elton blushed and covered his eyes, and I turned to Buster and asked, "Uh, did she happen to move to Ashes in 1999?"

"Yup," Buster said. "Missed her spaceship that year, but it's due again tonight." Then he honked his horn, and the naked woman waved at us before returning to Lotus position.

We parked outside Buster's cabin, which was somehow rustic and futuristic all at once. I'm talking a thatched roof with solar panels and log walls with LED lighting. It was like a Mad Lib you could live in.

"Did you build this place?" I asked.

"All by myself," Buster said. "Started it fifty years ago with a hammer and a saw. I'd like to say it's finished, but Sarah keeps pestering me to add a yoga studio."

Inside, the cabin was spartan, with handmade furniture, piles of books, an old turntable, and stacks of Grateful Dead albums. It looked just like I'd imagined Buster's cabin would look, apart from the kitchen, which even Martha Stewart would envy.

"Sarah likes to bake," Buster explained when he saw me gawking at his kitchen. "She wasn't so fond of running to the outhouse in the middle of winter either, so I ran us some indoor plumbing too." He thought for a moment and said, "I won't lie. I don't miss that outhouse much."

The three of us sat around the kitchen table I suspect Buster built with his bare hands, and our host took a deep breath and said, "Okay, tell me about Vance."

"I will, but you have to promise me you'll never tell anyone."

"What? Why?"

"Just promise, Buster."

He didn't like this but promised anyway, and I told him everything, first about Vance walking in on Aubrey and Tracie Ray, then about Mayor Benson blackmailing me into dropping my investigation and leaving town.

"And where is the Masters boy now?" Buster asked, wiping tears from both his cheeks.

I shrugged. "His boat is in Greece, but we never had any luck finding him. With his money, he could be anywhere."

We sat in silence for a long while, broken only occasionally by Buster's defeated sighs. "Dammit, Vance," he finally said, shaking his head. "Why didn't he run back to camp shouting to the rooftops what he saw happening in that shed? Why'd he have to try and be a hero? I mean, I know I raised him to be brave, but …"

"Raised him?" I asked.

"Taught him, raised him, you know what I …" Buster paused and smiled sadly. "Oh hell, what's it matter now. Y'all give me one second."

He returned with an ancient shoebox full of letters and photographs and set it on the table. "That … is Rosalind and me," he said, pulling out a black and white snapshot of a young couple sitting by a fireplace. "We took it right over there," he added, pointing across the room. "And here's the three of us right after Vance was born."

"You … you were Vance's father?" I asked in disbelief.

Buster shrugged. "Most likely. Wellington wasn't around much those days. I was. I guess nowadays we could have tested his DNA or whatnot, but one look at the boy's nose and you'd know he was mine."

"Did Wellington know?"

"About Rosalind and me? No, he'd have fired me on the spot, even though their marriage was a sham. He didn't care about Rosalind, you see, only appearances. He never sent her flowers. Never wrote her love letters. She was his wife, but she was my soulmate. She was—"

"She was your alibi," I guessed. "She was here the night Vance died, wasn't she?"

Buster bit his lip and nodded. "She was. She spent a night or two out here every week from 1963 until the day Vance died. I tried to get her to leave Wellington once, just a few years after Vance was born. Bought a ring and everything, but she couldn't do it. Couldn't leave all that money and security, I reckon."

"What about Vance? Did he know you were his father?"

"I never saw the boy much. Rosalind brought him out here some when he was little, but as he grew, she was afraid he'd start asking questions. But then he started getting bullied at camp, and Rosalind asked if he could sleep in my shed. That's when we got close. We'd sit up all night, talking about life, the sort of father-son talks Wellington was too busy to have with the boy. Those summer nights were the happiest of my life, but right before Vance left for Chapel Hill, I ruined everything. I told him about his mama and me. Told him who I really was. The boy lost it. Called me a liar. Called me every name in the book. I didn't talk to him again for ten years. Not until the day Tripp Aston nearly killed him and he wound up in my shed sipping moonshine. I tried to mend fences that morning, but Vance wasn't having it. He screamed at me again. Told me he hated every minute he'd ever spent with me. They found him dead the next morning."

Buster took a moment to wipe his eyes, but his lips kept quivering. "After the boy died, Rosalind only came back here once to tell me it was over. She said she thought God had punished her for cheating on her husband, but I suppose seeing me was just too painful. I only saw her a dozen times around town after that, but we never spoke. I didn't even go to her funeral last year. Didn't want to cause a scene."

Buster wept silently, and I stood and patted him on the back. "We'll go," I said. "I'm sorry we bothered you."

"First," Buster said, wiping his tears with his sleeve and smiling, "I've got to drive you back to your truck. There's booby traps along the way, and I don't want y'all losing a leg. And second, you gave this old man some closure. I only wish you'd found that Masters boy, but I guess I'll have to let God and the devil sort him out. So don't you worry your little red head. Y'all didn't bother me none."

"Well, in that case," I said as the three of us walked out the cabin door, "I'll come to visit every time I'm in Ashes."

"You can come, but I won't be here," Buster said with a wink. "Sarah said if I built her an indoor toilet, she'd book me a seat on her spaceship. If all goes to plan, I'm leaving this planet tonight."

Elton opened his mouth to argue, but I stopped him with an elbow to the ribs and said, "Well, in that case, happy trails, Buster."

CHAPTER THIRTY-NINE

An hour later, Elton and I were back in our office at Fuller Farms, him typing on the computer, me packing all our notes, photographs, and police reports into a box to give Mr. Fuller. In lieu of the murderer's identity, it was the best I could offer.

"You know," I said to Elton, "I think I prefer the cases where the bad guy goes to jail in the end."

Elton considered this with a grunt.

"Or at least drowns in the Thames," I added.

"This one lacks closure," Elton agreed, "but at least no one has held you at gunpoint."

"Well, Buster did, but we're buddies now, so I guess that doesn't count."

"By the way," Elton said. "I completed the important task you assigned me yesterday." He pulled a red spiral-bound notebook from his backpack and presented it to me like a priceless artifact. "It was under a twelfth-grade camper's mattress, as you predicted."

"Stupid boys hide everything under their mattress," I said, taking the notebook from Elton and opening it, and vomit, there it was. A ledger of every wager made by every boy camper at Fuller Farms that summer. I skimmed them until I found my name, well, my honorific, Queen of the Mountain. The son of a bitch. Not only would Sterling take home five grand if he could "Do Izzy" as the notebook so eloquently put it, but he'd made at least ten side bets with other boys, one for a thousand dollars. I almost regretted not being able to get in on the action earlier in the summer. I could have made a small fortune betting against him.

"And did you find the contact list I asked for?" I asked Elton.

"Affirmative."

"Sweet. Did you have to hack into the camp network or something?"

"No. I asked Wellington's secretary for a copy, and she handed it to me without question."

"I suppose that works too," I said with a laugh. "Okay, I'm going to break the news to Mr. Fuller. Will you make a few copies of this page for me?"

"How many do you consider a few?" Elton asked.

"Two hundred should do," I said. "And while you're at it, get that email ready to send. We won't have much time when the shit hits the fan.

Mr. Fuller buzzed me back to his office, but when I stepped inside, he didn't look up from his newspaper. So I stood there in purgatory, rocking on my heels and clearing my throat just to hear something besides the ticking clock on the wall. Wellington flipped over his paper, read some more, then folded it neatly and set it on his desk before saying, "Good afternoon, Miss Brown. To what do I owe the pleasure?"

"Mr. Fuller, this will be my last day at Fuller Farms."

"Oh, so you've solved Vance's murder?" Wellington asked, now examining a marble paperweight on his desk and acting like nothing in the world could interest him less than our current conversation.

"No, I'm afraid not," I said, eliciting zero reaction from the old man.

"Well, no worries, you still have time. Keep me updated," Wellington said, shuffling papers on his desk.

"No, Mr. Fuller, I don't have time. This is my last day at Fuller Farms. My brother and I are leaving tomorrow. We're going back to Nebraska to live with my father."

"Hmm," Wellington said without comment.

"But," I continued because the weird gaps in this conversation were killing me, and I had to try filling them with words, "even if I had more time, I don't believe I'd ever solve the case."

"Is that so?" Mr. Fuller said, finally looking up at me.

I nodded without conviction and felt like shit. I had solved the murder. I had the closure this man had sought for years. But I couldn't give it to him. "There's just so little evidence," I lied, "and so few suspects, and so much time has passed since the murder. Maybe the police, with their resources, could have solved the case back when it was fresh, but this one is beyond my abilities."

"Izzy, I must say, this is quite a change of tune from the last time we spoke when you were adamant Vance abused a boy who killed him in return."

"I ... I jumped the gun there. It was my first real lead, and I wanted it to be true. I wanted it to be true because I needed the reward money to hire my mom a better attorney."

Wellington shook his head. "I can't say I'm not disappointed."

Then don't hire a teenager to solve a murder next time, I thought. "I'm sorry," I said.

"Still, if you can't solve the case, you can't solve the case," Wellington said. "But before you leave, would you mind telling me where you and Mr. Jones-Davies went this morning?"

"We uh ... we went to Benson House," I said.

"Sightseeing?" Mr. Fuller asked. "I hear their hydrangeas are in bloom."

I forced a laugh. "No, we spoke with Jasper Benson. I wanted to talk to him one last time before I left. You know, leave no stone unturned."

Wellington nodded. "And Jasper, he was of no help?"

"No," I lied. "He wasn't."

"And from Benson House, you went ..."

"We stopped by the Ashes Inn, where I'm staying now, and then we came back here."

"Back here. To Fuller Farms?" Wellington asked, and I nodded. "Not to Buster McClellan's cabin on Sour Mash Road."

Dammit to hell.

"Izzy, I've grown concerned of late that you're taking my money but perhaps don't have my best interests at heart. So, I had a member of our grounds crew follow you today, and now my fears are realized."

"What? Because I went to tell Buster bye?"

"Tell him bye? You wanted to bid farewell to the man who murdered my son?"

"My God, you're not going to give that up, are you?" I snapped. "Buster McClellan didn't murder your son."

"Sure, I should just take your word for it. You've been so honest with me about everything else. I know folks around town think I've gone crazy, and perhaps they're right. In my right mind, I'd have never put so much faith in a skinny little pill popper like you."

My face flushed so hot I feared I'd burst into flames, but I held my tongue … for the moment.

"It makes sense you'd have fallen under Buster's spell. You two are peas in a pod. Just a couple of sinful devils. Two shameless, wicked, evil—"

"You knew, didn't you?"

"Knew what?" Wellington demanded.

I shook my head and laughed. "My God, of course. You knew about Buster and Rosalind. What, did you find her old love letters after she died?"

"I don't know the first thing you're talking about."

"Oh, I think you do. You may not know how long it went on— since the summer of 1963 if you're curious—but you figured it out, and you wanted to make Buster pay. So you hired me, not to find Vance's killer, but to find dirt on Buster McClellan. And to think, you just sat there calling me wicked and evil when you're trying to send an innocent man to prison for screwing your wife."

Wellington Fuller was on his feet and shouting. "I will not sit here and let you soil my late wife's good name. Either you get out of this office or—"

"Shut up, Wellington. I'm leaving."

I turned to leave, but Mr. Fuller called out from behind, "Say one word about Buster and Rosalind, and every college in the country gets a copy of the drug tests you failed this summer. I don't fish. I don't play golf. I hardly know what to do with myself most days. But ruining your sad little life would be a hobby I could really lose myself in."

At that moment, I could have chosen to drop the mother of all bombs on Wellington Fuller. I could have told him Buster McClellan was Vance's father. But in the end, I didn't feel like that secret was mine to reveal. It took some Olympic-level tongue-biting, though, because I've never wanted to make a grown man cry as much as I did that asshole. So I gave a middle finger salute instead and left him with, "Whatever."

CHAPTER FORTY

"Go pack your stuff," I said to Elton when I returned to our office. "You're coming with us. When we get to Nebraska, I'll call your mom and apologize, and she can fly you home from there, assuming Nebraska has an airport."

These travel plans were not as spur of the moment as they seemed. There was no way in hell I was about to leave Elton at that cesspool of a summer camp without me to protect him. Still, I feared when I told him he was leaving Fuller Farms without permission, he'd fight me tooth and nail. I was mistaken.

"Eppley Airfield in Omaha offers direct flights to over twenty destinations, including New York City's LaGuardia Airport," Elton said, because most of my jokes were still lost on him. Then he pointed at his suitcase and backpack in the corner and added, "And I am several steps ahead of you."

"Wait, so you're okay going AWOL?"

"Mother sent me here to be near you. If you are leaving, she would not expect me to stay." He then handed me the stack of copies I'd asked for. "Shall I send the email you requested?"

I checked the clock on the wall. "Give me ten minutes, then fire away."

"Aye, aye," Elton said with a salute before asking, "Where are you going?"

"To bum us a ride back to Ashes," I said. "Then blow this place to hell."

I found Shelby behind the dining hall, sitting on a bucket and smoking a cigarette while the campers dined inside.

"Hey, bitch," she said with a grin.

I waved back and took a seat on the bucket next to her. If ever there was a day to bum a cigarette and start smoking, this was it, but instead, I asked for one last ride back to Ashes.

"One last ride," she said, stubbing her Marlboro against the wall. "Does that mean you solved the murder?"

I shook my head. "Turns out, that's not exactly what Mr. Fuller hired me to do. Buster McClellan was sleeping with his wife for years, and—"

"Hold up. Old lady Fuller was a ho?" Shelby asked, laughter filling her eyes.

"No, she was a one-woman man," I said. "It's just the one man wasn't her husband. Mr. Fuller got wise to it after she died and wanted revenge. Wanted me to somehow pin Vance's murder on Buster, but I wouldn't do it."

"Good for you," Shelby said, then asked, "So, if not Buster, who killed Vance?"

I wanted to tell her the truth. She deserved it. Deserved to know that Aubrey Masters, the same boy who killed Vance Fuller, also hurt her mother. That Aubrey Masters, at least according to Jasper Benson, might even be her father. But it wasn't my place. Tracie Ray told me to keep her daughter out of this, and I promised I would. When Shelby drove me home the night before, I lied and said her mom didn't know who killed Vance, but she got scared when I showed up and began snooping around town. Afraid the killer might return and go after anyone who might have seen something at camp that night before they could speak to me.

"I … I don't know who killed Vance," I lied.

Shelby accepted this with a nod, then said, "Well, I do. It was those cave-dwelling devil worshippers." We both laughed, then she turned to me with tears welling in her eyes and asked, "When will my mom come home?"

"When she feels safe," I said, knowing that day might never come so long as Aubrey Masters walked the earth.

Shelby hung her head, and I put a hand on her shoulder. "I'm so sorry," I said. "I'm sorry I came here and kicked a hornet's nest and left." She smiled at me through tears, and I added, "But, I've got something that might cheer you up."

The campers were finishing their pecan pie when Shelby and I entered the dining hall. I like to think a hush fell over the room when they saw me. That the boys, sensing the destruction to come, had all choked on their dessert. But no one noticed me much besides Sterling, who stood and walked our way.

"Just have people take one and pass the rest down the table," I said, handing Shelby the stack of copies Elton made me.

"Hey, I've missed you," Sterling said, trying to give me a side hug that I squirmed away from so fast even Elton would be impressed. His smile dropped, and he said, "Look, Izzy, I'm sorry about the other night, but—"

Ignoring Sterling's bullshit, I watched as the stacks of paper reached the ends of the tables, marveling as the campers' faces morphed into a kaleidoscope of confusion, fear, and rage.

"May I have your attention," I said, putting a hand on Sterling's shoulder so he wouldn't walk away. The room turned to me expectantly, and I continued, "My name is Izzy Brown, and I've had the pleasure of washing your dishes for several weeks this summer. But not only that, I've also had the honor of serving as this year's Queen of the Mountain."

The girls still looked confused, but several guys exchanged wide-eyed glances, and one stood and quickly left the room. Sterling tried walking away, but I squeezed his shoulder and snarled, "Don't even think about it."

"For those unfamiliar," I continued, turning to face the girls, "Queen of the Mountain is an honor bestowed annually on a camp employee by your male peers here. During the eight weeks of camp, if any of them were fortunate enough to, as the sheet of paper in your hands so eloquently puts it, do me, they'd receive five thousand dollars." Gasps and murmurs filled the room, but I silenced them with a raised palm. "Sterling here tried very hard to earn that reward, getting downright rapey a couple nights ago at Doublehead Falls, but, alas, erectile dysfunction hits some men sooner than others."

Two more boys bolted for the exit as I continued. "But ladies, if you're feeling left out, don't despair, because several of you were also the subject of wagers this summer. Anna Grace Southerland?" I asked, scanning the room for a girl who wasn't about to identify herself. "When Marcus Albright, quote unquote, accidentally ran palm-first into your left boob two weeks ago, he earned a cool two hundred dollars. And Mary Kate Braswell, that incidental ass slap you received from Tyler Yates last week cost several boys twenty bucks each."

By now, the room was abuzz, and I had to shout to be heard over the fray. "Please, don't worry if you lose your sheet," I yelled, raising my copy of the summer's bets. "A copy was just emailed to your parents for their files. I suspect many of them will be in touch with you soon. Thank you all again for a memorable summer."

I turned to leave as the room devolved into chaos, girls screaming at boys with violent intent, boys running and cowering in fear. But Sterling, perhaps hoping I'd call his mom and tell her this was all a joke, stayed and gave it one last try with his bullshit. "Listen, Izzy, I know how bad this looks, but you've got to believe me. I never cared about the bet. I really liked you. I swear. Can't you forgive me?"

"Yeah, no," I said, walking past him with no intention of looking back. But then I heard a grunt and turned to see the aftermath of Shelby kneeing Sterling in the balls. I was thankful then that my last and lasting image of Sterling Masters was of him hunched over a table, moaning in indescribable pain.

"Izzy, I can't thank you enough. That was literally the best five minutes of my life," Shelby said between fits of laughter as we hurried across the commons. The shit had hit the fan, and we needed to get Elton and put as many miles between us and Fuller Farms as we could.

"Well, if I couldn't catch the killer, ruining the lives of a bunch of rich pricks is a nice consolation prize."

Elton was hunched over his phone when we entered the office, and without looking up, he asked, "Have you spoken to Tanner Cobb?"

"What?" No," I said, checking my phone and seeing several missed calls from Tanner and half a dozen texts. I called him back while telling Elton to grab his things.

"Pippi," Tanner said, answering after half a ring, "answer your damn phone."

"Sorry," I said, "I was out causing mischief. What time is it over there?"

"Like three in the damn morning," Tanner said. "Did Stretch fill you in?"

"No, what's happening?"

"I spoke to Lucas, the senior master on Aubrey's yacht. He came to town for groceries, and I pretended to bump into him. Two Americans far from home, we decided to go for a drink. I shit you not, that dude must spend his days taking tequila intravenously because it took a dozen rounds before he loosened up enough to talk. But once he started talking, he wouldn't stop, and do you know what he told me?"

"No, Tanner, what?"

"Aubrey Masters ain't here."

"Wait, what?"

"He ain't here, Pippi. Never was. Lucas hasn't seen him since the family last took the yacht out in 2007."

"What the hell?"

"Lucas suspects the Masters family might be in some tax trouble. A family attorney had him bring the yacht here last April and told him to wait for further instructions. Apparently, they're paying him a small fortune to just sit on that giant boat and eat gyros all day, so Lucas isn't complaining."

"Okay, but if Aubrey Masters isn't in Greece," I asked, "where is he?"

"Dead," Elton said.

"Dead?"

"Dead. Deceased. Departed."

"I know what dead means, you donkey. But why do you think Aubrey Masters is dead?"

Elton waved Shelby and me over to look at his phone. "This," he said, "is WhereAbout. For people who find the oversharing opportunities on Facebook inadequate, this mobile application allows users to share every location they visit. For instance, with the click of a button, I can check in and inform friends of my current location, Fuller Farms." Elton pressed the button and looked at us expectantly.

"O-kay, but why do you think Aubrey is dead? Did he check in at a cemetery?" I asked, and Tanner Cobb laughed over the phone.

"Aubrey Masters is not on WhereAbout," Elton said, "but Jasper Benson is, and he updates it continuously. Scrolling his feed gives you an almost exact accounting of his, pardon my pun, whereabouts since he began using the service in March 2008. Thirty minutes ago, Jasper checked in at Ristorante Balotelli in downtown Ashes. On May 16th, he attended the Preakness Stakes in Baltimore. And on April 12th, 2008, he stayed at the Waldorf Astoria in midtown Manhattan.

"The same day Quinn Westlake killed himself," I said.

Elton nodded and asked, "Do you happen to recall when Aubrey Masters supposedly left for Greece on his yacht?"

"April 15th," I said. "Sterling made a joke about his dad leaving town because he didn't want to pay taxes.

"And would you like to wager a guess on where Jasper Benson checked in on April 15th, 2008?"

There isn't shit in Northfork except oil wells and longhorn cattle. Seriously, the only restaurant within a hundred miles of our place is Gina's Diner, and I wouldn't eat there if I was starving.

I closed my eyes and guessed. "Gina's Diner. Northfork, Texas?"

"Correct."

My God.

1992

Jasper Benson never understood.

His family had more money than a small country, but they couldn't seem to enjoy it. Both of his parents had jobs. Like, they set an alarm, left the house, and actually worked for a paycheck they didn't need. His father ran Benson Properties, which boasted over 600 hotels and resorts worldwide. His mother taught Home Economics at Ashes High, showing mountain girls how to change the diapers of the babies they'd soon have. Even his sister got in on the act, scooping ice cream into waffle cones for the insufferable tourists. Einstein defined insanity as doing the same thing over and over and expecting different results, but Jasper had a better definition—working when you didn't have to.

When he retired in 1984, young Jasper thought perhaps his father would finally enjoy the fruits of his labor, but no. Upon leaving Benson Properties, Jeremy Benson founded the Twilight Rock Film Festival and devoted every waking hour to bringing Hollywood to North Carolina. The amount of groveling Jasper witnessed from his father was sickening. Billionaires shouldn't beg. Billionaires shouldn't give a damn what anyone thinks. Yet, there was Jeremy Benson, on his knees pleading with Hollywood to love him. He ran for mayor when the city council wouldn't approve tax incentives for any movie filmed in Ashes. He then packed the city council with his golf buddies over the following years, rubberstamping any proposal to raise the profile of his film festival. Jeremy Benson was busier and more stressed out now than when he ran a *Fortune* 500 company. His son thought it was about the stupidest thing he'd ever seen.

Sometimes Jasper wondered if he hadn't somehow descended directly from Willoughby Benson, his long-dead great-great-grandfather who made the family fortune, then built a house so big you could see it from space. Willoughby threw Gatsby-esque parties, slept with his friends' wives, and did what billionaires should do—anything they want.

That's what Jasper did—anything he wanted. And why not? He realized at a young age that the rules and norms guiding society didn't apply to the rich and powerful. His parents gave him warnings. Teachers gave him warnings. Police gave him warnings.

Don't do that again, or else.

Or else what?

Or else, well, nothing, that's what.

Jasper wouldn't receive monthly stipends from his trust fund until his twenty-fourth birthday. But first, he'd attend Southern California's film school at his father's insistence. Then Jasper would write and direct *Ghost of Judas*, a movie so historically bad it set Jeremy Benson's Tinseltown dreams back a decade. Only after Jeremy gave up any hope that his son might be his ticket to Hollywood did Jasper commence the life he'd dreamed of since puberty. Private jets, flashy cars, designer drugs, and sex. So much sex. All the sex with all the wannabe models and actresses frequenting the hottest clubs in the world, hoping to meet a rich, handsome guy like Jasper. He was James Bond without the license to kill. Hugh Hefner without the pajamas. Wilton Chamberlin without the 100-point game.

But back in Ashes, years before all of that, Jasper Benson had to entertain himself by doing whatever he could get away with—namely, everything.

Fuller Farms was punishment disguised as a gift. Who wouldn't want eight weeks spent swimming, hiking, and playing in the North Carolina mountains? Jasper Benson, that's who. Camp sucked. The counselors sucked harder. Two hours of free time each day meant twenty-two hours of captivity, and like all inmates, Jasper had to get creative to pass the time.

Gambling among the boys at Fuller Farms likely began on day one in 1963. Looking to add a little excitement to their morning archery lessons or the afternoon swim relay, they'd lay down a quarter here or a dollar there. But Jasper took things to the next level. He operated as Fuller Farms' first unofficial bookmaker, encouraging more bets, larger bets, and he even ran several card games on his bunk after lights out.

None of the boys needed the money they brought to camp, but they all hated losing. And no one hated losing more than Quinn Westlake, the all-state lacrosse player, who, by the third week of camp, owed Aubrey Masters a thousand dollars.

Sensing an opportunity for fun, Jasper encouraged Quinn to make the largest bet in the history of Fuller Farms. A bet Aubrey couldn't win but couldn't refuse. A bet so scandalous, so shocking, every boy at camp would want in on the action.

"Okay, Aubrey, a cool grand says you can't slay the Queen of the Mountain."

"Bet."

The betting wasn't even. Nearly everyone wagered on Aubrey's defeat, giving Jasper a rooting interest in his success.

Jasper stole the key to Buster's shed.

Jasper provided the wine.

Jasper spiked the bottle.

But then, it all fell apart. The pill worked as advertised, but apparently, Aubrey Masters didn't know what to do with a passed-out girl. When she hit the floor, he ran looking for help, and Jasper and Quinn ran back to the archery shed with him.

"See, she's unconscious," Aubrey said, almost hyperventilating.

"Yeah, that's the point," Jasper replied.

"You're sick," Aubrey shouted. "You're fucking sick."

"You say that like it's a bad thing," Jasper said with a snort, then he told Aubrey and Quinn to head back to camp before someone noticed they were missing. "Don't worry," he added, "I'll take care of the girl."

Jasper would never forget the fury with which Vance Fuller burst into the archery shed twenty minutes later, intent on saving the day. He looked a man possessed. An agent of divine vengeance. Or, perhaps, he was just hell-bent on restoring his own reputation at the expense of Jasper's.

"Hold your horses, Professor Molester," Jasper said, backing up against the wall with his hands raised, "you've got a choice. You can turn around and go back to camp and pretend this never happened. Or I can tell everyone that I caught you in here with an unconscious girl. You're the pervert, Vance, and it's my word versus yours." Jasper's shoulders relaxed as Vance seemed to consider the proposal, but then the weirdo came charging across the shed, screaming like a banshee. Jasper had just enough time to snatch the wine bottle off the floor and smash it upside Vance's head. Now he had an unconscious girl, an unconscious counselor, and a decision to make.

Jasper had gotten away with so much in life. He'd received warning after warning, full of sound and fury, signifying nothing. But this time was different. This crime would require more than a slap on the wrist. This would ruin his life.

Vance could never tell what he saw.

Jasper had to act.

And he did.

Nearly twenty years later, Jasper believed he'd covered all his bases. Those who knew what happened that night were either dead, terrified, or deep in the Benson family's pockets. He didn't understand that Vance Fuller's bones still called out from the grave. Didn't understand that the arc of the moral universe is long, but it bent toward raining down judgment on his sorry ass. Didn't understand that when there is hell to pay, the Devil doesn't accept cash.

Jasper Benson never understood … until today.

CHAPTER FORTY-ONE

"Let's go," I said, bolting toward the door.

"Go where?" Elton asked.

"That Italian place you said Jasper Benson checked into half an hour ago. If we hurry, we can catch him before his tiramisu arrives."

"Catch him and do what?" Shelby asked. "Do you think he's going to confess to murdering a bunch of people in the middle of a restaurant and turn himself in?"

"Yeah, Pippi, you might want to tell the police what you've figured out and let them handle it from there," Tanner Cobb said over speakerphone.

I looked around the room, incredulous no one shared my urgency. "Oh, do you mean the same Ashes Police Department that threatened to frame my mother for murder if I didn't leave town?" I asked. "Yeah, no thanks. The Benson Family thinks they've won, so their guard is down. If we tell the cops and word gets back to Jasper, he's gone. He's got the means to disappear forever, and I won't let him."

Tanner sighed because he couldn't argue my point, but then he tried anyway. "Still, Pippi, if this guy is as dangerous as he sounds, I don't feel too good about you and Stretch busting into—"

"What was that, Tanner? You're breaking up," I lied. "I'll call you back after we catch Jasper."

"Pippi, don't you dare—"

I hung up the phone and turned to Elton and Shelby. "This could be our only chance. We've got to try. For my mom. For Shelby's mom. For Vance Fuller."

"What the hell have you done?" Wellington Fuller boomed from the doorway, his face so flushed I feared a massive heart attack was imminent, his eyes glowing with Old Testament rage.

"Campers never take the time to write home these days," I said, "so I let their parents know what they've been up to this summer."

"You conniving little bitch," Wellington snarled. "I'm going to—"

"Listen, old man, I don't have time to stand here while you blather. Besides, you should probably be calling your lawyers because I can guarantee your campers' parents are calling theirs."

"You whore. You immoral, devious, manipulative little ..."

I said I didn't believe it was my place to share Buster's secret with Wellington Fuller, but after a solid thirty seconds of name calling, I just couldn't help myself.

"Are you finished?" I asked when Wellington stopped to catch his breath, "because I've got some good news and some bad news for you. The good news is we figured out who murdered your son. Vance caught Jasper Benson raping a girl from the kitchen, and Jasper murdered him to shut him up."

All the fury fell from Wellington Fuller's face as he processed this information, but it returned when I offered my parting shot. "The bad news is, Vance wasn't your son."

To look at Wellington Fuller, you'd never think he could move as fast as he did when I said this, but he charged like a bull, both hands raised, intending, I suspect, to strangle the life out of me. But, as fast as he was, Elton Jones-Davies was faster, and he snatched the old fart by the neck and slammed him against the wall so hard that several deer heads crashed to the floor.

"Elton, chill," I said, taken aback at how quickly this had escalated.

"He intended to harm you," Elton protested, tightening his grip on Wellington's neck.

"I know," I said, giving Elton a pat on the arm he didn't even notice. "But he's a hundred years old and probably can't open jars by himself."

Reluctantly, Elton let Wellington go, and the old man slid to the ground. Then Elton turned to me and said, "I won't let anyone harm you."

"I know, Elton. I know. Come on, let's go."

And the three of us left Wellington Fuller on the office floor while his kingdom went up in flames.

"Okay, so what's our plan again?" Shelby asked as we sped up the mountain toward Ashes.

"Jasper is at some Italian restaurant downtown."

"Ristorante Balotelli," Elton said.

"Yeah, there," I said.

"And?" Shelby asked when I failed to elaborate.

"And we're going to confront him," I said.

"Confront him with his WhereAbout check-ins?" Shelby asked, not sounding enthused at my half-ass plan."

"It's enough," I said. "Jasper and his father both told us Aubrey Masters killed Vance because he busted Aubrey assaulting a girl at Fuller Farms. They both went on and on about Aubrey being a psychopath and how terrified they were of the Masters family. So terrified, apparently, that Jasper went to Northfork, Texas, the day Aubrey disappeared. And that trip, not coincidentally, occurred just after Jasper visited Manhattan on the exact same day Quinn Westlake happened to jump off a building."

"It was my mother, wasn't it?" Shelby asked. "It was my mother Jasper raped?"

I hesitated before nodding yes. "She doesn't remember much. Just that she was with Aubrey in Buster's shed, then woke up hours later in the parking lot. Jasper talked to her the next morning. Told her Aubrey had lost his mind and killed Vance. Told her they could never say a word, or Aubrey would kill them too. I can't be sure, but I think Jasper, posing as Aubrey, has sent your mom threats and money ever since."

Shelby wiped her eyes, then laughed through her tears and said, "Well, he ain't been sending much money."

I shuddered as Jasper Benson's words from that morning came rushing back. *She's got a daughter, right? Sixteen or seventeen years old? You do the math.*

"What?" Shelby asked, the horror in my brain apparently visible on my face.

Your biological father is a murderer, I thought. "Nothing," I said. "I'm just trying to think this all through before we get there."

"Well, look, I believe you," Shelby said, "but you don't have proof.

You don't have a bloody glove or a dead body. What will you do if we walk in there and tell Jasper everything we know, and he shrugs and says we're wrong?"

"Izzy often resorts to half-truths and outright lies when interrogating suspects," Elton said.

"And that works?" Shelby asked.

I shrugged and said, "Sometimes," though I was struggling to think of a way to dupe Jasper Benson into telling the truth if our WhereAbout screenshots didn't do the trick. Then there was the unnerving fact we were about to confront a man who I believed had killed three people, one in a particularly grisly fashion.

"By the way," I asked Shelby, now wondering if perhaps going after Jasper
our own wasn't the best idea, "do you have a gun with you?"

"Of course," she said, looking at me like I was an idiot.

"Okay, cool," I said, unsure if walking into Ristorante Balotelli armed made me feel safer or not, so I called Axl.

"Let me make sure I have this straight," my brother said after I told him everything in one long breath, "the mayor told you to get out of town or he'd throw Mom in prison for life, but instead, you're going to accuse his son of murdering three people without any real evidence?"

"I feel like you're focusing on all the wrong parts, but yeah, pretty much."

Axl cursed and took a deep breath.

"Jasper did it," I said, "and if we take him and his dad down, Mom will be out of jail tomorrow." I'm not sure if I believed this, but I wanted it to be true, and Axl did too.

"Dad and I are on our way. Don't go in without us."

"Great. Bring anything you can use as a weapon. If this guy—"

"Just don't go in without us," Axl said, and I knew then he wasn't coming to help. He was coming to stop me.

We pulled into downtown on two wheels, sliding into a parking spot half a block from Ristorante Balotelli. Shelby and I were at the door when I noticed Elton wasn't with us. I turned and saw him talking on his phone next to the car.

"Elton, hurry up," I yelled, but he only raised a finger to show me he'd be a moment.

"Dude," I said when he finally caught up with us, "who were you talking to? We're about to confront a murderer, remember?"

"Zadie Carrick had an urgent query regarding Cranachan, a traditional Scottish dessert containing raspberries," Elton said, avoiding my glare.

I wanted to stay mad at him, but he had just rescued me from a raving billionaire, so I could only sigh and shake my head. "It's fine, come on."

The three of us stopped at the entrance to Ristorante Balotelli, where a sign on the window informed us the restaurant was closed for a private event. "Oh, please let it be Jasper's birthday party," I said, opening the door, and Elton and Shelby followed me inside.

The dining room was dark, but my eyes drifted toward the sound of conversation and silverware clinking on plates. Across the room, at a long table, I spotted Jasper Benson and his father, along with several faces I recognized from around town. In the corner, a large easel displayed a bright promotional poster for the Twilight Rock Film Festival, and next to it, five headless mannequins modeled T-shirts the town planned to sell for the big event.

I was about to speak when Shelby elbowed me in the ribs and whispered, "Whoa, is that who I think it is?"

And it was. Chase Foster and Bridget Bell, their big, beautiful movie star faces smiling at us from across the room, their giant bodyguard rushing across the room shouting, "No autographs."

It was then everyone at the table noticed us, and Mayor Benson jumped to his feet and demanded, "What is the meaning of this?"

"We know," I shouted back. "We know about Jasper."

Now all conversation screeched to a halt, and in the following silence, I tried frantically to think of a way to scare Jasper Benson into confessing. Maybe tell him a camper saw everything and had finally found the courage to come forward. Or perhaps he'd believe we'd acquired surveillance video from Quinn Westlake's building that proved his death was anything but suicide. But in the end, I didn't have to think of a lie.

I didn't have to think of a lie because Jasper Benson jumped from his chair and darted out the back door.

CHAPTER FORTY-TWO

After a moment's hesitation, where Elton, Shelby, and I exchanged disbelieving looks, we ran across the restaurant and out the rear exit in time to see Jasper duck down an alley heading back toward Main Street. Shelby chased after him, and Elton and I dashed back through Ristorante Balotelli, crashing into Axl and Dad as we burst out the front door.

"Where'd he go?" Shelby yelled, emerging from the alley about thirty yards from us, frantically scanning the street.

"Where'd who go?" Axl asked, as the unmistakable roar of a six-figure Italian sports car revved to life. Tires squealed as Jasper Benson backed onto Main Street faster than most cars can go forward, then he stomped the gas pedal and blew past us, leaving nothing but the smell of burning rubber in the cool mountain air.

"Follow us in your truck," I shouted to Axl and Dad. "We can't let him get away."

"Wait, Izzy," my brother protested, "we can't just—"

"No time to discuss this as a committee," I yelled, jumping into

Shelby's Honda. Seconds later, we hurtled down Main Street and had gone half a block before I realized Elton was behind the wheel.

"Why aren't you driving?" I yelled at Shelby from the backseat.

"Because I can't shoot and drive," she yelled back, leaning out the window with her pistol in hand.

I was about to argue we'd never get within range with speed-limit-loving Elton behind the wheel, but then I saw he'd pegged out the speedometer and was taking curves like Mario Andretti. My first instinct was to tell him to slow down, but I buckled up instead.

It wasn't much of a chase. Despite a noble effort from Shelby's twenty-year-old Japanese compact, the alien-looking taillights of Jasper's car faded in the distance on a straight stretch of road leaving Ashes. We'd have struggled to catch Jasper in a Cessna, much less a Civic, and I didn't particularly relish the thought of Elton chasing him down the mountain at full throttle, despite his apparent proficiency at highspeed driving. But then, we caught a break.

"He turned," Shelby said as Jasper's brake lights glowed bright and the car swerved left, disappearing from view. Seconds later, we reached the spot where Jasper left the road—the gravel parking lot for Twilight Rock.

The highest point on the Ashes Plateau, Twilight Rock sat a mile from downtown and offered stunning views of Ashes in the Pines and the surrounding peaks. A short, twenty-minute hike up the mountain from the parking lot led visitors through wooded trails to a massive granite slab that created a cliffside amphitheater. These days it's overrun with Instagram influencers taking duck face selfies, but back then, it was a lovely place to watch the sunset.

We slid into the parking lot for Twilight Rock, which was

surprisingly full, considering locals advised against hanging around too long after dark when all manner of wildlife arrived to eat the trash left behind by thoughtless tourists. Even so, Jasper's car wasn't hard to spot since it was neon yellow with doors that opened like seagull wings. Jasper, however, was nowhere in sight.

"He's gone up," Shelby said, pointing toward the trailhead that wound up and around the mountain to the cliffside. Higher up, where the trees thinned out, we saw Jasper scampering out of sight.

"Let's go," I said, running toward the trailhead, but Shelby and Elton balked.

"We should wait on your dad and brother," Shelby said.

"There's no time," I said, knowing Axl and Dad were more likely to wrestle me into their truck and take me home than charge up Twilight Rock to confront a murderer. "If we don't go now—"

"There's nowhere for him to go," Shelby said, trying to sound calm. "It's just woods and a cliff. We should wait for reinforcements. Or go back to town and stare at Chase Foster some more."

I ignored this and asked, "What if he keeps a helicopter stashed in a cave?"

"He is not Batman," Elton said.

"He's an eccentric billionaire who lives in a manor."

"Okay, he could be Batman," Elton conceded.

I didn't care to stay and argue with them any longer, so I took off up the trail, and after a moment's hesitation, they both followed. Five minutes later, we reached a fork in the trail, Shelby and I gasping for air like we'd just finished a marathon, Elton looking like he'd only walked to the mailbox and back."

"At least I smoke," Shelby said between heaving breaths. "What's your excuse?"

I didn't have enough oxygen in my lungs to laugh, so I just smiled and shot her a bird. Then, when I could finally talk again, I asked, "Where do these trails go?"

"They both wrap around the mountain to Twilight Rock," Shelby said.

"We should split up then. Meet in the middle."

"But we've only got one gun," Shelby argued.

"It's fine," I said. "You take the gun and go that way. I'll take Elton and go this way." Shelby shook her head uncertainly, and I added, "We'll be fine. He knows Tae Kwon Do."

"You know Tae Kwon Do?" Shelby asked, squinting at the gangly boy in wingtips.

"Izzy just told you I do," Elton said matter-of-factly.

"Okay, fine," Shelby said, though she wasn't happy about it. "I'll see you at Twilight Rock unless I see Jasper first."

Elton and I took the wooded trail to our right, and suddenly I felt very empty-handed without Shelby's gun. What if Jasper was armed? He could be hiding behind every tree or bend in the trail, waiting to ambush us. Of course, Elton talking at the top of his lungs wasn't helping matters.

"I still say, under the circumstances, waiting on your father and brother was the prudent decision. In fact, our odds of—"

An echoing gunshot pierced the silent night, and as Elton and I stood listening, we heard footsteps, then more footsteps, then a stampede of men and women wearing purples robes and neon green Nikes rushed past us, heading toward the parking lot.

"The doomsday cult," I said, breathing a sigh of relief, remembering their HomeGoing ceremony was tonight. But why were they running? Had Shelby shot Jasper? Had Jasper shot her?

After the last pair of Nikes ran past, Elton and I had no choice but to climb higher, the trail now falling off to our right without even a handrail to save us from tumbling into the abyss. This was a mistake. This was beyond stupid. If Jasper was hiding ahead with a gun, he wouldn't even have to shoot us. He could just start throwing pinecones, and we'd likely plunge to our deaths. But he wasn't, and we didn't, and soon the trail leveled off, winding around to a clearing and Twilight Rock.

Larger than a basketball court, the granite slab sloped for twenty-five yards before reaching a drop of three-hundred feet to the forest below. The view was as advertised. Elton and I walked out onto the rock, stepping over picnic dinners the cult members had abandoned, and together we looked down at the sparkling lights of Ashes, the moon rising giant and yellow above the mountains beyond. So stunned were we by the beauty of the scene before us, we both momentarily forgot why we'd climbed Twilight Rock in the first place. But then Jasper Benson stepped out of the woods behind us, and we remembered.

"Dizzy and Elvis," Jasper said, and we both spun to see him standing in the clearing with a pistol pointed in our direction.

"Hey look, Elton, it's like, the murderer or whatever," I said, impersonating Jasper.

Jasper snorted and said impatiently, "Okay, why don't you tell me exactly what it is you think you've figured out before we commence with the ugly business of the evening."

"You killed Vance Fuller, then you killed Quinn Westlake and Aubrey Masters to keep them quiet," I said. "And we know this because of your stupid WhereAbout app. You were in Manhattan the day Quinn died, and three days later, you were in Northfork when Aubrey disappeared."

Jasper's big dumb mouth opened slightly while he considered this, then he asked, "Wait, everyone can see those posts?"

"Negative. Only your friends," Elton said.

"Friends like Elya Petrovich here," I added, pointing to Elton.

To this, Jasper could only offer a dumbfounded "Huh."

The urge to tell him he was by far the stupidest murderer I'd ever caught was strong, but he currently had me trapped against a cliff, so I held my tongue.

"The western trail takes ten minutes longer," Jasper said when he caught me glancing behind him, looking for Shelby. "By the time your friend gets here you'll be dead. But I'm happy to relay any messages."

"You're not getting away with this," I said. "Half the town saw you run from that restaurant when we confronted you."

"Wrong," Jasper said, with a smirk. "Half the town saw two girls and a big Black dude storm a private event shouting threats at me. Surveillance video will later reveal two of these people have also trespassed into my private quarters at Benson House twice in the last month. Any reasonable person would totally understand why I ran from you. I was scared. I feared for my life. And they'd agree what I'm about to do, I did in self-defense." Jasper laughed and added, "It wouldn't surprise me if Chief Jenkins didn't already have his report written up."

Jasper still sounded like a stoner, but this was by far the most coherent I'd ever seen him, which scared me. He wasn't high now. He was, to borrow a phrase, like, totally in control or whatever. He waved his pistol back and forth between the two of us, settling on me. "Now, I think we'll start with Dizzy because I'm fucking sick of hearing you talk."

Elton's shout was so thunderous and primal I suspect the echo might still be reverberating around the Earth. He took two giant strides toward Jasper, making up so much ground the murderer didn't have time to aim, just shoot. The bullet struck the rock and ricocheted harmlessly into the night. But Elton slipped while taking evasive action, his wingtips not providing much traction on the smooth granite. His head hit hard, and he looked like a drunk stumbling to his feet, only to fall again and begin tumbling down the slope. It happened so fast, but I watched in horrible slow motion as Elton thrashed and flailed in a futile attempt to stop his momentum.

Then I screamed as he plunged over the ledge.

CHAPTER FORTY-THREE

As my scream faded into the mountain air, the night atop Twilight Rock grew eerily quiet. I gasped for air through sobs, but my lungs wouldn't fill. I feared I'd soon drown in my own tears and save Jasper the effort. But then Elton yelled from below, "Izzy, I have suffered an injury."

I ran to the cliffside and saw my friend perched perilously on a small ledge jutting out from the rock fifteen feet below. Elton raised his left arm, which, even in the moonlight, I could see he'd broken, and after examining it himself, he emitted a small gasp and passed out cold. He was hurt but alive. Elton Jones-Davies was alive. The relief was overwhelming but short-lived because there was still a killer behind me.

I scrambled to my feet to face Jasper, who stood twenty feet away, his gun aimed at my chest. It took every ounce of restraint I could muster to keep from charging him. Sure, I'd die, but at least my last act on Earth would be attempting to kill the bastard with my bare hands. There are worse ways to go. But I had to keep my wits. Had to keep

Jasper Benson talking. He was dumb. Perhaps not dumb enough to let Shelby sneak up from behind, but I had to try. I had to buy her time.

"You don't have to do this," I said, tasting the hot tears streaming down my cheeks. I'd need years of therapy to get over seeing Elton roll over that ledge.

"Dude, we can't exactly walk back down the mountain together and pretend nothing happened," Jasper said, taking a step toward me. "But I want you to know, I take no pleasure from it. I'm not a sicko. I'm not a serial killer or whatever."

"You've killed at least three people I know of. You're the dictionary definition of a serial killer."

Jasper shook his head, troubled by this distinction. "Except, I don't like, enjoy it," he said. "I find it kind of gnarly, to be honest."

He wanted to argue. This was promising. This meant he likely wouldn't kill me until he had proven his point. I kept pressing. "You shot Vance Fuller with a dozen arrows," I said. "Someone who didn't take pleasure in killing would have stopped at one."

"Wrong," Jasper snapped, growing annoyed, "because shooting arrows from fifty yards away like, removes the intimacy. It's like those drone pilots dropping bombs on Afghanistan from an office in Virginia, then going home for dinner with the wife and kids. Were they to spend their day stabbing Afghans with a butcher knife, they'd probably lose their appetite."

"That's not even remotely the same thing," I said.

"Fine, not exactly. But in Vance's case, it wasn't all my doing. Quinn shot some arrows. Aubrey did too."

"Wait, they did?"

"I made them," Jasper said, glancing back toward the clearing to look for Shelby. He hadn't forgotten about her yet. "You already know about the Queen of the Mountain."

"Yeah," I said, not hiding my disgust. "I was this year's."

Jasper seemed to appraise me with new eyes before snorting. "I suppose some years the pickings are slim."

The urge to charge him returned, but I fought it off.

"Anyway," he said, "the boys at camp have like, always placed bets to pass the time, and that summer, I acted as the unofficial camp bookie. Things were going well enough until Quinn bet Aubrey he couldn't slay the Queen of the Mountain. And by slay, we meant—"

"Yeah, I've got it, asshole."

Jasper ignored this and said, "Well, so many of the guys placed bets against Aubrey that I was set to lose a fortune if he couldn't pull it off, and if you'd met the dude, you'd have known there was no way he could pull it off. So I offered him my services, as it were. I swiped a key to the archery shed and hooked up Aubrey with a bottle of gas station wine containing a secret ingredient that made girls a little more willing or whatever. But when she passed out, Aubrey panicked and came running for Quinn and me."

Jasper shook his head, still disappointed in Aubrey's reluctance to take advantage of an unconscious girl. "I sent Aubrey and Quinn to the dorm. Told them I'd take care of the girl, and I—"

"And you raped her," I spat.

Jasper winced. "I don't like that word. Besides, a girl willing to sneak off to the archery shed and drink a bottle of wine totally knew what she'd signed up for. So, I slayed the Queen of the Mountain, which would have earned that five grand for myself, but then Vance Fuller burst in like some knight in shining armor trying to save the day.

I tried to talk him out of him. Told him it was my word against his, and everyone knew he was the perv. But the dude came after me anyway. I caught him upside his giant head with the wine bottle. Knocked his weird ass out cold, tied him up, and ran to find Aubrey and Quinn."

I shook my head in confusion. "Why'd you run for Aubrey and Quinn? You could have killed Vance without any witnesses."

"I could, sure," Jasper said with a shrug, "but are you familiar with the doctrine of mutually assured destruction?"

I nodded. I'd spent most of sixth grade freaking out over nuclear war after some terrifying video Mr. Lehman showed us in history class.

"It was all the news talked about when I was a kid in the eighties," Jasper said. "Maybe the Russians won't blow us to hell because they know we'd blow them to hell right back, or whatever. Well, if I killed Vance alone, I'd be vulnerable. The cops would question Aubrey and Quinn, and their answers could lead to me. But if we all killed Vance together, we'd be safe. Protected."

"And they just went along with that?" I asked.

"They didn't want to. Well, Aubrey didn't. Quinn was maybe too eager. He might have been a serial killer, come to think of it. But they both knew they didn't have a choice. If Vance told the police what he saw me doing, I'd tell the police Aubrey had drugged the girl with ill intent because Quinn bet him a thousand dollars that he wouldn't. A scandal like that would ruin our family names. A scandal like that would ruin our futures. Our only way out? Mutually assured destruction."

"But why all the arrows?" I asked, shaking my head. "Why'd you have to kill Vance in the most horrible way imaginable?"

"That was like, my idea," Jasper said, pointing to himself with a smug smirk. "You've heard the rumors of Satan worshippers living in the caves around Fuller Farms. I knew if Vance's death looked weird and ritualistic, those rumors would only grow. There's no way three kids would kill a man that way, but devil worshippers, oh yeah."

I wanted to tell Jasper this was the stupidest plan in the history of stupid plans. But half the town thought devil worshippers killed Vance Fuller, so maybe Jasper was so stupid he was brilliant.

"And now," Jasper said, closing one eye and aiming his pistol, "as much as I'd like to stay and play remember when—"

"Wait, why'd you kill Quinn and Aubrey if you knew they'd never tell?"

Jasper huffed impatiently but couldn't resist explaining just how brilliant he was. "We weren't super close or whatever. Didn't ring each other and talk about the good old days at Fuller Farms. But in the past couple of years, Aubrey must have grown a conscience because he'd call me late at night, going on about what we did and how he sees Vance in his dreams, shot full of arrows, wandering the woods looking for us. Then last March, he got passed over for the big job at Sterling Oil and he told me it was Vance's fault. Told me that Vance was getting his revenge from the grave. I knew then he'd cracked up, and there was no telling what he'd do or say. I went to New York to talk to Quinn about the Aubrey Problem, as we called it, and after smoking a little, I pushed him off the roof. He'd have never talked, but to be honest, I just felt safer without Quinn Westlake in the world. Next I paid Aubrey a visit, took him to dinner at the only restaurant within a thousand miles of his compound, and slipped something into his sweet potato pie. I buried him in the desert that night and had Tripp move his yacht to Greece, so everyone would think he—"

"Tripp? Tripp Aston?"

Jasper nodded but didn't elaborate. We wouldn't learn until later that Tripp Aston saw the three campers kill Vance Fuller that night on the archery range, then hatched his plan. A plan that involved blackmailing the Benson family into helping him get into law school and landing a job with a big Charlotte firm when he graduated.

"Tripp is an asshole," Jasper said, "but he's a hella smart attorney. He's certainly gotten me out of a jam or two. But he's not the sort of guy you want to know your secrets. Good thing we know his secrets too, so we're all protected. Protected by …"

"Mutually assured destruction," I said.

"Exactamundo," Jasper said with glee.

"Okay, but hold on," I said, "you were just a kid. You couldn't get Tripp into law school or land him a job with a big law firm. Your dad knew, didn't he?"

"From the jump," Jasper said. "Chief Morrison wasn't an idiot, and our stories, as much as we rehearsed them, had several inconsistencies. Chief came to Dad and told him things looked bad for us, and Dad came up with the idea to flip the script. Admit to killing Vance, but only because he'd abused all three of us that summer. Everyone in town knew Vance did something shady to get kicked out of Chapel Hill, so it wasn't much of a leap. Dad made sure Rosalind heard about it, and together they pressured Chief Morrison to let the case go cold and just fade away. I won't lie, I bet some money exchanged hands too, but I never asked. And that was that until Rosalind died, and Wellington got curious, and you started snooping around. I knew you'd never catch us, but Dad was paranoid. He read about those other cases you solved and got freaked out thinking you'd cause a big stink in Ashes and ruin his film festival. And dude, believe me, that film festival is all the man cares about. So, when your mom's drug-slinging boyfriend turned up dead, Dad saw an opportunity. First, he gave you an out, but you didn't take it. So he turned the screws, but you still didn't give up. I'm sure deep-down Dad admires your tenacity. He'd probably offer you a job if I weren't about to kill you."

"You don't have to kill me, Jasper. There has to be another way."

"You can jump," he said. "Save me the trouble."

"And you can go fuck yourself," I replied.

Jasper snorted a laugh, then held up a finger at the sound of footsteps on gravel. He moved toward me, keeping his gun aimed at my head, and after wrapping an arm around my neck, he stood behind me, and we watched Shelby emerge from the woods.

"Drop it," Jasper said, catching Shelby off guard. "Drop the gun right there and step toward me. Slowly."

Shelby had no choice. She put her pistol down and stepped out onto Twilight Rock.

"There, that's good," Jasper said when she was about ten feet away. "Now, on your knees. You too, Dizzy."

He let me go and stepped away, keeping his pistol trained on me and an eye on Shelby.

"Where's Elton?" Shelby asked.

"He fell," I said, my voice cracking. "He's okay, but—"

"But not for long," Jasper said. "I'll take care of him after you two."

"And Tracie Ray," I said, and they both looked at me.

"What?" Jasper demanded.

"Tracie Ray, Queen of the Mountain 1992. You know, the girl you raped."

Jasper flinched at the word *rape* and yelled, "I told you I don't like that word."

"But you raped her," I said. "Then you saw her the next morning and told her Aubrey killed Vance Fuller. Warned her if she ever told anyone, Aubrey would kill her too. And then I'm guessing you sent a few threats from Aubrey over the years, reminding her of what you're capable of if she ever talked."

"And money," Jasper said, suddenly on the defensive. "I heard she had a kid, so I sent a hundred bucks every now and then to help her out."

"How generous," I said, rolling my eyes. "Well, she did have a kid. A baby girl. She's kneeling right in front of you."

Jasper looked at Shelby again, and the color drained from his face.

"Tracie knows the truth now, so you'll have to kill her, and you'll have to kill your own daughter."

This was not how I wanted Shelby to learn who her father was, but I figured she'd forgive me if it kept us both from getting shot. Jasper, for his part, did not look well. I got the feeling he was being honest when he said he didn't enjoy killing. He'd kept talking for five minutes just to delay the inevitable bloodshed. And now, confronted with several more murders he'd have to commit, including his own daughter, his body revolted. I wondered then if perhaps guilt, not boredom, had brought him back to Benson House. If his early-nineties museum of a bedroom wasn't just a sad attempt to go back to a simpler time. A time before Jasper had doomed his soul to perdition with his evil acts.

"Then, you'll have to kill Tanner Cobb," I said, pouring it on thick.

"Who?" Jasper said, shaking his head back to the present.

"My attorney, who's been listening to and recording our entire conversation over speakerphone."

This was not true, but Jasper didn't know that, and any trace of smugness was gone from his stupid face. His secret was out, spreading like swine flu, and he'd never put it back in the bottle.

"Izzy, Elton, where are you?" my brother yelled from somewhere down the trail.

"It's Axl and Dad," I said to Shelby. "They brought the sheriffs."

Axl and Dad almost certainly hadn't brought the sheriffs, but the thought of more people arriving pushed Jasper over the edge. He began switching his aim between Shelby and me, muttering incomprehensibly.

"Dammit," he finally screamed at me, his hands shaking with rage. "You've ruined everything. This had nothing to do with you. Nothing!"

"Izzy!" my father shouted, his voice closer than Axl's. "Where are you?"

Time was out, and Jasper knew it. He raised the pistol to his temple, and I closed my eyes, not wanting to watch. But then he said, "No, fuck that. If I go, so do you." He aimed his pistol at my head, and I closed my eyes again, wincing in anticipation of the end. But instead of a gunshot, I heard something unexpected.

A whistle and a thud.

Shelby screamed, and I opened my eyes to see Jasper, an arrow sticking out of his chest, a look of complete shock on his face. He took a stumbling step backward, then another, all the while reaching for a helping hand that wasn't there. Then Jasper Benson fell like the devil, off Twilight Rock, into hell.

Shelby and I scrambled to our feet and turned toward the clearing to see Buster McClellan in a purple robe and neon green Nikes holding a bow.

"You girls are lucky as hell," he said, checking his watch with a smile. "Our spaceship was late again."

CHAPTER FORTY-FOUR

Several hours later, Shelby, Buster, Axl, Dad, and I sat in the Highlands-Cashiers Hospital ER, waiting to hear about Elton. To my surprise, Axl and Dad had, in fact, called the Jackson County sheriffs, and dozens of them arrived minutes after Jasper Benson fell off Twilight Rock. An EMS team came soon after and lifted Elton from the ledge in some sort of rescue sled, and I hugged him until one of the medics made me stop. He'd nearly died charging an armed man and trying to protect me. I loved him so much.

The sheriffs questioned us for the better part of eternity in the parking lot below Twilight Rock, trying to wrap their heads around a laundry list of rape, murder, and extortion allegations. Tomorrow held the promise of even more interviews with more sheriffs at their office in Sylva, but for now, they had warrants to obtain and arrests to make.

"So," Dad asked Buster as the five of us snacked on vending machine food while waiting for news about Elton, "what's up with the purple robe again?"

"Sarah could explain it better than me," Buster said, "but she don't make it to town much on account of folks insisting she wear clothes."

Dad looked to me for an explanation, but I could only shrug.

"But," Buster continued, "it boils down to her spaceship having a rather strict dress code during the boarding process."

"Oh," Dad said, because what else could he say?

"I'm sorry we ruined the HomeGoing ceremony," I said, but Buster waved me off.

"Don't you worry about that. There's always next year. Besides, those things are usually boring as hell. At least this one was memorable. Plus, you caught Vance's killer. I don't think I could ever repay you."

"Well, saving my life was a good start," I said with a grin.

"So, will Mr. Fuller pay you the fifty grand now?" Axl asked.

Shelby whistled, and I looked skyward.

"Izzy, what did you do?"

"Sort of started a riot at camp, then informed Mr. Fuller Vance wasn't his son."

"Dammit, Izzy," Axl said, dropping his head into his hands.

"Sorry," I said to Buster. "I know that wasn't my secret to tell."

"It's alright," Buster said. "Some secrets ain't meant to be kept forever."

"And I'm sorry you had to find out about Jasper the way you did," I said, turning to Shelby.

"No," she said, shaking her head, "he'd have shot me if you hadn't said something. It's a lot to process, but I ain't mad."

"And I'm sure your mom will be back soon," I told her. "Once she sees the news, she'll know she never has to fear those boys from camp again."

"But what about us?" Axl asked. "Without that money, how will we get—"

"Mom!" I yelled as our mother walked into the emergency room, escorted by two smiling Jackson County sheriff's deputies.

Axl and I leaped from our seats and ran across the room, wrapping our arms around our mother, both of us bursting into tears.

"How'd you get out?"

"How'd you know we were here?"

"How'd you—"

"Hold on, you two," Mom said, hugging us a little longer before pulling away. "They released me about an hour ago. The Macon County sheriffs caught Lenny's killer. It was some guy named Jasper Benson who lives in a big house outside Franklin."

"Wait, what?" Axl and I said in unison.

Mom shrugged. "Someone called the anonymous tip line tonight, and the sheriffs followed up. They found the knife used to kill Lenny in this Jasper guy's bedroom, along with some medicine he took from the van."

"Mom, Jasper Benson is dead. He's the man who killed Vance Fuller at camp all those years ago, and he was about to kill me tonight, but Buster shot him in the heart with an arrow, and he fell off Twilight Rock."

"That man in the purple nightgown and green sneakers?" Mom asked.

"Yeah, that'll all make more sense later," I said, but Axl shook his head to say it wouldn't.

"Baby girl," Mom said, turning to me, "do you not recall me asking you to try and stay out of trouble this summer?"

"I tried," I said, my lips curling into a smile, and Mom could only shake her head.

"Well, I guess in the end you—" Mom began to say, but then looked past us and said, "Is that Rodney Brown?"

"Yeah, Mom, he came as soon as—"

Mom tried to push past us, but Axl blocked her way while I tried to calm her down.

"Mom, please don't hurt him. He's been really good to us and—"

"I ain't gonna hurt him," Mom said, raising both hands in a gesture of goodwill. "We just need to talk, that's all."

Reluctantly, Axl let her pass, and she walked over to the corner, where she and Dad exchanged an awkward half-handshake half-hug before going outside to talk.

"I'm going outside to smoke," Shelby said, walking past us.

"Will you make sure my parents don't kill each other?" I asked.

"Sure thing. You coming, Sweet Cheeks?" she asked Axl.

"I'll be right there," he said, and when I shook my head at him, he said, "What? She's hot."

I laughed and sat next to Buster, who offered me some of his Doritos and said, "So, it sounds like Jasper and his daddy killed your mama's boyfriend and framed her for the murder, hoping it would run y'all out of town."

"Maybe, but I don't think so," I said.

"You don't?" he asked. "Well, who do you think—"

"Mr. Jones-Davies has requested to see you," a nurse said, waving me back to the exam rooms.

"Go on," Buster said, "I won't leave without saying goodbye."

Elton was lying in bed, his head wrapped like a mummy, his arm in a sling. I hugged him until his heart rate monitor went berserk, then backed up several steps and just smiled at him.

"I have fractured my radius and ulna," Elton said, the pain medicine making him sound tipsy. "The doctor said my injury will not require surgery, but I must wear a cast for several weeks. I would like for you to sign it."

"Sure," I said, smiling to the point of tears.

"I also suffered a grade 2 concussion, but the doctor does not believe there is any permanent brain damage."

"Good to hear," I said, and we sat there in silence, me holding his hand, him seemingly not caring.

"Have you spoken to your mother?" I asked after a while.

"Briefly," Elton said. "She is on her way here now. She somehow sounded both happy and angry."

I already dreaded trying to explain to Holly Jones-Davies how I'd managed to endanger her son's life once again. She'd be furious, but she'd also be proud. The boy was a hero.

"Elton," I said, squeezing his hand, "you tried to save my life. You charged a man with a gun and tried to save my life."

"Affirmative," Elton replied.

"That was incredibly brave."

"On the contrary, it was a calculated decision. Jasper was armed, we were not, and our odds of survival were low. A frontal attack was the best of several poor choices." Elton's phone dinged, and he glanced at the screen. "Zadie Carrick sends her greetings and says she worries our friendship is hazardous to my health."

"It's hard to argue," I said with a laugh and patted him on the arm. "I should let you rest. Besides, Mom and Dad are outside having a conversation that could devolve into armed conflict at any moment."

"Send your mother my regards," Elton said as I turned to leave, but then I stopped.

"Elton," I said, sitting back down, "you knew my mother was in jail, but you didn't seem surprised to hear she's here in the parking lot."

"I … I assumed she was released. And, as you recall, I have also recently suffered a concussion, which has hindered my ability to think critically."

"I suppose so, but do you recall when exactly you discovered Jasper Benson's WhereAbout account?"

He hesitated. "Today."

"Friends don't lie, Elton."

"Several nights ago, soon after he accepted a friend request from Elya Petrovich."

I closed my eyes and shook my head. "You know, I didn't put it all together until tonight when I saw how fast you drove chasing Jasper. Until then, I didn't believe you were physically capable of breaking the speed limit."

"We were pursuing a murderer," Elton said. "Under the circumstances, law enforcement would likely—"

"Elton, I'm not upset you were speeding. I'm not upset about anything. But the night Lenny died, a truck nearly ran Axl and me off the road when we stopped for gas. I didn't get a good look at the driver because my life flashed before my eyes, but the truck looked a lot like the one from Fuller Farms we've been using the past few weeks. A truck I didn't even know you could operate until you told me you'd driven to the Ashes PD to look over some files by yourself. Then, the next time I saw you, you had a bandage on your arm, and you were wearing wingtips."

"Affirmative. Nike is one of my father's endorsement sponsors, and I no longer wish to—"

"No, no, I remember what you said. And I remember reaching into your backpack a few days ago for some Skittles and you biting my head off."

"The word *personal* in personal property implies—"

"You were so eager to go back to Benson House after Jasper accepted Elya's friend request, but you couldn't tell me why. Then, when I suggested visiting Jasper the next day, you were all about it, even though I was going to blackmail him, something you'd usually try and talk me out of." I shook my head and smiled. "I figured you were looking for clues this morning when you crawled around under Jasper's bed and dug through all of his stuff. But now I think I know what was in your backpack. I think there was a bloody knife and some pill bottles. And I suspect your Nikes got blood on them too, and that's why you spent the rest of camp running around in church shoes. And I think you figured out Jasper Benson killed Vance, Aubrey, and Quinn several days before I did, but you couldn't tell me until you'd had a chance to plant evidence in his bedroom."

Elton opened his mouth to reply, but he couldn't find the words this time.

"You weren't talking to Zadie tonight outside of Ristorante Balotelli, were you? You were on the phone with the Macon County Sheriff's department, leaving an anonymous tip."

"Negative," Elton said. "I was on the phone with Zadie outside Ristorante Balotelli. She had an urgent query regarding Cranachan, as I said." He hesitated for a moment before adding, "I contacted the Macon County Sheriff's office from the pay phone at Fuller Farms so they would not trace the call to me."

I gasped and covered my mouth.

"That night, I knew your family was discussing how to expel Lenny from the apartment over dinner, so he would be home alone. Knowing your mother's poor dating history, I feared a violent altercation was likely, so I went to talk to Lenny myself. I informed him he was to never lay a hand on you or your mother again and he should vacate the premises immediately. Unfortunately, that is when he became unhinged. He stomped and screamed and called me several names I will not repeat, and he attempted to shove me out the door but lacked the strength to do so. He then took a butcher's knife from the kitchen and rushed me with ill intent. Having taken Tae Kwon Do for several years, I am trained to defend myself against basic knife attacks, even though I did receive a slight laceration on my arm, as you noted. Lenny Roach, however, was not a particularly skilled fighter. As I attempted to disarm him, he stumbled and fell, and the knife plunged into his chest, killing him instantly."

"Oh my God," I whispered over and over, rubbing my face and blinking in disbelief.

"Having acted in self-defense, I did not commit a crime," Elton said. "However, I was hesitant to report this incident and place my life in the hands of the Ashes Police Department."

"And with good reason," I said.

"But please know, I never meant for your mother to go to jail. And now that Jasper is dead, I will confess to—"

"Absolutely not," I said. "You did nothing wrong. Well, nothing wrong with Lenny. You'd definitely get in trouble for planting evidence and fleeing the scene and the rest of it, but I won't let you. I need you, you donkey, and you need me. We're a team, remember? We're all we've got."

Elton tolerated another hug for as long as he could, then said, "While I appreciate your loyal friendship, knowing what you know makes you an accessory after the fact to my crimes and leaves you susceptible to punishment of your own."

"Which guarantees you I'll never tell," I said with a wink, "and guarantees me you won't tell either."

Elton considered this for a moment and said, "Mutually assured destruction."

"Yeah," I said, "something like that."

EPILOGUE

The night Jasper fell from Twilight Rock, Jackson County sheriffs came for Mayor Jeremy Benson at his 7,321 square foot rustic mountain mansion in Ashes. While famous houseguests Chase Foster and Bridget Bell watched in horror, the mayor jumped from his back deck and fell over twenty feet in a daring but stupid escape attempt, breaking both legs and greatly hindering his ability to run away. Charged with breaking nearly every law in North Carolina, a jury of his peers convicted Mayor Benson of most of these crimes, and his sentence, handed down by the same judge who presided over my mother's arraignment, ensured the asshole would never again see the light of day. Years later, in a glorious twist of fate, Netflix developed a limited series based on that summer's events called *Murder in the Pines*. Chase Foster would win an Emmy for his portrayal of Mayor Jeremy Benson.

North Carolina has no statute of limitations for felony sex crimes. However, victims only have three years to file civil suits against their abusers, and Tracie Ray's window had long since closed. So instead, Shelby Ray sued the Benson family after paternity tests revealed she was the rightful heir to Jasper's share of the family fortune. The court battle raged for years, though public opinion of the Bensons remained low, especially after an ill-fated appearance on *Jerry Springer* in which Mrs. Benson attacked Shelby with a chair. Finally, in 2017, the North Carolina Supreme Court upheld a district court's decision to award Shelby 49.3 million dollars. She would have received much more, but seven more of Jasper's illegitimate children had come forward in the interim.

Dennis Strewberry was disbarred. Facing pressure from Mayor Benson, he'd lied to Mom about almost every aspect of her case, including telling her the cops had a murder weapon, and that she was forbidden to call home and speak with her family. Tripp Aston was disbarred too, though that was the least of his worries. As a high-ranking member of Charlotte society, Tripp's trial was the talk of the town. His conviction is most remembered for Tripp crying like a baby as the judge delivered a tongue-lashing that has since been viewed over 200 million times on YouTube. Several members of the Ashes police force also served time for their misdeeds, including Chief Jenkins, who, after his release, moved to Arizona and currently portrays Ike Clanton in reenactments of the O.K. Corral Gunfight.

Parents filed the first lawsuits against Fuller Farms just minutes after my email hit their inboxes. From there, the floodgates opened, and campers from five decades came forward alleging all manner of abuse. Internal documents would prove Wellington Fuller knew of and attempted to cover up some of these horrors, including Mitch, the counselor who abused Vance and countless others in the summer of

'79. Too cowardly to face his reckoning, Wellington Fuller suffered a stroke and died in 2011. Courts soon scattered Wellington's fortune to the wind to pay victims and their attorneys, and the camp that once bore his family name now sits abandoned. However, locals insist it's overrun with devil worshippers.

Ashes in the Pines canceled the Twilight Rock Film Festival as the spigot of tourism ran dry. Residents sold their homes and moved to Highlands or Cashiers, and restaurants, boutiques, and specialty grocery stores, including Fraîche, soon shuttered their doors. But then something strange happened. As news of the local doomsday cult and their belated spaceship spread, more and more true believers flocked to town. These days, Ashes is home to hundreds of paranormal investigators, UFO hunters, psychics, mystics, witches, wizards, and, oddly enough, a large contingent of Portland Trailblazers fans. The HomeGoing Festival and Parade now attracts thousands of visitors each June, and in 2013, the parade's grand marshal was none other than Buster McClellan. I suspect he hated every second of it.

Mom and Dad reconciled and were married at a small ceremony in Destin later that year. Ha! Just kidding. They got into such a loud shouting match that night outside the Highlands-Cashiers Hospital that the sheriffs who'd just dropped Mom off had to turn around and break them up. But they did patch things up in the end. Dad sends checks now, and Mom doesn't send them back covered in expletives. He calls us too, usually on Sunday afternoons, to see how we're doing. And there's even talk of a visit next spring break if he can convince us there is anything fun to do in Nebraska.

Elton returned to New York, where his parents' bitter divorce continued to dominate tabloid headlines. I hoped our summer escapades wouldn't arm his father's attorney with even more ammunition, but I knew they would. Even so, he rarely seemed troubled when we spoke, mostly because he was too busy telling me about the new Manhattan private school he'd attend in the fall, which sounded a little like Xavier's School for Gifted Youngsters in the X-Men comics. A private school, it goes without saying, that Holly Jones-Davies did not offer for me to attend as well.

We moved back to Dandridge, because of course we did. Mom landed her old job at Waffle King and found us an apartment at Pineview Chateau. Axl rejoined the Dandridge High Manatees who named him their starting quarterback six seconds later. And I got a part-time job bagging groceries at the Piggly Wiggly in Chipley, which, I soon realized, was only a block away from something called the Panhandle Pain Clinic. Two days later, I had a prescription for OxyContin 20mg with my name on it.

Summer gave way to autumn, my junior year began, and life settled into routine. Axl threw touchdowns and dated cheerleaders. Mom started seeing a man named Freddy who seemed alright until his wife found out and tried to set our car on fire. And I got by the best I could, taking pills when the shittiness felt unmanageable and trying to cut back after crossing arbitrarily drawn red lines. River Lewis took me to the homecoming dance and asked me out almost every other weekend, but I always found an excuse to say no. The boy was too sweet. Too nice and kind to get mixed up with someone like me. I was doing him a favor.

And as for murders, I assumed I was done. I'd solved three before my seventeenth birthday, which seemed enough for one lifetime. I certainly didn't go looking for them. Didn't scan the crime section of the *Walton Observer*. Didn't surf the web for a new cold case. By December, I figured my days of sticking my freckled little nose where it didn't belong and being a pain in the ass to anyone hiding the truth were behind me. But then I woke up a few days before Christmas break and saw this headline on my phone—

Hall of Fame Running Back Mustang Jones Found Stabbed in the Bronx.

Here we go again.

THE END

Izzy and Elton will return in
THE BLADES OF BROTHER ISLAND
2024

For updates visit www.chadalangibbs.com

ACKNOWLEDGMENTS

Thanks to my wife, Tricia, who works hard every day healing sick children while I stay home and write silly books. I would trade places with you, but there would be a lot more sick children in the world ... and some pretty terrible novels.

Thanks to my sons, Linus and Oliver. Your busy soccer/choir/piano schedules delayed this book by several weeks, but I wouldn't trade it for the world.

Thanks to my friend and editor, Becky Philpott, who never laughs at me for making the same grammatical mistakes for fourteen consecutive years. Your magic red pen does wonders for these books. I cannot thank you enough.

Thanks to everyone who read an early version of this book, including my Swiftie nieces, Ava and Morgan, my sister-in-law and brother-in-law, Lori and Johnny, and my mother-in-law, Karen.

Thanks to Tricia's aunt and uncle, Phyllis and Tom Davis, for hosting us in Highlands, North Carolina, which is a lot like Ashes in the Pines, minus the doomsday cult and all the murders.

Thanks to Andrew Stanley for not calling the police when I asked for legal advice regarding stabbing an abusive drug dealer boyfriend. And thanks to his wife Sarah for giving me Andrew's number on the condition I name a character after her.

And finally, thanks to my readers. I'm still humbled to think anyone would spend their precious free time reading something I wrote. Your kind words and encouragement mean the world to me. Thank you.